Someone to Care

Mary Balogh

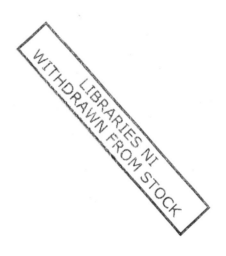

W F HOWES LTD

This large print edition published in 2019 by
W F Howes Ltd
Unit 5, St George's House, Rearsby Business Park,
Gaddesby Lane, Rearsby, Leicester LE7 4YH

1 3 5 7 9 10 8 6 4 2

First published in the United Kingdom in 2018
by Piatkus

A CIP catalogue record for this book is available
from the British Library

ISBN 978 1 52886 157 1

Typeset by Palimpsest Book Production Limited,
Falkirk, Stirlingshire

Printed and bound by
T J International in the UK

CHAPTER 1

Marcel Lamarr, Marquess of Dorchester, was not at all pleased when his carriage turned abruptly into the yard of an undistinguished country inn on the edge of an undistinguished country village and rocked to a halt. He made his displeasure felt, not in words, but rather in a cold, steady gaze, his quizzing glass raised almost but not quite to his eye, when his coachman opened the door and peered apologetically within.

'One of the leaders has a shoe coming loose, my lord,' he explained.

'You did not check when we stopped for a change of horses an hour ago that all was in order?' his lordship asked. But he did not wait for an answer. 'How long?'

His coachman glanced dubiously at the inn and the stables off to one side, from which no groom or ostler had yet emerged eagerly rushing to their aid. 'Not long, my lord,' he assured his employer.

'A firm and precise answer,' his lordship said curtly, lowering his glass. 'Shall we say one hour? And not a moment longer? We will step inside while we wait, André, and sample the quality of

1

the ale served here.' His tone suggested that he was not expecting to be impressed.

'A glass or two will not come amiss,' his brother, André, replied cheerfully. 'It has been a dashed long time since breakfast. I never understand why you always have to make such an early start and then remain obstinately inside the carriage when the horses are being changed.'

The quality of the ale was indeed not impressive, but the quantity could not be argued with. It was served in large tankards, which foamed over to leave wet rings on the table. Quantity was perhaps the inn's claim to fame. The landlord, unbidden, brought them fresh meat pasties, which filled the two plates and even hung over the edges. They had been cooked by his own good wife, he informed them, bowing and beaming as he did so, though his lordship gave him no encouragement beyond a cool, indifferent nod. The good woman apparently made the best meat pasties, and, indeed, the best pies of any and all descriptions, for twenty miles around, probably more, though the proud husband did not want to give the appearance of being boastful in the singing of his woman's praises. Their lordships must judge for themselves, though he had no doubt they would agree with him and perhaps even suggest that they were the finest in all England – possibly even in Wales and Scotland and Ireland too. He would not be at all surprised. Had their lordships ever traveled to those remote regions? He had heard—

They were rescued from having to listen to what-ever it was he had heard, however, when the outer door beyond the taproom opened and a trio of people, followed almost immediately by a steady stream of others, turned into the room. They were presumably villagers, all clad in their Sunday best, though it was not Sunday, all cheerful and noisy in their greetings to the landlord and one another. All were as dry as the desert and as empty as a beggar's bowl in a famine – according to the loudest of them – and in need of sustenance in the form of ale and pasties, it being not far off noon and the day's festivities not due to begin for another hour or so yet. They fully expected to be stuffed for the rest of the day once the festivities *did* begin, of course, but in the meanwhile . . .

But someone at that point – with a chorus of hasty agreement from everyone else – remembered to assure the host that nothing would or could compare to his wife's cooking. That was why they were here.

Each of the new arrivals became quickly aware that there were two strangers in their midst. A few averted their eyes in some confusion and scurried off to sit at tables as far removed from the stran-gers as the size of the room allowed. Others, somewhat bolder, nodded respectfully as they took their seats. One brave soul spoke up with the hope that their worships had come to enjoy the enter-tainments their humble village was to have on offer for the rest of the day. The room grew hushed as all attention was turned upon their worships in anticipation of a reply.

The Marquess of Dorchester, who neither knew the name of the village nor cared, looked about the dark, shabby taproom with disfavor and ignored everyone. It was possible he had not even heard the question or noticed the hush. His brother, more gregarious by nature, and more ready to be delighted by any novelty that presented itself, nodded amiably to the gathering in general and asked the inevitable question.

'And what entertainments would those be?' he asked.

It was all the encouragement those gathered there needed. They were about to celebrate the end of the harvest with contests in everything under the sun – singing, fiddle playing, dancing, arm wrestling, archery, wood sawing, to name a few. There were to be races for the children and pony rides and contests in needlework and cooking for the women. And displays of garden produce, of course, and prizes for the best. There was going to be something for everyone. And all sorts of booths with everything one could wish for upon which to spend one's money. Most of the garden produce and the women's items were to be sold or auctioned after the judging. There was to be a grand feast in the church hall in the late afternoon before general dancing in the evening. All the proceeds from the day were to go into the fund for the church roof.

The church roof apparently leaked like a sieve whenever there was a good rain, and only five or six of the pews were safe to sit upon. They got mighty crowded on a wet day.

'Not that some of our younger folk complain too loud about the crowding,' someone offered.

'Some of them pray all week for rain on Sunday,' someone else added.

André Lamarr joined in the general guffaw that succeeded these witticisms. 'Perhaps we will stay an hour or two to watch some of the contests,' he said. 'Log sawing, did you say? And arm wrestling? I might even try a bout myself.'

All eyes turned upon his companion, who had neither spoken nor shown any spark of interest in all the supposedly irresistible delights the day held in store.

They offered a marked contrast to the beholder, these two brothers. There was a gap of almost thirteen years in their ages, but it was not just a contrast in years. Marcel Lamarr, Marquess of Dorchester, was tall, well formed, impeccably elegant, and austerely handsome. His dark hair was silvering at the temples. His face was narrow, with high cheekbones and a somewhat hawkish nose and thin lips. His eyes were dark and hooded. He looked upon the world with cynical disdain, and the world looked back upon him – when it dared look at all – with something bordering upon fear. He had a reputation as a hard man, one who did not suffer fools gladly or at all. He also had a reputation for hard living and deep gambling among other vices. He was reputed to have left behind a string of brokenhearted mistresses and courtesans and hopeful widows during the course of his almost forty years. As for unmarried ladies and their ambitious mamas and hopeful papas, they had long ago given up hope of netting him. One quelling glance from those dark eyes of his could freeze even the most determined among them in their tracks. They consoled themselves by fanning the flames of the rumor that he lacked either a heart or a conscience, and he did nothing to disabuse them of such a notion.

André Lamarr, by contrast, was a personable young man, shorter, slightly broader, fairer of hair and complexion, and altogether more open and congenial of countenance than his brother. He liked people, and people generally liked him. He was always ready to be amused, and he was not always discriminating about where that amusement came from. At present he was charmed by these cheerful country folk and the simple pleasures they antici-pated with such open delight. He would be perfectly happy to delay their journey by an hour or three – they had started out damnably early, after all. He glanced inquiringly at his brother and drew breath to speak. He was forestalled.

'No,' his lordship said softly.

The attention of the masses had already been taken by a couple of new arrivals, who were greeted with a hearty exchange of pleasantries and comments upon the kindness the weather was showing them and a few lame flights of wit, which drew disproportionate shouts of merry laughter. Marcel could not imagine anything more shudderingly tedious than an afternoon spent at the insipid entertainment of a country fair, admiring large cabbages and crocheted doilies and watching troops of heavy-footed dancers prancing about the village green.

'Dash it all, Marc,' André said, his eyebrows knitting into a frown. 'I thought you were none too eager to get home.'

'Nor am I,' Marcel assured him. 'Redcliffe Court is too full of persons for whom I feel very little fondness.'

'With the exception of Bertrand and Estelle, I would hope,' André said, his frown deepening.

'With the exception of the twins,' Marcel conceded with a slight shrug as the innkeeper arrived to refill their glasses. Once more they brimmed over with foam, which swamped the table around them. The man did not pause to wipe the table.

The twins. Those two were going to have to be dealt with when he arrived home. They were soon to turn eighteen. In the natural course of events Estelle would be making her come-out during the London Season next year and would be married to someone suitably eligible within a year or so after that, while Bertrand would go up to Oxford, idle away three or four years there, absorbing as little knowledge as possible, and then take up a career as

7

a fashionable young man about town. *In the natural course of events* . . . There was, in fact, nothing natural about his children. They were both almost morbidly serious minded, perhaps even pious, perish the thought. Sometimes it was hard to believe he could have begotten them. But then he had not had a great deal to do with their upbringing, and doubtless that was where the problem lay.

'I am going to have to exert myself with them,' he added.

'They are not likely to give you any trouble,' André assured him. 'They are a credit to Jane and Charles.'

Marcel did not reply. For *that* was precisely the trouble. Jane Morrow was his late wife's elder sister – straitlaced and humorless and managing in her ways. Adeline, who had been a careless, fun-loving girl, had detested her. He still thought of his late wife as a girl, for she had died at the age of twenty when the twins were barely a year old. Jane and her husband had stepped dutifully into the breach to take care of the children while Marcel fled as though the hounds of hell were at his heels and as though he could outpace his grief and guilt and responsibilities. Actually, he had more or less succeeded with that last. His children had grown up with their aunt and uncle and older cousins, albeit at his home. He had seen them twice a year since their mother's death, almost always for fairly short spans of time. That home had borne too many bad memories. One memory, actually, but that one was very bad indeed. Fortunately, that home in Sussex had been abandoned and leased out after he inherited the title. They all now lived at Redcliffe Court in Northamptonshire.

'Which I am not,' André continued with a rueful grin after taking a long pull at his glass and wiping froth off his upper lip with the back of his hand, 'Not that anyone would expect me to be a credit to Jane and Charles, it is true. But I am not much of a credit to you either, am I, Marc?'

Marcel did not reply. It would not have been easy to do even if he had wanted to. The noise in the taproom was deafening. Everyone was trying to speak over everyone else, and it seemed that every second utterance was hilarious enough to be deserving of a prolonged burst of merriment. It was time to be on their way. Surely his coachman had had sufficient time to secure one loose shoe on one leg of one horse. He had probably done it in five minutes and was enjoying a tankard of ale of his own.

Beyond the open door of the taproom, Marcel could see that someone else had arrived. A woman. A lady, in fact. Undoubtedly a lady, though surprisingly she seemed to be alone. She was standing at the desk out in the hallway, looking down at the register the innkeeper was turning in her direction. She was well formed and elegant, though not young, at a guess. His eyes rested upon her with indifference until she half turned her head as though something at the main doors had taken her attention and he saw her face in profile. Beautiful. Though definitely not young. And . . . familiar? He looked more intently, but she had turned back to the desk to write in the register before stooping to pick up a bag and turning in the direction of the staircase. She was soon lost to view.

'Not that you are much of a credit to yourself sometimes,' André said, apparently oblivious to Marcel's inattention to their conversation.

Marcel fixed his brother with a cool gaze. 'I would remind you that my affairs are none of your concern,' he said.

His brother added to the general din by throwing back his head and laughing. 'An apt choice of words, Marc,' he said.

'But still not your concern,' Marcel told him.

'Oh, it may yet be,' André said, 'if a certain husband and his brothers and brothers-in-law and other assorted relatives and neighbors should happen to be in pursuit and burst in upon us.'

They were coming from Somerset, where they had spent a few weeks at a house party hosted by a mutual acquaintance. Marcel had alleviated his boredom by flirting with a neighbor of his host who was a frequent visitor to the house, though he had stopped well short of any sexual intimacy with her. He had kissed the back of her hand once in full view of at least twenty other guests, and once when they were alone on the terrace beyond the drawing room. He had a reputation for ruthless and heartless womanizing, but he did make a point of not encouraging married ladies, and she was married. Someone, however – he suspected it was the lady herself – had told some highly embellished tale to the husband, and that worthy had chosen to take umbrage. All his male relatives to the third and fourth generations, not to mention his neighbors and several local dignitaries, had taken collective umbrage too, and soon it had been rumored that half the county was out for the blood of the lecherous Marquess of Dorchester. A challenge to a duel was not out of the question, ridiculous as it had seemed. Indeed, André and three of the other male houseguests had offered their services as his second.

Marcel had written to Redcliffe Court to give notice of his intention to return home within the week and had left the house party before all the foolishness could descend into downright farce. He had no desire whatsoever either to kill a hotheaded farmer who neglected his wife or to allow himself to be killed. And he did not care the snap of two fingers if his departure was interpreted as cowardice.

He had been planning to go home anyway, even though home was full of people who had never been invited to take up residence there – or perhaps because of that fact. He had inherited the title from his uncle less than two years ago, and with it Redcliffe Court. He had inherited its residents too – the marchioness, his widowed aunt, and her daughter, and the daughter's husband with their youngest daughter. The three elder ones had already married and – mercifully – flown the nest with their husbands. Since he had little interest in making his home at Redcliffe, Marcel had not deemed it important to suggest that they remove to the dower house, which had been built at some time in the past for just this sort of situation. Now Jane and Charles Morrow were there too with their son and daughter, both of whom were adults but neither of whom had shown any sign of launching out into a life independent of their parents. The twins were at Redcliffe too, of course, since it was now rightfully their home.

One big, happy family.

'What *is* my concern,' Marcel said into a slight lull in the noise level after the landlord had distributed steaming pasties from a giant platter and everyone had tucked in, 'is your debts, André.'

'Yes, I thought we would get to those,' his brother said with a resigned sigh. 'I would have had them paid off long before now if I had not had a run of bad luck at the tables just before we left for the country. I will come about, though, never fear. I always do. You know that. *You* always come about. If my creditors have the sheer impudence to come after you again, just ignore 'em. I always do.'

'I have heard that debtors' prison is not the most comfortable of residences,' Marcel said.

'Oh, I say, Marc. That was uncalled for.' His brother sounded both shocked and indignant. 'You surely do not expect me to appear in company dressed in rags and wearing scuffed boots, do you?

12

I would be a reproach to you if I patronized an inferior tailor or bootmaker. Or, worse, none at all. I really cannot be faulted on *those* bills. As for the gaming, what is a fellow supposed to do for amusement? Read improving books at his fireside each night? Besides, it is a family failing, you must confess. Annemarie is forever living beyond her means and then dropping a whole quarter's allowance at the tables.'

'Our sister,' Marcel said, 'has been the concern of William Cornish for the past eight or nine years.' Though that did not stop her from begging the occasional loan when she had been more than usually extravagant or unlucky and quailed at the prospect of confessing all to her sober-minded husband. 'He knew what he was getting into when he married her.'

'She tells me he never scolds and never threatens her with debtors' prison,' André said. 'Extend me a loan, if you will be so good, Marc. Just enough to cover the gaming debts and perhaps a bit extra to get the more pressing of my creditors off my back, damn their eyes. I will pay back every penny. With interest,' he added magnanimously.

The lady had reappeared. The door from the taproom into the dining room was also open, and Marcel could see her seating herself at a table in there, the room's sole occupant as far as he could see. She was facing him, though there was the width of two rooms and many persons between them. And by God, he really did know her. The

13

marble goddess whom he had once upon a time tried his damnedest to turn to flesh and blood – with no success whatsoever. Well, almost none. She had been married at the time, of course, but he had tried flirting with her nevertheless. He was an accomplished flirt and rarely failed when he set his mind to a conquest. He had begun to think that she might possibly be interested, but then she had told him to go away. Just that, in those exact words.

Go away, Mr Lamarr, she had said.

And he had gone, his pride badly bruised. For a while he had feared that his heart had been too, but he had been mistaken. His heart had already been stone-cold dead.

Now, all these years later, she had fallen a long way from the pedestal of pride from which she had ruled her world then. And she was no longer young. But she was still beautiful, by God. The Countess of Riverdale. No, not that. She was no longer the countess, or even the dowager countess. He did not know what she called herself now. Mrs Westcott? She was not that either. Mrs Somebody Else? He could take a look at the inn register, he supposed. If he was sufficiently interested, that was.

'You do not believe me,' André said, sounding aggrieved. 'I know I did not repay you the last time. Or the time before, if I am going to be perfectly honest, though I would not have lost such a vast sum at the races if the horse I bet on had not run lame out of the starting gate. He was as

14

sure a thing as there ever was, Marc. You would have bet a bundle on him yourself if you had been there. It was just dashed rotten luck. But *this* time I will definitely repay you. I have a tip on a sure thing coming up next month. A *real* sure thing this time,' he added when he saw his brother's skeptically raised eyebrow. 'You ought to take a look at the horse yourself.'

Hers was a face that had suffered, Marcel thought, and was strangely more beautiful as a result. Not that he was interested in suffering women. Or women who must be close to forty or even past it, for all he knew. She was taking a look around, first at the presumably empty dining room and then through the door at the noisy crowd gathered in the taproom. Her eyes alit upon him for a moment, passed onward, and then returned. She looked directly at him for a second, perhaps two, and then turned sharply away as the innkeeper appeared at her elbow with the coffeepot.

She had both seen him and recognized him. If he was not mistaken – he did not raise his quizzing glass to observe more closely – there was a flush of color in her cheeks.

'I hate it,' André said, 'when you give me the silent treatment, Marc. It is dashed unfair, you know. You of all people.'

'Me of all people?' Marcel turned his attention to his brother, who squirmed under his gaze.

'Well, you are not exactly a saint, are you?' he said. 'Never have been. Throughout my boyhood

I listened to tales of your extravagance and woman-izing and reckless exploits. You were my idol, Marc. I did not expect that you would stand in judgment when I do only what you have always done.'

André was twenty-seven, their sister two years older. They all had the same mother, but there had been an eleven-year span during which no live child had been born to her. And then, when she had given up hope of adding to her family, along had come first Annemarie and then André.

'Someone was careless in allowing such unsavory gossip to reach the ears of children,' Marcel said. 'And to make it sound like something that ought to be emulated.'

'Not so young either,' André said. 'We used to listen at doors. Don't all children? Annemarie adored you too. She still does. I have no idea why she married Cornish. Every time he moves he is obscured by a cloud of dust.'

'Dear me,' Marcel said. 'Not literally, I hope.'

'Oh, I say,' André said, suddenly distracted. 'There is Miss Kingsley. I wonder what she is doing here.'

Marcel followed the line of his gaze – toward the dining room. Kingsley. *Miss* Kingsley. But she had never been married, except bigamously for twenty years or so to the Earl of Riverdale. He wondered if she had known. Probably not, though. Undoubtedly not, in fact. Her son had inherited his father's title and property after the latter's death and then been disinherited in spectacular fashion when his illegitimacy was exposed. Her daughters had been disinherited too and cast out of society like lepers. Had not one of them been betrothed and dropped like a hot potato?

Across the two rooms, he saw her look up and directly at him this time before looking away, though not hurriedly.

She was aware of him, then. Not just as someone she had recognized. She was *aware* of him. He was almost certain of it, just as he had been all those years ago, though her final words to him had seemed to belie that impression. *Go away, Mr Lamarr.*

'Well,' André said cheerfully, picking up his tankard and draining its contents. 'You can come and visit me in debtors' prison, Marc. Bring some clean linen when you come, will you? And take the soiled away with you to be laundered and deloused. But as for today, are we going to stay for a while and watch some of the contests? We are in no big hurry, after all, are we?'

'Your debts will be paid,' Marcel said. 'All of them. As you know very well, André.' He did not add that the debt to him would also be forgiven. That went without saying, but his brother must be left with some pride.

'I am much obliged to you,' André said. 'I will pay you back within the month, Marc. Depend upon it. At least you are unlikely ever to have a similar problem with Bertrand. Or Estelle.'

Quite right. Perhaps it was illogical to half wish that he would.

'But then,' André added with a laugh, 'they would not have been brought up to idolize you or emulate you, would they? If there is one person more dusty than William Cornish, it is Jane Morrow. And Charles. A well-matched couple, those two. *Are* we staying?'

Marcel did not answer immediately. He was looking at the former Countess of Riverdale, whom he could not quite think of as Miss Kingsley. She was eating, though he did not think that was one of the landlady's famous but somewhat over-hearty meat pasties on her plate. And she was glancing up to look straight at him again, a sand-wich suspended a short distance from her mouth. She half frowned, and he cocked one eyebrow before she looked away once more.

'I am staying,' he said on a sudden impulse. 'You are not, however. You may take the carriage.'

'Eh?' André said inelegantly.

'I am staying,' Marcel repeated. 'You are not.'

She was not wearing her bonnet and there was no other outdoor garment in sight. He could not see her bag beside her. She had signed the register – he had seen her do it – surely proof that she was staying, though why on earth she had chosen this particular inn in this particular village he could not imagine. Carriage trouble? Nor could he imagine why she was alone. Surely she had not fallen on such hard times that she could not afford servants. It was hardly likely she had come for the express purpose of participating in the harvest celebrations. He might soon be kicking himself from here to eternity, though, if she was *not* staying. Or if she repeated her famous reproof and sent him away.

But since when had he lacked confidence in himself, especially when it came to women? Not since Lady Riverdale herself, surely, and that must be fifteen years or more ago.

'Miss Kingsley,' André said suddenly and with a clicking of his fingers and great indignation. He looked from his brother to her and back again. 'Marc! Surely you are not . . .'

Marcel turned a cold gaze upon his brother, eyebrows raised, and the sentence was not completed. 'You may take the carriage,' he said again. 'Indeed, you *will* take it. When you reach Redcliffe Court, you will inform Jane and Charles and anyone else who may be interested that I will arrive when I arrive.'

'What sort of message is that?' André asked. 'Charles will turn purple in the face and Jane's lips will disappear, and one of them is sure to say it is just like you. And Bertrand and Estelle will be disappointed.'

Marcel doubted it. Did he wish André was right? For a moment he hesitated, but only for a moment. He had done nothing to earn their disappointment, and it was a bit late now to think of yearning for it.

'You hate this sort of country entertainment,' André said. 'Really, this is too bad of you, Marc. I am the one who suggested staying awhile. And I left that house party before I intended to in order to give you my company just when I was making some progress with the redhead.'

'Did I ask for your company?' Marcel asked, his quizzing glass in his hand.

'Oh, I say. Next time I will know better,' his brother told him. 'I might as well go on my way, then. I always know when arguing with you is useless, Marc, which is most of the time. Or all the time. I hope she intends to be back on the road within the half hour. I hope she will have nothing to do with you. I hope she spits in your eye.'

'Do you?' Marcel asked softly.

'Marc,' his brother said. 'She is *old*.'

Marcel raised his eyebrows. 'But so am I, brother,' he said. 'Forty on my next birthday, which is lamentably close. Positively decrepit.'

'It is different for a man,' his brother said, 'and you very well know it. Good Lord, Marc.'

He left a few minutes later, striding off without a backward glance and only a cursory wave of the hand for the villager who asked redundantly if he was leaving. Marcel did not accompany him out to the innyard. He heard his carriage leave five minutes or so after that. He was stranded here, then. That was more than a bit foolish of him. The crowd was eyeing him uncertainly and then began to disperse, the platter of meat pasties having been reduced to a few crumbs and the festivities beyond the inn doors apparently being imminent. The former countess was drinking her coffee. Soon there were a mere half dozen villagers left in the taproom, and none of them occupied the tables between him and her. He gazed steadily at her, and she looked back once over the rim of her cup and held his gaze for a few moments.

Marcel got to his feet, strolled out into the hallway, turned the register to observe that yes, she had indeed signed it for a one-night stay as Miss Kingsley, and then strolled to the outside door to glance out. He crossed to the dining room and entered it by the hallway door. She looked up as he closed the door behind him and then set her cup down carefully in its saucer, her eyes on what she was doing. Her hair, swept back and upward into an elegant chignon, was still the color of honey. Unless his advanced age had dimmed his excellent eyesight, there was not a single strand of gray there yet. Or any lines on her face or sagging of chin. Or of bosom.

'You told me to go away,' he said. 'But that was fifteen years or so ago. Was there a time limit?'

CHAPTER 2

The hired carriage in which Viola Kingsley had been traveling just a short while before the Marquess of Dorchester spoke to her at the country inn not only had been uncomfortable with its hard seats and surely nonexistent springs and its drafty windows and door and its innumerable squeaks and groans and pervading smell of oldness and staleness. It had also developed a severe limp and was proceeding at less than half its former speed and was listing somewhat to one side. Try as she would to sit upright, she had kept finding her left shoulder pressed up against the hard wood panel beside the seat. At any moment she had expected that the carriage would stop altogether and she would be stranded in the middle of nowhere.

And it was all her fault. She would have no one to blame but herself.

Two years before, something truly catastrophic had happened to Viola. She had been Viola Westcott, Countess of Riverdale, at the time and had recently suffered the loss of the earl, her husband of twenty-three years. Her son, Harry, had succeeded to the title. He had been only twenty years old at the time and had therefore been placed under the guardianship of Avery Archer, Duke of Netherby, and of Viola herself. Her elder daughter, Camille, had already made her debut into society and was respectably betrothed to Viscount Uxbury. Her younger daughter, Abigail, was looking forward to her own come-out Season the following spring. Viola had been satisfied with her life despite the necessity of wearing deep mourning. She had not been fond of her husband and felt no great grief at his passing.

There had been just one loose end to be tied up, and she had made an attempt to tie it. There was a girl, a young woman by then, whom her husband had kept and secretly supported – he had *thought* it was a secret, anyway – at an orphanage in Bath for as long as Viola had known him. She had made the understandable assumption that the female was his natural daughter by a mistress, and had done what she had considered the right thing after his death by sending her solicitor to Bath to find the woman, inform her of her father's death, and make a final settlement upon her.

That was when the catastrophe had hit.

For it had been discovered that the young woman concerned, Anna Snow, then twenty-five years old and a teacher at the orphanage, was in fact the late earl's legitimate daughter by a previous wife. By his *only* wife as it happened. He had married Viola a few months before Anna Snow's mother died of consumption. Viola's marriage had been a bigamous one. Worse, her son and her daughters were illegitimate. Harry was stripped of his title and fortune – the title had passed to his second cousin, Alexander Westcott, and the fortune to Anna. All of it. The earl had made only one will, and that had been drawn up while he was still with his first wife. Everything that was not entailed went to his daughter by that marriage. Camille and Abigail lost their titles and their portions. Camille was cast off by Lord Uxbury. Abigail would have no come-out Season or any prospect of making the sort of marriage she had been brought up to expect. They had been left destitute, though Anna had tried to insist that her fortune be divided equally among her half siblings and herself. But at the time, she was a stranger to them. In their pride and hurt and bewilderment, they had all refused. Viola had resumed her maiden name.

To say that the bottom had fallen out of her world would be severely to understate the case. The enormity of what had happened to her and her children had been too much for her mind to bear. She had lived on. How could she not, short of putting an end to her own existence? And in the two years since then her life had settled into a new order that was really more bearable than she could have expected. Harry was serving as a captain with a rifle regiment in the Peninsula and was forever cheerful in his insistence that it was just the life for him. Camille was married to a much better man than her former betrothed and they had three children – two adopted and one their own. Abigail lived with Viola at Hinsford Manor in Hampshire, where Viola had spent most of her marriage. What had truly been unexpected after the whole mess was that Anna Snow would end up marrying Harry's guardian, Avery, Duke of Netherby. But she had, and was a duchess now herself. She had insisted she would never live at Hinsford Manor herself and had begged Viola not to let it sit empty. She had even written into her will that the house would pass to Harry and his descendants after her time if he would not accept it before then. The large dowry Viola's father had given when she married Humphrey had been returned, with all the interest it would have accrued since then. Anna had insisted upon it and taken care of it even before Viola could think of it for herself.

Meanwhile, the rest of the Westcott family, far from shunning Viola and her children after the truth became known, had made every effort to draw them back into the fold. As one, they had made it clear to Viola and her children that they were no less loved and valued now than they ever had been, and no less a part of the family. Two of Viola's sisters-in-law, the earl's sisters, were still fond of saying that they dearly wished Humphrey were still alive so that they could have the pleasure of killing him themselves.

All was well, in fact. Or as well as it would ever be after a few necessary adjustments had been made. Viola, who had lived her whole adult life according to the two guiding principles of duty and dignity, appeared to be back to normal, albeit with a different name. She had convinced herself that she was back to normal, anyway.

Until she was not.

Until she snapped – unexpectedly and for no apparent reason. The trauma of what she had experienced had stealthily crept up behind her and then pounced. And she knew that she had not healed at all. She had only suppressed the pain and the hurt. And the anger.

She had snapped at the worst possible time, when the family had all gathered in Bath for the christening of Jacob Cunningham, Camille and Joel's newborn son. They had all agreed to stay on afterward for two weeks of family activities. But two days after the event, Viola, the baby's own proud grandmother, had fled.

She had left Bath feeling guilty and out of sorts and sorry for herself and hurt and angry and all sorts of other nasty, negative things that had no rational explanation. She had simply behaved badly, and that was something she rarely did. Through all her forty-two years she had been known for her graciousness of manner and the evenness of her temper. Yet now she had hurt and bewildered those who were dearest to her in the world. And she had done it deliberately, almost spitefully. She had insisted upon returning home to Hinsford against all reason and against the pleadings of her daughters and son-in-law and the protests of her mother and brother and the Westcott family.

She had announced her intention of returning home. Alone. In a hired carriage. She had pointedly insisted upon leaving her own carriage and servants, even her personal maid, for the use of Abigail when she should decide to return home. She had ignored the shocked protestations of Camille and Joel that they would *of course* see Abby properly conveyed and escorted home when the time came. She had ignored the kindness of the Dowager Countess of Riverdale, her former mother-in-law, who had come all the way to Bath, though she was in her seventies. She had ignored the kind effort Wren, the present countess, Alexander's wife, had made to come to Bath despite the fact that she was herself in expectation of a happy event, as Matilda, the eldest of Viola's former sisters-in-law, liked to describe pregnancy.

Viola had told them all to mind their own business. Yes, she had used those exact words. She had probably never in her life used them before. And she had spoken sharply, without humor or consideration for the feelings she was hurting. She wanted to be *left alone*. She had told them that too.

Leave me alone, she had said more than once – like a petulant child.

And she had no idea why she had so suddenly snapped.

She had gone to Bath with Abigail just before

Jacob's birth, brimful of anxiety and excitement at the imminent arrival of a new grandchild, and she had been happier when it had happened than she had been in a long while. Camille and Joel Cunningham lived in a manor in the hills above Bath with Winifred and Sarah, their adopted daughters, and now with their son too. They used the house for a variety of purposes – for artistic or writing retreats, for workshops in music and dance and painting and other arts, for plays and concerts, and for visits varying from one day to several days of the children from the orphanage in Bath where both Anna and Joel had grown up and Camille had taught briefly before her marriage. The house and extensive garden were always teeming with life and activity. Even just before and after Jacob's birth, it had remained a busy, noisy place.

The amazing thing was that Camille appeared to be thriving. She had not yet lost all the weight she had gained when she was expecting Jacob, and she often looked slightly untidy, some of her hair fallen out of its pins, her sleeves pushed halfway to her elbows, her feet as often as not unshod, even when she stepped outdoors. She always seemed to have Jacob bundled up in her arms while Sarah clung to her skirt and Winifred hovered close – except when Joel was around to share the parenting, as he often was. She never seemed harried.

Sometimes it was hard for Viola to recognize in her elder daughter the severe, straitlaced, always rigidly correct former Lady Camille Westcott, who had never set a foot wrong and had lacked any discernible sense of humor. Now she seemed vividly happy in a life that was as different from the one she had expected as it could possibly be.

Everything had gone well with the birth and the plans for the christening and the event itself. Abigail had been ecstatic, for her dearest friend came too for the occasion – her cousin Jessica Archer, daughter of one of Humphrey's sisters. Viola had been happy. She had developed a close friendship with Alexander's wife, Wren, the year before, and she was delighted to renew it this year. She was happy that her brother and his wife had come from Dorset. Dinners, parties, teas, excursions, walks, concerts – any number of family events had been planned. Viola had been looking forward to them.

Until she snapped.

And had to get away.

Alone.

She had behaved badly. She knew it. She had left at dawn before the family on both sides could gather to hug her and say their farewells and express their concern and wave her on her way. And she had held steady on her determination to travel by hired carriage, though she had had the offer of half a dozen private carriages and servants to go with them to give her company and protection and respectability.

Leave me alone, she had said to more than one of them.

But then suddenly there was something wrong with the hired carriage. And finally it had been creaking and moaning more than ever and leaning ever harder to one side as it turned into the yard of an inn, though surely not a major posting inn. The carriage had ground to a halt.

'What is amiss?' she had asked the coachman when he opened the door and set down the steps. The carriage had hovered over them at an alarming angle.

'Axle about to bust, missus,' he had said.

'Oh.' She had accepted his hand and climbed down to the cobbles of the yard. 'Can it be mended quickly?'

'Not likely, missus,' he had said. 'She's going to need to be replaced, she is.'

'How long?' she had asked.

He had lifted his hat to scratch his head as he went down on his haunches to assess the damage. An ostler belonging to the inn had come ambling up to stand at his shoulder and purse his lips and shake his head. 'You was lucky,' he had said, 'not to be tipped on the open road miles from anywhere for highwaymen and wolves to find you. You might have got yourselves killed if you'd been springing 'em. That there axle ain't going to be held together with no piece of string tied around it, I'm here to tell you. It's got to go and a new one put in its place.'

'Which is exactly what I can see for myself,' the coachman had said testily.

'How long will that take?' Viola had asked again, realizing anew how foolish she had been to go against all advice by venturing on her journey without even a maid to lend her countenance. Oh, she deserved this.

The coachman had shaken his head. 'I dunno, missus. All the rest of today, anyway,' he had said. 'We won't get back on the road till tomorrow morning at the earliest, and a blessed unlucky thing it is for me. I was to go straight back to Bath tonight, I was. I have another customer booked for tomorrow, and a right classy gent he is too, a regular. Always pays a lot more than the fare if I gets him where he's going with time to spare. Now someone else will get to take him and he may never ask for me again.'

'Tomorrow?' Viola had said in dismay. 'But I need to be home today.'

'Well, so do I, missus,' the coachman had said. 'But neither one of us gets to have our wish, do we? You had better speak to the innkeeper here for a room for yourself before they all gets taken, though I doubt that happens too often in this place.' He had looked up at the inn with some contempt.

A smart traveling carriage had been standing to one side of the inn door. It must not be an entirely decrepit place, then. The thought of entering it unaccompanied, however, had caused Viola to quail inside. Whatever would they think of her lone state? But she had caught herself in the thought. Good heavens, she was thinking like the Countess of Riverdale, for whom all had had to be rigid respectability. What did it matter what anyone thought of plain Viola Kingsley? She had reached into the carriage to pull out the bag she had kept inside with her and made her way toward the inn, leaving her trunk to be fetched later.

Noise had greeted her as she opened the door, as well as the odors of ale and cooking. The double doors into the taproom to her left had been wide open, and she had seen that the room, dark and shabby though it appeared, was filled with people, all of whom had seemed to be in high spirits – perhaps in more ways than one. It was surprising for so early in the day. But all had been clarified when the innkeeper came to tend to her and explained that if she had to be stranded by a near-bust axle, for which he expressed his sincere sympathies, at least she was fortunate that it was here and today that it had happened. The village was about to celebrate the end of the harvest, though they did not do it every year. But the church roof was leaking something bad whenever it rained, and that always seemed to happen on a Sunday morning when people were sitting in their pews, trying to listen to the vicar's sermon. Someone had had the idea of organizing an after-the-harvest event to raise money. What better way was there to gather funds than to give people a rollicking good time in exchange for their good, hard-earned cash?

Viola had been able to offer no better suggestion, and the innkeeper had nodded at her with pleased satisfaction when she had said so. She had paid for one night's stay and signed the register before taking a large key from his hand. She had assured him that she did not need any help with her bag but would be obliged if someone would bring up her trunk, and she climbed the stairs to her room, feeling sick at heart.

Whatever was she going to do here for a whole afternoon and evening? Go to watch these village celebrations and make her contribution to the repair of the church roof? It was a far from appealing prospect, but it would be better, perhaps, than remaining in her room until tomorrow morning. There was nothing in here except a bed, a large old dresser, and a washstand and commode behind a faded curtain. There was no chair, no table. But first things first. She was growing hungry and would go back down to see if there was anything decent to eat. Something certainly smelled good. She only hoped she would not have to step inside that taproom to get it. The noise was deafening even up here in her room.

Fortunately the inn also sported a dining room, which she had been relieved to discover was empty, though not quiet. It adjoined the taproom, and the door between the two rooms stood open. The innkeeper had not offered to shut it after seating her. What he had offered was a meat pasty, but though he had spent some time extolling its virtues and those of his good wife, she had settled for a cold beef sandwich and a cup of coffee.

Goodness, the people in the taproom were loud. But it was a happy, good-natured loudness and did not sound in any way drunken. There was a great deal of bellowing laughter. She had wondered what could be so funny. It must feel good to have not a care in the world. Though perhaps everyone did have cares. It was surely self-indulgent to imagine that only she did. And what really *were* her cares? She had a home and an income. She had children and grandchildren who loved her and whom she loved. She had family and friends.

But it was not so easy to reason herself out of the dismals. She still felt guilty about upsetting everyone and leaving Bath so abruptly. She felt guilty about making Abigail feel bad about not accompanying her – and about rubbing salt in the wound by insisting upon leaving the carriage and her maid behind. The truth was that she had not even wanted Abigail to come with her. She wanted to be alone – but did not know why. Was her life not lonely enough without deliberately seeking out solitude?

She did not know what was happening to her. Except that she felt . . . empty. Utterly and totally empty. A black hole yawned inside her, but she could not see to the bottom of it and was frightened at what she might discover there if she could.

What did she have to show for her forty-two years on this earth? Anything at all? She had a dead husband who had not even been her husband. She had never loved him or even liked or respected

34

him after the first month or so of their marriage. But she had remained faithful to him, and she had cultivated dignity and respectability as twin virtues. She had brought up her children to share those values. All for what? What remained to her but a leftover life she did not know what to do with? And what of Harry, her beloved son, who had been home for a few months earlier in the year recovering from wounds and a recurring fever before insisting upon going back for more? He was surely too determinedly cheerful about the change in his fortunes. How did he really feel about it all? And . . . would he survive? Fear was a constant in her life since Avery, as his guardian, had purchased his commission. And what of Abigail, pretty, sweet, uncomplaining, aged twenty but with no prospects?

Viola had pretended until as recently as two days ago that she was happy with her new life. Or if not quite happy, then at least contented. Happiness was not something she missed, after all, since she had never known it, except for one brief flaring of euphoria when she was sixteen and had fallen in love with the seventeen-year-old son of an acquaintance of her mother's. That budding romance had not lasted. When she was seventeen her father had had a chance to marry her to the son and heir of the Earl of Riverdale, and he had talked her into it. It had not been difficult. She had always been a biddable, obedient daughter.

Viola had sighed as she took a bite of her

sandwich and found it unexpectedly tasty. The bread was freshly baked, the beef moist and tender.

Who was she? The question, which popped so unexpectedly into her head, was a little frightening because it had no obvious answer. For many years she had thought she was the Countess of Riverdale and had identified herself with that title and everything that went with it – the social position, the obligations, the respect. She had become, in effect, not a person, but . . . but what? A mere label? A mere title? She had become something that had no basis in fact. She had never been the Countess of Riverdale.

Was she really nothing at all, then? Nobody? Like a ghost?

Who *was* she? And did no one care that she did not know the answer? That she had no identity? Except more labels – mother, mother-in-law, daughter, sister, sister-in-law, grandmother?

Who was *she*? At the back of it all, beyond it all, beneath it all, *who was she?* She had taken another bite and chewed determinedly, though the sandwich no longer tasted delicious. She had felt very close to hysteria. She recognized the panic, though she had never experienced it before – even just after the catastrophe. She had been simply numb then.

There was a certain coziness about the inn, she had noticed when she looked about in a deliberate attempt to steady herself. It was small and shabby, but it appeared to be clean, and it was a happy place, at least at present. She had moved her gaze to the open door and the crowd beyond it in the taproom. They were villagers, she supposed, all wearing their best clothes in anticipation of a day of revelry in one another's company. She had felt a wave of unexpected nostalgia for the days when, as the countess, she had hosted picnics and open days at Hinsford and everyone had come from miles around. They had been . . . Yes, really, they had been happy times. Her adult life had not been one of unalloyed gloom.

Her eyes had moved idly from person to person of those she could see. On the far side of the room, facing her, were two gentlemen, clearly not belonging to the rest of the crowd, though both had a glass of ale in hand and one of them, the younger of the two, was smiling and nodding in response to something that had been said. They had probably arrived in that smart traveling carriage outside. Her eyes had moved over them and beyond with little curiosity until they snapped back to the other gentleman . . .

Oh.

Oh, goodness me.

It was a long time since she had last seen him. For many years she had avoided him altogether whenever she could and studiously kept her distance from him when she had found herself attending the same social event as he. By what bizarre coincidence . . .

He had seen her too. He was gazing back at her with those hooded, penetrating eyes of his, and she was aware suddenly – annoyingly – of her age

37

and her lone state and the relative shabbiness of her appearance. She had not worn her best clothes for a journey by hired carriage, and she had left too early to have dressed her hair in anything more elaborate than a simple chignon.

She had looked sharply away when the landlord came to refill her coffee cup and tried to keep her eyes from straying again to that doorway. Why had she not sat at a table from which she could neither see nor be seen?

It seemed unfair that men – some men at least – aged far better than women and ended up at the age of forty or so even more attractive than they had been in their twenties. That was what he had been when she had fallen in love with him. Oh, and she had fallen hard. It had been nothing like the joy she had experienced with her first love at the age of sixteen, but she had never doubted that she was in love with Mr Lamarr. It had not mattered that he was rumored to have been responsible for his wife's death or that he cared so little for her memory that he had abandoned home and children almost immediately after her passing and lost no time in establishing a reputation for hard living and relentless womanizing, for coldness and a callous disregard for the conventions of society or the feelings of others. It had not mattered that despite his dark, lean good looks and surface charm it had been easy enough to detect the lack of real feeling or humanity in him. Women fell before him like grass before the scythe, and Viola had been no exception. He had singled her out for dalliance and, oh, she had been tempted, even though she had known perfectly well that dalliance was all it was or would ever be. Even though she had known he would abandon her the morning after she gave in to him.

She had been tempted.

Her marriage, even though it had produced three children, had been a sterile, joyless thing, and other wives strayed. It was even considered acceptable, provided the wife concerned had already done her duty and presented her husband with an heir, and provided her liaisons were carried out with sufficient discretion that the *ton* could pretend not to know.

Viola had sent him away.

Oh, to her shame she had done so not from any great moral conviction but because she had fallen in love with a rake and a rogue and knew that her heart would be broken if she allowed him to bed and then abandon her. She had sent him away and had her heart broken anyway. It had taken her a long, long time to get over him. Every new conquest of his she heard about and every known courtesan he paraded in Hyde Park to the outraged scrutiny of the *ton* had been like a spear to her heart.

He had been handsome beyond belief.

Now he was attractive beyond reason, even as he looked austere and aloof and more than a little intimidating. She could not resist stealing another look at him. His hair was silvering at the temples gorgeously. He was still looking steadily back at her.

He had made her feel young again – at the grand age of twenty-eight – and beautiful.

Now he made her feel old and . . . weary. As though life had passed her by and now it was too late to live it. All the years of her youth and early womanhood were gone and could never be brought back to be lived differently. Not that she would live them differently even if she could go back, she supposed. For she would still obey her father's wishes, and she still would have married a bigamist and remained faithful and unhappy and ultimately a nothing and a nobody.

She had caught Mr Lamarr's eye again over the rim of her coffee cup and refused to be the first to look away. Why should she? She was forty-two years old and probably looked it. So what? Was her age something to be ashamed of?

Perhaps Harry was wounded again. Or dead. Ah, where had that thought come from? She dropped her gaze, Mr Lamarr forgotten. She wondered how many mothers and wives across Britain were plagued with such fears every hour of every day of their lives. And sisters and grandmothers and aunts. For every soldier who was killed in battle there must be a dozen or more women who had worried themselves sick for years and might end up mourning for the rest of their lives. There was nothing so special about her. Or about Harry. Except that he was her son and sometimes love felt like the cruelest thing in the world.

He had gone. Mr Lamarr, that was, and his

companion. They had left when she was not looking. How foolish of her to feel disappointment that he had gone without a word or a parting glance. Most of the other people in the taproom had left too, she realized, and the noise had subsided considerably. It must be past noon by now. No doubt they had gone out into the village for the start of the festivities. Would she go out there too? Wander around to see what was to be seen? Or would she go up to her room, lie down for a while, and wallow in her self-pitying misery? How dreadful it was to be self-pitying. And to have had the feeling intensified by the sight of an attractive man who had once pursued her and wanted to bed her but had gone away today without a word. She had not even had to tell him to leave this time.

Then the dining room door opened – the one into the hallway – and she turned her head to inform the innkeeper that she did not want more coffee. But it was not the innkeeper.

She had forgotten how tall he was, how perfectly formed. She had forgotten how elegantly he dressed, how at ease he was in all his finery. And how harsh and cynical his face was.

She had not forgotten his magnetism. She had felt it across the width of two rooms. Now it was palpable.

'You told me to go away,' he said. 'But that was fifteen years or so ago. Was there a time limit?'

CHAPTER 3

'Fourteen,' she said. 'It was fourteen years ago.'

It felt like a lifetime. Or like something from another life altogether. But here he was, fourteen years older and fourteen years more attractive, though there was a greater hardness now to the handsome, austere features. She wondered, as she had wondered at the time, why he had taken her literally at her word. He did not seem like a man who took kindly to being told no. But she had told him to go away and he had gone. His feelings for her, of course, had not run more than skin-deep. Or groin deep, to be more blunt about it. And there had been plenty of other women only too happy to jump to his every command.

'I stand corrected,' he said in that soft voice she remembered well. He had never been a man who needed to raise his voice. '*Was* there a time limit?'

How did one answer such a question? Well, with a simple no, she supposed. There was no time limit. She had sent him away and had intended that it be forever. But here she was, alone in a room with him fourteen years later, and he had spoken to her again and asked a question. He did not wait for the answer, though.

'Now how am I to interpret your silence?' He strolled to the table nearest the door, pulled out a chair, and sat on it, crossing one elegantly booted leg over the other as he did so. 'Having sent me away once, you have nothing more to say to me? But you have already said something. You have corrected my defective memory. Could it be, then, that you hate to repeat yourself by inviting me yet again to go to the devil? Or could it be that you do not wish to admit that company – *any* company, even mine – is preferable to none at all when one is stranded in a godforsaken village somewhere in the wilds of England? I assume you *are* stranded and have not come here with the express purpose of jollificating with the locals and helping save them from being rained upon on Sunday mornings?'

The mere sound of his voice sent chills up her spine. Just because it was so soft? And because he spoke unhurriedly, with the absolute certainty that no one would dream of cutting him off?

'*Jollificating?*' she said. 'Is it a word?'

'If it is not,' he said, his eyebrows lifting, 'then it ought to be. Perhaps I should give serious consideration to writing a dictionary. What do you think? Do you believe it would rival Dr Johnson's?'

'With a one-word entry?' she said. 'I very much doubt it, Mr Lamarr.'

'Ah, but you do me an injustice,' he said. 'I could

think of ten words without having to frown in thought and pummel my brow. But why is it you will not answer a direct question? *Was* there a time limit? And *are* you stranded? All alone?'

'The axle of the carriage in which I am traveling came perilously close to breaking,' she said. 'The coachman does not believe we will be able to resume the journey until tomorrow morning at the earliest.' Why was she explaining?

'I took a glance out into the innyard before stepping in here,' he said. 'There is no sign of a private carriage. Has yours by chance made off without you, the imperiled axle story just one big hoax to be rid of you? But that is unlikely, I must admit. You did not – surely – arrive here in that apology for a conveyance that is listing hard to the north-west and looking for all the world as though it will not be fit to go anywhere for the next eternity or two. Or did you? A hired carriage, Lady Riverdale?'

'That is no longer my name,' she said.

'A hired carriage, *Miss Kingsley*?' He sounded pained.

'How are the mighty fallen?' she said. 'Was that your meaning, Mr Lamarr? Then why not say so?'

Long, elegant fingers closed about the handle of his quizzing glass, but he did not raise it to his eye. 'Riverdale was a blackguard,' he said. 'If it was your idea to completely disassociate yourself from him, even in name, then I congratulate you. You are better off without the connection. Kingsley is your maiden name, I assume?'

She did not answer. She looked down at her coffee in order to break eye contact with him. There was still half a cup left. It would be cold by now, though. Besides, she was not sure her hand would be steady enough to lift the cup without revealing her agitation.

'Miss Kingsley,' he said after a few moments of silence had passed. '*Are* you going to send me away again? And spend the rest of the day alone?'

'How I spend the rest of the day is none of your concern, Mr Lamarr,' she said. 'I do not suppose *you* are stranded here. I will not keep you, then. You must be eager to be on your way.'

'Must I?' His eyebrows rose again and he rotated the quizzing glass in his hand a few times. 'But I *am* stranded. My brother was eager to be back on the road and left all of fifteen minutes ago. Too eager, perhaps. One wonders how long it will be before he realizes he has forgotten me, and whether when he does so he will deem it necessary to turn back to retrieve me. It is doubtful. The young are ever careless of their elders, do you not find? André is still in his twenties. A mere puppy.'

What? Whatever was he talking about?

'Your carriage has left without you?' She stared at him in disbelief. If it was true, then there could be only one explanation, and the absurd story he had just told was not it. 'You sent it and your brother away? Because of me?'

His eyebrows rose again and he turned his glass once more. 'But yes,' he said. 'Why else?'

Her head turned cold. For one nasty moment she thought she was about to faint.

'Having done so,' he said, 'I hope you will not force me to spend the rest of the day alone. The thought of attending a village fair unaccompanied is singularly unappealing. The prospect of whiling away the hours by trudging along country lanes trying to identify flora and fauna has even less appeal. If you are willing to suspend your dismissal of me, even just for today, Miss Kingsley, then perhaps we may step outside together either to jollificate or to wander and thus save each other from a day of unutterable boredom. Assuming, that is, you do not find me unutterably boring. Or worse.'

She stared at him and wondered, as she had done numerous times before – even after she had sent him away, even as she had avoided him and studiously averted her eyes from him whenever they happened to be in the same ballroom or theater – what it was about him that both powerfully repelled and attracted her. He was not a classically handsome man. His face was surely too thin and angular and unamiable. Instead he was . . . gorgeous. But that said almost nothing at all about him, only about her reaction to him. She had never been able to come up with quite the right word to describe him accurately. For with him it had never been just looks. It was . . . everything. Presence. Charisma. Power. Ruthlessness. Sexuality – though that was not a word very common to her vocabulary.

He expected her to spend the rest of the day in his company. Yes, *expected*. He had gambled on her compliance by sending his carriage on its way without him, though it was altogether likely it was waiting somewhere nearby and would return for him later tonight or tomorrow. It would be madness for her to comply, especially given the mood she was in.

Or perhaps it was exactly what she *needed* given the mood she was in – to do something unexpected and outrageous to fill in the hours and take her mind off herself. The alternative was to hide away in her room and brood. And it was not as though she were going to be deceived or seduced or left brokenhearted tomorrow.

'I will attend the fair with you for an hour or two of the afternoon,' she said.

He released his hold on his quizzing glass. 'There is to be a feast of sorts at the church hall later,' he said. 'There will be nothing at all served here, alas. Both the taproom and the dining room are to be closed so that mine host and his good wife may mingle and feast with their neighbors. The banquet is to be followed by dancing on the village green this evening. It all sounds quite, quite irresistible, does it not?'

'I will most certainly draw the line at dancing,' she said.

'Ah, but you were always so lovely to dance with,' he told her. And oh, goodness, *how* had he done that? For with the mere dropping of a tone in his voice and a somewhat more intense focusing of his eyes upon hers, he had made it sound as if he were talking about a different sort of dance altogether from what would be performed on the village green this evening.

And of course – oh, *of course* – his words had their effect, as they always had. They half robbed her lungs of breath and her mind of good sense. She got firmly to her feet. Enough of this. 'I shall go and fetch a bonnet and shawl,' she said, 'and see if my baggage has been taken up to my room yet.'

He reached the door ahead of her and held it open. 'And I will bespeak a room for myself since it would appear unlikely that my brother will return for me this side of nightfall,' he said. 'So much for brotherly devotion. Shall we meet here again in fifteen minutes?'

'Fifteen minutes,' she agreed, and swept by him and on up the stairs. She paused on the first landing and looked back. He was still standing in the dining room doorway, gazing lazily after her.

This, she thought, was not a good idea.

But its companion thought came unprompted: *Why not?*

It was a brisk and breezy September day, halfway between summer and autumn. The sky was predominantly blue, but white clouds scudded across it and made of the land below an ever-moving chessboard of sunshine and shade. Marcel could think of a dozen things – at the very least! – he would rather be doing than standing at the edge of a village green, waiting with a largish crowd of expectant villagers and their darting children and prancing dogs for the grand opening of a harvest fair. The ceremony was apparently to include some sort of recital by the church choir. They were gathering and lining up on the green, all clad in billowing gowns. However, he had chosen quite deliberately to be here and had no cause for complaint. He had even quite rashly deprived himself of the means of leaving here.

But, so far at least, the annoyance of it all was outweighed by the triumph of the fact that he had the former Countess of Riverdale at his side. Let no one ever say that life was without its little co-incidences. Actually, a giant coincidence in this case. What were the odds . . .?

She had put on weight in the past fourteen years. She would doubtless be horrified if she knew he had noticed, but really the extra pounds were evenly distributed over all the right places and made her even more attractive than she had been then. More womanly. Or perhaps it was merely that he was looking at her now through eyes and sensibilities that were fourteen years older than they had been then. What twenty-five-year-old male would look upon a fortyish woman with lust, after all? And it was certainly lust he was feeling for Miss Somebody Kingsley. Strangely – he was just now struck with the thought – he did not know her first name.

She was looking aloof and dignified, the very look that had so intrigued him then. For he had wondered if what he saw told the whole story, or if she was in fact a powder keg of passion that no one, least of all Riverdale, had ever ignited. He wondered the same thing now.

'What would you guess their average age to be?' he asked, nodding in the direction of the choir. 'Sixty-five? Seventy?' Had no one here heard of choir boys?

'Their age is surely immaterial,' she said in just the cool, reproving tone he would expect of her.

'The quality of voice will matter, though,' he said. 'I would wager upon plenty of warble and vibrato, with some off-key would-be soloist ruining the collective effect. That will be the one who has grown deaf and cannot hear the tuning fork or his fellow choristers.'

'That is very disrespectful of you,' she said with a frown. 'People cannot help being elderly.'

'But they can help remaining part of a church choir long after they ought to retire with some grace,' he said.

'Perhaps it is a younger member who will prove to be tone deaf,' she said. 'If anyone *is*. Good heavens, we have not even heard them yet. Perhaps they will be sublime.'

'Perhaps,' he agreed. 'I will stand corrected if you prove to be right. I seriously doubt it, however.'

Her lips twitched and she almost smiled. A memory struck him then of trying – and failing – to make her smile all those years ago. He could not remember ever seeing her do so, in fact, and wondered if she ever did.

'Ah,' he said. 'The moment is upon us.'

A man of great self-importance who did not introduce himself but doubtless held some position of authority in the church – though he was not the vicar – delivered a long and pompous and repetitive speech while people grabbed their children and tried to grab their dogs and keep them more or less still and quiet. He made a point of welcoming visitors to their humble festivities and professed himself and his fellow churchgoers honored indeed to have them. Every eye in the village, except perhaps those belonging to the babies and dogs, turned upon the only two obvious visitors. The church dignitary was followed by the vicar, fully vested, who offered a mercifully short prayer of thanksgiving for the harvest and the fine weather and the hard work and generosity of his flock. The choir sang about Christian soldiers and archangels on high and other holy things that had nothing whatsoever to do with either harvest or church roofs. But Marcel's prediction proved undeniably correct. There were both warbles and vibrato, and one dominant male voice was off-key by a crucial half tone.

'You need not say it,' Miss Kingsley said after the vicar's wife, with gracious smiles and nods for everyone, had declared the fete open. 'I heard. And the singing was lovely. They were doing their best.'

'If ever I did something to please you,' he said, 'and you told me afterward that I had done my best, I would crawl into the nearest deep hole and sulk for the next fourteen years or so, Miss Kingsley.'

The wind had whipped some color into her cheeks. Even so, he had a strong suspicion that she was blushing. She had thought he was making some risqué remark, then, had she? He had not been, as it happened, but he was perfectly willing to take credit for it. Her eyes were as blue as he remembered them. They had always been one of her finest features – a real blue, not one of the varying shades of gray that often pass for blue.

'I see a booth over there that is positively spilling over with jewels,' he said. 'Allow me to escort you.' He offered his arm.

She looked at it before taking it, as though she suspected some sort of trap. He must have touched her before. Of course he had. He had danced with her on more than one occasion. But the touch of her hand on his arm now felt unfamiliar. Light. Neither leaning nor clinging. But it brought her shoulder close to his arm, and her dress brushed against his Hessian boots. It brought the faintly fragrant scent of her to his nostrils. Not too floral, not too spicy. Just right. Perfect for her.

He was glad he had sent André away.

'Absolutely,' she said. 'The church congregation must be rescued from being rained upon. Besides, I am partial to sparkling jewels. Let us see if there are any diamonds among them. *Large* diamonds.'

The former Lady Riverdale being lighthearted? Actually joking? This was intriguing. He raised his eyebrows but made no comment.

There were diamonds and emeralds and rubies and sapphires. There were topazes and garnets. There were silver and gold. And there were pearls. All of them large and sparkling – even the pearls – and perfectly shaped. All of them unutterably vulgar and not even convincing fakes. He decked her out in some of the more ostentatious of them and paid three times what the two flustered ladies who ran the booth asked of him. She glittered and sparkled at ears, bosom, wrists, and fingers – and admired the effect and preened herself under the admiration of the two ladies and the small crowd that had gathered about at a respectful distance to watch. There was a smattering of admiring applause. She thanked him and told him she would have considered the sapphire bracelet too if only she had one more wrist.

'An ankle?' he suggested, looking down toward the hem of her dress.

'Ah, no,' she said. 'One would not wish to look overdressed.'

She had set aside at least some of her legendary dignity, it seemed, in favor of something approaching gaiety, and he was enslaved. She did not immediately snatch off the jewelry as soon as they were out of sight of the booth and hide it away in the darkest depths of her reticule. Rather, she kept fingering it and admiring it.

They had their portraits sketched in charcoal by a bearded, wild-haired artist who made Marcel look like a cadaverous devil minus his pitchfork and Miss Kingsley like a moon-faced ghost with a pearl necklace. They bought two iced cakes after the baking had been judged and they had been awarded third prize. They were as hard as granite.

'But very pretty with their twirled icing, you must admit,' she said when he grimaced.

'I might,' he said, 'if I did not feel as though every tooth in my head had just snapped in two.'

'But not by the icing,' she said.

'But not by the icing.'

'Well, then . . .'

They watched the wood-sawing contest, in which a group of brawny, sweating young men with shirt-sleeves rolled well above the elbow showed off their muscles and their prowess for a gaggle of giggling village maidens – and for the two of them, the visitors, the outsiders. They examined – at least she did – the needlework stall after the judging had been completed, and she bought him a man's coarse cotton handkerchief, across one corner of which a large *L* had been embroidered in the midst of curlicues and stemless, leafless blossoms. The handkerchief had not placed among the winners – one fact that impelled her to buy it, he suspected, the other being that the *L* could stand for Lamarr. She seemed not to know about his marquess's title.

He bought her a crocheted drawstring bag in a hideous shade of pink – also not a winner – in which to keep all the jeweled finery now bedecking her person.

'I will treasure it all,' she assured him, and he wondered idly if she really would. He considered how long he would keep the handkerchief. He suspected that he *would* keep it, though he would never use it and thus display it to the shocked eyes of the *ton*.

They watched and listened to the fiddle contest. He refrained from tapping his foot or clapping his hands in time to the music, as most of the spectators did, but she did not so refrain, he noticed. She appeared to be genuinely enjoying herself. As, strangely enough, was he.

They watched a singing contest for little girls and one boy soprano, who had somehow escaped the dreadful fate of being a member of the church choir, before moving on to watch the archery contest and then to have their fortunes told. He was to expect long life and prosperity and happiness. No surprise there. Did fortune-tellers ever predict anything different? He did not know what she was to expect. She did not tell him.

They drank weak, tepid lemonade from a table run by a Sunday school class. It must be many years since he had drunk any sort of lemonade. It would be many more before he would indulge again.

She became more lighthearted as the afternoon wore on. But she did not flirt with him. And that surely had been part of the attraction when they were younger. Although he had wondered too about the possibility of hidden passions; maybe he had seen in her a potentially steadying influence as his life had careened more and more out of control – and even as he had flirted outrageously with her. And even as he had known she was married and therefore out of bounds for anything more than dalliance. It had not occurred to him at the time that just maybe he could have made a friend of her.

But he did not make friends with women. Or even with men for that matter. Friendship involved a certain degree of intimacy, an opening of self to another, and he chose not to share himself with anyone.

She was not married now. Ironically, she never had been.

And he wanted her. Still. And he wondered still.

They watched a dancing contest about the maypole that had been erected in the center of the green. Two teams had come from other villages to challenge the dancers from this village, and crowds gathered around to cheer on their favorites and to applaud appreciatively every intricate move in which the colorful ribbons twined themselves about the tall pole in seemingly hopeless entanglement while the dancers who held them were forced closer and closer to it and to one another – and then smoothly extricated themselves, weaving in and out as they circled to the spirited scraping of the fiddles until each dancer held an unencumbered ribbon and the maypole was bare.

'The maypole is like a symbol of life, is it not?' the former countess said at the end of one such dance, and he turned an inquiring gaze upon her. She was flushed and bright-eyed – not just from the wind, he guessed – almost as though she had been out there dancing herself.

'It is?' He raised his eyebrows.

'Around and around,' she said, 'seemingly getting nowhere but becoming more and more entangled in troubles and cares, not all of them of one's own making.'

'That is a gloomy assessment of life with which to entertain yourself on a festive afternoon, Lady Riverdale,' he said.

'But the maypole dances do not end in chaos,' she said. 'And I am not the countess. The Countess of Riverdale is married to the present earl and is a friend of mine.'

'I will not be distracted with trivialities,' he said. 'Complete your analogy.'

'Everything works out,' she said. 'If one faithfully follows the pattern of the dance, it all works out.' She was frowning.

'But what would happen,' he asked her, 'if just one of the dancers bobbed when all the others weaved? The whole pattern would be ruined, all the ribbons would be hopelessly tangled with one another, and all the dancers would be doomed to weave and wander in eternal befuddlement. I am afraid your analogy is a naively romantic one, Miss Kingsley. It is simplistic. It suggests that there is such a thing as happily-ever-after if one but lives a virtuous and dutiful life.'

'Very well,' she said. 'It was a foolish and impulsive idea, and it has annoyed you. I am sorry.'

Had she annoyed him with her oh-so-simplistic suggestion that unwavering virtue was always rewarded? By God, she had. But how could anyone in her right mind believe even for an impulsive moment that life turned out right if one but followed the rules? Especially when such a belief depended upon the companion theory that everyone else in one's orbit could be relied upon to do likewise. How could she of all people believe it?

'Annoyed?' he said. 'Rather say *charmed*, Miss Kingsley. I am charmed by your naïve optimism.' He possessed himself of her hand and raised it to his lips. She was not wearing gloves, as she had not all afternoon. She was, however, wearing a ridiculously large diamond ring, which sparkled in the sunlight. 'And dazzled,' he added.

She . . . smiled. And he really was. Dazzled, that was. Years fell away from her face even as lines appeared at the outer corners of her eyes.

'It is rather splendid, is it not?' she said, extending her hand and spreading her fingers. 'The poor emerald on my other hand is dwarfed.' She raised that hand too and shook it to make the ruby bracelet jangle on her wrist. 'Optimism? Do I believe in it?'

It was a rhetorical question, it seemed. She turned away rather abruptly before he could answer in order to listen to the lengthy adjudication of the maypole dancing. She kept her face turned away from him. He had offended her, perhaps, by calling her naïve.

What would he do tomorrow? Hire a horse? *Buy* a horse? André had had the presence of mind to have the largest of his bags taken into the inn, but that in itself posed a problem. Hire a gig, then? A curricle? A carriage? Were any such conveyances available in such a place? He doubted it. Would he find himself walking home, or at least to the nearest sizable town? But he would think of that tomorrow.

'Shall we make our way to the church hall and the feast?' he suggested. That was where everyone else seemed to be headed.

'I suppose there is little choice if we wish to eat,' she said.

'I most certainly do not choose to go hungry.' He offered his arm. 'Do you?'

She gave him that look again, the one that suggested he had just said something risqué, though he had not done so intentionally.

'No,' she said, and took his arm.

CHAPTER 4

It seemed to Viola that she had stepped out of time. There had been the seemingly disastrous delay in a journey that should have been completed by nightfall; the almost incredible coincidence of finding Mr Lamarr stranded – albeit deliberately – at the same small country inn as she; the fact that a village fair had been arranged for this exact day; his suggestion that they enjoy whatever it had to offer together; and the excellence of the weather for the time of year. It was all so strange that it was hard to believe in the reality of it. So she did not. It was a time out of time, as though she had been given the chance to step off the world for a short while and had taken it.

Tomorrow everything would return to normal and so would she. She would resume both the journey and the life she had cast off for today. She would face the demons that had cracked her surface calm in Bath and sent her scurrying homeward, alone. She would face all that when tomorrow came.

In the meanwhile . . . Oh, she had enjoyed this afternoon as she could not remember enjoying any other. She had left her old self back at the inn and become someone new, someone she had never before allowed herself to be. She had been decked out in tasteless, garish jewelry, the very sight of which would normally make her cringe. Worse, she had allowed Mr Lamarr to pay for it. She had bought him a gift too – a hideous handkerchief hideously embroidered. She had clapped her hands and tapped her foot in time to fiddle music and to the intricate maneuvers of the maypole dancing instead of observing with quiet, gracious dignity. She had shamelessly admired a few brawny, sweating young men as they sawed wood and showed off for the young women. She had had her fortune told and was apparently to expect long life and continued bliss with her handsome husband – she had not corrected the misconception. She had sat for her portrait even though she had seen some of the artist's earlier efforts and knew he had no talent whatsoever. She knew artistic excellence. Joel, her son-in-law, was fast gaining fame as one of the country's most talented portrait painters. She had continued to sit even when a crowd had gathered around to watch and comment.

They had certainly not gone unnoticed or unre-marked upon, she and Mr Lamarr. Far from it. She had felt very much on display all afternoon and had chosen to enjoy the attention and even to play up to it. She had flashed her cheap false jewels before anyone who looked at her with admiration and pointed out to a few people where they could purchase some for themselves.

The vicar's wife met them at the door of the church hall with smiling formality and insisted upon seating them at a private table, while most people squeezed onto the benches flanking the long tables that stretched from one end of the hall to the other. And unlike everyone else, who had to line up for their food, they were served heaping plates of every dish known to man – according to Mr Lamarr.

'Or woman,' Viola added.

'It is hardly surprising, of course,' he said, 'when the harvest has just been gathered in from fields and gardens. But dear me, I do not recall ever before having been presented with such a vast pyramid of innumerable foods all piled onto one plate.'

The presentation did indeed lack something in elegance. It lacked nothing in either quantity or flavor, however. Viola, normally a dainty eater, cleaned off her plate, as did he. And then they both ate a generous wedge of apple tart smothered with thick, sweet custard.

And that was that, she thought with more than a little regret as she set her spoon down on the empty dish. Not just the banquet, but this whole precious day of escape from herself and her world. She would remember it for a long time, even for the rest of her life, she suspected. Perhaps the memory of it would somehow cheer her up, help her get her life back together at last.

Or perhaps it would do just the opposite.

'Miss Kingsley.' He was turning his cup of coffee

in his hands, and she was aware again of the well-manicured elegance of his fingers and of the gold ring – *real* gold – on his right hand. 'Are you going to doom me to an evening spent alone in my room, stretched out on my bed, hands clasped behind my head, toes pointing at the ceiling while I count the cracks up there and entertain the fear that it is about to fall on my head? Or are you going to dance with me?'

The image of him lying stretched out on his bed, hands clasped behind his head, was enough to turn her hot inside. But the idea of dancing with him did no less. She had agreed to spend the afternoon in his company and had added the meal because there was to be no alternative at the inn. It had been enough. More than enough. She must not be tempted . . .

But why not? Who was going to be harmed?

'If it will serve as an act of mercy,' she said, 'then I will dance with you.'

'Ah.' He set down his cup and leaned back in his chair.

'Though my main reason for agreeing,' she added, 'is that the evening would be long and tedious for me too if I were forced to spend it alone in my room.'

'How very flattering, Lady Riverdale,' he said. 'But you are not Lady Riverdale. I cannot think of you as Miss Kingsley either, however. The name makes you sound like someone's governess. Will you entrust me with your given name?'

It was an imposition. They were near strangers. Only her family members had ever called her by her first name.

'It is Viola,' she said.

'Ah,' he said. 'The loveliest of the stringed instruments. Of a lower tone than the violin but not as low as the cello. It suits you even though the pronunciation is different. I am Marcel. Marc to my family and intimates.'

Strangely, one did not think of him as a man with family. But he had a brother. And had there not been children with his late wife?

The church dignitary who had opened the afternoon's activities with a lengthy speech earlier in the afternoon was on his feet again now and raising both arms to draw everyone's attention. After the room had hushed he delivered another rambling speech before announcing to a cheer from the gathering that the dancing would begin on the village green in half an hour.

'I need to return to the inn first,' Viola said. 'I would like to change my dress and comb my hair.' Among other things.

'I will do myself the honor of escorting you,' he said, getting to his feet and coming around the table to draw back her chair. 'I need to comb my hair too.'

They walked back to the inn, her arm drawn through his, and went upstairs together. She paused outside her door, and he bowed and suggested that they meet downstairs in half an hour. The inn appeared to be deserted apart from the two of them. Before she closed her door, Viola was aware of him letting himself into the room opposite and one door down from her own.

It was probably foolish of her to prolong this unexpected gift of a carefree, happy day, she thought as she leaned back against her door after closing it. But why? Why not suspend reality for a few hours longer and dance with him on the village green? It was not as though she was going to fall in love with him and have her heart broken all over again, after all. Why not snatch a little more joy from this time-out-of-time adventure with which fate had gifted her? She was no longer a young woman, but she was not old either. She was only forty-two. The thought made her smile ruefully.

She changed into a dress that was suitable for evening wear but was neither too flimsy nor overly elaborate. She styled her hair as well as she could without the services of her maid. It was a little more fussy than the simple chignon in which she had worn it all day. She hesitated over her box of jewelry, but finally decked herself out in her newly acquired finery. Her family and acquaintances would be scandalized. But she actually liked it. It made her feel lighthearted, as though just the wearing of it could make her smile inside. She slid her feet into dancing slippers instead of the more sensible shoes she had worn all day, added a heavier woolen shawl for warmth, and bent to look at herself in the tarnished glass over the washstand. If the pearls of her necklace and matching earrings were real, she would surely be one of the richest women in the world. Perhaps *the* richest. She surprised herself by chuckling aloud.

She felt breathless by the time she left her room. And inexplicably nervous, as though there were something clandestine about going with him to join a large gathering of villagers on a very public village green. She had often attended *ton* events in the company of gentlemen who were not her husband. As far as she knew she had never so much as raised an eyebrow in the *ton* by doing so. It was perfectly acceptable.

But never with Mr Lamarr.

He was waiting for her in the hall. He had changed too. Like her, he had avoided donning the sort of finery he would surely have worn to a *ton* ball, but he was immaculately turned out even so in black and white, with an intricately tied neckcloth despite the fact that he did not have a valet with him. A diamond solitaire winked from its folds. A real diamond.

'My diamond is larger than yours,' she said, waggling her fingers at him, making a jest because she was feeling awkward and self-conscious even though she had spent all afternoon in his company.

'And it shines brighter too,' he said, his eyes gleaming at her. They were dark eyes, like liquid chocolate. 'But then the giver has immaculate taste.'

'And is the epitome of modesty too,' she said as his eyes moved over her from head to foot, not even making a pretense of being discreet.

'The pearls are a nice touch too,' he said. 'Viola.'

The sound of her name on his lips sent shivers down her spine. Again. She was behaving like a gauche girl. It felt rather good.

'They do not clash with the diamond or the rubies?' she asked, displaying one wrist. 'Or the garnets?' She raised the other.

'Clash?' he said, all astonishment. 'Certainly not. One cannot wear too many jewels. Why have them if one is not to display them? But to be perfectly frank with you, Viola, I scarcely noticed your fine jewels until you drew my attention to them. The beauty of the woman who wears them shines brighter.'

'Oh, well-done,' she said, brushing past him in the direction of the door. Foolishly, though the compliment had been too outrageous to be taken remotely seriously, she was absurdly pleased.

She was only forty-two, after all.

He caught up to her and offered his arm. Fiddles and pipes were already playing with great enthusiasm beside the village green, from which the maypole had been removed, and a vigorous reel was in progress, boots thumping on the hard ground, skirts swaying, voices whooping, hands clapping, and voices calling out encouragement. Children dashed noisily about, probably overtired after the day's unaccustomed excitement. Lamps along

67

the street on their side of the green provided some light in the gathering dusk.

They were drawing attention again, Viola was aware. And a few shy smiles. And some comments.

'Are you going to dance with your lady, guv?' someone called out boldly, and Mr Lamarr grasped the handle of his quizzing glass and raised it halfway to his eye. He did not reply.

'If you aren't, I will,' someone else added to a general burst of merriment from those who heard.

'I believe I can manage without assistance,' Mr Lamarr said in a languid voice. 'But I thank you for the offer.'

'That's putting you in your place, 'lijah,' someone shouted to another gust of laughter.

They joined the lines for a country dance, less vigorous, more intricate than the reel. He was an elegant, accomplished dancer, as Viola well remembered. He also had a gift for focusing his attention upon his partner, even when he was performing some figures of the set with another.

How wonderful it was, she thought as she danced, the cool evening air on her face and arms below her shawl, to be someone's focus of attention, to be made to feel even for just a short while that she was the only person in the world who really mattered. It was not that she craved attention all the time. Far from it. She never had. But oh, sometimes it felt wonderful. They were surrounded by pretty, laughing young women, several of whom were darting half-frightened, half-appreciative glances at the formidable stranger in their midst, but he appeared to see no one but her.

It was all artifice, of course. It was part of his appeal, and part of the danger. But it did not matter. She was not for a moment deceived by it. When the dancing was over for the evening, or perhaps even before it ended, they would return to their rooms at the inn, and tomorrow they would be on their separate ways and would very probably never see each other again. She did not mingle with the *ton* any longer.

So tonight – this evening – was to be enjoyed for what it was. A brief escape offered by fate.

All the sets were country dances or reels. They were what the villagers and farmers from the surrounding countryside knew and wanted. Viola and Mr Lamarr – Marcel – danced two of them and watched a few more. But when one tune started he lifted a finger as though to stop her from saying anything, listened intently for a moment, and then turned to her.

'One could dance a waltz to this,' he said.

She listened too and agreed. But no one else was waltzing. The dancers were in line, performing steps with which Viola was unfamiliar.

'We will waltz.' It was an imperious command.

'Oh, hardly,' she protested.

But he was holding out a hand for hers. 'I believe waltzing is something you and I never did together, Viola,' he said. 'We will right that wrong. Come.'

'Marcel.' She frowned.

'Ah,' he said. 'I like it – the sound of you speaking my name. But come.' He took her hand, and she did not resist as he led her about the green to the side nearest the church, where there were no people, perhaps because full night had fallen and the light from the lamps did not penetrate this far. Here there was heavy shade, though not total darkness. It was a clear night, illumined by both moonlight and starlight.

'You will waltz with me here,' he said. It was still not a question. He was offering her no choice. Neither, of course, was he coercing her.

'But people will see,' she protested.

'And?' She was aware that his eyebrows were raised. 'They will see us dancing together. Scandalous goings-on indeed.'

'Oh, very well,' she said, raising her left hand to set on his shoulder as his right arm came about her waist. How could she possibly resist? She had always thought the waltz the most romantic dance ever invented, yet there had been no such thing when she was young. There were still people who thought there was something scandalous about it, a man and a woman dancing a whole set exclusively with each other, face-to-face, their hands touching each other.

He took her free hand in his, listened a moment, and then led her into a waltz, twirling about the uneven ground of the village green, the sounds of voices and laughter seeming far away though they were only just beyond the shadows. She was very aware of his hands, the one resting firmly against the arch of her back at the waist, the other clasped about hers. She was aware that there was only an inch of space between his evening coat and her bosom, that their legs occasionally touched, that he was looking down at her, that she was looking back. She could not see him clearly in the darkness, but she knew his eyes were on hers. She could feel his body heat, smell his cologne, feel his magnetism. She could hear his breath.

She did not know how long it went on. Probably no longer than ten minutes. The dance had already been in progress, after all, when they started. It might have been forever. Viola forgot everything except the waltz and the man with whom she danced it in silence.

'Viola,' he said softly next to her ear when the music stopped. He did not immediately release her, and she made no move to extricate herself from his arms. 'Let us go see what is behind the church, shall we?'

A churchyard, she supposed. But actually there was a sort of meadow beyond that, sloping downward to a river she had only half noticed this morning from the carriage window. A willow tree leaned over from the bank and almost touched the water. A humpbacked stone bridge crossed the river a short way to their left. It must all be very picturesque in the daylight. But so was the rest of the village.

They stood halfway between the low churchyard

wall and the river, which winked in the moonlight, and listened to the slight rushing sound of water. The music began again, but the sound of it and of voices and laughter seemed far away now, part of some other world that did not concern them. His arm, through which her hand had been drawn, came about her waist to draw her to his side, and she wondered idly, not if she ought to allow it, but if she would. She made no move to bat his arm away or to take a step to the side. Rather, she leaned against him.

She would allow it, then. But she was in no danger. She knew what he was about. She understood. It did not matter.

He nudged her head onto his shoulder, lifted her chin with his long fingers, and bent his face to hers to kiss her.

Ah, it was a shock. She was so very unkissed. The boy she had loved when she was sixteen had kissed her once – a fumbling, guilty, swift smacking of lips that had left her in rapture for weeks afterward. And Humphrey had kissed her a few times in the early years of their marriage when he came to her bed. But the kisses had always been a prelude to the bedding and had never been offered with anything resembling conviction or affection or even lust. He had never lusted after her. He had married her – bigamously – for her money because he had none with which to pay off his many debts, but her father had pots of it that he was willing to give in exchange for the titles and

72

prestige that would come through marrying his daughter to an earl's heir.

She had never been kissed with any expertise. Until now. The first shock was the lightness of it, the unthreatening nature of it. He did not grab her or grind his lips against hers. He did not even turn her and pull her against him. His lips were soft, warm, slightly parted, and he teased her own until they parted too. His breath was warm against her cheek. His hand moved from beneath her chin to cup the back of her head. He took his time. There was no urgency, no hurry, no agenda, no destination. No threat. It was she who turned at last in his arms to come against him – knees, abdomen, bosom. Her hands came to his shoulders.

The second shock was that it did not end, not after a moment, not even after several moments, though he did move his mouth from hers to kiss her face and her throat, to murmur soft words her mind did not even try to decipher. Then he was kissing her mouth again, but again without urgency, teasing her lips farther apart, touching the flesh within with his tongue, reaching his tongue slowly into her mouth, stroking its tip over the sensitive roof.

That was when desire stabbed through her like a raw wound, and she knew herself to be in peril. She was, she understood, an almost complete innocent. She had been married – or had thought herself married – for more than twenty years. She had borne three children. She was a grandmother.

But she knew virtually nothing. She had not even had . . . relations for almost twenty years. Soon after Abigail had turned out to be another girl and not the spare for Harry that Humphrey had hoped for, he had given up on their marriage in all but name – and even that was false.

She knew nothing about desire.

If she had thought about it at all, she had expected it to be a fierce thing. On the part of the man, that was. With willing submission on the part of the woman.

But this was not fierce. This was . . .

Expertise.

This was seduction.

She drew back, but only with the upper part of her body. Her hands were still on his shoulders. She could see him only faintly in the moonlight. His eyes were dark and heavy lidded. 'We ought not to be doing this,' she said.

'Ought we not?' His voice was low. 'Why not?'

She drew breath and . . . could not think of a single reason. 'We ought not.' She was almost whispering.

'Then we will not,' said the master seducer, and he released his hold on her, took her hand in his, laced their fingers, and strolled closer to the water with her and along the bank toward the bridge. He led her to the middle of it, and they stood by the low parapet and gazed into the dark water that flowed beneath. The sounds of merriment seemed louder from here. The light of the lamps from the street on the far side of the green was visible again.

She was bewildered and . . . disappointed. That was all? He would answer so promptly the voice of protest? But why was she surprised? When she had told him fourteen years ago to go away, he had gone without argument, and without returning. She remembered now that she had been both bewildered and disappointed then too.

Perhaps this was why he was so successful. He might be a seducer, but he was not a coercer. No woman would ever be able to accuse him of tricking her, of persuading her against her will, of refusing to take no for an answer. At least, Viola assumed he approached all his conquests this same way.

But their hands were clasped, their fingers laced. Perhaps because this time she had not told him to go away. Should she? Undoubtedly. But would she? Where was the harm in strolling alone with him thus? In holding his hand? In kissing him? In allowing him to kiss her? Whom was she harming? Her children? Hardly.

Herself?

She had been depressed for so long that she scarcely knew any other state. So she would be depressed again tomorrow looking back upon today. So what? At least she would have a few memories of pleasure, of desire. Even happiness. There had been so little happiness . . .

'When you told me to go away,' he said, almost

as if he were reading her thoughts, 'did you expect me to obey?'

'Why would you stay where you were not wanted?' she asked. 'You had plenty of other choices.'

'Cruel,' he said softly.

'Oh, nonsense,' she said.

'Did you *want* me to obey?' he asked.

'Why else would I have asked you to leave me alone?' she said.

'Have you noticed,' he asked, 'how some people will almost invariably answer a question with another? Did you want me to obey, Viola?'

She hesitated. 'Yes,' she said. 'I was a married lady, Marcel. Or thought I was.'

'Was that the only reason?' he asked.

She hesitated again. 'I had young children,' she said, 'and a reputation to protect.'

'And was it worth protecting,' he asked, 'at the expense of personal inclination?'

'We cannot always do what we want,' she said.

'Why not?' he asked.

'And have you noticed,' she asked him, 'that some people ask interminable questions and are never satisfied with the answers they are given?'

'Touché,' he said.

Two people – a man and woman – were approaching from the village. A couple of children darted and danced about them. They came across the bridge.

'Good night, ma'am, sir,' the man said respect-fully, pulling on his forelock. 'Me and my missus here hope you have enjoyed your day. We are honored to have had you with us.'

The woman bobbed an awkward curtsy and the children gathered closer to her skirts and fell silent.

'Well, thank you,' Viola said. 'We have indeed enjoyed ourselves. And it has been our pleasure to have been included in your festivities.'

The man cleared his throat. 'And Vicar told us about your very generous donation to the roof repairs, sir,' he said. 'May I make so bold as to express my personal thanks?'

Mr Lamarr nodded curtly, Viola saw when she turned her head rather sharply to look at him. When had he done that? He bade the couple a good evening, and they went on their way.

'Some people,' he murmured, 'would be unable to hold their tongues if their life depended upon it.'

Presumably he was talking about the vicar.

'It was very kind of you to be generous,' she said.

'Viola.' He released her hand and offered his arm, turning back in the direction of the village as he did so. 'One thing no one will ever be able to accuse me of with any conviction is kindness. The cool of evening is rapidly turning to the chill of night. Do you wish to dance something vigorous and warming on the green? Or would you prefer to return to the inn?'

'The inn, please.' But she said it with regret. Was her day of escape finally over, then? And what would tomorrow bring? Would the carriage be ready to take her home? She dreaded the possibility that she might be stranded here for another day. But she dreaded going home too. She would think about it all tomorrow.

They walked back to the inn without talking, though they did have to pass numerous people as they skirted the village green, and exchanged good night greetings with some of them – at least Viola did. At some time since they had left to go to the dance, the innkeeper had returned and the taproom had been opened up. It was half filled with men imbibing ale and hiding away from would-be dancing partners, Viola suspected. Everyone seemed to be in just as jovial spirits as they had been this morning, however.

He escorted her upstairs to her room, took the key from her hand, unlocked the door, and stood in the doorway with her.

'Thank you—' she began, but he set one forefinger across her lips.

'No absurdities, Viola,' he said. 'Has it been worthwhile to you, a blameless life of virtue and dignity and self-denial? Has it brought you happiness?'

'Happiness is not everything,' she said.

'Ah. I have my answer,' he told her.

'And has it been worthwhile to you, a life of debauchery and self-indulgence?' she asked. 'Has it brought you happiness?'

His face turned blank and cold, and for a moment she thought he would simply turn and walk away. He did not do so, however.

'Happiness,' he said softly, 'is not everything.'

'Touché,' she whispered softly. And then more loudly, 'Good night, Mr Lamarr.'

'Shall we make it an even better night?' he asked, his voice velvet soft.

And she felt that sharp stabbing of longing again. Somewhere too there was a feeling of shock and outrage, but it was far back in her consciousness, more a token showing of how she ought to react than a reflection of her true feelings. She would – she *must* – of course say no. But oh, the temptation. Just once in her life to do what she *wanted* to do, no matter how outrageous, rather than what she *ought* to do. Or twice in her life, perhaps she meant. She had done what she wanted to do this afternoon and this evening. But this was different. It would mean nothing at all to him, while to her it might mean everything in the world. She dared not risk it. But did it matter that it would mean nothing to him? She would not expect it to, after all. And would it matter if it meant far more to her? At least she would have the memory. At least she would *know*.

The silence between them had stretched.

'You do have a hard time answering questions,' he said. 'Has the path of your life been such a predictable one, Viola, that you have never had to make any serious decisions?'

'The revelation after my husband's death that he was married to someone else when he wed me was unpredictable,' she said. 'So was the fact that he had fathered a daughter with that first wife and that she inherited everything from him. And what is a serious decision? Is this one of them? The suggestion that we make it a better night than it has already been? Or is it more trivial than anything else I have ever had to decide?'

One corner of his mouth lifted in a mockery of a smile. 'I will not trouble you further,' he said. 'When you told me to go away, you meant it. Today was but a temporary reprieve. I cannot argue with virtue, Viola. I wish you a good night and a good rest of your life.' He lowered his head and kissed her softly on the lips.

'Yes,' she said when he lifted his head, and she listened to the echo of the word, almost as though someone else had spoken it. 'Yes, let us make it an even better night, Marcel.'

There was an arrested look on his face. And her mind was catching up to her words. This was *Mr Lamarr* standing before her, the ruthless, dangerous Mr Lamarr, one of England's most notorious libertines, among other vices. Suddenly he looked like a forbidding stranger, all dark and brooding and attractive beyond bearing.

'I shall go down to the taproom for a while and make myself seen,' he said. 'If when I come back up I find your door locked, I will know you have regretted the words you just spoke. If I find the door unlocked, I shall indeed give you a very good night. And you will give me the same in return. It is give and take with me, Viola, in equal measures. It will be a night you will not regret – if your door remains unlocked.'

He turned and went back to the staircase and down to the taproom below. It was a strange seduction, giving her space and time to change her mind, to lock her door firmly against him. Or perhaps it was the most effective seduction of all. No coercion. There could be no looking back afterward to claim that she had been deceived by a practiced rake.

The decision was all hers.

. . . I shall indeed give you a very good night.

Would he? Was it possible? She had no idea what to expect except for the basics. Could *that* ever be good?

. . . a night you will not regret.

Oh, she very much doubted that. Which begged the question – why go through with something she knew very well she would bitterly regret?

She stepped inside her room after lighting the candle on her dresser from the larger candle in the wall sconce in the corridor and shut the door behind her. She set down the candlestick and stood watching the flame gutter and then grow steady.

I shall indeed give you a very good night . . . It will be a night you will not regret.

Would her door be unlocked when he came back upstairs? She really did not know. But the choice – the decision – would be hers.

CHAPTER 5

The noise in the taproom subsided somewhat when Marcel walked in and seated himself at a small table close to the fire. But when it became clear that he wanted neither to contribute to the conversation nor to listen to it, the men recovered from their self-consciousness in the presence of such upper-class splendor and the noise level resumed its former pitch. He drank his ale and stared into the coals.

He wondered idly if her door would be unlocked when he went back up. He laid private and conflicting bets with himself. Yes, it would be. She had made her decision, and it would go against her dignity to change her mind and hide behind a locked door. But no, it would not. She would think twice – and very probably thirty-two times after that – and decide that a sordid coupling with a near stranger, and a rake to boot, at a third-class inn was not at all the thing, and she would conclude that a locked door was what he thoroughly deserved.

He did not much care either way. If the door was unlocked, he would have a night of unexpected sport. If it was locked, he would have a decent night's sleep . . . perhaps. There would be nothing else to do, and the bed in his room looked clean and comfortable enough. Tomorrow he would be on his way by some means or other. He was not worried about being stranded here indefinitely.

And he was indeed in no hurry to arrive home. He was going to have to assert himself when he got there over matters in which he really had very little interest. He ought of course to have done it two years ago immediately after he had inherited his title and Redcliffe Court and all the encumbrances that went with it. But it had seemed too much bother at the time. He had been content to settle the twins there with their aunt and uncle and to pay them his usual twice-yearly visits while leaving everything else to be sorted out by those who lived there. It had been too optimistic an expectation. Lately he had been inundated with an increasingly frequent stream of increasingly lengthy and discontented letters, and it was too much to be borne. He would not bear it. He was going to have to put a stop to it.

The marchioness, his elderly aunt, complained that her authority was being usurped by *that upstart Mrs Morrow*, his sister-in-law. She – Marcel had assumed his aunt was referring to herself – had had the running of Redcliffe for more than fifty years and no one had ever found fault with her management until she – Marcel had assumed the marchioness was referring to Jane Morrow – had come upon the scene with the idea that she could just take over everything simply because she had the care of Estelle and Bertrand. Marcel had not bothered to keep track of which *she* or *her* was being referred to. Neither had he read on to find out. Obviously there was friction between the two women, and of course Jane wrote of it too, at great and indignant length, emphasizing her superior role as guardian of Marcel's heir and her longtime experience in running his household. He had not read that letter to its conclusion either, though there had been three pages of it left.

He nevertheless had been made aware – by Jane in another letter – that his cousin Isabelle, who also lived at Redcliffe with her husband, the excuse being that the marchioness was elderly and frail and needed her daughter on hand to administer tender care, was also trying to assert an authority over the running of the house that she did not in any way have. She was also planning a lavish wedding for her youngest daughter, Margaret, doubtless at Marcel's expense, and no one had yet answered Jane's perfectly reasonable question about where the couple planned to take up residence after the wedding. He had stopped reading, but clearly he needed to go there in person, though he would rather be setting out for the North Pole unless there was somewhere farther away and more remote. The South Pole?

The steward complained that Mr Morrow and his son were attempting to interfere with the running of the estate with ideas that were asinine. The man had been too diplomatic to use that exact word, but Marcel had understood him well enough. Even the housekeeper had written to ask him if it really was his wish that the cook serve late and inferior breakfasts – which some people she would not be so disrespectful as to name then proceeded to complain about – because she was required, along with all the other servants, who had better things to do with their mornings, to attend prayers with the family in the drawing room for all of half an hour, sometimes longer.

There was only one way to stop the flow of such letters, and he was doing it. But he was in no hurry nonetheless. A day or two here or there would be of no great consequence. At least no further letters could reach him while he was on the road.

The noise level rose, and along with it came an increased swell of laughter with the arrival of three more men, one of whom complained that their feet were all blisters from so much dancing and there was only one sure cure they knew of.

'Bring on the ale,' he bellowed cheerfully to the innkeeper. 'A jug, man, and none of your tankards.'

And then there were the twins, who had been brought up in the mold of their maternal aunt and uncle. Adeline would turn over in her grave if she could know. He would turn over in his too if he were in it already. He was going to have to do something about them, though the devil knew what. Perhaps it was too late to do anything meaningful.

And perhaps it was just as well they were not taking after their father. Or their mother for that matter, he thought with a guilty start. The trouble with sitting up late was that one's mind became undisciplined and maudlin. Not that it was really late. His evening would probably be just starting now if he were in London. It just felt late.

He went back upstairs after half an hour and undressed in his room. He belted a silk dressing gown about his waist and crossed the passageway to Viola Kingsley's room. Would the door be unlocked? Or would it not? He wondered why he had given her time to cool off and think about what she was about to do. That had been uncharacteristically foolish of him. Why stoke a fire to warm a room, after all, and then leave all the windows and doors open to the winter cold?

But he had done it, he knew, because she was not at all his usual type of woman. He had no doubt of her virtue, not just because she had rejected his advances fourteen years ago, but because . . . Well, there was something about her. She was a virtuous woman all right, a fact that would normally depress any spark of interest he might have in her. And then there was her age. She could not be more than a year or two younger than he. She might even be older. He was not a cradle snatcher, but very few of his women were ever much above the age of thirty.

Had he been in love with her fourteen years ago? It seemed highly improbable and quite unlike him.

His pride had been hurt, though. There was no denying that. Perhaps that would explain today – and tonight. Perhaps he wanted the satisfaction of having his way with her without exerting any sort of coercion. If the door was unlocked, she would have made the decision herself with the cool head half an hour alone would have induced.

But was it unlocked?

He turned the knob slowly and – he hoped – silently. He had no desire to wake her and alarm her if she had fallen asleep. Or to make an idiot of himself. He pushed gently inward. It was not locked. She was not in bed either. She was standing facing the window, though it was pitch-dark out there. Clouds must have moved over the moon and stars. There was a candle burning on the dresser behind her. She was looking back over her shoulder at him.

She was wearing a white nightgown, very little different from any dress she might have worn except that it fell loose from the bosom. It was modestly scooped at the neckline. The sleeves were short. She had unpinned and brushed her hair so that it fell in honey-colored waves over her shoulders and halfway to her waist.

Lust, which he had kept in check lest the door be locked, surged. He closed the door and locked it before strolling toward her and reaching beyond her to draw the curtains across the window. He dipped his head and kissed her.

She took a step toward him, as she had out on

the riverbank, and twined her arms about his waist as she held the kiss and deepened it. It was different this time. There were no stays beneath her nightgown to mask the soft curves of waist and hip or to push up her breasts. And he had no layers of garments beneath the thin silk of his dressing gown. He savored the embrace, the warmth of her body, the slightly fragrant smell of her, the feel of her thighs and abdomen and bosom pressed to his as one of his hands twined in her hair to hold the back of her head and the other moved down her back and drew her closer. His lips teased hers. His tongue explored her mouth and found the pleasure spots. She sucked gently on it.

He was in no hurry. This was not about release. It rarely was. He had promised her a night of pleasure she would not regret, and he would give her just that. Not five minutes, ten, or half an hour, but a whole night. He had rarely looked forward to a night of sex with such anticipation. Perhaps because he suspected she was not vastly experienced, as most of his women were. Strange thought when she must have been married for more than twenty years. He wondered if there had ever been anyone else in addition to Riverdale, but doubted it. Which led to the question, Why him? Just because of this strange set of circumstances? Because she saw this as a sort of time away from reality, outside the normal realm of her moral standards?

It was not that she was unaware of his reputation,

of the fact that he had few scruples and no heart. He had nothing to give, in fact, except his body and his expertise in bed. Was that enough for her? But if it was not, that was her problem, not his. He had given her enough chance, after all, to choose differently.

He drew back his head and looked into her eyes – dreamy with desire and blue even in the shadows cast by the candle. 'You are sure, Viola?' he asked. What the devil was this?

'Yes,' she said.

They were the only words they spoke in the first hour of that night, apart from some indecipherable murmurings as they coupled. They were on the bed by then, the bedcovers pushed to the foot, the candle still burning, her nightgown and his dressing gown in a heap on the floor.

She was hot. Eager and uninhibited. Having made her decision, she gave herself with abandon and demanded pleasure in return. He slowed her down, showing her that the pleasure given and taken with hands and fingertips and mouth and tongue and even teeth was as sexual as the final feast. And seeking out pleasure points on her body and guiding her to pleasure points on his.

When he finally mounted her, turning her onto her back first and coming between her thighs as he covered her, she was slick and ready and he was hard and eager. But even then he slowed them, thrusting with measured strokes, avoiding too great a depth until the final moments, sliding his hands beneath her as she lifted herself toward him and matched his rhythm.

And then the final drive toward the shared and ultimate pleasure of release and the little oblivion that always followed upon the best of couplings.

This was surely the very best.

He lay on her for several moments, his weight pressing her to the mattress while his heartbeat slowed and consciousness returned. She was warm and relaxed and sweaty beneath him. He moved off her and reached down for the covers before settling beside her and sliding an arm beneath her neck.

The Countess of Riverdale. Viola Kingsley. He still could not quite believe it. She had been worth the fourteen-year wait. Not that he would have had her this way back then even if she had been willing. She had been a married lady – apparently married, that was.

She was asleep. Her hair was untidy, her face flushed, her lips slightly parted. She had drawn the sheet up to cover her breasts in a belated nod to modesty. Beneath the covers her naked body touched his from bosom to ankles. She was beautiful in every way it was possible for a woman to be beautiful. Fourteen years had not robbed her of any of her allure. They had merely added to it.

What strange fate had thrown them together here, one of his hired horses having acquired a loose shoe, her hired carriage having developed a cracked axle? He still did not know the name of either the village or the inn. But he did not believe

90

in fate or coincidence. It had happened and they had made the most of it – were making. The night was far from over. It was probably not even midnight yet.

There was still much pleasure to be had.

The noisy revelries were still continuing downstairs.

And there was no hurry.

Viola did not sleep deeply, though she did perhaps drift for a few minutes, exhausted and satiated. It had been so very long, and never like this. Oh, never even close. It would be laughable even to try comparing.

She knew beyond a doubt that she had made a grave mistake. For she had allowed something vivid into her life, something . . . joyful, and she would never, ever be able to forget. For a while perhaps she would not want to, but eventually she surely would. For vivid living and joy were not for her. Any possibility of either had been killed in her when she was seventeen and married Humphrey, and there was no changing the world and the persona she had created for herself since then.

Her life would become dull and decorous and blameless again tomorrow and for all her tomorrows after that. She had run from Bath in a sort of panicked attempt to escape all that had happened during the past two years, when it had all accumulated in her spirit and become too much for her. Perhaps she had wanted to escape everything

91

that had happened before that too. Perhaps she had wanted to escape from the whole of her life, even from herself. And something – call it fate? – had arranged all this. She had run far from her usual reality this afternoon when she went to the village fair with a known libertine and enjoyed every single vivid moment of it. She had run further yet tonight when she had waltzed with him on the village green and kissed him on the river-bank and left her door unlocked. But if it *was* fate that had set up today, she was not at all sure it had been kind to her. Perhaps it had not intended to be. Perhaps it had intended to teach her a harsh lesson. For there was no permanent escape. Ultimately she must take herself with her wherever she went, and there was no changing herself except during brief, wistful, defiant moments.

But oh – *she was not sorry.*

Not yet. And why anticipate sorrow and guilt?

She must have drifted again. She awoke to the touch of his hand moving featherlight up her body, between her breasts, over one of them, beneath it. He set the pad of his thumb over her nipple and rubbed so lightly that she felt the effect more than the touch. Desire stabbed down inside her and upward so that both her womb and her throat ached.

She turned her head on his arm and saw the hard, austere, cynical, silver-templed Mr Lamarr, with whom no woman of sense would allow herself to become personally involved. But almost in the same moment she saw Marcel, the lover in whom she had found escape and delight and no peril at all. Except that there was the certain knowledge of a bleaker-than-ever future.

And the rest of tonight.

She realized suddenly that the inn had fallen silent and there was no further sound of music coming from outside. She must have dozed for longer than she thought. Time was passing. This night was passing.

He kissed her.

And again she marveled that kisses and touches could be so light, so seemingly lazy and yet so purposeful too. For there was no doubt in her mind that every touch of his – of palm and fingertips and lips and tongue – was knowledgeable and deliberate and designed to bring her to full readiness again. Not that that was going to be a hard task. She turned onto her side and touched him, one of her hands spreading over his chest with its light dusting of hair, while the other moved over him, feeling the hardness of muscles, the pulsing warmth within. She had never touched a man's body . . .

'Viola,' he murmured against her lips, and he took her hand by the wrist and moved it low between them. She first balked at the very idea, then touched him lightly, and then closed her hand about him. Long, thick, hard. But she had known that. She had had him inside her. It was different to touch him with her hand, though. With her thumb she stroked the tip, and he inhaled slowly and audibly and moved his mouth to her throat and slid his hand between her thighs to work magic with his fingers there.

He lifted her on top of him this time and slid his hands down her thighs to grasp her behind the knees and bring them up to hug his hips. She knelt above him and spread her hands over his chest and looked down at him. The candle was still burning on the dresser. He gazed back at her, his eyes dark and hooded, and she was fully aware for the first time that she was naked and unembarrassed. She ought to be. She hated to be seen naked, even by her maid. Indeed, no one else had seen her unclothed since she was a child. And she was no longer young.

He was perfect physically. It seemed unfair. But she was unembarrassed by her own imperfections. After tomorrow she would probably never see him again, and she doubted he would remember this or her for long. She had no illusions about that. Unlike her. She would always remember. It did not matter. She had made her decision quite knowingly and without any coercion on his part. Quite the contrary.

And she was not sorry. *She would not be sorry.*

'Mount me,' he said softly. 'Ride me, Viola. Ride me to a standstill.'

Even the words were deliberately chosen, deliberately spoken. For desire, already roiling in her, surged. Her nipples tightened and so did her inner muscles against the ache of wanting. And it did not matter that she was sore so soon after the last time, or that it had never occurred to her that the woman could take the lead in a sexual encounter. She lowered herself until she could feel him, and she circled about him until he was there at her opening, and she lowered herself onto him, slowly, savoring every moment, every sensation, until she was filled. She clenched her muscles about him, reveling in the hiss of his inward breath.

'Witch,' he whispered.

And she rode while he lay quite still. And rode and rode, her eyes closed, her hands braced on his chest, all her concentration *there* where exquisite pleasure built to exquisite pain. She made circular motions with her hips, grinding about him as she rode, until she thought she must surely go mad and it seemed he must be made of granite—

Until it was clear he was not. His hands came to her hips and pulled hard downward, holding her still while he pressed deeper than it seemed possible to come and the pain burst into something that would surely be unbearable until . . . it was not. Her mind had a vivid image of a rose bursting open in the sunlight to reveal all the glory of its inner beauty, and then the image was gone with every other coherent thought.

He relaxed beneath her, his chest damp with sweat, his breathing ragged and audible. He was looking up at her with lazy eyes. 'The magnificent Lady Riverdale,' he murmured.

The dangerous Mr Lamarr. But she did not speak the words aloud or correct him for wrongly naming her. She stretched out on him, turning her head on his shoulder while he hooked the bedcovers with one foot and brought them back up over them. They were still coupled.

How strange that life could be this way and she had never known it. Not really. She had imagined, perhaps, what passion must be like, but imagination was inadequate. One had to experience it. Did some people live all their lives like this? *Alive?* Did he? A night like this one must, of course, be not very different for him. There must be nothing so very unusual about it. It was just a part of his normal way of being.

But she did not want to dwell upon that. It was not as if she had not known. There was no point now in lamenting the fact that she had got herself involved with a man who would never be involved with her.

But she would never forget. Even when she wanted to, she never would.

They loved the night away. She tested his stamina, as he did hers, but they both lived up to the challenge. Tomorrow was moving inexorably toward them, however. Indeed, tomorrow was already today. Hardly had he noticed that the candle had burned itself out than he was aware of dawn graying the window behind the curtains and then of daylight illumining the room.

It was a damnable apology for an inn room. The wallpaper was faded almost to extinction, and there were indeed cracks on the ceiling – cracks involving only the paint up there and not the structure, he hoped. The room smelled faintly of oldness. And less faintly of sex.

It had been good. Very good indeed. Perhaps the best. He had had no more than a couple of winks of sleep. Why waste a night that had offered – and delivered – such pleasure? She was inexperienced, he had discovered early. There was no real surprise there. She was also without inhibition. That had been a bit more of a surprise when he had sometimes thought of her – after her rejection and rather spitefully, he had to confess – as an ice queen. But of course he had often wondered if her unfailingly cool dignity was a mere veil over a powder keg of passion.

It was.

She was curled onto her side, facing away from him, and he turned too and curled about her, spoon fashion, with one arm over her waist. She had slept more than he had.

Today they would go their separate ways. And next spring, more than likely, he was going to have Estelle in town with him making her come-out during the Season. And if Estelle was going to be there, then so – perish the thought – was Jane Morrow as her official sponsor and chaperon. He was going to have to be far more circumspect about his own behavior. He would not be able to continue his accustomed way of living when it might affect his daughter's chances of making a good marriage.

Viola would not even be in town next spring. Through no fault of her own she had fallen out of favor with some members of the *ton* and was no longer accepted as unconditionally as the Countess of Riverdale had been. She had not been seen in town since soon after the death of Riverdale, or, if she had, he had not heard of it. She was unlikely to return.

So there was no chance of an ongoing affair with her. Perhaps it was just as well, however. He doubted she knew the unwritten rules of dalliance. Its inevitable ending might be messy. And to be quite honest with himself, he was not sure he could treat an affair with her as lightly as he did with other women. He was not sure what he meant by that, and he was certainly not going to puzzle over it at this precise moment.

She drew a deep breath and let it out on a low, self-satisfied sigh. Her hand came over his about her waist.

'Daylight,' she muttered a few moments later. She did not sound too pleased.

'It is an abomination, is it not?' he agreed.

She turned to lie on her back the better to look at him. 'How are you going to get home?' she asked.

'Ah, we are looking ahead to the day, are we?' he said. 'I have no idea, but I very much doubt I will be stranded here for the rest of my natural-born days, attractive as the prospect might be if I could have a fellow strandee of my own choosing. That is unlikely, however. I took a stroll out into the yard yesterday while waiting for a certain lady to get ready to go dancing. The coachman of that dreadful hired vehicle was confident that it would be ready to proceed by the middle of this morning. You will be home before nightfall.'

'Provided a couple of wheels do not fall off,' she said.

'Do you look forward to being at home?' he asked.

'Of course,' she said, and looked unutterably bleak.

'And who is awaiting you there?' he asked.

'No one,' she said. 'Only peace and quiet. I left behind all my family in Bath – except my son, who recently returned to the Peninsula to rejoin his regiment. I left behind my daughters and my son-in-law and grandchildren. I left my mother and my brother and his wife. I left all the Westcotts, who came for the christening of my newest grand-child. I had to get away.'

Had to?

'Too much family?' he asked. 'I know the feeling.'

'It sounds so very ungrateful put that way,' she said. 'I love my children and grandchildren dearly, and everyone else too. The Westcotts in particular have been unwaveringly supportive and kind since the discovery that I am not really one of them after all. But . . . I had to get away.'

'In a hired carriage,' he said. 'Did no one offer a private one for your use? And servants to accompany you?' They sounded like a grim lot, her family.

'I had my own carriage with me,' she explained. 'I left it for Abigail, my younger daughter. She lives with me at Hinsford. I was offered the loan of several others. I believe I even hurt a few feelings by refusing, but . . . I had to get away.'

He was beginning to understand yesterday afternoon a little better. And last night. It sounded to him as though, surrounded by her loving, concerned family, she had cracked.

He knew all about that – cracking, that was.

'Are you looking forward to going home?' she asked.

'It is full of . . . people,' he said. 'Family. All of whom need to be sorted out and put in their place. By me. I have a severe aversion to being forced to exert myself in domestic matters.'

'It is all quite sufficient to make one want to run away and hide, is it not?' she said with a smile.

Ah, that smile. So rare with her.

'It is indeed,' he agreed.

He kissed her and wondered if they could or should have sex again. How many times would that make? Five? Six?

Did it matter? The night was all but over, and there would be no other. Not with her, anyway. There was something melancholy in the thought, though melancholia was not something he was in the habit of indulging.

They made love again.

CHAPTER 6

Viola was seated in the dining room again, eating breakfast. The carriage was indeed ready to resume the journey. She would be home well before nightfall, barring any further accident. One of her eggs was too soft, the other too hard. The toast was dry, the coffee too bitter. Or was it all just her? Was there in fact nothing wrong with the food? Her stomach felt a bit queasy. She ate only because she believed she ought to before embarking upon a longish journey.

And perhaps to prove to herself that she was fine, that she had had a bad few days followed by an unexpectedly pleasant day and night and was now cheerfully back to normal. Perhaps she would be better able to convince herself once she was actually on her way. She did not know if she would see him again before she left. He had gone from her room an hour ago without giving any indication of whether he intended seeing her on her way or not. She would not press the issue. She would not linger in the hope that he would come down, and she would not knock on his door. When she was ready to leave, she would simply go.

She set down her coffee cup with a grimace. She had added more milk to counter the bitterness, and now it was too weak.

It is all quite sufficient to make one want to run away and hide, is it not? she had said earlier, before they made love for the last time. She supposed she would continue to hide, as she had done all her adult life, deep inside herself. She had burrowed deeper after the great catastrophe that had followed Humphrey's death – only to have everything erupt out of her for no apparent reason a few days ago. She would press it all deep again and deeper yet from today on, and she would go inward with it. She would go so deep no one would ever find her again. Perhaps she would not even find herself.

The thought made her bite her upper lip to stop herself from crying – or laughing – and for a moment she thought the panic was going to return. But the dining room door opened and saved her.

'Good morning,' he said, all elegant formality. 'Or have I already said that?'

'Good morning,' she said.

The innkeeper came hurrying in behind him and indicated a table a little removed from Viola's.

'Perhaps, Mr Lamarr,' she said, 'you would care to join me?'

'Thank you,' he said. 'I would.'

The innkeeper went to fetch more toast and coffee.

'Nothing else,' Marcel said firmly when the man tried to suggest eggs and beefsteak and kidneys.

They spoke of the weather until the innkeeper

returned and had gone again. Viola was not sure if she was glad Marcel had come down or if she would have preferred him to stay in his room until after she had left. Her stomach was clenching about the little food she had eaten.

She hated goodbyes, especially when they were forever.

'Well, Viola.' He was leaning back in his chair, the fingers of one hand playing with his quizzing glass, a habit that was becoming familiar to her. He was making no effort to butter his toast.

'Well.' She made the effort to smile. There was never anything to say when there was all the world to say. She had to remind herself that there was nothing unusual about this to him.

'Well,' he said softly again. '*Shall* we run away?'

The absurdity of the suggestion struck her at the same moment as a great wave of yearning washed over her. Oh, if only . . .

If only life were that simple.

'Why not?' she said lightly.

'We will travel in your hired monstrosity of a carriage until we can replace it with something altogether more roadworthy,' he said. 'And then we will go somewhere, anywhere, everywhere until we are ready to return. Next week, next month, next year. Whenever the urge to run away wears thin, if it ever does.'

'Well, I would like to see my grandchildren again before they grow up,' she said.

'Then we will return in fourteen years,' he said.

'All the time we have not spent together since you commanded me to go away.'

'And where exactly will we go?' she asked. '*Somewhere, anywhere, everywhere* sounds a trifle vague.'

'But enticing, one must admit,' he said. 'There are no limits upon where we can go. Scotland? The Highlands, of course. Wales? Within sight of Mount Snowdon, that is, or Harlech Castle. Ireland? America? Devonshire? I own a cottage there, nestled on a hillside above a river valley, not far from the sea. An ideal place for an escape. No one else lives nearby. Let us go there for a start, and if it proves to be not far enough, then we will move on. There are no permanent destinations in the land of running away.'

'That would be a splendid title for a children's story,' she said. '"The Land of Running Away." Though I am not sure it would teach a worthy lesson in life.'

'Why not?' he asked. 'Do not all people, especially children, need to escape from their lives now and then – or all the time? Even if just through their imagination? Why else do people read? Or listen to music? Or travel?'

'Or dance.' He had still not touched his breakfast or even his coffee. 'Do you read?'

'I am better at running away,' he told her.

'That can be done through reading,' she said. 'You have just said so yourself.'

'But it is all too easy to be intruded upon when

one is reading,' he said. 'Or listening to music. Or traveling according to a planned itinerary one has shared for the convenience of all one's relatives and friends who may wish to join one or call one back on some flimsy excuse.'

'Ah. We would send no notice of our intent to our families, then?' she asked. 'Nothing to allay their anxieties, should they miss us?'

'That is exactly why it is called running away,' he said. 'My family will not think of the Devonshire cottage, even supposing they think at all, which is highly unlikely. Your family does not even know about it. Or about me.'

He was gazing steadily at her, and she felt that wave of yearning again.

'How very tempting you make it sound,' she said with a sigh.

'But . . .?' His eyebrows rose.

'Yes, but,' she said. 'It is time for me to leave. Time to go home.'

'You are a coward, Viola?' he said.

And for the first time – oh, foolish, when she was dealing with a man she very well knew to be selfish and reckless and a law unto himself – for the first time it occurred to her that perhaps he was serious. That he was in truth asking her to run away with him to his remote cottage by the sea. Without a word to their families. Without any long-term plan. Without any careful consideration. He was seriously suggesting that she do the most irresponsible thing she had ever done in her life.

'You are serious,' she said.

'About your being a coward?' he said. 'What would you call yourself, Viola? A virtuous, dutiful woman? What end does your virtue serve? And virtuous by whose standards? Dutiful to what or to whom? To a family that has allowed you to leave Bath alone when you are clearly in deep distress?'

'I am not in distress,' she protested. Oh, surely she had not shown any outer sign . . . But she had told him she had had to get away, that she had rejected all offers of a loaned carriage and servants. It was unlike her to confide so much to a virtual stranger.

'Perhaps it was not clear to them,' he said. 'Perhaps they merely believed you were being stubborn and deliberately awkward. Perhaps they have not noticed your distress. You are very good at hiding inside yourself, are you not?'

All her insides clenched, and she grew cold. How did he—? What did he think—? 'What else am I supposed to do?' she asked, stung. 'What else could I have done all my life? Be an emotional, hysterical, vaporish burden upon all who know me?'

'Many women are,' he said. 'Such behavior is their call for help, or at least attention. But not you. You have chosen all your life instead to keep a stiff upper lip and a rigid backbone. You have character, Viola, and that is admirable. But even strong characters have their limits of endurance. You have reached yours, I believe.'

How could he know her so well when he did not know her at all? 'And the answer is to throw all responsibility to the wind and run off with you without a word to anyone?' she asked him. 'For the pleasure of more days like yesterday and more nights than last night?'

He tipped his head slightly to one side in apparent thought, and his eyes narrowed. 'In a word, yes,' he said. 'Why end something that has been so very pleasant when one does not wish or need to end it? Why not prolong the pleasure until it reaches its natural limit? For it will, you know. All passion has an arc. We should enjoy it while it lasts and part amicably, without pain or regret, when it is over. When all is said and done, you owe more to yourself than you do to anyone else, much as you may love all those someone elses, and much as they may love you.'

Oh, she knew what was happening right enough. His words were far more dangerous than his love-making during the night had been. For his lovemaking had been all physical sensation and emotion. His words appealed to her reason and seemed, on the surface at least, very persuasive. But it was seduction pure and simple.

When had she ever done anything just for herself? Everything in her upbringing and life experience had taught her that pleasing herself was the ulti-mate selfishness. Her life as a woman had always had but two guiding principles: duty and dignity. Duty to her family, dignity in the face of society. And where had it got her? Was the love her family felt for her enough? Did they *need* her? Even

Abigail? Even Harry? She would die for either of them – she knew she would – if doing so would take away their hurt and ensure them a happy life. But it could not be done. Her death would in no way ease their living. They would somehow forge their own lives without any real help from her.

Who would die for her? Or give up all personal gratification for her? Perhaps her children would. Perhaps her mother would. Even her brother. But would it make any difference? Would she want any such sacrifice? It had never occurred to her that she might need anyone to *care* for her. She did not.

Why should she not care for herself, then? Where did selfishness end and the need to live one's precious, only life begin?

Who would suffer if she ran away with Marcel Lamarr for a short while?

But was she merely reacting predictably to what she recognized as expert seduction? Dancing as a puppet to his strings? Rationalizing?

'Yes,' she said in answer to her own questions, but she spoke the word aloud, and her voice sounded quite firm. 'Let us do it. Let's run away.'

Marcel Lamarr, Marquess of Dorchester – he had omitted the title when signing the inn register – took a look at the axle on the hired carriage. It was new and appeared to be sound enough. He looked closely at the horses, which had already been hitched to the carriage, without actually lifting any legs to examine the shoes, and judged them to be sorry creatures, though probably adequate to their appointed task, at least for a few miles. He ignored the shabby outer appearance of the vehicle and opened the door nearest to him. Threadbare stained seats, fraying at the edges, met his disapproving eye and a smell of staleness his nose.

'I need the lady out here and in there without further ado,' an impatient, impertinent voice said from behind him. The coachman, presumably, wearing soiled linen beneath an ill-fitting stained coat, and a greasy-looking hat upon greasy-looking hair.

The Marquess of Dorchester turned and looked the man over, his eyes moving from oily head to scuffed, mud-caked boots and back again. 'Indeed?' he said.

The coachman had frozen in place, and Marcel had the satisfaction of seeing fear in his eyes as he snatched off his hat and held it to his chest with both hands. 'If you please, Your Honor,' he said. 'I need to get the lady where she's going and get myself back to Bath for more business tomorrow. It's my livelihood. Your Honor, sir,' he added.

'The lady will come when the lady is ready,' Marcel informed him. 'Until then you will wait, whether it be five minutes or five hours. When she does come, you will convey us to the nearest town. I have been told it is eight miles distant. There the lady and I will remove to a different carriage. We will refrain from insisting upon a return of the unused portion of the fare the lady paid you in advance and upon demanding compensation for the extra expense she has incurred as a result of your negligence in leaving Bath with a defective vehicle. I may, if you conduct yourself with professional decorum from this moment on, pay you a small bonus before you spring your horses in the direction of Bath and further business. I trust I have made myself clear.'

The man bobbed his head and tugged at his greasy forelock and could not seem to find his tongue.

'I thought so too,' his lordship murmured, and strolled back inside the inn to give instructions that his bag be loaded onto the hired carriage and that someone be sent up to carry down Miss Kingsley's bags. He hoped his nose would survive the eight-mile journey ahead, not to mention his spine and every other bone in his body. He would wager there was not an operational spring in that vehicle, and English roads were unkind to those who did not ride in well-sprung conveyances.

She had said yes. She might not repeat it when the time came to change carriages, of course, but he would take the risk and give her the choice. It had never been his way to drag women about by the hair just to cater to his lusts. But, however it was, she would complete her journey in a carriage that offered both cleanliness and comfort and under the protection of a competent, deferential driver. If she chose to return home alone, he would also send a maid with her. Her family had obviously not insisted. He would.

He was both surprised and gratified that she had

said yes. It was a long time since he had had an extended affair with any woman. He had never run away in order to enjoy one. He had never taken a woman to the Devonshire cottage. He had not spent much time there himself. It had belonged to a childless great-aunt, upon whose lap he had apparently climbed unbidden when he was three. She had adored him ever after and left him everything when she died. It was indeed a remote location, a fact that had not endeared the place to him until now. Had he not been inherently lazy about such matters, he would doubtless have sold the property long ago. But now he was glad he had not done so. He rather fancied the idea of escaping there with a lover he thought might hold his interest for a week or two at the very least. It would be up to him, of course, to make sure that he held her interest for as long as she held his.

They were on their way less than half an hour later, seated side by side on the appallingly hard seat, as much space between them as she could possibly contrive by clinging to the fraying strap beside her head.

'Has the coachman agreed to take us all the way to Devonshire?' she asked.

'Heaven forbid. I believe I might end up with a permanent case of the shakes if I were to allow any such thing,' he said. 'You must be made of stern stuff to have come all the way from Bath in this, Viola. We will find something better to hire as soon as we possibly can. If you put too much trust in that strap, you know, it may let you down and snap and catapult you across the seat to collide with me.'

'This all feels very . . . strange,' she said by way of explanation.

Yes, it did. Even for him it felt strange.

She did not relinquish her hold of the strap. Or relax the tension in her body. Or attempt to make any further conversation. He rather suspected that in another hour or so they were going to be going their separate ways, she in one carriage to her home, he in another to his.

Except that last night she had left her door unlocked.

They stopped at a reputable-looking posting inn in a bustling country town. He settled Viola in a private parlor under the care of a bowing, smiling innkeeper and a bobbing, smiling, spotlessly clad serving girl before dismissing the Bath coachman with a generous bonus he had done nothing to earn. Soon after that, he joined her for a cup of coffee. She was looking rather pale and grim.

'There is a carriage here for hire,' he said. 'It is plain, but it is also clean and looks serviceable. It even has a few springs. There are also horses of decent quality for a stage or two. I suspect there are more and better elsewhere in town. You must tell me your wish, Viola. Shall I hire two carriages and send you home in one of them? Or shall it be one carriage to take us to Devonshire?'

She set her cup down, watching what she was doing. 'All morning,' she said, 'ever since breakfast,

I have been trying to think of a way to tell you that I have changed my mind.'

'Ah,' he said, and he leaned back in his chair.

She raised her eyes to his. 'It is not in my nature,' she said, 'to reach out for what I want.'

'Then we are quite incompatible,' he told her. 'It is not in my nature to do anything else. What do you see in your future, Viola? What will your life be like?'

'Safe,' she said. 'Respectable. I have friends and neighbors at Hinsford. I have my daughters and son-in-law and grandchildren. Perhaps there will be more. Abigail will surely marry in time. And perhaps Harry—'

'Your son?' he said when she stopped abruptly.

'Perhaps he will survive the wars,' she said. 'Perhaps he will come home and marry and— But I must not say *perhaps*. He *will* come home.'

'And will you marry again?' he asked.

'Oh, goodness, no,' she said. 'Though the word *again* does not apply, does it? Another marriage, even a *real* one this time, is the very last thing I want. Besides, who would have me?'

In the name of respectability she was going to live a very lonely rest of her life, then? But it had probably always been like that. Lonely and dreary. It often seemed to be a woman's lot in life to endure. Simply that. He was very glad he was not a woman.

He did not break the silence that stretched between them while she held her cup in both hands but did not drink from it.

113

'I wish,' she said once, but did not continue.

'I wish,' she said a minute or so later, 'I could be selfish like you.' She looked up at him and flushed. 'I beg your pardon. I was thinking aloud.'

Still he said nothing. She looked back down into her cup.

'I would want to come back.' She set the cup down in its saucer and looked up at him again. 'I would not want to run away forever. But it would not be forever, would it? We would tire of each other after a while. You said so yourself. A week, perhaps? Two?'

Some women believed in permanence, in happily-ever-after and all that nonsense. He had believed in it himself once upon a time, and look where that had got him. He always made clear to any woman with whom he was embarking upon a liaison that it would not be forever or even for very long. It was not cruelty. It would be cruel to promise forever and not be able to deliver more than a few weeks.

'It would be good while it lasted,' he said.

'Like yesterday and last night?' she asked.

'I cannot promise you jewels every day,' he said. 'I would be beggared.'

'Not even pearls?' she asked, and . . . smiled.

He might, he thought, fall in love with that smile. Again. He had fallen in love with it fourteen years ago. Strange. Yesterday he could not remember her having ever smiled. But she must have. He had fallen in love with her smile. And with her. There must still have been traces of his old self left when he met her that he had used that phrase in his own mind.

'Perhaps a single pearl every second day,' he said.

'A bracelet to match my necklace and earrings,' she said. 'How many pearls, do you suppose? Twelve? Twenty-four days, then. Will we have tired of each other by then?'

'If not,' he said, 'we will add a pearl ring. And perhaps that ankle bracelet you resisted yesterday.'

She closed her eyes briefly. 'One carriage,' she said. 'Hire one.'

'I shall find a better one than this inn has to offer,' he said, getting to his feet.

'I will wait,' she promised.

He was gone an hour. An hour during which to change her mind. But she would not do so. She used the time instead to write brief notes, one to Camille and Abigail in Bath and one to Mrs Sullivan, her housekeeper at Hinsford. She could not after all reconcile it with her conscience to disappear without a word to anyone. She told her daughters that she was going away somewhere private for a while – perhaps for a week or two – and they were not to worry about her. She would write again as soon as she returned. She informed Mrs Sullivan that her return to Hinsford had been delayed indefinitely and that she would write again before she came home. She apologized for the inconvenience she must have caused when she did not arrive yesterday.

She gave the letters with money to cover the cost

of sending them and an additional tip to the maid who had been serving her. The girl put them in the pocket of her apron and promised with a warm smile to set them in the bag for outgoing mail right away.

And so Viola waited to run away. To disappear where no one would find her. To do something just for herself. She was not going to think any longer about whether she was being selfish and self-indulgent. She was not going to think about the moral implications of what she was doing – and had done last night. She had not harmed anyone – except perhaps herself – and was not going to do so by going away for a while. She was not going to think about being hurt or about what would come after. She would think of that when the time came. She had lived a life of the utmost rectitude and propriety and been hurt anyway. And she had no illusions. The affair would come to an end and that would be that. If she ended up unhappy – well, what would be so new about that?

Marcel returned with a black, yellow-trimmed traveling carriage that was smart and shining with newness. And he came with horses that were a definite cut above the quality of the ones available at most posting inns, including this one. He also brought a burly coachman, who was clean shaven and well groomed and smartly dressed and quietly deferential.

'You did not hire this,' Viola said when she stepped out into the innyard. 'You purchased it.'

116

He raised his eyebrows in that arrogant way he had and held out a hand to help her up the steps. Their bags, she could see, were already strapped on behind. What must it be like to have that much money? But she had known once upon a time. It seemed a long time ago. He had stranded himself yesterday by sending his own carriage on its way with his brother – *so that he could spend the rest of the day with her.* And he had solved his dilemma today by simply buying a new carriage.

'Does the coachman come with it?' she asked as he got in after her and seated himself beside her. 'Did you employ him too?'

'It seemed wise,' he said. 'If I had hired him merely for the journey, I would have had to pay his stage-coach fare back here, and it might have put a strain upon my purse. Besides, what if we wish to use the carriage while we are in Devonshire? Or run away to Wales or Scotland? Would you ride up on the box with me if I were forced to take the ribbons myself? I might die of loneliness if you would not.'

'Very well,' she said. 'It was a foolish question.' A stagecoach ticket might put a strain upon his purse, but a coachman's salary for an indefinite length of time would not?

The coachman had put up the steps and shut the door. Moments later the carriage rocked into motion on what were obviously excellent springs. There was the pleasant smell of newness inside – wood and leather and fabric. And there was instant luxurious comfort.

He took her hand in his and laced their fingers – as he had done last evening before they returned to the inn. And he dipped his head and kissed her. 'The strap beside your head looks far more reliable than the one in the other carriage did,' he said. 'But I hope you will not find it necessary to use it. I am the same man I was last night. The same man I will be tonight.'

They were deliberately seductive words, and of course had an immediate effect upon her body. She felt the ache of wanting, as he had known very well she would. His head was still turned toward her, his dark, apparently lazy eyes boring into hers. But she no longer had to fight the seduction. She had surrendered to it. And it was not even seduction, for that implied that she was unaware of what was happening and would be an unwilling victim if she were. She was fully aware, and she was fully complicit.

There was something freeing in the thought.

'What?' she said. 'You do not improve with practice?'

She had the satisfaction of seeing a startled, arrested look on his face before he laughed. And, goodness, she did not believe she had ever seen or heard him laugh before. Laughter made him look more youthful, less hard, more human – whatever she meant by that.

At the inn they had just left, the maid who had taken Viola's letters and her generous tip was called to some busy work in the kitchen before she could go to the office and the post bag. And as bad luck would have it, the elbow of the cook's helper standing next to her sent a bowl of gravy spilling down the front of her frock and apron. She was sent off to change in a hurry since she was still needed urgently in the kitchen. She dropped the dirty garments into the laundry basket on her way back to work and forgot the letters until a couple of hours later, when it was too late to save them. They came out of the laundry tub still inside the apron pocket but reduced to a soggy clump.

It was impossible to smooth out the clump into anything resembling paper, much less individual pages. And even if it had been possible, there were no words left to be read. The ink had turned the inside of the pocket and some of the outside too a mottled gray and black and ruined one perfectly good apron.

The poor girl felt quite sick, not least because the cost of a new apron would be taken out of her wages. But she did not confess to the soggy clump's having once been letters entrusted to her by a lady customer who had already departed. She claimed instead that it had been a letter she had written to her sister, who worked at a private home twelve miles away.

The letters had probably not been important anyway. Letters rarely were. Or so she consoled her conscience.

CHAPTER 7

They took their time. There was no hurry, after all. They were running *away*, not *to* anything in particular. The journey was as much a part of it all as was the destination. They stopped for practical purposes – to change horses, to partake of meals. The latter they did at their leisure, and sometimes they went walking afterward if the place where they had stopped seemed of interest. They explored a castle, descending to the dungeons down long, spiraling stone steps and then climbing to the battlements in the same manner to gaze out over the surrounding countryside, the wind threatening to blow his tall hat into the next county. They looked about churches and churchyards. She liked to read all the old monuments and gravestones to discover what age those buried there had been when they died and how they were related to one another. She liked to work out how they had been related to others in the graveyard.

'You have a morbid mind,' he told her.

'I do not,' she protested. 'Graveyards remind me of the continuity of life and family and community.

In this cemetery the same four or five last names keep recurring. Have you noticed? I am sure if we were to ask in the village we would find that the same names predominate even now. Is that not fascinating?'

'Wondrously so.' He favored her with a deliberately blank look. 'It would certainly seem to indicate that people on the whole do not do much running away.'

'Or else they run but then return,' she said, 'as we will do after a while.'

'A good long while, it is to be hoped,' he said.

He was in no hurry to think about returning. After a few days and nights in her company, he was still enchanted by her. It was a strange word to pop into his head – *enchanted* – but no other more appropriate word presented itself. *Lusted after* was too earthy and did not quite capture how he felt.

Sometimes they wandered through markets and often bought cheap frivolities that would have repelled him, and probably her too, in a more rational frame of mind. He bought her a pea green string bag to hold their purchases like the ones other women were carrying and a sky blue cotton sunbonnet with a wide, floppy brim and a neck flap. He suggested that they look for a three-legged stool to go with it and a pail and a milking cow, but she called him silly and pointed out that they would be unable to squeeze the cow into the carriage and it would be unreasonable to expect it to trot behind and still be ready to fill the pail with milk whenever they stopped. He conceded the point.

She bought him a black umbrella with hideous gold tassels all around the edge that dripped water everywhere, mainly down the neck of the holder when he tried to keep it over himself and his companion on a rainy day. She suggested that he keep it for future use as a sunshade. He suggested that he cut the tassels off but did not do so. He bought himself a gnarled and sturdy wooden staff with which to trudge about the hills of Devon like a seasoned countryman. It snapped in two with a loud crack when he put the smallest amount of weight upon it in their inn room later that evening. Fortunately for his dignity, he maintained his balance, but she collapsed into giggles anyway on the side of their bed and he shook the jagged stump at her and would perhaps have fallen in love if he had been twenty years younger and twenty times more foolish.

'I paid good money for this, madam,' he told her.

'You paid almost nothing for it,' she reminded him. 'Even so, you did not get your money's worth, and I sympathize.'

'A great deal of good your sympathy does me,' he grumbled.

'You poor dear,' she said, opening her arms wide. 'Let me show you.'

Poor dear?

He cast aside the remnants of his rustic staff and let her show him.

When they were on the road, they were sometimes silent, but it was a companionable silence. They often sat hand in hand, their shoulders touching. Occasionally she dozed, her head on his shoulder. He had never been able to sleep in a moving carriage. Once he suggested they pull down the leather curtains and make love, but there were limits to what he could expect from the former Countess of Riverdale. She said a firm no and was not to be budged.

'Prude,' he said.

'Agreed,' she retorted.

There was no answer to that. Clever woman not to try besting him on the exchange of insults. He pointedly admired the countryside instead of making love to her.

'Annoyed?' she asked after some time had elapsed.

'Very,' he said.

Her head stayed facing toward him for a few moments, presumably to discover if he meant it. Then she turned and admired the countryside on her side of the carriage.

'It would be decidedly uncomfortable,' she said after a while.

'And undignified,' he added.

'And that too.'

A moment later she laughed softly and settled for sleep against his shoulder. But they never did make love in his new carriage.

Sometimes they talked. He was wary of conversation at first. He did not converse with women. Not *really* converse, that was. Frankly, he was not interested in women as people, though to be fair to himself, he did not expect them to be interested in him as a person either. His dealings with women were to fulfill a very specific need in their lives and his own. It was not that he disliked them or did not respect them any more than he believed they disliked or did not respect him. It was just that . . . Well, he had no interest in relationships. Again to be fair to himself, he avoided close friendships with men too. He had numerous friendly acquaintances, but no one to whom he bared his soul. The very thought was anathema to him.

They talked about their families. Or she did, anyway. She obviously felt a deep attachment to her family, though he wondered if they knew how deep her feelings ran. She could be very reserved, very cool, in manner. He had often wondered how much feeling there was behind that reserve. He had already discovered the passion. But there were genuine emotions too.

Her heart was torn in shreds with worry over her son, who was a captain with a rifle regiment in the Peninsula. She did not put her feelings into quite those words, but it was not difficult to interpret what she said that way. She spoke with hope of her elder daughter, who had been stripped of her title and place in society and robbed of her betrothal after her illegitimacy had been exposed.

She had apparently taught at an orphanage school and then married a schoolmaster and artist who had just inherited a modest fortune and a home outside Bath. It all sounded very complicated to him. They had adopted two of the children from the orphanage and recently had one of their own – her reason for having been in Bath. They had opened their home as a sort of retreat/conference/concert/gallery venue that was always buzzing with activity and teeming with people. Artist types, Marcel guessed. It all sounded quite ghastly, but apparently the daughter was happy, one indication being that she went about barefoot more often than she was shod.

'I suppose,' he said, 'her former self would have shuddered with horror at the mere thought of anyone except her maid seeing her *feet*.'

'Yes,' she said, apparently having taken his question seriously.

She was worried about her younger daughter, who had been deprived, with her title and social status, of any chance of making her come-out at a Season in London and of all hope of contracting the sort of marriage she had grown up to expect. The girl was apparently sweet and gentle and quite accepting of her lot in life – a fact that deeply worried her mother.

'Perhaps she really is,' he said. 'Accepting, that is.' Were not women raised to accept whatever life cared to throw their way? The devil but he was glad all over again that he had not been born female.

She gave him a speaking glance, and he kissed her hard so that he would not have to look into her deeply wounded eyes. Good God, he did not need this. He had run away with her so that they could put all their cares behind them for a while, forget everything but each other and the pleasure they could derive from each other and their immediate surroundings. So that they could enjoy a week or three of stress-free living and lusty sex.

Yet when he had finished kissing her and had sat back beside her again, he took her hand in his and settled it on his thigh, turned his head to look into her face, and so tacitly encouraged her to go on talking. He sensed that she needed to talk, and it struck him that no one ever seemed eager to talk to him – unless they were peppering him with complaints, that is, and pleas that he do something to put matters right.

She had gone to London earlier in the year to attend the wedding of the new Earl of Riverdale. He had not heard of her being in town. She had gone at the specific invitation of the earl himself – the very one who had usurped her son's title, though that had not been his fault – and of his mother and sister. The bride had also written to urge her to go, though the woman was about to assume the title that had been Viola's for more than twenty years.

Had she been taunting Viola? He had not met the new countess, but he was instantly biased against her. Why had Viola gone? Duty? Dignity? Pride? Good God.

'That must have been painful for you,' he said.

'Sometimes,' she said, 'doing what is most painful is the only thing to do.'

'Is it?' he asked, looking at her in some astonishment. 'I have always thought it is the very last thing to do. Surely pain is to be avoided at all costs.'

'I tried that for a while,' she said. 'I fled. I fled London and then Hinsford Manor, which was no longer either mine or Harry's. I even fled my daughters, with the explanation that it was for their own good that they live with my mother in Bath rather than with me. I fled to Dorset to stay with my brother. He is a clergyman and was still a widower at the time. But fleeing was not enough, for I took myself and my pain with me. Finally I had to go back and face at least some of it. I still sometimes find it difficult to look into the eyes of my daughters – and my son. He was home for a few months this year recovering from serious injuries.'

'I suppose,' he said, 'you felt guilty. Correction: I suppose you feel guilty.'

'I suppose I do occasionally,' she admitted. 'As though I ought to have known. But mainly I felt . . . mainly I feel helpless. I would die for them if by doing so I could ensure their happiness. But even that would not be enough. There is really nothing I can do for them.'

'Except love them,' he said. Now where had that come from?

'Love never seems to be enough either,' she said.

'It is said to be everything, but I am not sure I believe that.'

He felt a bit chilled. This was not the first time she had run away, then. She had carried all her bewilderment and pain and guilt with her the first time. And this time? The very fact that she was talking about it suggested that she had not come unencumbered, as he had. Did he really want to be doing this? Yet he made no effort to stop the flow of her words. He lifted their clasped hands and set his lips to the back of hers. He kept his eyes on her face.

She was telling him that she had gone to London and made friends with the new Countess of Riverdale.

What the devil? Did she delight in punishing herself?

'It was possible?' he asked.

'They are a lovely family,' she told him. 'Alexander is good and kind and has a strong sense of duty and responsibility. Wren is warm and earnest and truly generous. She is also strong and independent. She is a wealthy businesswoman in her own right and continues to be, with Alexander's blessing. They epitomize for me what a true marriage ought to be but very few marriages are.'

Ah, yes. He remembered now reading about it. Riverdale had married the Heyden china heiress, said to be fabulously wealthy.

'You find both of them impossible to hate, then,' he said. 'That must be a severe annoyance.'

She darted a look of amazed incomprehension at him and then . . . smiled. 'Well,' she said. 'I suppose it would be a comfort if I could dislike them. But I cannot. None of what happened was their fault. Alexander was genuinely dismayed when he was told the title was his. I know. I was there. I cannot dislike any of the Westcotts. None of it was their fault either, and they have gone out of their way to draw us back into the family. They have even all traveled to Bath several times in the last two years for our sakes. They are there now to spend a couple of weeks together following the christening of Camille and Joel's son.'

'But you do not use the Westcott name,' he said.

'No.' She shrugged.

'And when I met you, you were running again from all this kindness and generosity and love,' he said.

'Yes,' she said. 'Again. I had not thought of it that way. And now – yet again. Perhaps I have just turned into a runner. A shirker of reality.'

'Reality can be much overestimated,' he said.

She sighed, and they were silent for a while. Tall trees lining the road on both sides obscured the view of fields and meadows beyond and shut out much of the sunlight.

'And you, Marcel,' she said. 'What are you fleeing from?'

He had listened with unexpected interest to the tangle of love and hope and drama and fear and tedium that was her life. But listening was a passive thing. Her life was her own. It did not directly concern him. He had no real interest in her children, her mother, her brother, or the Westcotts – except as they affected her. Not that he was interested in shouldering her burdens and making them his own. Indeed, it was a little alarming to realize that she had brought them with her on this journey of supposedly mindless pleasure. But it was only because she had lived through such experiences and been involved in those relationships that she was the person she was now, he realized in a moment of strange insight. And somehow he was interested in the person who was Viola Kingsley. His interest in her should be entirely about sex if this affair was to proceed true to type. It did not feel quite like any type, however. It had not from the start.

What was he fleeing from?

'Merely the tedium of a visit home,' he said. 'There are too many feuding women there. And men who want to take charge in my absence, and a steward who is complaining about them. And a housekeeper who is grumbling about being forced to pray. It is a place to be avoided whenever possible, though just occasionally one feels obliged to put in an appearance to assert one's authority.'

'And does that work?' she asked.

'Oh, assuredly.' He looked at her, eyebrows raised. 'I do not suffer fools gladly. Or at all, in fact.'

'Your family and servants are fools?' she asked him.

He gave the matter some thought. 'I can see,'

he said, 'that I am going to have to choose my words carefully with you, Viola. No, they are not fools. At least, not all of them are. They are merely . . . tedious. Is that a more acceptable word?'

'I do not know the people concerned,' she said. 'Are they all your family? Do you not have children? Surely your own children are not tedious.'

He sighed and settled his shoulders across the corner of the carriage seat, putting a little distance between them. He folded his arms over his chest. 'They are not,' he said. 'But those who have the charge of them would make them tedious if they could.'

'But can they?' she asked. 'Do you not have the charge of them yourself?'

'Perhaps,' he said, 'I am tedious, Viola.'

'How old are they?' She was not to be deterred, it seemed.

'Seventeen, almost eighteen,' he said.

'All of them?' It was the turn of her eyebrows to shoot up.

'Two,' he said. 'Twins. Male and female.'

'And are they not—' She got no further. He had set one finger across her lips. Enough was enough.

'I am running away,' he said. 'With you. I have the necessary baggage with me in the form of a few changes of clothes and my shaving gear. It is all I need. And your company. But not your probing questions.'

'Just my body,' she said, drawing back from his silencing finger.

'That,' he said softly, refolding his arms, 'was uncalled for.'

'Was it?' she asked.

'I suppose that now we are embarked upon a thoroughly satisfactory affair you want more?' he said.

'Like most women?' She smiled, but the expression did not reach her eyes. 'That is what your question implied. No, Marcel, I do not want to own your soul. I certainly do not want to own your name. But is an affair only about—' She stopped and frowned.

'Sex?' he said. 'But sex is very pleasurable when it is good, Viola. As I believe you would agree.'

'Yes,' she said, and laid her head back against the cushions and closed her eyes. Shutting him out. Leaving him feeling somehow shallow for wanting nothing but sex from this brief escape from responsibility. She was the ice queen of memory, lips in a thin, straight line. He wanted her.

'None of them will miss us,' he said after a few minutes of irritated silence – irritated from his point of view, anyway. She looked perfectly serene, apart from her lips. He might almost have thought she had dozed off except that her head had not flopped to the side. 'Do you realize that, Viola? None of your numerous family members will even notice you are gone. They think you have returned to whatever-the-devil house you live in—'

'Hinsford Manor,' she said without opening her eyes.

'Hinsford Manor,' he said. 'They will continue to enjoy themselves in Bath and not spare you another thought.'

She had no comment on that. No protest to make. She knew he was right.

'And no one will miss me,' he said. 'When André arrives with word that I have fallen by the wayside but will put in an appearance when I put in an appearance, they will breathe a collective sigh of relief and carry on with their lives. Their tedious, sometimes fractious lives. And they will all write me another letter of complaint, and then complain to one another when they realize there is nowhere to send it.'

Her lips softened and curled at the corners in the suggestion of a smile. 'You are out of sorts,' she said.

He pursed his lips and glared at her, but she would not give him the satisfaction of opening her eyes. And he would not give her the satisfaction of speaking another word, even to deny her charge.

He was not out of sorts.

After a few minutes her head tipped to the left. He unfolded his arms, slid away from his corner, and lifted her head to rest on his shoulder.

They had had their first quarrel.

But he was right. No one would miss them. And he was *not* going to start feeling self-pitying about that. Though he did permit himself some small indignation on her part. They had let her go – in a hired carriage, no less – when the raw wound of what she had suffered a few years ago had not even begun to heal. They had let her go, and they would not even miss her.

He would miss her when she left him, he thought. Which was, of course, utter nonsense.

CHAPTER 8

Viola's family began to miss her after just a few days, when no letter came from Hampshire to inform them that she had arrived home safely. It was unlike her not to let at least her daughters know, especially when she must realize they would be more anxious than usual. They had tried everything they could to dissuade her from leaving in a hired carriage with no servant for protection or company, not to mention respectability.

Camille and Abigail had each since written to her. So had their maternal grandmother and Viola's sister-in-law on the Kingsley side and two of her erstwhile sisters-in-law on the Westcott side, they discovered when they mentioned the matter during a family dinner at their grandmother's home on the Royal Crescent. And so had Wren, the Countess of Riverdale, and Elizabeth, Lady Overfield, Wren's sister-in-law, Alexander's sister. One of a lady's daily duties, after all, was to write letters, and they had all been concerned about Viola and her abrupt decision to return home so soon after the christening of her grandson.

135

A little more than a week after her departure a letter finally did arrive from Hinsford, addressed to both Camille and Abigail. It was beside Camille's plate in the breakfast parlor when they arrived there together, having come directly from the nursery. It was not from their mother, however, but from Mrs Sullivan, the housekeeper, who explained that she had got in a whole pile of provisions in expectation of her ladyship's return home – she had flatly refused to stop addressing Viola thus even after the title was no longer hers. She had given most of the food away after a couple of days before it could go bad, as she was sure her ladyship would have wished her to do. It was unusual for her ladyship not to let her know she had changed her mind about coming, but Mrs Sullivan had not been too concerned until a number of letters started arriving for her, all from Bath. Her question for Mrs Cunningham and Miss Westcott, then, if she might make so bold, was this: If her ladyship was not either in Bath or at Hinsford, where was she?

The realization that their mother had neither arrived home nor written to explain why was alarming indeed to the sisters. Joel Cunningham found them severely agitated when he strolled into the breakfast parlor five minutes after them with a cheerful smile on his face and good morning greetings on his lips.

'Mama has disappeared,' Camille told him without preamble, the letter open in her hand,

136

her face ashen. 'She has not arrived home yet, and she has not written either to us or to Mrs Sullivan.'

'I *knew* I ought to have gone with her,' Abigail wailed. 'She was behaving very strangely – we all noticed it. How could we not? She was abrupt and even rude with a few of us, and she is never either of those things. It was selfish of me to remain here and let her go alone.'

'It was no such thing,' Joel assured her. 'I think she actually wanted to be alone for a while, Abby. Now where would she have gone if not home? To stay with some relative?'

Both ladies gazed at him in incomprehension. 'But everyone is here in Bath,' Camille said.

'Right.' He rubbed his hands together. 'Some particular friend, then?'

'There is no one who does not live within a couple of miles of Hinsford,' Abigail said. 'There is nowhere she could have gone.'

'Well clearly,' he said, 'there is *somewhere*. She cannot just have disappeared off the face of the globe.'

'But she has not even *written*.' Abigail covered her mouth with one hand while tears welled in her eyes and threatened to spill over.

'Perhaps she has arrived by now,' Camille said, handing the letter to her husband and making a visible effort to pull herself together. 'Perhaps there was carriage trouble and she was delayed. I daresay she is home by now.'

'But for a whole *week*? And if it was that, why did she not *write*?' Abigail asked.

No one could think of an explanation. Camille set an arm about her sister's shoulders while Joel read the letter, a frown on his face. There was no further enlightenment to be found from that single page, however.

'I tell you what I will do,' he said, folding it as he spoke. 'I will go down into Bath and see if the hired carriage that took her has returned. If it has, I will talk to the man who drove it. He is bound to know where she went.'

'Oh yes,' Camille said with visible relief while Abigail gazed hopefully at her brother-in-law. 'Of course he will. Let us go and find him.'

An argument ensued about whether he would go alone, as he wished to do for the sake of speed, or if his wife and sister-in-law would accompany him. As he pointed out, if Camille went, she would have to take Jacob with her, since it was impossible to predict how long they would be, and if Jacob was going, it would be difficult to leave Sarah and Winifred behind. In the end, they all had their way. Joel went ahead on horseback, and the rest of the family followed in the carriage, for, as Abigail pointed out, their grandmother would want to know about their letter and about what Joel discovered, as would the rest of the family, who were staying at the Royal York.

Joel rode down the long hill into Bath and left his horse at a livery stable before striding off on foot. He passed Bath Abbey on the way and was hailed by someone in a group of people standing and conversing outside the Pump Room. He recognized Anna, his dearest friend when they were growing up together at the orphanage and for a number of years afterward. She was now the Duchess of Netherby. The duke was with her, as were Camille's aunt Louise, the Dowager Duchess of Netherby, and Elizabeth, the widowed Lady Overfield. He hesitated for a moment, but then turned in their direction and returned Anna's hug when she stepped forward to greet him.

'You look as if you are in a vast hurry over something,' she said.

'Is anything amiss, Joel?' Elizabeth asked, a frown of concern on her face. 'One of the children?'

'Camille and Abby are worried sick,' he said. 'There was a letter this morning from the house-keeper at Hinsford. She wants to know where my mother-in-law is. She still had not arrived there.'

'Hired carriages are an abomination,' the Dowager Duchess of Netherby said. 'You may depend upon it that it broke down somewhere. She should have accepted the loan of my carriage. I have no use for it while I am here, as I was at pains to explain to her. But dearly as I love Viola, I have to say she is one of the most stubborn women of my acquaintance. She was bound and determined to do it her way.'

'But why has she not written to say so?' Anna asked.

'I daresay,' Avery, Duke of Netherby, said, 'that before we delayed him, Joel was on his way to demand answers of the coachman who drove her.'

'I was,' Joel said. 'I still am. If the carriage has returned, that is.'

'*If.*' Anna's hand crept to her throat.

'I shall come with you,' Avery said. 'If you will excuse me, that is, my love?'

'Oh yes, do go, Avery,' Anna urged. 'We will return to the hotel and wait to hear what you discover. Oh, what on earth could have happened?'

'Camille and Abigail are on their way to the Royal Crescent,' Joel said. 'They were too worried to wait at home.'

'Then we will go there too and wait for you,' the dowager said.

The coachman who had driven the hired carriage was not present when they arrived at the company's office. He was out on a call, but it was a local one and he could be expected back at any moment. *Any moment* proved to be an hour long. When he finally arrived, the man removed his greasy hat in order to scratch his greasy hair after Joel had hailed him and explained why he was there.

'I lost a good-paying customer back here on account of that there fare,' he said. 'Had to replace the axle, I did, though the old one wasn't exactly broke. Not good enough to fix, though. I lost a whole day and a pile of money. That gent did not make good for the day I lost either. I suppose a day's pay is neither here nor there to the likes of him. Some has it easy.'

'The gent?' Joel said.

'My carriage wasn't good enough for Mr High and Mighty,' the coachman said bitterly. 'Oh no, not him. He had to go looking for another one, he did, even after I went and changed the axle. Got me to take him to where he could find one. I only hope he got fleeced and all the wheels fell off before it had gone five miles.'

'You left Bath with Miss Kingsley,' Joel said. 'Who is this gentleman you speak of? And what happened to Miss Kingsley after the mishap with the axle?'

The coachman scratched his head again. 'Didn't know him from Adam,' he said. 'But he thought he was the king of England, he did. She was with him when I took him into town after the carriage was fixed. He had the cheek to say he wouldn't insist that I pay her back for the cost of the night at the inn. Can you believe it? I hope that after I left them they couldn't find nothing else to hire for the wheels to fall off of. It would serve him right, it would, if they was stranded there for the rest of their lives.'

'My temper would be considerably happier if you would confine your remarks to answering the questions that have been put to you,' Avery said, regarding the man with languid disfavor. 'Where exactly did this slight accident with the axle occur? Where exactly was Miss Kingsley stranded for the night? To which town did you convey her and the mysterious male stranger the following day?'

More head scratching. 'Some village,' the coachman said vaguely. 'Can't remember what it was called, if I ever knew. They was having some big fair there over something or other. The church roof, maybe.' He did, however, remember the name of the town to which he had taken his passengers the following day. 'I really ought to have been paid more for my trouble,' he added, squinting shrewdly at Joel. 'Cost me a bundle, that trip did.'

'I believe you got off lightly,' Joel told him. 'Your journey, for which you had been paid in full, was cut short when you were no longer required to go the whole distance, and Miss Kingsley apparently did not insist upon either a refund for the untraveled portion of the journey or recompense for the unexpected night she was forced to spend at an inn. Did she say anything to you the next day? About who the gentleman was or where she was planning to go in another carriage?'

But there was no further information to be got out of the man, and he dropped no more hints about the losses he had incurred during the ill-fated journey. He seemed somewhat disconcerted by Avery's languid mention of his unhappy temper and Joel's grim displeasure.

When Joel and Avery arrived at Mrs Kingsley's house on the Royal Crescent, they found every member of both families gathered in the sitting room, all looking identically anxious, with the exception of the children. Jacob was asleep in Abigail's arms, and Sarah, the younger of Camille and Joel's adopted daughters, was curled up on her mother's lap, hovering between sleeping and waking, though she roused herself sufficiently to greet her papa with a wide smile. Winifred, the elder of the adopted daughters, was tickling and smoothing a hand over the bald head of Josephine, Anna and Avery's baby.

As soon as Joel had given his report, the whole family would have gone tearing off in pursuit of Viola and the mysterious gentleman, who quickly assumed sinister proportions in the eyes of many of them, if Avery had not imposed silence and then reason upon the gathering with the mere lifting of one finger. He then observed that they would resemble a traveling circus and would surely move across the countryside at the speed of one if they all went together.

'I will go alone,' Joel said.

'I'll come too, Joel,' Alexander, Earl of Riverdale, told him. 'I am head of the family, after all, and you may need some assistance. This . . . man is an unknown quantity.'

'You are not going without me, Joel,' Abigail announced with a voice that quavered slightly. 'I blame myself for all this. If I had gone with Mama, everything would have been different.'

'If she had taken my carriage and a few hefty servants and a maid,' her aunt Louise, the dowager duchess, said, 'everything would certainly have been different. They would have dealt with the pretensions of that man, whoever he is, and sent him packing in some disarray.'

'I am going with you,' Abigail said again.

'And I will accompany you to give you countenance, Abby,' Elizabeth, Lady Overfield, said. 'Oh, do not look at me that way, Alex. Of course Abby wants to go search for her mama. And of course another lady must go with her. Wren cannot go in her condition. Why not your sister, then? And, Joel, do not *you* look at me that way. We may all be needed in one way or another.'

'I do think that is sensible, Elizabeth,' Lady Matilda Westcott, the eldest of Viola's former sisters-in-law, said in her strident voice. 'It would be most improper for two gentlemen to go alone, even if they are Viola's relatives. What would they do when they find her? And it would be out of the question for Abigail to accompany them without a chaperon.'

That settled the matter. All four of them would go in pursuit, though it was very possible the trail would run cold at the town where Viola had last been seen. Where she had gone no one could begin to guess. *Or with whom.* That was the question that loomed largest.

They set off before midafternoon in the earl's carriage, waved on their way by the other family members gathered outside the house on the Royal Crescent. Some of them were tearful, including Camille and Winifred. Sarah clung to Camille's

144

skirts, looking soulful after her father had hugged and kissed her and climbed into the carriage without taking her too. Jacob was asleep again in his great-aunt Mary Kingsley's arms.

Marcel, Marquess of Dorchester, was not missed at first. André arrived duly at Redcliffe Court, bringing with him the explanation that his brother had been unavoidably detained but would follow shortly. No one peppered him with awkward questions. No one was particularly surprised. That did not mean they were all happy.

Jane and Charles Morrow, as Marcel had predicted, were more relieved than chagrined over the delay. They were not fond of their brother-in-law. Worse, they had strong moral reservations about his possible influence over his children. If Adeline had not been such a silly ninnyhammer, they often assured each other, she would have married someone of altogether stronger moral fiber and there would be no danger of her children backsliding into sin and debauchery. However, she had been both silly and a ninnyhammer, and they could only hope that their brother-in-law's visits remained both brief and infrequent and that the strength of their own moral influence over their niece and nephew would prove stronger than the effect of heredity.

The marchioness, Marcel's elderly aunt, and Isabelle, Lady Ortt, her daughter, were more divided in their feelings. On the one hand, they were disappointed that they must wait longer for the marquess's return and the blistering setdown he was sure to deal the upstart Morrows, who behaved for all the world as though they owned Redcliffe and everyone and everything in it. The two ladies detested the couple heartily. Lord Ortt merely stayed out of their way and had no known opinion of Marcel, whom he avoided even more diligently when they happened to be beneath the same roof. On the other hand, the dowager and her daughter were deeply immersed in the planning of an increasingly elaborate wedding for Margaret, Isabelle's youngest daughter, and both entertained a gnawing anxiety that the marquess, without saying a word but with a mere lifting of his eyebrows in that way he had of expressing displeasure, might spell doom to their carefully laid schemes.

André was reasonably content, at least at first, to hide out from his creditors and from the shame of his gaming debts until his brother should choose to amble homeward.

It was the normally placid, biddable twins who were the problem.

All the ladies had been in the drawing room when André arrived, all usefully employed with needlework or tatting or knitting. Lord Ortt was there too, his head hidden behind a newspaper. And Bertrand Lamarr, Viscount Watley, was reading a book until the sound of an approaching carriage caused them all to raise their heads. He got to his feet and went to look out the window.

'Is it he, Bert?' Lady Estelle Lamarr asked eagerly.
'It looks like his carriage,' he said. 'Yes, it is.'

Estelle would have run downstairs to greet her father on the terrace, but she looked toward her aunt first, and that lady shook her head slightly and smiled fondly. It was not seemly for a young lady to go dashing about the house, displaying unbridled emotion. Estelle looked at Bertrand, who had turned from the window, and a silent message passed between them, as it often did. They were not identical twins, of course, so there was not that almost psychic bond that many identical twins shared. Nevertheless, they knew each other very well indeed, having been almost inseparable since birth. Estelle returned her attention to her embroidery, and Bertrand stayed where he was, much as he would have loved to dash down to meet his father himself.

Lord Ortt slipped from the room unnoticed.

And then their uncle André strode into the room. Alone.

'Father is not with you?' Estelle asked in clear dismay.

That was when he gave his vague explanation about his brother's having been unavoidably delayed.

'But he wrote to say he was on the way,' Estelle said. 'I have planned a party here for his fortieth birthday the week after next. I begged Aunt Jane to let me, and she said it would be good training for me.'

'I daresay he will be here long before then,' André assured her cheerfully. 'How do you do, Aunt Olwen? And Isabelle? Margaret?' He did the rounds of the room, bowing to each of the ladies in turn.

'I knew he would not come,' Bertrand said. 'I told you so, Stell.'

'Oh you did not,' she protested.

'And I warned you that your father is sometimes unpredictable,' their aunt Jane said kindly. 'I warned you too, Estelle, that he may not be as delighted as you hope at the prospect of a party in his honor here in the country. The company is bound to seem insipid to a man of his tastes. It will probably be just as well if he does not come in time, though I hate to see you spurned and disappointed.'

'Yes, Aunt Jane,' Estelle said as she resumed work on her embroidery.

'He has never *spurned* us,' Bertrand said, but he spoke quietly enough that his aunt either genuinely did not hear or wisely chose not to comment.

Their father had still not come after a week had passed or sent word to say when he would be there – if he came at all. Estelle grew steadily unhappier as the hope that he would arrive in time for his birthday grew slimmer. Bertrand, unhappy on his own account but even unhappier on his sister's, tackled their uncle André about the true cause of the unavoidable delay – and then reported to his sister in her room.

148

By the time he had finished, Estelle had grown unaccustomedly angry – she had been taught that a lady never allowed strong feeling to rob her of a calm dignity. 'I suppose,' she said, 'that if he set off with Uncle André and then decided to stay in some godforsaken village – were those his exact words, Bert? – I suppose that if he did that and even deliberately stranded himself there without his carriage, there can be only one of two explanations.'

'He found a card game or a cockfight or some such thing,' he said.

'Or a *woman*.' She spoke with great bitterness.

'I say, Stell, Aunt Jane would have a fit of the vapors if she could hear you say that,' he said.

Her eyes were swimming with tears when she lifted her face to his. 'I think it was a woman,' she said.

'Are you thinking what I am thinking?' he asked after they had stared at each other glumly for a few moments. His nostrils flared with a sudden anger to match hers.

'Yes, I certainly am,' she said. 'It is time we went to *find* him. And bring him home. He is *not* going to ruin the only party I have ever planned. He is simply *not*. I have had *enough*.'

'That's the spirit, Stell,' he said, clapping a hand on her shoulder and squeezing. 'We are not children any longer. It is time we asserted ourselves. Let's go find Uncle André again. He was in the billiard room five minutes ago.'

He still was.

'He could be anywhere by now,' André told them, chalking the end of his cue as though hopeful he was going to be able to resume his solitary game. 'I really cannot imagine him staying in that village for longer than a day or two at most. The Lord knows where he went after leaving there or where he is now. There is never any knowing with your father.'

But they went anyway. They set off the following day on a journey they were fully aware might very well prove fruitless. Four of them. Estelle and Bertrand had insisted that their uncle go with them in order to lead them to the village where he had left their father, since he could not remember the name of it. To be fair, he went without any great protest. Redcliffe did not offer much by way of entertainment or congenial company, but he could not go off anywhere alone, since his pockets were sadly to let and creditors might pounce if he went to his rooms in London or to any of his usual haunts. And it was in his own interest as well as that of his niece and nephew to find his brother and persuade him to come home and make good on his promise to lend the money to pay the more pressing of André's debts. The fourth in their company was Jane Morrow, who went after the failure of all her attempts to dissuade, command, wheedle, and threaten two young people who had never before in their lives given her a moment's trouble.

'I cannot think what has got into them,' she had

complained to her husband when he too had failed to talk sense into his wife's niece and nephew. 'Unless it is bad blood showing itself at last. I shall do all in my power to prevent that from prevailing, however, for Adeline's sake. Oh, I could cheerfully wring that man's neck, and I may do it too if we find him, which is very unlikely. It would be easier to find a needle in a haystack, I daresay.'

She was more annoyed than she could remember being since Adeline had insisted upon marrying a young man whose only claim to fame apart from extraordinary good looks had been his wildness. On this occasion she had even threatened to wash her hands of the twins if they defied her wishes. But she went. Duty was too strongly ingrained in her to be ignored. Oh, and affection too, though she did not like to admit to any gentle feelings for such disobedient children.

But she would have a word or two to say to her brother-in-law the very next time she saw him, even though she was very well aware that he would merely *look* at her in that way he had and finger the handle of his quizzing glass and make her feel like a worm crawling across the dirt before his feet.

How dared he disappoint his children?

CHAPTER 9

The Marquess of Dorchester employed a man of business to manage his investments and numerous properties, among them the cottage in Devonshire. He considered the man upright, honest, and trustworthy, and therefore did not bother his own head too much with details. However, he did seem to recall that the Devonshire property was tended and maintained by a resident housekeeper and a handyman, conveniently husband and wife, who had stayed on after his great-aunt's death. He could not remember their name when he sent a letter notifying them of his imminent arrival with a guest and of his intent to remain there for a couple of weeks or so. He addressed the letter simply to the housekeeper. As far as he remembered from a few boyhood visits, there were no other dwellings close by, and the nearest town was several miles to the west. Reaching it entailed either a lengthy and tedious journey northward by carriage to a ford and a sturdy bridge across the river, or a more direct descent of the steep hillside below the cottage by foot or on horseback to a narrow stone bridge and a steep ascent of the hill on the other side.

In either case, one did not simply dash into town to purchase an item or two whenever the whim took one. It would not seem wise, then, to arrive unannounced to the discovery that there was virtually no food in the house or other essential supplies.

They arrived on a warm, sunny afternoon, though there had been a hint of autumn in the air earlier. It was much as Marcel remembered it, though he had forgotten the small village on the eastern side of the valley, closer to the house than the town on the other side. The village was really little more than a church and a tavern and a cluster of houses, however, in a slight dip of land with a view out to sea. What the people who lived there did for a living and for entertainment was anyone's guess. His guess was that the tavern did a roaring trade, and perhaps the church too.

The valley itself was obscured for the beholder by a slight rise and a few clusters of trees until one came upon it suddenly, a wide swath of greenery sliced into the land with a river flowing through the bottom of it. Its long slopes were carpeted in rich green ferns and shaded by trees, some of which were beginning to show signs of autumn. The cottage, just as he remembered it, was on the near hillside, far enough down the slope to be invisible until one could see the whole valley plunging beneath one's feet. It had no private garden, though its stone walls were festooned with ivy and other climbing plants. The valley was its garden.

There was a way down to it even for the carriage.

A wide dirt laneway approached it from some distance to the north rather than from directly above, in order to minimize the slope. It really was quite impressive if one favored remote rural living. Or if one were seeking out a cozy love nest where one was unlikely to be distracted or disturbed.

For his purposes it was perfection itself.

'Oh my goodness.' Viola sat forward in her seat as the carriage topped the rise and began its careful descent to the house. 'This is magnificent, Marcel.' She was looking from side to side through the windows, trying to see everything at once.

And it really was. Calling the house a cottage was somewhat misleading, for it was no hovel. Neither was it a mansion, however. There were six – or was it eight? – bedchambers abovestairs and an equivalent number of rooms downstairs, variously designated in his great-aunt's time by names like parlor, sewing room, morning room, and writing room. It was built of yellowish stone with a tile roof, in which there were dormer windows, presumably belonging to the servants' quarters. The plants that grew on the walls looked well tended. A thread of smoke rose straight into the sky from a wide chimney. There was a stable block off to one side and a chicken coop.

'What a beautiful house,' she said. 'But it must surely have been built originally by a recluse. There is no other building in sight.'

'Or by a romantic,' he said. 'Perhaps by a man who wished to escape the bothers of life with a woman of his choosing.'

She turned her head to look at him. There had been a strange tension between them all day with the knowledge that they were approaching their destination. He had been thinking that perhaps he ought not to have suggested this place or any specific destination. For the very nature of running away surely implied no fixed direction, but rather a constant wandering onward as inclination led. They had had a taste of the pleasures of it on the way here.

'Perhaps,' she said, 'we are being disrespectful to your great-aunt's memory.'

'Family lore has it,' he told her, 'whispered behind hands, I might add, but children have ears at full attention when they hear whispers. Family lore has it that she lived here for years and years with another woman, euphemistically known as her dearest friend and companion, until that other woman died. And then she lived on here, solitary and doubtless lonely and respectable enough once more to be visited by family members. Respectable *and* rich. It was during those later years that I was brought here and climbed onto her lap and into her heart – and her will.'

The carriage had drawn to a halt, and a buxom, red-cheeked woman in a mobcap and spotless white apron tied about a voluminous dress was standing on the stone doorsill outside the open front door, smiling and bobbing curtsies while the coachman opened the door and set down the steps.

'Good day to you, sir,' she said when Marcel had

descended to the hardened dirt terrace before the door. 'I had your letter, and I sent Jimmy into town yesterday with a list as long as your arm. I have a meat-and-vegetable stew bubbling away on the hob and ready whenever you are hungry, and fresh baked bread to go with it, and I took the liberty of hiring Maisie from the village – Jimmy's niece's girl – to help me put clean linen on the beds and beat the rugs and dust the furniture and polish the brass, though I always do that once a fortnight anyway. With your permission I will keep her on while you are here to help with the extra work. Jimmy has fixed the door on the carriage house and mended the leak in the roof, and he has mucked out all the stalls for the extra horses and got in plenty of fresh straw and feed for them. And how do you do, ma'am? I daresay you are ready for a nice cup of tea and some of my fresh scones. Jimmy got some more tea yesterday, and I have filled the caddy so there will be plenty whenever you fancy a pot.'

Marcel groped for the handle of his quizzing glass.

'Good afternoon,' Viola said. 'I am Viola Kingsley.'

'Edna Prewitt, ma'am,' the housekeeper said, curtsying again. 'And pleased I am to make your acquaintance and to have someone staying at the house again. It has been too long a time, as I am always saying to Jimmy. Maisie can give you a hand if you do not have a ladies' maid with you. She does hair a treat. And she doesn't chatter all the time, which I daresay ladies don't always want to listen to.'

Marcel had his glass halfway to his eye.

'A cup of tea would be very welcome, Mrs Prewitt,' Viola said. 'And perhaps a scone or two. No more, though. We would not wish to spoil our appetites for your stew, which smells quite heavenly from here.'

'It smells better from inside,' the housekeeper said. 'And what am I doing keeping you standing out here when you must want to be settling in your rooms and washing your hands? Jimmy always says I talk too much, but I wanted to welcome you properly and make you feel at home, even though it *is* your home, isn't it, sir? You haven't been here for so long, though, that I felt I needed to—'

'Thank you, Mrs Prewitt,' he said. 'We would indeed like to wash our hands.'

Good God.

She bustled upstairs ahead of them and indicated one room for him before taking Viola into another. They were side by side, both rooms facing out over the valley. 'I will have Maisie bring up two pitchers of hot water, Mrs Kingsley, ma'am,' he heard her say before she bustled back downstairs. 'It is all ready. I always keep plenty on hand because you never know when you are going to need it, and if there is one thing I hate it is having to wash in cold water. And do dishes.'

Marcel went into Viola's room after the woman had left. She was standing at the window, looking out.

'She did not seem offended,' she said.

'Offended?' He went to stand beside her at the window and dipped his head to look into her face. '*Offended*, Viola? Why should she be? She is a servant.'

She did not withdraw her gaze to look back at him. 'Is there a color more soothing than green?' she asked. It sounded like a rhetorical question, and he did not attempt to answer. 'Flowers would be superfluous here, would they not, when nature is so prolific with greenery. They would look almost gaudy. This is all far lovelier than I imagined.'

Marcel had heard the girl going into his room. Now she came into Viola's and set a pitcher of water on the washstand before bobbing a curtsy. She did not launch into a chat, however, which was something of a relief.

'Thank you, Maisie,' Viola said, turning toward her, and the girl bobbed another curtsy before leaving. She looked like a younger version of her great-aunt even down to the rosy cheeks. A *silent* version of her great-aunt. Though come to think of it, she was not a blood relative of Mrs Prewitt's, was she? She was Jimmy's great-niece. It must be a wholesome country look they shared.

'Viola,' he asked, 'are you regretting this?'

She glanced at him before turning back to the window and opening one half of it to let in fresh air and birdsong and the distant sound of flowing water. She closed her eyes and inhaled slowly. She had been generally lighthearted during their journey, willing to enjoy herself and enjoy him.

'I have never done anything like this before,' she told him. 'Virtuous women do not, you know. We are taught that our happiness is to be found in virtue and in doing our duty with cheerful dignity. Only men are allowed to do what they want while their women look the other way and . . . endure.'

'Why do more women not simply shoot themselves?' he asked.

'Because we know no different,' she told him.

'You believe you have become an *un*virtuous woman, then?' he asked.

'Oh, I more than believe it,' she said. 'I have quite knowingly abandoned virtue and stepped into the unknown. All this is . . . normal to you, Marcel. It would not occur to you to regret it or wonder about the moral implications of what you are doing or the effect it will have on your character for the rest of your life. It is not at all normal to me. I do not regret what I have done. Neither do I applaud my boldness. But I do not deceive myself. I am doing this. For myself. The future will decide how I will be affected by it all. I will not think of it until I reach that future. It would be better if you do not keep asking. I am here. By choice. Your servants here do not appear to be scandalized. And I am enchanted with this cottage and everything that is out there.'

'Are you enchanted with me?' he asked.

When she looked at him this time, her eyes were laughing. 'You sound like a little boy begging for approval,' she said.

The devil he did! He reached out a hand and pulled her into his arms before kissing her thoroughly.

'Yes,' she said against his mouth when he gentled the embrace. 'I am enchanted with you. But I very much need to wash my hands, behind closed door, if you please. And then I would like that cup of tea Mrs Prewitt is brewing for us.'

And thus dismissed, he withdrew to his own room until she was ready to go back downstairs.

You sound like a little boy begging for approval. Good God!

The window of Viola's bedchamber had been ajar all night. Now she flung it wide and stood before it, breathing in the crisp autumn air as she drew her shawl more closely about her shoulders. There were trails of mist in the valley and pale blue sky above. It was surely impossible to get closer to paradise than this while one still lived. She allowed her heart a conscious welling of happiness . . .

. . . and wondered if there was a letter from Harry awaiting her at home. *Or a letter about Harry.* She wondered if her brother and sister-in-law and all the Westcotts were still in Bath, celebrating family. For that was what they had been doing more and more in the last couple of years, since the great catastrophe, which might just as easily have broken them asunder into bitter disunity. For one moment she regretted having left Bath so abruptly and thus having spoiled things a bit for everyone.

160

This was so typical of her. So very typical. Even now, when she had made the conscious decision to do something for herself, she could not quite stop herself from looking back and fearing that she had inconvenienced or hurt others. She had *hurt* no one. And no one would worry unduly. She did wish she could go back and rewrite that letter to Camille and Abigail, though. She ought to have explained that she had met a friend and been persuaded to spend a couple of weeks or so at that friend's house. They would wonder, but they would not worry. But at least she had written, and they would know that she had not just disappeared off the face of the earth.

And so she could permit herself this time of unalloyed . . . happiness. It was a rash word to use, perhaps, and a rash thing to feel. But why not? This was what she had run away for. This was what her heart had surely yearned for all her life. Just simply to be happy, however fleetingly. She was not so foolish as to believe in happily-ever-after. That did not mean happiness was to be spurned when it offered itself for brief, vivid moments, as it did now.

Oh, this really was paradise. The ferns above the mist gleamed wetly in the morning sunlight.

'Something,' a voice said from behind her, 'is reminding me of winter days at school, when we were hauled from our beds at an ungodly hour each morning in order to run twenty laps about the playing fields before returning to a refreshing wash in icy water and a descent to the unheated stone chapel for half an hour of prayers and moral harangues from the headmaster. I believe it must be— Yes, indeed it is. It is the Arctic air billowing through that window.'

She turned to smile at him. He was lying naked in her bed, his fingers laced behind his head, the bedcovers bunched about his hips.

'Are you a hothouse plant, Marcel?' she asked him. 'I want to go out there. I want to run in the ferns. I want to run through the mist. I want to stand in the middle of that bridge and twirl slowly about and breathe in the wonder of it all. Such a feast for the senses.'

'I perceive a compatibility problem,' he murmured, and closed his eyes. But he made no move to cover himself.

'It was you,' she reminded him, 'who wanted to dance on the village green.'

'Ah, but that was a means to an end,' he said, his eyes still closed. 'I hoped to lure you into bed.'

'It was a trick that worked like a dream,' she said, turning back to the window. 'I hope you are proud of yourself.'

'Indeed I am.' She jumped slightly, for his voice came from just behind her, and his arms came about her and drew her back against him. 'It was one of the greater successes of my life.'

'Not the greatest? I am crushed.' She rested her head on his shoulder and sighed with contentment.

'Viola,' he said, 'this is a little akin to shutting the stable doors after the horse has bolted, I suppose, but do you know – and practice – ways to prevent conception?'

She was very glad he could not see her face. She had rarely been more embarrassed in her life. Women never discussed . . . even with one another. But why was prudery still dogging her footsteps when she was standing here with her naked lover in a remote love nest the morning after a night of loving?

'I stopped having my—' Oh dear. She tried putting it another way. 'I stopped being fertile a couple of years ago, after all the upset. It has never come back. I will not conceive.'

'Was that not a very young age for it to happen?' he asked.

'Yes, I believe so,' she said. 'I was forty.'

'Ah, so I am bedding an older woman, am I?' he said. 'I will pass that dreaded landmark in a short while. At present I am still in my youthful thirties.'

She did the subtraction in her head. He had been only twenty-five, then, when he had so pointedly flirted with her and so tempted her twenty-eight-year-old self. He must have been awfully young when he married and when his wife died. He did not seem at all the sort of man to marry young. Had he been essentially the same man then as he was now? Had he married for practical reasons, perhaps, as she had? Or had he changed quite drastically? But he would not talk about his family, not even his children. Twins. A boy and a girl.

It was strange how someone she had always

summed up with a single label – *libertine* – and the assumption that there was nothing else to know had become a person, though she still knew hardly anything about him. He was a man of mystery, of depths she suspected were dark. Though she could be wrong. But she did not need to know him, except in this way – as the lover with whom she had run away from her dreary life for a short spell. It would be as well if she did not probe deeper. The point of this idyll was not to get to know each other but to *enjoy* each other.

It sounded very shallow put that way.

Did it matter? Sometimes the human spirit needed the shallows. Sunshine danced on the shallows but was absorbed beyond trace by the depths.

'Those ferns are going to be wet,' he said, 'and knee-high. They are going to slap about you from all directions and in all their cold wetness and splash your hands and face and cause you unutterable discomfort.'

'Coward,' she said.

'I have boots,' he said. 'I will wager you do not.'

'I have stout shoes,' she told him. 'They and the hems of my clothes will dry. So will my person. I am going out there. If you would prefer to remain here, nibbling on your toast—'

'Ten minutes,' he said, snatching up his dressing gown from the floor and striding toward the door. 'I will meet you downstairs. Just be warned. I do not want to hear any whining or complaining for the next hour or so.'

She poked her tongue out at him, something she could never remember doing before, even as a child. But he did not turn back to see.

Ten minutes later she watched him come downstairs, all elegant practicality in a greatcoat with too many capes to count at a glance and top boots that gleamed with polish and reached almost to his knees. She hoped he would expire from the heat before they returned to the house. She hoped his boots would be ruined beyond repair. She smiled at him and felt that welling of happiness again.

'A punctual woman,' he said. 'No, a woman who is early. A rarity indeed.'

'You were never a woman in *my* household, Mr Lamarr,' she said.

He made her a courtly bow, unlocked and opened the door, and offered his arm.

They walked sedately along the dirt terrace that would take them onto the driveway to the top of the valley if they continued. But she did not want to go up to the top. She had seen the view from there yesterday. She slipped her hand from his arm and stepped off the path among the ferns. They did indeed reach her knees, some of them even higher than that, and, yes, they were beaded prettily with moisture, as she had seen from her window. The moisture did not feel nearly as pretty when transferred to her dress and cloak and even her stockings and legs, however. There was still a chill in the air, but there was warmth in the sun too and the promise of another lovely afternoon.

'Are you satisfied, ma'am?' he asked, all right-eous and smug inside his top boots. 'Shall we go back in for breakfast?'

She smiled dazzlingly at him and turned back to the valley. She spread her arms wide, lifted her face to the sky, whooped with delight, and began to run downhill. It did not take long to discover that it was not as easy as it looked. The carpet of the ferns suggested a smooth slope, but the ground under them was anything but. It was also spongy from the mist and the dew. The slope was a lot steeper than it had looked from above, and certainly longer. After a few moments she needed both hands to hold up her skirts so she would not trip over them. With her eyes she tried to map out a path ahead, but it was virtually impossible to see all the dips and rises and rocks and mud patches. Even the trees were dripping water. She found herself laughing helplessly. It was either that or scream. Somehow she kept her feet under her all the way down, but she was very thankful that the slope leveled off to a grassy bank for a few yards this side of the river. She was able to slow down in time to save herself from the shock of an early-morning swim.

Good heavens, she did not even know how to swim.

And when had she behaved with such little regard for dignity and propriety and even safety? Probably never. There were hills aplenty in Bath. She had never run down any of them as a child.

Or spread her arms or whooped or laughed helplessly.

He was still standing on the terrace where she had left him, his arms folded across his chest, looking handsome and virile and disapproving. Oh goodness, oh goodness, when had she ever felt so free? When had she ever felt so happy? There had been fleeting moments – her first love when she was sixteen, the births of her children, Camille's wedding, Jacob's christening . . . For the life of her she could not recall any other such moments until she had waltzed on the village green.

Every day since had been crammed with such moments. And every night too.

He was descending the slope with measured steps and great dignity. 'You ruined my morning,' he said when he was close enough to be heard. 'I was waiting for the giant splash and the shriek as you dashed into the water.'

'And you would have rushed to the rescue like a knight-errant,' she said.

'I must caution you, ma'am,' he said, 'against making a gallant hero of me in your imagination.'

She had the satisfaction of seeing that his buff-colored breeches were wet above his boot tops as well as the lower third of his coat. She was soaked almost to the waist, and there was nothing remotely warm about the moisture. Her feet, half frozen, were squelching inside her shoes.

'You still wish to do your ecstatic pirouette on the bridge, I assume?' he asked, offering his arm.

It was some distance away.

'Perhaps we ought to keep that treat for another day,' she said. 'Breakfast seems like a lovely idea, does it not?'

'It seemed even lovelier from the top of the hill,' he told her.

'I believe,' she said, 'you are not a lover of country living, are you, Marcel?'

'I am not renowned for tramping about my fields admiring my crops,' he admitted, 'a faithful hound panting at my heels.'

'How can you look about this valley,' she said, indicating it with one sweeping arm, 'and not feel something . . . here?' She tapped her heart.

'I would rather look at the woman in the valley,' he said, his eyes following her hand.

'Would you?' She gazed at him, his face harsh and cynical, his dark, hooded eyes unfathomable, and despite her earlier resolve, wondered what lay behind them. Or *who* lay behind them.

He set his hands at her waist, drew her against him, and kissed her openmouthed and at some length. His mouth was hot in contrast to the uncomfortable coldness of her person.

You must not fall in love, an inner voice of reason cautioned. *You really must not.*

Oh, but there is no fear of that, she protested silently. *I am merely enjoying a brief escape from my life.*

'There is a law of duality,' he said, 'that insists, as laws often do, that what goes up must come down. Sometimes, however, when one least wants the law to reverse itself, it does.'

She looked up the hillside to the cottage, so idyllic and picturesque among the trees and ferns, climbing plants adorning its walls. It also looked welcoming with the one bedchamber window wide open and a line of smoke rising out of the chimney. Some of the leaves about them were changing color.

'It does look like rather a long climb,' she admitted.

She was out of breath halfway up and had to pause and cling to a tree trunk while pretending she had stopped to admire the view. She was out of breath again at the top and puffing inelegantly. He was breathing as though he had just taken a leisurely stroll along Bond Street in London – except that his boots had lost some of their luster.

'Your cheeks are becomingly rosy, Viola,' he said. 'And so is your nose – perhaps not quite as becomingly.'

'Gallantry is really not your forte, is it?' she said.

'As I warned you,' he reminded her. 'I believe it would be more accurate to describe your nose as *adorably* rosy.'

'Oh, well-done,' she said, and turned to precede him into the house.

'Never let it be said,' he murmured from behind her, 'that I do not think quickly on my feet.'

She laughed.

CHAPTER 10

After a week at the cottage, Marcel discovered with something of a surprise not only that he was still deeply immersed in this new affair of his, but that he was also thoroughly enjoying himself. Not enjoying just the affair – he would expect that. It never took him any time at all to put an end to any liaison he was *not* enjoying. No, he was enjoying . . . himself.

When he had thought of coming to the Devonshire cottage, it had seemed to him that it was the ideal place for the uninterrupted conduct of the affair. He had pictured them cozily ensconced in the house, the valley merely the secluded background that would cut them off from prying eyes and the distractions of civilization and the normal course of their lives. His family would not in a million years think of searching for him there, even if for some unfathomable reason they should consider searching at all, and her family would not even know of its existence.

He had *not* considered the place in terms of wild natural beauty and fresh – sometimes cold – air and bracing walks and conversation that stretched his mind to its limits. The very thought would have given him pause.

He had been right in his main expectation. They enjoyed long nights of sensual pleasures, which had not yet even begun to pall upon him. Quite the contrary, in fact. He was even growing slightly uneasy at the possibility that they never would, though he was being ridiculous, of course. Any day now he was going to grow restless, not just to return to civilization, but to regain his freedom so that he could look about him for some new source of pleasure.

The sexual delights, however, had been confined to the nights, while their days had been filled with almost nothing but the bracing outdoors, God help him. They went up and down the steep valley sides on both sides of the river as other people might ascend and descend stairs within a house. They walked pathways and *no* pathways and rough headlands. They almost got blown to glory one afternoon while tramping along the top of towering cliffs overlooking the sea, the wind in their faces before they turned back to be blown home. One morning they walked up to the village and through it to descend a steep flight of rough-hewn steps and an equally steep fall of large rocks and smaller pebbles to a small sandy cove. All they got for their pains on that occasion was sand inside her shoes and caked on the outside of his boots, and sand inside every piece of clothing on their persons and even in their hair. Oh, and there was the enormous pleasure of huffing their way back up to the village afterward and from there back to the cottage.

'Are you trying to wear my legs down to the knees, Viola?' he asked when they were almost home. But she just laughed at him. She did a lot of that during the week – laughing at him. Oh, and with him too.

He took great delight in her laughter. Even more in her smiles.

'I want to walk along beside the river to the sea one day,' she said. 'I hope you will not be worn down to the knees, Marcel. You would be shorter than I am, and I should dislike that.'

'I would think you would enjoy the sense of power towering over me would bring you,' he said, and she laughed again.

And they talked. They were standing in the middle of the bridge one day at the end of their first week there and she had executed her long-promised pirouette and made the expected comments upon the breathtaking beauty of their surroundings. Actually he agreed with her, though he did not fling his arms wide, an ecstatic look on his face, as he turned once about. He would have been quite content to stand there in silent companionship with her with all his senses alive. Good God, he had senses he had never even suspected before. But she decided to talk.

'Why do you think we were born?' she asked, her arms resting along the waist-high parapet of the bridge as she gazed down into the water. 'What do you think is the point of it all?'

If any other woman had asked him such asinine questions, he would have bundled her into his carriage without further ado, sprung the horses in the direction of London, and lost her somewhere in its busiest midst, never to be found again.

'I suppose we were born because our parents fancied each other one night nine months or so before it happened,' he said. 'And the point of it all is that thereby the world will remain populated and we will not expire as a species.'

She chose to take his flippancy seriously. She was no longer looking down into the water or up at the valley sides surrounding them. She was gazing at him instead, and he was beginning to believe his colossal lie that her rosy nose was adorable. 'But why?' she asked. 'Why deliberately perpetuate something if it has no inherent value?'

Her words were a bit chilling if she meant that human life really was not worth living. He had not given much thought to the matter. Not for many years anyway. He did not particularly want to break that habit.

'You had children,' he reminded her.

'Yes,' she said, 'because it was expected of me. It was my duty. Camille was a disappointment to Humphrey because she was not the heir he had anticipated. And after Harry, Abigail was a disappointment because she was not the spare to go with the heir.'

'It was only duty?' He raised his eyebrows.

'Well, no.' She turned to gaze with a frown along the river in the direction of the sea, which was not visible from here. 'They were my joy.'

'Your *only* joy?' he asked. 'The only things that have given meaning to your life?'

She considered her answer, her gloved fingers rubbing back and forth over the stones. 'Yes,' she said. 'Almost. But why did I feel joyful when I was merely delivering them to all the pains that awaited them in this life?'

'Their lives have been nothing but misery, then?' he asked.

'Camille was an unhappy child,' she told him. 'She wanted what she could not have – her father's love and approval. She is happy now. So happy that I almost fear for her. Harry insists that being in the Peninsula being constantly shot at is a great lark while I wait at home in constant fear of what the news might be when I next hear from him – or of him. Abigail is sweet and quiet and serene, and I fear what lies beneath it all and what the future holds for her.' With that, she turned to him abruptly. 'Why did you have children, Marcel?'

'Because I was young and married and it happened in the natural course of what young married people do,' he said. And he had been so fiercely joyful that he still could not bear to think about it.

'Do you ever feel weighed down by the burden

of fatherhood?' she asked him. 'Not because you do not love them but because you do?'

He really did *not* want to be talking about this. This was not why he had come here. He had run away with her for a week or three of pleasure. *Mindless* pleasure. He had come because he did not want to go home and see evidence of his own failure as a father and as a human being. They were almost grown-up, Estelle and Bertrand, those much-adored babies.

They were almost grown-up.

He stared back at her, resentment mingling with something else he did not try to analyze. She lifted both hands and cupped his face with them. She brushed her gloved thumbs over his cheeks. For one moment he feared they were wet, but they were not.

'Sometimes,' she said, 'your face turns hard and your eyes turn opaque, and I am almost frightened.'

'Of me?' he said.

'Of not being able to see you,' she said.

He did not ask what she meant. He did not want to know.

'I was not fit to raise my children,' he told her curtly. 'I still am not, though there is not much raising left to do. They are seventeen.'

'Who *does* raise them?' she asked.

'Their aunt and uncle,' he told her. 'My late wife's sister and her husband. And yes, they *were* fit and *are* fit and my children are fine young people who will be fine and worthy adults.' It was not often he admitted that Jane and Charles had been good for his children.

'Do you love them?' Her voice was a mere breath of sound.

He grasped her none too gently by the wrists and removed her hands from his face. 'That is a typical *woman's* question,' he said. 'I fathered them and have seen to it that they have the proper care. I have provided a home and the means for them to grow up according to their station in life. I have visited them twice a year since they were one year old. I will see to it that they are suitably established in life, and then my job, such as it has been, will be done.' He was still gripping her wrists.

'You were on your way to see them.' Her eyes, damn it all, had filled with tears.

'They will still be there when—'

'When we are finished?' she said when he stopped abruptly.

'I resent this, Viola,' he told her. 'We came here to escape, to put our everyday lives behind us, to enjoy each other's company, not to bare our souls.'

'I have enjoyed your company,' she said softly.

'Past tense?' It had not occurred to him that perhaps she would tire of him before he tired of her. Arrogant of him, that. And alarming if it was true.

'No,' she said, 'not past tense. When I asked about the purpose of life, I was not really expecting an answer. I asked because sometimes one can be happy, so vividly happy that there seems a point

176

to everything. So happy that one is fiercely glad one was born. Happiness that intense never lasts, of course, and even what there is of it often comes at the expense of conscience and responsibility. I have been very happy with you.'

He felt that unease again and released his hold on her wrists. She was still using the past tense.

'Oh, you must not fear,' she said with a fleeting smile. 'I have just admitted that I know it cannot last. But are fleeting moments enough anyway, Marcel? Are times like these sufficient to make the whole of life worth living?'

He sighed and set his hands on her shoulders briefly before gathering her loosely into his arms. 'Up and down, down and up, light and shade, happiness and unhappiness,' he said. 'They are life, Viola. *Why* we are so seemingly helpless in the face of these opposites, I do not know. I am no philosopher. But seeking happiness – or pleasure – while avoiding pain is human nature. There is nothing selfish about it.'

'Happiness and pleasure are the same thing to you,' she said. 'Is seeking them never selfish? What about duty?'

'I suppose,' he said, 'indeed I *know* that you spent more than twenty years of your life ignoring the fact that Riverdale was a scoundrel of the first order and keeping up appearances before your family and the *ton*. Doing your duty. Being unselfish. And unhappy.'

'Foolish, was it not?' she said. 'I ought to have

177

had an affair with you. I wanted to, you know.' She rested the side of her head against his shoulder.

He was arrested for the moment by her admission.

'No, you would not have,' he said. 'That was not who you were, Viola. And it was not who I was. You would not have had an affair with me because you were married – *apparently* married – and had young children. I would not have had an affair with you because you were married. I would have done no more than flirt.'

'You would not?' She drew back her head to look into his face. She sounded surprised. 'You did have some principles, then?'

Something in him turned cold. 'Precious few,' he said. 'Principles are tedious, Viola. They interfere with personal gratification.'

'But sometimes they are part of who a person is,' she said. 'You have never seduced a married woman?'

He raised both eyebrows. 'I have never *seduced* any woman,' he said. 'It just happens for some reason I have not quite fathomed that a flatteringly large number of them wish to share my bed without having to be seduced there. No, I have never bedded a married woman, except my wife.'

She smiled fleetingly again but did not take the opening he had unwittingly offered her. She did not ask about Adeline.

'It may seem strange,' she told him, 'but I do

not believe I was actively unhappy during all those years of my marriage. Not all the time, anyway, or even most of the time. It was only afterward, when I knew what an empty shell the whole fabric of my life had been, and when my children had been irreparably hurt, that I saw the emptiness of those years. I was forty years old, more than half my life gone in all probability. But if I could go back and relive it, I cannot think that I would live differently. What havoc I would have caused to so many lives, my own included, if I had behaved just as I wanted. And I would never have been happy. Now is a little different.'

'Only a little?' he asked.

'There are still people to be hurt,' she said.

'This is but a brief idyll, Viola,' he reminded her.

'Yes,' she said. He held her close and kissed her deeply, sensing that somehow this was the beginning of the end. Not the end yet. They had still not finished with each other. But some corner had been turned, and they had begun the journey back to where they had started.

'I do not believe I am willing to wait for tonight,' he said against her lips. It was approaching the middle of the afternoon. They had come down here after luncheon.

'I am not either,' she told him.

And so the affair resumed as it had been proceeding for the past week and more – except that they did not often make love in the daytime. They climbed the hillside together to the cottage and went to bed and made slow, skilled, wonderfully satisfying love.

With perhaps just an edge of desperation.

The weather turned overnight. It grew chillier and more blustery. Clouds hung low over the valley, and there were frequent sharp showers. More trees were turning color.

'Autumn always makes me feel a bit sad,' Viola said at breakfast one morning during a brief sunny break. 'It is so beautiful but so very fleeting. One knows that winter is not far off.'

'And spring not so far beyond that,' he said with a shrug.

'True,' she said. 'But sometimes it seems very far off.'

'Viola,' he said, reaching across the table to take her hand in his. 'There is much to be said for winter. Rainy days, snowy days, cold days.' He grinned suddenly, and her heart turned over. 'Nothing to do but remain indoors and love.'

He meant *make* love, of course. He did not know much if anything of love. Though that was perhaps unfair and not necessarily right. She would have said it of him a week or so ago with some confidence. Now she was not so sure. He did not want to talk about his children or about his brief marriage as a young man. His very reticence suggested to her that there was pain there. And where there was pain, perhaps there was love. He had neglected his children since they were infants – not materially, but in ways that mattered. He had *visited* them twice a year. It was a strange verb to use of time spent with his own children. And the word suggested a stay of days or brief weeks rather than of months.

Humphrey had neglected his children. He had not loved them. She had always thought he was scarcely aware of their existence. Sometimes, when she and they were at Hinsford and he was else-where – London, Brighton, or wherever he went during his frequent absences – he would not return home or even write for weeks on end. He missed first steps and first teeth and birthdays. She wondered if Marcel's neglect of his children was of that nature, but suspected it was not. Perhaps that was because she did not want to believe that his neglect stemmed from indifference. She wanted to believe that there was a person hidden behind the handsome, harsh, often cynical exterior that had so captivated her.

Perhaps it was just that she needed to believe there was. For her own sake. Perhaps she needed to believe that he was not without all heart, as she had always thought. She had flung aside everything she had believed of herself in order to come here with him for a few intense weeks of . . . love.

Nothing to do but love.

'There are always things to do,' she said. 'Reading, painting, sketching, making music, conversing, writing, taking the air, sewing, embroidering.'

'And making love,' he said.

'And making love.' She smiled. Ah, how was she

going to do without when this was over? How had she done without for most of her adult life?

'Taking the air?' He shuddered. 'Is it not enough that you insist upon sleeping with an open window? Or is that what you meant by *taking the air*?'

'No,' she said. 'I meant walking or riding or driving out. Yes, even in winter. Perhaps visiting neighbors and friends.'

'And yet,' he said, 'you say the thought of winter's approach makes you sad.'

It would be many times worse this year. She would be without him. Was she just needy? Or was she in love with him? Well, of course she was *in love* with him. But did she *love* him? There was a world of difference. How could she, though? He had given her precious little reason to love him. She really did not know him, and he was making good and sure that she never would.

She wondered if he was lonely.

'It is raining again,' he said, and she turned her head to look out through the window. 'Even you cannot wish to go out in this.'

No. She had no boots. Besides, it was cold and windy and wet. Miserable. Yet cozy to look out upon.

'Your silence is ominous,' he said. 'Please do not tell me the ferns are calling to you again, Viola. My instinct for gallantry would be put severely to the test. I suspect I would feel compelled to follow you out there.' He removed his hand from hers in order to finish his breakfast.

'I do not wish to go out,' she said.

They spent two full days indoors, enjoying the warmth of log and coal fires. They read – his great-aunt had been a reader and had left behind a whole wall of bookshelves in the writing room, all of them filled with books. They played cards with a faded deck they discovered in the writing desk. They even tried playing charades and kept it going for all of an hour before she collapsed in laughter and he told her she had lost the famed dignity he had always so admired and she threw a cushion at him. They talked. She told him about her childhood in Bath, incidents she had not thought of in years. He told her about various hair-raising exploits in which he had been a key player while at Oxford. She suspected the stories were much embellished, though perhaps not. And they were certainly amusing. They kissed, warmly and languidly, but never went beyond kisses, as either Mr or Mrs Prewitt was forever popping into the room after the most perfunctory of knocks, he to bring fresh coals for the fire, she to bring a constant supply of tea or coffee with biscuits or cakes or scones. She inevitably stayed to chat – or, rather, to deliver one of her monologues – while pouring their beverages and pressing food upon them.

Sometimes Viola dozed, his arm about her shoulders as they sat side by side on the sofa. He had told her he could never sleep unless he was horizontal on a bed, but once when she awoke his breathing was suspiciously deep, almost on the verge of a snore. She kept still and smiled into the fire while she indulged herself with one of those moments of total happiness.

They looked out at the valley and the weather. Or she did, at least, nestled on the window seat, her knees drawn up before her, her arms clasped about them – the sort of casual pose she had never before allowed herself. The valley was endlessly beautiful, even when clouds hung over it and wind and rain lashed it.

What if she . . . What if *they* lived here all the time, though? Would she continue to be enthralled by it all? Or would it become tedious and confining? But never that, surely. She could be happy here forever. But – cut off from all she knew? From *everyone* she knew?

And she was assailed by a stabbing of fear bordering upon terror for Harry. And by a dull ache of love for her daughters. Was Camille still going outdoors barefoot? Was Abigail still enjoying being in Bath? And her *grandchildren*. Was Jacob sleeping for longer stretches at night yet? Had Winifred finished reading *A Pilgrim's Progress*? And did she still feel the need to summarize each chapter for anyone willing to listen? Oh, Viola was always, *always* willing to listen. Did Sarah still like to be cuddled? *Was there a letter from Harry?*

A hand closed warmly about her shoulder, and she covered it with one of her own and turned her head to smile up at him.

'What a marvelous invention glass is,' he said.

'One can observe the inclemency of the outdoors while enjoying all the comforts of the indoors.'

He affected a dislike of fresh air and the outdoors for her amusement, she suspected. She did not for a moment believe that he was the hothouse plant he pretended to be – and she had once accused him of being.

'Mmm.' She turned her head to kiss the back of his hand.

'What do you want of life, Viola?' he asked her. 'What do you *most* want?'

It was unlike him to ask such questions. He must be in a mellow mood. She turned her head to look through the window again. It was not easy to answer. The simplest questions very rarely were. What *did* she want? Happiness? But that was far too vague. Love? Still too vague. Meaning? But no one was ever going to spell out the meaning of life for her. What, then? She could not seem to focus upon anything specific. Except—

'Someone to care,' she said. 'Are we all identified by labels, Marcel? I have always been daughter or sister, wife, mother, sister-in-law, grandmother, countess, mother-in-law. Perhaps it is why I was so disoriented when the truth came out after Humphrey's death and some of those labels were stripped away from me, even my name. Oh, I know there are people who care for me. I am not self-pitying enough to imagine myself unloved and unappreciated. I am very well blessed with family and friends. But— Well, I am going to sound self-pitying anyway. It seems to me there has never been anyone who cares about *me*, the person who dwells within the daughter and mother and all the rest. No one even knows me. Everyone thinks they do, but no one really does. Sometimes it feels as though I do not even know myself. I am so sorry. I do not know quite what I am talking about. But you did ask.'

'I did, indeed.' His hand was gripping her shoulder more tightly.

The rain had stopped. For a few moments there was a glimpse of blue sky through a break in the clouds. A few multicolored leaves, blown far too soon from their branches, were strewn over the ferns, which were tossing wildly in the wind.

'And you,' she said. 'What do you want most of life, Marcel?'

'Pleasure,' he said after a few moments of silence. 'It is the only sensible thing to wish for.' And yet it seemed to her there was a sort of bleakness in his voice.

'Like this?' she asked, resting her cheek against his hand. 'This escape?'

'Yes,' he said. 'Precisely like this. Come to bed, Viola.'

It was the only time they went to bed during those two days, though they retired early both nights. He made love to her in silence and more swiftly than usual, without the lengthy foreplay at which he was so skilled. Yet she came to a shattering climax a few moments before he did – he always waited for her. He rolled off her almost immediately but kept his arms about her as he drew the bedcovers warmly up about them. He settled her head on his shoulder and laid his cheek against the top of her head before they both pretended to sleep. She was sure it was pretense on both sides.

There was so much pleasure, so much . . . vividness in these days of physical passion she was living through. She was nowhere near having had enough of him. She never would be. She knew that now beyond any doubt. And he was not done with her yet either. She would know if he were. She would sense withdrawal, loss of intensity and interest. He was not done with her. But there was something . . .

An edge of melancholy had crept into their affair with the autumn.

She suspected – no, she *knew* – that they had arrived at the beginning of the end.

CHAPTER 11

The Earl of Riverdale's carriage made excellent progress after it left Bath and arrived without incident at the town where Viola had last been seen. They did not have the name of the inn at which the hired coachman had set down his passengers, it was true, but it did not take them long to find it. They were there by the middle of the evening.

The innkeeper remembered the two passengers concerned, a lady and a gentleman. He did not remember their name, however, if he had ever heard it. They had not taken a room and therefore had not signed the register. The reason he remembered was that the gentleman had made inquiries about the hire of a carriage, and there had been one here, a perfectly decent one. Far more decent than the one in which they had arrived, that was for sure. But the gentleman had gone off into the town anyway to look for something better and had come back with a spanking new carriage and horses – and even a coachman to drive it. The gentleman's wife had remained at the inn, drinking coffee in the private parlor. The innkeeper had no idea where they had gone once they left. Perhaps one of the ostlers who had been on duty then would remember, or perhaps the maid who had served the lady had heard something. But she was off duty now.

The group from Bath took rooms for the night, and after an early breakfast the following morning Joel and Alexander went into the town while Abigail and Elizabeth had another cup of coffee in the private parlor and questioned the serving girl, who had been sent in by the innkeeper. She was looking pale and saucer eyed as she curtsied.

'Yes, I do remember her, my lady,' she said, addressing herself to Elizabeth. 'She was waiting for the gentleman to return. But I do not remember their name. I don't think she said.'

'She left no message?' Elizabeth asked hopefully.

If the girl hesitated for a moment, neither of her two listeners noticed or made anything of it. 'No, my lady,' she said while her hands twisted the sides of her apron – the new one that had cost her so dearly out of her wages. 'But she wouldn't have left one with me anyway. I only brought the coffee. You could ask at the desk.'

'She did not arrive home that day or any day since,' Abigail explained, 'and we are worried about her.'

'If you are worried about her, miss,' the maid asked, frowning, 'how is it you do not know her name?'

'I do know it,' Abigail said. 'She is my mother. It is the gentleman whose name we do not know.'

'Ohhh,' the girl said as understanding dawned – and with it gossip for the kitchen when she returned there.

'I daresay he was either her brother or her cousin,' Elizabeth said with a swift glance at Abigail, who had flushed and was biting her lip. 'Both live not far from here. And it would be so typical of either one of them not to think of letting us know.'

'Yes, it would,' Abigail added. 'Especially Uncle Ernest. I am sure you are right, Cousin Elizabeth.'

The girl withdrew to the kitchen, but she did not after all share the juicy piece of gossip she had just acquired. She was feeling even more sick than she had felt when she discovered that the letters with which the lady had entrusted her had turned to pulp in the laundry tub. Obviously they had been important letters. That terribly haughty, frightening-looking gentleman who had been with the lady was *not* her husband, as she and everyone else had assumed, and the maid did not for a moment believe the brother-or-cousin story. Why would he have wanted a new carriage and horses if he lived close by, after all? No, the lady had been running away with him, whoever he was. Though she had written to someone – to two persons actually – probably so they would not worry about her.

It did not take Joel and Alexander long to discover where the mysterious gentleman had bought his carriage and horses. He had offered employment to his new coachman at the same place. But even the seller of the carriage did not know the gentleman's name or where he had been intending to go with the carriage. No one at the inn knew the answer to either question either, though none of the ostlers thought to mention the one who was absent because it was his day off. No one could recall even the direction the carriage had taken when it left the inn.

'North, south, east, or west,' Alexander said when he and Joel had returned to the parlor. 'We can take our pick.'

'And all points in between,' Elizabeth added while her brother grimaced.

'Who was he?' Abigail set her elbows on the table and cupped her hands over her face. 'Who *is* he? And why was she with him? Where were they going? Why did she not *write*? Why has she not written since?'

They were rhetorical questions. She did not expect an answer. None of them would have had any to offer even if she had. Joel patted her shoulder while he exchanged grim glances with Alexander.

'London seems the most likely destination,' Alexander suggested.

'Oh, do you think so, Alex?' Elizabeth was frowning in thought. 'It would seem to me the most unlikely place Viola would agree to go. She has shunned it for two years, except for that brief visit earlier this year for your wedding. And she could not leave fast enough afterward even though we all tried to persuade her to stay longer.'

'Where, then?' he asked.

But she had no better suggestion to offer.

'She was the same in Bath after Jacob's christening,' Joel said. 'She could not leave fast enough. She has been smothered in love ever since . . . since Anna was summoned to London and everything changed for so many of us.'

'*Smothered?*' Abigail lowered her hands and turned a pale, frowning face on her brother-in-law.

'Yes, I think it is the right word,' he said. 'All anyone has been able to think to do is reach out to her, and to you and Camille too, Abby, with assurances that you are all still loved and still an integral part of the Westcott family. Perhaps I can see a bit more clearly than any of you because I came from the outside quite recently. You did not all react the same way. Camille steeled her nerve and marched off to the orphanage to teach where Anna had taught, determined to remake herself and her world. Anna steeled her nerve and stepped into the world of the *ton*, so alien to a girl who grew up in an orphanage. She even had the courage to fall in love with Avery and marry him. I am not sure about you, Abby. But unlike Camille and Anna, your mother has not charged forward to best these changes. She has kept herself to herself. She has been stifled. I have seen it. The whole family has been concerned about her, but everyone's answer has been simply to love her more.'

'Which has stifled her instead,' Abigail said quietly.

'Love is not enough?' Elizabeth said with a sigh. 'Oh, how wretchedly complex life is. It ought to be simple. Love ought to solve all problems. But of course it does not. The trouble is . . . what else is there except love?'

'There is giving her some space,' Joel said.

'Space,' Alexander repeated, pouring himself lukewarm coffee from the pot, which was still on the table. 'You mean anywhere in the world that is not Hinsford or Bath, Joel?'

Abigail moaned and set a hand over her mouth.

'Oh, we certainly need to find her, for our own peace of mind,' Joel said. 'But once we do and can assure ourselves beyond any doubt that she is safe and where she wishes to be, then we ought to allow her to remain there untroubled. Don't you all agree?'

'With a man she met only the day before she fled with him,' Alexander said, his voice unusually harsh.

Abigail moaned again.

'Perhaps she knew him, Alex,' Elizabeth said.

'Does that make the situation any more acceptable?' he asked.

'Alex.' Abigail was gripping the edge of the table and gazing steadily at him from a face that was even paler than it had been before but was set in stubborn lines now. 'I will not allow anyone to stand in judgment upon my mother, not even you. You may be the head of the Westcott family, but strictly speaking, Mama is not and never has been a Westcott. And even if she were . . . Oh, even if she were, I agree with Joel.'

Joel gripped her shoulder again and Elizabeth patted her hand.

'I am sorry, Abigail,' Alexander said, running the fingers of one hand through his hair. 'You are perfectly right. So is Joel. I am sorry. Wren would say I am reverting to my natural self. I always want to manage and protect those close to me, especially the women. Wren has been good for me, though I often need reminding. But let us go and find your mother.'

'Where?' she asked.

They decided upon the road to London and wasted a day and a half traveling east, stopping at every likely inn and tavern and even a few unlikely ones to ask if anyone had seen a shiny new black carriage with yellow trim and a fair-haired lady of middle years and a tall, dark gentleman. But though several people had seen carriages of a different color or design or trim conveying a gentleman and a lady – or, in one instance, two ladies and a child – none of them were helpful.

'*Someone* must have seen them,' Joel said when they stopped for a change of horses and a late luncheon. 'It is impossible that they could have traveled so far in total invisibility.'

'I have been reaching the same conclusion,' Elizabeth said. 'They did not come this way.'

There was always the chance, of course, that someone at the very next village or town would remember, but they had been playing that game all morning.

'It was my suggestion that we come this way,' Alexander said. 'Now it is my suggestion that we go back and take a different road. Does anyone disagree?'

No one did.

It took them less time to return to the town where Viola had last been seen, but even so it seemed an endless journey. This time when they arrived there, though, they had better luck. The ostler whose day off had coincided with their last stop there was on duty again, and he recalled the coachman of the new rig saying that they were headed for the west country. The coachman had made a particular point of it because he had hoped they were not going to London, a noisy, filthy, smelly place he had been to only once and hoped never to go to again.

And so Alexander's carriage set off at last in the right direction, though *west country* was a vague enough description of a destination. It could be Somerset or Devonshire or Cornwall or Wales, or even Gloucestershire. They had to proceed, as they had before, by stopping far more frequently than they would have liked, asking about the carriage and its occupants. At least this time, though, their questions bore results. By gradual degrees they arrived in Devonshire.

'We could have traveled just as fast,' Joel said in some frustration one afternoon, 'if we had boarded a snail in Bath and told it to move at its briskest pace.'

'But we would have been a bit crowded riding on its back,' Elizabeth said, a twinkle in her eye.

'And the shell would have made a hard seat,' Alexander added. 'As far as I know, there are no springs beneath snail shells.'

'I have never seen any for hire in Bath, anyway' Abigail said. 'You would have had to go hunting for one, Joel.'

But in truth it was hard to retain their sense of humor when they seemed to have been traveling forever and still did not know when or whether they would reach their journey's end – or what they would discover when or if they got there.

She has run away with a man, Abigail kept thinking. *Whatever will Camille think? And Harry if he ever finds out?* Harry would kill the man.

Twice over.

The carriage from Redcliffe was several days behind the Earl of Riverdale's to start with, though it did gradually narrow the gap. At first the search was slow and André regretted not having insisted upon bringing his brother's carriage or at least his coachman. He did not find it as easy as he expected to recognize the place where he had left Marcel. Most villages looked essentially alike to him, and he had not observed scenery and landmarks with the sort of attention he would have paid them if he had known he would have to find his way back.

When they finally reached the right one, however, he recognized it with some relief and knocked on the front panel to signal the coachman to stop outside the inn at the end of the street.

The Marquess of Dorchester was no longer there, of course, and never had been there under that name. But the innkeeper recognized André and was able to inform him that Mr Lamarr had indeed stayed there – and had left the next morning with Miss Kingsley.

André wished he had settled the ladies, and perhaps Bertrand too, in the dining room before he asked his questions.

'*What?*' Jane Morrow said. 'And who, may I ask, is Miss Kingsley? Bertrand, take your sister into one of these rooms behind us if you will. She will be ready for some refreshment.'

But it was too late to shield them from looming scandal. Neither twin moved.

'She is an acquaintance of his,' André explained. 'And of mine. A perfectly respectable lady, Jane. I daresay she gave him a ride to somewhere where he could hire a carriage for his own use since I had taken his.'

Jane was not about to question her brother-in-law's ramshackle brother while the innkeeper was an interested spectator – or in the hearing of her niece and nephew. But her mind reeled. Why exactly *had* Dorchester sent his brother and his carriage out of the way? And who exactly was this woman André insisted was respectable? Was it respectable to take a man who was not one's husband up into one's carriage? And *had they both spent the night at the inn?* In separate rooms? Oh, she ought to have locked the twins in their rooms at home and embarked on this journey with Charles and André.

The innkeeper was able to direct them to the town where Miss Kingsley's hired carriage had been bound.

'But where did he go from there?' Estelle asked of no one in particular. 'Why did he not come home, as he had promised he would?'

Jane could think of one excellent reason, but she held her peace.

André rubbed the side of his nose with one finger and held his peace too.

'I daresay something happened to make him change his mind, Stell,' Bertrand said. 'Maybe we will find out what that is when we reach that town.'

Jane Morrow looked at André with narrowed eyes while the twins climbed into the carriage again. 'You knew about that woman,' she said quietly enough not to be overheard by her nephew and niece. 'You ought not to have brought them here. I suppose it did not occur to you that it was highly improper to do so. You are no better than your brother.'

'Oh, I say,' he said indignantly. 'I did not bring them here. I had no wish to come here at all. It stood to reason that Marcel would be long gone. *They* brought *me*.'

'We really have no choice now,' she said, raising her voice to address the twins inside the carriage, 'but to return home and wait for your father there. He will come in his own good time. He always does.'

'But the party,' Estelle protested.

'We do have a choice, Aunt Jane,' Bertrand said. 'We can go and find out where he went, or at least try. We have come this far. Why go back now without at least making an effort to track him down?'

Jane could have offered a very good answer, but how could she speak bluntly to her two young charges? 'He is probably busy and will resent the intrusion,' she said.

'You think he is with that woman, Aunt Jane,' Estelle said. 'Well, what if he is? I daresay it is not the first time and will not be the last. But I want him to know that I have arranged a birthday party for him. I want to tell him to his face that he has . . . inconvenienced me.'

Her aunt stared at her in some exasperation. It was so very unlike Estelle to be stubborn. What a shame it was that children had to grow up.

'Onward with the search, then?' André asked cheerfully, offering his hand to help Jane into the carriage.

'Yes,' Estelle and Bertrand said in unison.

After that, the pursuit was relatively easy. They found the inn at which Miss Kingsley's hired carriage had set down its passengers, and they found out about the newly purchased carriage without having to leave the inn. They spoke with the ostler who knew which direction the carriage had taken – with both the lady and the gentleman. All of Jane's worst fears were confirmed. The same ostler was obliging enough to mention that four other people – two gentlemen and two ladies – had gone in pursuit of that same carriage two days earlier. Even more obligingly he gave them a description of that carriage too.

It was merely a case after that of following a trail that fairly blazed before them. Almost everyone they spoke with remembered one or other of the two carriages, or, in many cases, both. They were further assured that they were going in the right direction when André suddenly remembered something.

'Oh, I say,' he said with a loud clicking of his fingers. 'I will wager Marc has gone to the cottage.'

'Cottage?' Jane asked.

And André told the story his mother had told him of the great-aunt on their father's side who had taken a fancy to Marcel when he was an infant long before he, André, was born, and of her making him her heir and leaving him her cottage some-where in the wilds of Devonshire.

'It seems a likely sort of place to take a wo—' André said before being cut off too late by a pointed glare from Jane and a sharp elbow in the ribs.

'*Woman,*' Estelle said. '*Where* in Devonshire, Uncle André?'

He rubbed one side of his nose, but doing so did not prompt his memory further. Or perhaps, he admitted, he had never known. Close to the sea, perhaps?

That was very little help.

CHAPTER 12

The sky had cleared and the wind had died down, at least in the valley. The hillsides and the valley floor had had a day to dry out. It was time to go out again, Viola announced, to take a long, brisk walk along the valley to the sea.

'There will be mud,' Marcel predicted.

'It can be stepped around,' she said. 'Coward.'

It turned out to be not the brisk hike she had anticipated. The valley floor beside the river was spongy at best after all the rain, muddy at worst. In places, old, dead branches and even whole, rotted-out tree trunks were strewn across what had not really been a path in the first place. It was all very wild and overgrown. It was possible, even probable, that no one had walked here for years. But it was an exhilarating exercise anyway as they weaved about obstacles, clambered over a few, avoided the worst of the mud, and stopped frequently just to look about at the glory that was the early autumn trees and to listen to the birds.

'Is it not amazing,' she said, 'how they make so much noise but are barely visible?'

'Amazing,' he agreed in the deliberately flat voice he used whenever he was teasing her enthusiasm.

She was not deterred. She had discovered this enthusiasm during the past couple of weeks and wondered why she had considered it so important all her life to quell it in the name of dignity.

It took them more than an hour to reach the sand of the beach – and the wind again. It slanted across the sea from the southwest unobstructed, ruffling the waves, taking their breath away, and flattening their clothes against them. He had to hold his hat on. The river, as it widened to flow in shallow runnels to the sea, had cut the beach in two. They strolled along their side of it, hand in hand, not talking. Often they did not. But it was never because they had run out of things to say. Sometimes there could be a more companionable feel to silence than to conversation. High cliffs rose to one side of them. The sea stretched to infinity on the other.

'I am glad the cottage was built in the valley, out of sight of all this,' she said.

'You do not like the sea?' he asked.

'Oh, I do.' She drew her hand from his and turned to see the whole panorama. The beach stretched for miles in both directions. Endlessly long waves were breaking in foam and flowing onto the wet sand some distance away before being sucked back into the deep. The air was cold and salty. A lone gull, buffeted by the wind, cried mournfully, or so it seemed. She must not ascribe human feelings to other creatures, though. 'But I do not believe I would like to live close to it. It is too . . . elemental.'

'On that at least we are agreed.' He came to stand in front of her and dipped his head to kiss her. She leaned into him and kissed him back, seeking comfort and forgetfulness from him as well as warmth. They had been so very good, these weeks. The best of her life. Oh, by far the best. Why, then, had there been a thread of melancholy dragging at her spirits for the last few days, like a faintly throbbing bass note in an otherwise light and joyful melody?

'At least?' she said. 'Are we not agreed upon most subjects?'

She had not meant it as a serious question. She was not sure he had taken it seriously. Except that suddenly it seemed to hang between them like a tangible thing. Were they not, in almost every way that mattered, very different from each other? It was easy to ignore that basic fact for a short idyll of a romantic affair. But it would not remain masked forever. Fortunately they did not have forever.

Fortunately?

She took a step to one side, fighting a certain inexplicable panic. 'I am going to walk down to the edge of the wet sand,' she said.

I am going to . . . Not *Let us* . . . It had not been deliberate. Maybe he had not taken it that way.

But he did not come with her. He remained where he was or he walked onward. She did not look back to see. Were affairs always this way? He would know. She did not. Did one suddenly *know*, without warning or any particular reason, that it was over? There *was* no reason. She was desperately happy here. She was deeply satisfied with their relationship, if it could be called that. But of course it could, however brief it would be. She was invigorated by his company and had come alive to his lovemaking. She still did not know how she was going to do without him once it was all over.

Soon, very soon, she would find out.

She stopped when she came to the edge of the wet sand. The tide must be on its way out, but the sand it had covered a short while ago had not dried yet. It gleamed with wetness in places. She felt isolated here, cut off from everything but her thoughts. She did not turn to look back. The wind whipped mercilessly at her.

Her daughters would be starting to worry. She had given no hint of where she was going or with whom, only that she *was* going. They would be starting to wonder what they would do if she never came back. She had not written again since she came here. Her great escape was seeming more and more like her great selfishness. And she was starting to worry about them, or at least to wonder. She was missing them. She was missing her grandchildren, or at least the frequent news she always had of them in Camille's letters.

She was worried about Harry. Always, always, always. Pointlessly worried. There was nothing she could do to ensure his safety. But she should at least be there to read any letter that came from the Peninsula. Oh, would the wars never end?

And what had happened to her moral core? Morality had been her compass through her life until . . . how long ago? Two weeks? Three? She was losing track of time. But in that time she had been living a life of sin. Or had she? *Was* it sinful to love a man and to allow him to love her? It was not love, though, what was between them. It was lust.

It felt like more than lust. But that was self-deception. He had never pretended that this was anything more than business as usual for him. How many days ago had he told her what he wanted most out of life was pleasure? She had known it from the start, though. She had not been deceived. She had come with him because she had wanted pleasure too.

Because she had lusted after him, and still did.

She lifted her face to the wind and closed her eyes. A gull – the same one? – cried mournfully again. She felt horribly, despicably lonely. But she deserved no better. She turned and walked back up the beach. He was standing surely in the very spot where she had left him. She stopped a short distance away.

'I need to go home,' she said.

And then felt sheer, raw panic.

He looked very large with his tall hat pulled firmly onto his head, in his many-caped greatcoat and his top boots. He looked remote, austere. His eyes, hooded as they often were, looked darker than usual in the shadow of the brim of his hat. He looked curiously like a stranger, a rather grim stranger.

'I am glad you said it first, Viola,' he said. 'I never like to hurt my women.'

Even his light, soft voice sounded unfamiliar. She felt hurt anyway. Had he intended that – to hurt her even as he denied any wish to do so? Or was he merely speaking the truth? He had tired of her and was glad she had announced the end of the affair before he had to do it himself.

'I miss my family,' she said. 'They will be worried about me.'

'I thought you said you had written to them,' he said.

She had mentioned it soon after their arrival.

'But without any detail or explanation,' she said. 'And it has been longer than two weeks.'

'Has it?' he said. 'It is amazing how time flies when one is immersed in pleasure.'

Was he insulting her? There was no insult in the words themselves, but something in his tone chilled her. 'It has been a pleasure,' she said.

'Indeed,' he agreed. 'I have rarely known better.'

Was that word *rarely* carefully chosen to cut into her? But she had no reason to be offended. This had never been anything else but an affair, and only for her was that a momentous thing.

'You will be glad to go home to your children,' she said.

'Indeed I will,' he said. 'I will need to recover some stamina. You have come near to exhausting me, Viola.'

Oh, he *was* insulting her. In the subtlest of ways. He was telling her that she had been a thoroughly satisfactory mistress, but that now he was ready to move on to the next one – or would be after a short spell in which to recuperate. He was suggesting that she had been insatiable – as she had.

'There does not need to be any bitterness in our parting, does there?' she asked.

'Bitterness?' His eyebrows rose and he raised one hand as though to clasp the handle of his quizzing glass. But it was hidden beneath his great-coat. 'I certainly hope I never arouse bitterness in any of my women, Viola. We will part as friends, and it will be my hope that you will have fond memories of our liaison after you return to the respectability of your life.'

. . . any of my women.

He made no mention of any fond memories he would have. In a month's time he would probably have forgotten all about her.

She had known that from the start.

'Tomorrow?' she said. 'We will set out for home tomorrow?'

He did not reply for a few moments. His face looked a bit like granite, his eyes hard and

208

opaque. And, fool that she was, she hoped he would beg for a few more days.

'With these longer nights I suppose it would be wiser to wait until tomorrow,' he said. 'Yes, we will leave early.'

It felt like a slap to the face. He would have preferred to leave today.

It took them less than an hour to make their way back up the valley. They did not stop to look around or listen to the birds or catch their breath. They skirted muddy puddles and scrambled over fallen tree branches without fuss – and without touching. The only time he stopped to help her over a tree trunk, she pretended not to notice his hand. The next time he did not offer it. They spoke not a word to each other.

They had not quarreled. There was no reason in the world why they should not still converse amiably and be easy with each other. There was the rest of the day to live through, after all, and the night and then however many days it would take them to travel back. She would have him take her to Bath rather than all the way to Hinsford. It would surely not take many days to get there. They would not be traveling in anything like the leisurely manner they had when they came here.

But every hour was going to seem an eternity. She had not thought ahead to this. When she had thought of the end of their affair, she had envisaged herself back at home, alone and lonely and picking up the threads of her life. She had not thought of the actual getting from here to there. She wondered if she should suggest traveling by stagecoach from the town on the far side of the valley.

But it would seem like an insult on her part.

He stopped walking suddenly and uttered an oath so startling that she stopped too and looked at him in surprise. But he was not looking at her. He was gazing, narrow-eyed, upward to the cottage, which had just come into sight. She looked up there too and froze.

There was a carriage drawn up on the dirt terrace before the door. Not his carriage. And nothing local either, surely. It was altogether too grand. They were still too far away to see any detail, but . . .

'We have company,' he said, the words coming from between his teeth and sounding savage.

'Who?' she asked foolishly. How could he be expected to know any more than she did? But even as she asked the question, three figures stepped into view – two men and one woman.

One of the men was Alexander.

The other – Joel? – was pointing in their direction.

The woman was Abigail.

Marcel swore viciously again – and again did not apologize.

He swore silently to himself as they climbed the hillside toward the cottage. How the *devil* had they found this place? Viola had admitted to writing to her daughters while he was out purchasing the carriage that had brought them here, but she had assured him she had said only that she was going away for a week or two – and he had believed her. He had recognized the crest on the door of Riverdale's carriage before he recognized the man himself. Head of the Westcott family, no less. And he did not doubt that the young lady was one of her daughters. His eyes confirmed the suspicion as they drew closer. She looked a bit like Viola. He had never seen the other man before, but he would wager upon his being the schoolteacher artist son-in-law.

His considerable arsenal of profane language had been exhausted. He began repeating himself. This hill seemed to grow steeper and longer every time he climbed it. Viola had gone a little way ahead of him. Her question – *Who?* – of a couple of minutes ago was the only word she had spoken since they left the beach.

He wondered if it was going to be pistols at dawn tomorrow, and which of the two men would claim the honor. What a disaster it would be to put a bullet through the heart of one of Viola's kinsmen or wing him in the right arm the day after the ending of the affair. Or perhaps the kinsman would kill him. Perhaps this was about to turn into a romantic tragedy – with comic elements.

The young lady had stepped off the terrace to stand knee deep among the ferns. She was all willowy slenderness and big eyes and pale complexion

211

with two spots of color in her cheeks and anxious vulnerability. No, she was not like her mother except in coloring and a certain similarity of features. Even from the back view he had of her he knew that Viola had donned the mantle of her habitual cool dignity. There was a moment when they might have rushed into each other's arms, but the girl hesitated and Viola did not press it, and they ended up merely clasping hands for a few moments.

'Mama?' the young woman said. Her voice was high pitched and slightly trembling. Probably not her usual voice.

'Abby,' Viola said. 'My dear. I was about to scold you for coming alone with Alexander and Joel. Or, rather, I was about to scold them for bringing you. But I see that Elizabeth had the good sense to come too.'

Another somewhat older lady had stepped out from behind the carriage. She must have just come out of the house. She looked vaguely familiar, though he could not recall her name at the moment. Elizabeth Somebody.

'Viola,' she said with a warm smile. 'How good it is to see you. And you are looking well. What a breathtakingly beautiful place this is.' A sensible lady, trying to create some normalcy out of this situation, as though she and her companions had merely called in for tea as they were passing.

The men had not taken their eyes off Marcel.

'And so the mystery is solved,' the Earl of Riverdale said, his voice stiff and cold. 'Dorchester.

The Marquess of Dorchester,' he explained to the man beside him.

Viola turned her head sharply and regarded Marcel with wide, surprised eyes. He shrugged. 'Riverdale?' he said. 'What kept you so long?'

'Mama,' the young lady said – she was Abigail, the younger daughter, then. 'Whatever happened? Why did you not go home? Why did you come here? Why did you come with . . . *him*? Why did you not *write* to us? We have been worried out of our minds. The whole family has.'

'I ought to have written again,' Viola said, 'to explain that I was quite safe at the home of a friend. It was remiss of me not to do so, Abby. But . . . to come after me like this? However did you find me?'

'*Again?*' Abigail asked. 'What do you mean by *again*?'

'Well.' Viola sounded a bit puzzled. 'You must have received the note I sent you and Camille. And Mrs Sullivan must have received hers.'

The color had receded from the young lady's cheeks to leave her face uniformly pale. 'No,' she said, her voice little more than a whisper. 'None of us did.'

Riverdale had not been distracted. He had not removed his eyes from Marcel. Neither had the other man. They looked like two avenging angels if ever Marcel had seen any. And sure enough—

'I will want satisfaction for this, Dorchester,' Riverdale said softly.

'Then you will have to stand in line behind me,' the other man said. 'You may be head of the Westcott family, Alexander, but the lady is Camille's *mother*. My mother-in-law.'

They had drawn the attention of the ladies. 'That is nonsense, Joel,' Viola said. 'You too, Alexander. I was not abducted. I came here of my own free will. And I am no green girl to be cosseted by the family men. I am forty-two years old.'

Riverdale turned his cold gaze upon her.

'Oh, Mama,' Abigail said. 'How *could* you?'

'I suggest we all step inside and see if the very pleasant housekeeper is willing to make a pot of tea for all of us,' the woman called Elizabeth said. 'There is a very welcome-looking fire burning in the parlor.'

Everyone ignored her.

'It is not nonsense, Mama,' Viola's son-in-law said. Marcel could not recall his name. Had he ever heard it? 'What you have done has hurt Camille. And Abby. And Winifred, who is old enough to understand a few things. And your mother and your brother, who is a *clergyman*. And the whole of the Westcott family, who consider you one of their own even though you behave sometimes as though you would rather they did not. It is not nonsense to wish to punish the man who led you astray.'

'Joel,' Viola began, and her voice was cold now too.

'I believe,' Marcel said in the rather soft voice

that he knew always commanded attention. It did not fail him now. Everyone stopped talking, and everyone turned their attention upon him. *Hostile* attention, perhaps, but attention nonetheless. 'I believe everyone is under a misapprehension, Viola. You must introduce me to your family in a moment, but first we really must explain that we are betrothed, that we were betrothed even before we began our journey here.'

For a few moments the scene outside the cottage must have looked like a well-contrived tableau. No one moved or said a thing. Before Viola could break free of the spell his words had cast, he moved up beside her, took her hand in his, laced their fingers rather tightly, and raised her hand to his lips.

'Ours has been an attachment of long standing,' he said. 'To use the vulgar parlance, we fell in love at a time when honor would permit neither of us to admit it – or to see each other again. We did see each other again, however, at a certain country inn a few weeks ago when each of us had been stranded by carriage woes. It took no longer than one exchange of glances to rekindle a passion that had never really died. Before that day ended we had decided not to spend a day more of our lives apart. We were betrothed. We made the impulsive though perhaps rash decision to run away here to celebrate our happiness alone together for a short while before beginning the lengthy process of informing our families and making the necessary announcements and planning a wedding. Is that not the way it was, my love?'

He looked into her face at last. It was as pale as her daughter's. Pale and utterly expressionless. Her eyes met his. She gazed and then . . . smiled.

'I cannot even blame you for the rashness of it all, Marcel,' she said. 'I am the one who first suggested that we run away.'

'Ah, but I did not put up a single argument to the contrary, did I?' he said. 'We will accept mutual responsibility, then. Introduce me, my love.'

Her daughter was Abigail Westcott. The older lady – though she was still younger than he and Viola – was Lady Overfield, Riverdale's sister. And yes, he had seen her a few times in London, though he did not believe they had ever been formally introduced until now. He had known her late husband. The son-in-law was Joel Cunningham.

'Mama,' Abigail said, 'you are going to *marry* the Marquess of Dorchester?'

'Viola—' Riverdale began.

'Elizabeth is the most sensible one among us,' Viola said in the firm, cool voice of the former Countess of Riverdale. 'Let us go inside and have some tea. It is chilly out here. We may all talk as much as we wish once we are settled about the fire.'

She withdrew her hand from Marcel's and gave him a cool, blank look, which did not deceive him for a moment. Beneath the practiced layers of gracious dignity, she was seething.

Did she think he was not?

He had rarely been angrier in his life. Perhaps never.

Marcel did not immediately follow everyone else into the parlor. He went upstairs, presumably to remove his hat and greatcoat. Viola followed him up, making the excuse that she needed to wash her hands and comb her hair and change her shoes. She followed him into his bedchamber and shut the door behind her. He turned to face her, his raised eyebrows and half-lowered eyelids giving his face an arrogant, almost sneering appearance. It was the look he usually presented to society.

'*Marquess of Dorchester?*' she said. Of all the things with which she might have begun, it was the detail that somehow stung the most. Who *was* this man with whom she had been having an affair? Did she know him at all?

He shrugged again as he had shrugged outside. 'My uncle died two years ago,' he said. 'He was a very old man. I daresay he could not help it. I happened to be next in the line of fire since in all his long years he had produced only daughters. I have always considered the title a cumbersome appendage, but what was I to do? I do not believe I would have convinced anyone that my brother was older than I.'

She let it go. There was so much else. *So much.*

'What did you mean,' she said, 'by announcing that we are *betrothed?* The very idea is laughable.'

'Laughable?' He was speaking softly in that way he always had in public, even though she was the only other person in the room. 'You wound me, Viola. Am I no more than a figure of fun in your eyes?'

'Alexander must know it is laughable,' she said. 'Elizabeth must know. Everyone, the whole world will know it if word ever gets out.'

'Word will surely get out, my love,' he said. 'The marriage of an aristocrat always does. There is little privacy when one is the Marquess of Dorchester. Or the marchioness.'

'You cannot be *serious*,' she said. 'You could hardly wait until tomorrow to be rid of me.'

'Did I say that, Viola?' he replied in a pained way that came across as mocking. 'How very ungallant of me. I would call you a liar, but that would be equally ungallant. What am I to say?'

'You do not want to *marry* me,' she said.

The mocking look disappeared to be replaced by something more grim. 'What I *want* is no longer of any significance,' he said. 'Neither is what *you* want. We embarked upon a great indiscretion a few weeks ago, Viola, and we have been caught out and must pay the price.'

'That is nonsense,' she said, 'and you must know it. Alexander will not breathe a word of any of this. Neither will the others.'

'Let me see,' he said. 'Riverdale will whisper it to his wife. Cunningham will tell *his* wife, and she and Miss Abigail Westcott will inform your mother in the strictest confidence. Your mother will inform your brother. All the Westcotts, who are so worried about you, will have to have their minds set at rest, and my guess is that they will not be told lies and that, even if they are, they will see through them in a moment. Servants will hear the story, as servants inevitably do. And servants will tell it in the strictest confidence to other servants, who will pass it on to their employers. Is my point becoming clear? Your virtue has been compromised, Viola, and I am the compromiser. I must, then, as I occasionally manage, do the honorable thing and marry you. You have no cause for complaint. *I* did not write to *my* family. *My* family has not put in an appearance here, breathing fire and brimstone, have they?'

They both heard it at the same moment. It would have been hard not to despite the fact that the window was closed. The valley was normally so very quiet. Viola hurried to look out, expecting to see that it was just Alexander's carriage being moved out of the way. But it was still outside the doors of the house, no orders having been given for its disposal. No, what they had heard was the arrival of another carriage. It came to a halt on the driveway, still partially on the slope. Marcel had stepped up beside her. He swore, as he had down in the valley.

The coachman descended from the box to open the door and set down the steps. A familiar figure stepped down and looked out over the valley. He was the young gentleman who had been with Marcel at that inn. His brother. But he was not alone. A much younger man, really no more than a boy, tall, slender, dark, with all the promise of heartbreaking good looks, got out after him and turned back to hand out an older lady and then a mere girl, whose face was hidden by the brim of her bonnet.

'Sometimes,' Marcel said, 'the farce at the end of a play is overdone and loses any amusing quality it might otherwise have had. Have you observed that, Viola?'

My family has not put in an appearance here, breathing fire and brimstone, have they?

Apparently, they had.

CHAPTER 13

What in thunder had got into André that he had come here – and brought Estelle and Bertrand of all people? And *Jane*. Had the world gone mad? Marcel turned from the window, strode downstairs, and stepped onto the terrace.

'I say,' he heard André say, 'there is not another building in sight. This must be the loneliest place on earth. I could not see myself wanting to spend much time here.'

'Fortunately perhaps,' Marcel said, 'you have not been invited to do so, André.'

'Oh, I say.' His brother swung about to face him. 'You *are* here, Marc.'

The others had turned in his direction too. Jane was tight-lipped and ramrod straight, a look and posture she surely reserved for him. She made no pretense of either liking or approving of him and never had from the moment of his announcing his intention of marrying Adeline. Bertrand, slender and very tall after a sudden growth spurt a couple of years ago, took a few steps toward him. Estelle, smaller but just as slender, narrow faced, big eyed,

221

not really pretty but with the potential for extra-ordinary beauty, came striding toward him in a manner that was surely forbidden in Jane's rules for the proper conduct and deportment of young ladies.

'Father,' she cried, and he realized in some surprise that she was furiously angry. 'You have ruined everything. You *said* you were coming home, and I *believed* you, fool that I was. I ought to know by now that you *never* do what you say you are going to do. I believed you because it was going to be your special birthday, and I thought you would want to spend it with us. I organized a party to surprise you – my first ever. I planned everything down to the finest detail. I made long lists so I would not forget anything. And *you did not come.* You sent Uncle André home in your carriage, which showed that you had no intention of coming at all. Which was *fine*, but you ought not to have said you were coming in the first place. I came to find you because I wanted you to know that I will never believe another word you say – *ever*. But that is all right because I do not *care*.'

Marcel was too taken aback even to reach for his quizzing glass. He had just heard possibly more words from his daughter than he had in all the almost eighteen years since she was born.

'My sister is upset, sir,' Bertrand told him. 'She put her heart and soul into planning that party to surprise you.'

'Estelle, my love,' Jane was saying, 'that is hardly the way a genteel young lady speaks to her f—'

'Silence,' Marcel said softly, and she stopped abruptly.

André was clearing his throat. 'Good day, Miss Kingsley,' he said, and in a glance over his shoulder Marcel could see that she had indeed stepped outside, though she was keeping her distance.

'Who—' Estelle was looking even more stormy as her eyes went beyond him to Viola, but he had held up a hand and she too fell silent.

He turned and extended one arm toward Viola and watched her approach, all cool marble dignity. 'My family too has found us,' he said to her, 'just as we were about to set off to find them. Mrs Morrow is my late wife's sister and has had the chief care of my children since her passing. André is my brother. Estelle and Bertrand are my daughter and son.'

André nodded genially. The others stood like statues as Viola inclined her head and bade them all a good afternoon.

'I have known Miss Kingsley and admired her for many years,' he said, turning his attention to them. 'When we met again by chance a few weeks ago, we no longer needed to hide our regard for each other and she agreed to marry me. We ought to have proceeded immediately to inform both her family and mine, of course. We ought to have made a public announcement of our betrothal and begun to plan our wedding. That is what we ought to have done. What we actually decided upon instead was a couple of weeks alone together.'

Jane's nostrils had flared, though she remained silent.

He had taken Viola's hand in his and raised it now to his lips. It was icy cold.

'It was thoughtless and self-indulgent of us,' she said. 'One of my daughters arrived here a short while ago with my son-in-law and other members of my family, and you were not far behind them. We owe you all apologies.'

Estelle's dark eyes had widened as she looked from one to the other of them, and for one moment Marcel thought she was more infuriated than ever. But then, in a total reversal of mood, she smiled – radiantly.

'Papa?' she said. 'You are going to be *married?* Then you will be coming home to live. All the time.' At first Marcel thought she was going to launch herself at him, but she merely swayed where she stood and clasped her ungloved hands to her bosom. They were white knuckled.

He could not remember a time when either of his children had touched him voluntarily. He could not remember a time when he had hugged them or kissed them – except during that first enchanted year before Adeline died. He could not remember either of them calling him Papa.

Bertrand was bowing stiffly. 'Congratulations, sir,' he said. 'Congratulations, ma'am.'

'Oh, I say,' André said.

Jane still said nothing.

'It is a chilly day,' Viola said. 'Do come inside. We are all about to have tea in the parlor. There is a fire in there. Mrs Morrow, let me show you the way.'

'*Miss* Kingsley?' Jane said without moving. 'You have a daughter?'

'Two of them and a son,' Viola said. 'And three grandchildren. There is a story behind it all that I will gladly share with you after I have set a cup of hot tea in your hands. Do come. Marcel, bring your children and Mr Lamarr.'

'Miss Kingsley was once a Westcott, Jane,' André explained, 'and the Countess of Riverdale.'

Jane allowed herself to be taken into the house. Estelle followed with Bertrand, her hand drawn through his arm. André lingered and grinned at his brother.

'I say, Marc,' he said, 'has the arrival of two avenging families caught you in parson's mouse-trap at last?'

'I trust,' Marcel said softly, 'you have a good reason for bringing my children here, André.' But how the devil had he known where to come?

'You were devilish difficult to find,' his brother told him. 'It might have taken us another day or two to get here if Miss Kingsley's family had not left a blazing trail for us to follow. Which of them have come in addition to one of her daughters and her son-in-law?'

Marcel ignored the question. 'Why did you

bring them?' he asked. 'They are *seventeen*, André, and have had the strictest and narrowest of upbringings.'

'Whose fault is that?' André said. 'I did not bring anyone, Marc. *They* brought *me*. I think your little Estelle is growing up. I have never seen her upset before or anything but a placid, quiet mouse of a girl. After a week or so of fretting and watching for your arrival every hour of every day, she would have come in search of you alone if she could not have persuaded anyone else to accompany her. Bertrand would have come with her, of course, and Jane had no choice short of locking the girl in her room and feeding her bread and water. They dragged me along because I could lead them to where you had last been seen, though that village was dashed difficult to find. They all look alike. How was I to know that you did not merely enjoy Miss Kingsley for a night or two before wandering off somewhere else alone in search of further diversion? You are not known for liaisons that last more than a few days, after all.'

'We had better go inside,' Marcel said curtly. He would rather do anything else on earth. For two pins he would saddle one of the horses in the stables and ride off in the direction of the farthest horizon. But Estelle was here. And Bertrand.

'You have acquired a leg shackle.' André grinned again. 'This will be the joke of the *ton*, Marc.'

'If I should hear of Miss Kingsley being the subject of any off-color humor,' Marcel said as they followed the others into the cottage, 'someone is going to be answerable to me, André.'

But his brother only chuckled.

The truly bizarre thing about the following hour, Viola thought later as she looked back upon it, was that it quickly became a perfectly civil social occasion, a group of persons representing two families seated together in the parlor of a country house partaking of tea and cakes together and conversing about the Devonshire countryside, the state of the roads, the secluded beauty of the valley, the sturdy coziness of the cottage, and the upcoming wedding. She wondered if anyone had noticed that she and Marcel did not participate a great deal in that particular strand of the conversation – or in any other, for that matter.

She at least was able to busy herself with the pouring of tea and the distribution of cakes, having assured Mrs Prewitt that her presence was not needed. Marcel merely stood, first before the fire and then at the window, though he did not give in to any temptation he might have felt to turn his back and look outward.

He was looking austere, anything he might be feeling well hidden inside himself. But the same was true of her. She fell back upon a demeanor that had been second nature to her during the more than twenty years of her marriage. She played the part of the gracious hostess.

They would marry in London – at St George's

on Hanover Square, of course, where all society weddings were solemnized during the months of the Season. Alexander had suggested it. It was where he and Wren had married earlier this year despite, or perhaps because of, the fact that Wren had lived almost the whole of her life as a recluse, her face hidden behind a heavy veil to mask the birthmark that covered virtually the whole of one side of her face. Perhaps Alexander thought the only way to silence any scandal that might erupt in response to this sudden marriage announcement was to brazen it out and take the wedding there.

No one else liked the idea. Viola would have vetoed it anyway had her wishes been consulted.

They would marry here by special license, either in the village church or in the nearest town, as soon as it could be arranged, with eight members of their families in attendance – to add an air of respectability, of course, though Mrs Morrow, whose suggestion it was, did not say so.

Joel did not like that idea. No one else seemed thrilled with it either.

'Camille will want to attend her mother's wedding,' Joel said. 'And Mrs Kingsley will want to attend her daughter's wedding.'

They would marry in Bath, then, where everyone could come and find good hotels to stay at. Perhaps in Bath Abbey, where Camille and Joel had married last year. Bath, after all, was Viola's original home. The suggestion was made by Abigail, who had been quiet and listless until she spoke up. Joel and Alexander and Elizabeth looked upon the suggestion with some favor, but the others did not. It would be too impersonal with all the guests spread over Bath in various hotels and neither the bride nor the groom having a home of their own there.

They would marry at Redcliffe Court, Lady Estelle Lamarr decided. She appeared to be the only one who was contemplating the wedding with any enthusiasm. It was because she hoped marriage would settle her father down and keep him at home, Viola realized with a sinking heart. The girl was somehow or other going to end up terribly hurt. She was probably already carrying around a lifetime of hurt inside her. The wedding would be solemnized within the next few weeks and would replace the birthday party she had planned. She would adapt the plans and expand upon them. It would be a wonderful challenge – and Bertrand would help. She was quite sure her aunt would too, though she was going to take the lead herself.

'I am going to organize a grand wedding breakfast,' she said, smiling at all the solemn faces about her, 'in the ballroom.'

'A wedding on the scale you imagine would be impossible to plan so quickly, Estelle,' her aunt said. 'You have no idea of all the work it would involve, my love. And your father's aunt and cousin are already deep into the planning of a wedding for Margaret. Very elaborate and costly plans, I might add.'

'The wedding must be celebrated at Brambledean Court,' Alexander said. 'At Christmastime. It is the appropriate place for it, as Viola was once Countess of Riverdale and Brambledean was her official residence. And my wife and I are the appropriate people to host the event, since I am head of the Westcott family. Wren will be delighted. She and Viola became particular friends earlier this year. And there will be plenty of time between now and Christmas to make all the necessary plans and send out all the invitations.'

Viola did not bother to point out that she was not a Westcott.

'That does seem like an excellent idea, Alex,' Elizabeth said. 'And since you are now starting to restore Brambledean to its former splendor, you can make a sort of housewarming of Christmas and Viola's and Lord Dorchester's wedding.'

'I do think the Earl of Riverdale's suggestion the wiser one, Estelle,' Mrs Morrow said.

'Yes, Aunt,' the girl said, but she looked suddenly crestfallen. Elizabeth must have noticed it too.

'What I would suggest,' she said, 'is that you convert the birthday party you have so carefully planned into a betrothal party, Lady Estelle. It could still be a birthday party too, though somewhat belated perhaps.'

The girl's face lit up in response. 'Oh,' she said, 'that is a splendid idea, Lady Overfield. Is it not, Bert? Is it not, Papa?'

He entered the conversation for the first time. 'I

am fast learning,' he said, his voice soft and languid, 'that a wedding belongs to everyone except the bride and groom. Arrange your party, Estelle. Arrange your Christmas wedding, Riverdale. I will do my part by attending both. My betrothed, I do not doubt, will do likewise.'

'Of course,' Viola said.

And so it was all settled – a betrothal party at Redcliffe in the next few weeks, a wedding at Brambledean at Christmas.

There was going to be horrible turmoil, Viola thought, and some hurt feelings when neither event took place. She looked from Abigail to Estelle to Bertrand.

For of course there was no betrothal.

And there would be no marriage.

It was evident to everyone that despite the fact that the cottage boasted eight bedchambers and they could all conceivably have squeezed into them, it was really not a practical idea for everyone to spend the night there. At first it was suggested that Marcel and his family remove to an inn in the town across the river, while Viola and her family remained at the cottage. It was ultimately decided, however, that the men would move to town and the ladies remain where they were. Either way, Marcel was to leave his own home, presumably because it was deemed improper for him to sleep under the same roof as his betrothed.

Riverdale made the final decision, explaining that

231

he needed to have a few private words with Dorchester. Marcel assumed he was to be interrogated on his eligibility by a man ten years his junior and a rank below his on the social scale – but with all the damned dignity of head of the family, no doubt.

So they drove off, the five of them squashed together in Riverdale's carriage, to an inn that mercifully could provide them with a room each. They dined together on boiled beef, potatoes, and cabbage. And they conversed on a variety of topics, not one of which touched upon betrothals or weddings or prewedding honeymoons. It was all very amiable and very civil. But after they had finished their suet pudding with something drizzled over it that was not custard but was not anything else recognizable either, André got to his feet and clapped Bertrand on the shoulder.

'Come along, Bert,' he said. 'We will go and see what the taproom has to offer. I daresay your father will not object to your quaffing a glass of ale. Join us, Cunningham.'

'Thank you,' Joel Cunningham said, 'but I will remain here.'

So he was to have two interrogators, was he? Marcel leaned back in his chair and played with the handle of his coffee cup as uncle and nephew left the dining room.

He was still feeling savage.

I am going to walk down to the edge of the wet sand, and just like that, with the choice of a singular pronoun – *I*, when she might have said *shall we?* – he had felt the chill of an ending. He had let her go alone and had stood watching her for he did not know how long until she turned and came back.

I need to go home, she had said then, and he had known instantly why her words had so upset him. It was the first time – he was almost certain of it – the woman in one of his affairs had been the one to end it. Just as she had ended a budding flirtation fourteen years ago by telling him to go away. Had he not learned his lesson then?

Clearly not. He had behaved badly down there on the beach. He had been hurt, and so he had set out to hurt in return. Oh, only in words and insinuations, of course. He had not laid a finger on her. But had that really been his intention? To return hurt for hurt? He knew it had.

And now they were doomed to spend the rest of their lives together. Or at least to spend the rest of their lives married to each other, which was not necessarily the same thing. He spoke before Riverdale could launch into the speech he had no doubt prepared.

'I have title and fortune,' he said. 'The lady's lack of either does not matter more than the snap of my fingers. The daughter's lack of fortune will be remedied. And the lady, if any reminder is needed, is of age and needs no permission from anyone to marry whom she chooses.'

'The daughter,' Cunningham said, 'has a name.'

'So does the lady,' Riverdale added.

The gloves had come off, it seemed, and he had been cast in the role of villain. Marcel lifted the cup and sipped his coffee, which was too weak and too cool. Why the devil had none of them thought to have wine or port brought in?

'I will be marrying Viola at Christmastime, presumably at Brambledean,' he said. 'It will be a valid marriage. I have no secret wife hidden away somewhere. I will care for all her needs for the rest of her life and make provision for her in the event that I predecease her. Miss Abigail Westcott will be welcome in my home and will be more than adequately provided for.'

'*All* her needs?' Riverdale said. It was a quietly, courteously posed question, but it was pure venom, Marcel decided. He was beginning heartily to dislike this oh-so-correct, oh-so-dutiful earl, who was not a blood relative of Viola's or even a relative by marriage.

It took effort not to answer as he would have liked to answer. He did not need the goodwill of any of Viola's relatives. He could live very well without it, in fact. But she could not. She had proved that down on the beach. She was missing them, damn it all. She had chosen them over him.

'*All*,' he said with quiet emphasis.

'Abigail is illegitimate,' Cunningham said, 'just as my wife is. Just as I am. You are willing to taint your children by having her live in your home with them?'

234

Marcel looked at the man with a new respect. He wanted the answer to a question that delicacy might well have led the lot of them to ignore – until it became a possible problem later.

'And my mother-in-law was in a bigamous marriage for longer than twenty years,' Cunningham added. 'Though it was no fault of hers, the *ton* has been inclined to treat her as they would a leper. You are willing to face what this may mean after your marriage?'

'If the *ton* should treat my wife with anything less than the full respect due the Marchioness of Dorchester,' Marcel said, 'then the *ton* will have me to reckon with. And I can assure you those are no idle words. And I treat with contempt any idea that Abigail's illegitimacy somehow disqualifies her from full participation in the sort of life for which she was raised.'

They all looked at one another for a few moments.

'There was no betrothal was there,' Riverdale said at last, 'until you saw us outside the cottage from down in the valley this afternoon.'

'Does it matter?' Marcel asked.

'Yes,' Cunningham said. 'She is my mother-in-law. My wife and my sister-in-law love her dearly. So do my daughters. I hold her in the deepest affection. If the price of her happiness is some arrangement made among the ten of us to tell a plausible story and never divulge the full truth, then I am prepared to pay it.'

Riverdale said nothing.

It was his way out, Marcel thought. And Viola's too. A way out of a situation that was intolerable to them both. No one need know of her disgrace, though what a ridiculous way that was of looking at an affair a woman older than forty had entered into quite freely and enjoyed immensely – until she was enjoying it no longer. No one need know except the eight people who had found them at the cottage this afternoon. And – as he had said to Viola earlier – all the people to whom those eight would confide the truth, and all the people in whom *they* would confide. And the Prewitts and Jimmy Prewitt's great-niece.

Besides, he was at heart a gentleman, he supposed, and at the heart of every gentleman even partway worthy of the name, there was a core of honor.

'Your mother-in-law will be happy with me,' he told Cunningham with a glance at Riverdale. 'I will see to it.'

They looked far from convinced. He ought to have left it at that.

'I fell in love with her fourteen years ago,' he added, embellishing the story he had told earlier at the cottage, 'and she with me, though she was far too dutiful a wife to admit any such thing at the time. She sent me away before our attraction could ever be put into words or deed, and I went. She was a married lady – or so we both thought. Sometimes, however, if it is real, love does not die. It only lies dormant.'

'From what I know of your reputation,

236

Dorchester,' Riverdale said, 'your definition of *love* is not mine.'

'Ah,' Marcel said, 'I have another word for my dictionary, then. I plan to write one, you know, though Viola is skeptical, since until now I have had only one word to go in it – the verb *to jollificate*. Now I can add *love* with all its myriad meanings and shades of meaning. Just the one word should be good for several pages, do you not think?' He was becoming angry. He deliberately drew a few slow breaths.

'I would settle for your assurance that you will treat her honorably,' Cunningham said.

The anger almost broke through his control – until he realized what was happening here. He was in the presence of very real love. Here were two men, neither of whom had any blood relationship to Viola but both of whom *cared*. Because she was a member of their family, and family mattered to them. Family stood together and defended its own.

For a few moments he felt unutterably bleak. What had he squandered in the name of guilt and self-loathing and staying out of the way of what he was not worthy to claim as his own?

'You have my assurance,' he said curtly. 'I suppose you speak of fidelity. You have my assurance.'

'Perhaps,' Riverdale said, 'you should add the word *fidelity* to your dictionary too, Dorchester. It has far more meanings than the obvious one.'

Marcel got to his feet. 'I must rescue my son from the taproom,' he said, 'and the chance that he is sampling the ale too freely.'

They made no move to follow him.

He could cheerfully break a few chairs and a few tables and smash a few windows, Marcel thought. But as it turned out he could not even relieve his feelings by scolding Bertrand or berating André. His son was drinking water.

'Bert never touches alcohol,' André said, clapping the boy on the shoulder, 'or intends ever to do so. I think it is time, Marc, that you rescued him from the clutches of his uncle and aunt.'

Marcel looked at his son, whose nostrils were slightly flared, though he said nothing. Marcel agreed with his brother – or did he? And he wished André had not picked up Estelle's pet name for her twin.

'Bertrand is seventeen years old,' he said. 'Almost eighteen. Old enough, I believe, to make his own decisions.'

His son flashed him an indecipherable look before picking up his glass. He must have looked just like Bertrand when he was seventeen, Marcel thought. And yes, old enough to make his own decisions, good or bad. His anger had been converted to melancholy.

But he still wished he could smash a few chairs.

The evening at the cottage was long and unutterably tedious, though somehow civility was maintained.

Perhaps, Viola thought when it was over, that was because they were all ladies and had been brought up to deal with even the most awkward of social situations.

Though there could not be many more awkward than this one.

Mrs Morrow was icily civil. But Viola could not blame her for the hostility that obviously seethed just below the surface of her good manners. She had been forced into the company of a woman she must consider beneath contempt. And despite the fact that she showed no real emotion, it seemed to Viola that the woman cared for her young niece, whom she had brought up almost from the girl's birth. Lady Estelle Lamarr's modest, docile manners in the presence of her elders were testament to her aunt's training.

Viola's training and long experience as a society hostess stood her in good stead too. She was able to rise to the ghastly situation of being hostess at a cottage that belonged to her lover. She was able to organize dinner and refreshments and converse with practiced and apparent ease.

Elizabeth, as usual, was a gem of warm amiability and sensible conversation. She was able to find common ground on a number of topics dear to Mrs Morrow's heart, and she was able to draw Lady Estelle into some conversation. It was Elizabeth who pointed out to her that she and Abigail would be sisters after the wedding of their parents. Estelle, who had been stealing glances at Abigail all evening with obvious interest and admiration, looked suddenly pleased.

'Oh yes,' she said, addressing Abigail. 'And you will be coming to live with us, of course. We will perhaps be special friends. I have cousins at Redcliffe, but none of them have ever felt like a sister or brother, apart from Bert, of course. I have often thought I would have liked having a sister if only my mother had not died.'

Abby was kind, though she was obviously very unhappy. 'It is lovely having a sister,' she said. 'I have always been close to Camille, my elder sister. But she is married now – to Joel, whom you met earlier – and I do not see as much of her as I would like. And I have a half sister, whom I met for the first time only a couple of years ago. She is Anna, the Duchess of Netherby.'

'It is going to be a great pleasure to meet and get to know them all,' the girl said. 'I have wished – oh, for years and years – that Papa would marry again and come home to stay.'

Viola went to bed feeling more wretched than she had felt in two years. And her bed looked so very vast and empty. She expected Abigail to come for a private talk, but it did not happen. And that made her feel even more wretched. Abby was too hurt, it seemed, even for confrontation.

And that poor child, his daughter, whom he had neglected so shamelessly all her life. Whom he had neglected just recently after sending word that he was on his way home. She was going to be hurt even more when she discovered that there was to be no wedding after all and that her father was not going to go home to stay. And the boy too. He looked achingly like a very young Marcel – and he called him *sir*.

I am glad you said it first, Viola. I never like to hurt my women.

It was what he had said down on the beach when she had told him she needed to go home.

My women.

Reducing her to nothing more than a temporary mistress, just like all the others who had preceded her.

As, of course, she was. As she had known from the start. But putting it into words that way had been a deliberate insult. And, fool that she was, she had allowed it to hurt.

Only an hour later he had announced their betrothal.

Well. He would not have things all his way. There *was* no betrothal and there would be no wedding. She would be very clear on that and quite immovable. She would put a dent in his pride, perhaps, even though he would also feel an enormous relief.

He did not want the marriage any more than she did.

It was the last thing she wanted.

CHAPTER 14

At least, Marcel thought during the long journey home, he had his own carriage in which to travel, though André insisted upon bearing him company.

'It is dashed trying to be confined to close quarters with Jane Morrow,' he explained. 'A more Friday-faced female it would be hard to find, Marc. Every time she so much as glances at me it is with a look that says I am no better than a toad about to wriggle out from under a stone and that if she had her wish I would stay under it for the next eternity or so. How Estelle and Bertrand stand it I do not know.'

'They have been given no choice,' Marcel said curtly.

'You are in a blue mood,' his brother observed cheerfully. 'Feeling lovelorn already, are you, Marc, after being parted from your lady for all of an hour?' He grinned. 'Or are you merely feeling the noose tighten about your neck?'

'Let me make one thing clear,' Marcel said. 'You may talk about the weather if you must talk at all or about your own health or that of any or all your acquaintances. You may talk about politics or the

242

war or art or religion or all the books you have never read or the man in the moon. You may even talk about my betrothal and the state of my heart – *if*, that is, you enjoy talking to yourself as you trudge along beside an empty road or dash along it to try to catch up to the other carriage. What you may *not* do is talk upon either topic inside this carriage or anywhere else within my hearing. And I have excellent hearing.'

André continued to grin, but he held his peace.

Another fortunate thing about the journey was that Jane was as bent upon completing it as Marcel was and was therefore just as eager to press onward each day until the light was too poor to make for continued safe travel. She insisted that Estelle travel with her, and Marcel did not argue. Bertrand chose to remain with his sister. Perhaps he would have chosen the other carriage anyway.

The birthday-turned-betrothal party was to be held in three weeks' time, well after Marcel's actual birthday. He was not sure if Estelle had noticed that no one else felt an enthusiasm for the occasion anywhere near matching her own. She had pressed on with her plans even after Viola had informed her that she would come and bring her younger daughter with her if Abigail wished, but that no one else from her family could be expected to attend.

'They have all recently spent a few weeks in Bath for my grandson's christening,' she had explained gently enough. 'Christmas will be upon us before we know it and they will all wish to go to Brambledean. It would be too much to expect them to travel to Redcliffe Court too.'

Estelle had been disappointed, though she had brightened when Abigail assured her that she would indeed accompany her mother. 'I will have you all to myself for a short while, then,' his daughter had said, 'and will have a chance to get to know you better before we become sisters.'

Marcel knew very well what Viola was up to, of course. Amid all the bustle of departure after the men had returned to the cottage soon after breakfast, she had insisted that they talk in private. They had walked a little way down the hill among the ferns before he stopped and crossed his arms.

'This is a waking nightmare,' she had said coldly. 'While I appreciated your gallantry yesterday, it was unnecessary and it very much complicates the situation. It was an embarrassment to be found here together, especially by our children, but no one was going to make a fuss. Oh, there were rumblings from Alexander and Joel about a duel, but I would have put an end to that silliness in a matter of moments. Good heavens, the very idea! None of these people were going to spread the story, and if any of them did, so what? I have no great reputation to lose, and you have a reputation that would only be enhanced.'

'You believe that you lost your reputation along with your marriage two years ago, then?' he had asked.

She had made an impatient gesture with one hand. 'It does not take much when one is dealing with the *ton*,' she had said, 'and when one is female. I do not care. And if my family and even the Westcotts – *who are not my family* – cannot accept the fact that at the age of forty-two I am free to take a little time for myself and to spend it in any manner I choose and with whomever I choose, then they have a problem. It is not mine.'

'I believe, Viola,' he had said, 'you deceive yourself.'

'If I do,' she had said, 'it is none of your concern. *I* am none of your concern. I am not going to marry you, Marcel. It would be kinder, especially for your daughter, if everyone were informed of that fact now before we leave.'

Yet she had not threatened to go and do it herself. He wondered if she had realized that. And he wondered why he had not stridden back up the hill to do exactly what she demanded. He had no wish whatsoever to tie himself down in matrimony again, after all, and to live in tame domestication at Redcliffe for the rest of his life, pretending to himself that she had not grown tired of him even before they were betrothed.

'The horses are champing at the bit,' he had said, 'and so are all the humans in the cottage. We will resume this discussion, if we must, at Redcliffe.'

'It will be too late then,' she had said. 'It will be general knowledge that we are betrothed even if no official announcement has been made. Estelle will have planned her party and invited guests. Do you not care that her feelings will be more terribly hurt then than they would be now?'

'It is because of my daughter and my son,' he had said, 'and because of your daughters and your son too that we must do the decent thing, Viola, regardless of our own feelings on the matter.'

'Since when,' she had asked him, all incredulity, 'have you cared one iota for your children's feelings?'

It was a good question.

Since Estelle had called him *Papa* the day before, perhaps. She had only ever called him *Father* before that, and all her life had rarely raised her eyes to his or spoken to him beyond largely mono-syllabic answers to any direct questions he had asked her. He had often wondered if she was actu-ally afraid of him or if she simply disliked him. He had almost always cut his visits shorter than he had planned. Bertrand was still calling him *sir* and was still behaving with stiff good manners.

'It is a fair question,' he had said, forcing himself to speak with cool arrogance instead of allowing himself to lash out in bitterness. 'Call it the auto-crat in me, then, this insistence of mine upon not having my will thwarted. You will marry me, Viola – for your own sake and for that of your children. You may not care about the loss of your own reputation, though I am not at all sure I believe you – or even that your reputation has been lost. But I am very sure you care about your children's.

246

Do you want them to have to deal with yet another scandal to pile upon what they dealt with not so long ago? Do you wish them to hear their mother called a slut?'

He had heard the sharp intake of her breath. 'How dare you!' she had said.

'You see?' He had raised his eyebrows. 'I rest my case. I will see you in Northamptonshire, Viola. Every day between now and then will seem like a week.'

'You do mockery awfully well.' She had not done as well as he. She could not hide the bitterness from her voice.

He wondered what had happened to the man he had been just three weeks ago – the man who did not care a tinker's damn for what anyone thought or said of him, the man who looked upon the world and its rules and conventions and judgments with cynical indifference. But his mind shied away from any answers that might have presented themselves.

If only there had been a few more days – and a few more nights. He would surely have worked her out of his system and would no doubt have taken a different course upon the arrival of the search parties. He would have thought of every argument there was – and a few there were not – to avoid having to marry her. Or perhaps he would have used no argument at all. That would have been more like him. If he had been forced into a duel with either Riverdale or Cunningham, he would have shot contemptuously into the air and taken his chances on what they chose to do – and on the accuracy of their aim.

Had he broken with his usual practice, then, and insisted upon marriage because of some leftover lust? He had missed her like a gnawing toothache since their last night together, and it kept occurring to him that the last time he had traveled this road she had been beside him, her hand often in his, her head sometimes upon his shoulder, the whole of their glorious escape ahead of them.

He felt vicious.

It was a feeling that was threatening to become habitual.

Everyone had remained in Bath. It was the final humiliation. Even Michael, Viola's brother, had stayed, though he had had to make hurried arrangements to have another clergyman carry out his duties in his parish. For those staying at the Royal York hotel it was a huge extra expense they had not planned for.

The carriage stopped at Joel's house first before making its descent into Bath, and Camille, who must have been watching for it, came dashing out in her thin slippers despite the cold, Sarah balanced on one hip, Winifred close behind her. She grabbed her mother in a one-armed hug as soon as Viola's feet touched solid ground.

'Mama,' she cried. 'Oh, Mama, I have been sick with worry. Oh, Mama. I have been so worried. Wherever have you been?'

'Papa!' Sarah was exclaiming as she held out her arms and leaned away from Camille.

And this was the daughter who had outdone her mother just a couple of years ago in very correct, icily controlled demeanor?

There was a cluster of strangers out on the lawn, huddled inside warm cloaks before their easels as they worked on their paintings.

'She did write, Cam,' Abigail cried, scrambling down from the carriage unassisted, as Joel had been distracted, first by Winifred, who wrapped an arm about his waist and raised a beaming face to his, and then by Sarah, who clasped her arms tightly about his neck and gave him a smacking kiss on the lips. 'To us and to Mrs Sullivan. Somehow both letters were lost. Mama is *betrothed*, Cam.'

And after all, Viola could not set the record straight, as she had intended to do the moment she arrived. Neither Camille nor the rest of the family when they all came to the house within the hour was thrilled by the announcement, especially when they knew the identity of her betrothed, but none of them protested loudly or demanded or even suggested that she change her mind before it was too late. For there was no hiding the fact that she and the Marquess of Dorchester had lived together for a few weeks before Alexander and the others had found her, though no one spoke of it. Everyone believed, or pretended to believe, the story that they had been betrothed before they decided to go to Devonshire for some time alone together and that therefore their behavior was less scandalous than it would otherwise have been.

It was after all impossible to tell the truth, though she had steeled herself throughout the journey home to do just that. For these were decent, much-loved, respectable people – her mother, well-known for most of her life in Bath society; her brother, a man of the cloth, and his wife; the Dowager Countess of Riverdale, her former mother-in-law, who at the age of seventy-one had made the effort to come all the way to Bath; her former sisters-in-law; Avery, Duke of Netherby, who had once been Harry's guardian, and his duchess, Anna, who was Humphrey's only legitimate child; Jessica, Avery's half sister and Abigail's dearest friend.

And her own daughters. And her grandchildren. Had they not all suffered enough in the past two years without . . . How had he phrased it? But it took no great effort of memory to remember. Had her children not suffered enough without having their mother known as a slut?

She hated him, she hated him, she hated him.

She believed she really did.

And she would *not* marry him. But now was not the time to announce that.

When would be the time, then?

Oh, she was being justly punished. She had no one to blame but herself for her own unhappiness. The trouble was that one sometimes dragged inno-cent people down into one's own misery and guilt.

Marcel. She closed her eyes for a moment while the noise of conversation proceeded about her in Camille and Joel's drawing room. Why had they had to be stranded at the same country inn? What were the chances?

Why did you stay instead of leaving with your brother?

Why did you speak to me?

Why did I reply?

She felt a shoulder pressed to her arm and opened her eyes to smile down at Winifred and set an arm about her thin shoulders.

'I finished *A Pilgrim's Progress,* Grandmama,' she said. 'It was very instructional. Are you proud of me? Will you help me choose my next book?'

While they were still at the cottage in Devonshire together, Estelle had asked Abigail for a list of all her family members and where they lived. Abigail and her mother were to come for the party, and Estelle's father had told her that that would be quite sufficient to make the betrothal aspect of the party a grand occasion for their neighbors. Bertrand had agreed that it was all she could reasonably expect when the wedding itself was to follow in just a couple of months and involve everyone from both families in traveling all the way to Brambledean in Wiltshire. Aunt Jane had reminded her niece that this was the first party she had organized and was a remarkably ambitious undertaking even as it was.

'Anything on a grander scale would simply over-whelm you, my love,' she said, kindly enough. 'You have no idea.'

Estelle dutifully took the guest list she had made for her father's birthday party and added Miss Kingsley's and Abigail Westcott's names. She would have added her aunt Annemarie and uncle William Cornish, who lived a mere twenty miles away, if she had not noticed that, of course, their names were already there. If everyone came, as surely they would, they would be well over thirty in number. That included the thirteen people who were already living at the house, it was true, but even so, it was an impressive number for a country party in October. It was all very exciting.

But oh, it was not as exciting as it would be if only . . .

Having discovered her wings only very recently, Estelle was eager to spread them again to see if she could fly. She was very nearly a woman, even if she was not quite eighteen. She wanted . . . Well. Without any real expectation of success, she added Abigail's list to her own and began the laborious task of writing the invitations. She refused all help, even though both Bertrand and Aunt Jane offered, and even Cousin Ellen, Aunt Jane's daughter.

In Bath, Camille handed the invitation to Joel without any comment and watched his face as he read it.

'Unless memory is failing me,' he said, 'we do not have any official booking here that week.'

'We do not,' she said.

'It would be a long journey for the children,' he said.

'And for us.' She smiled at him. 'And you have only recently returned from another long journey, you poor thing.'

'Winifred would be thrilled,' he said.

'Yes,' she agreed. 'So would Sarah. And Jacob would sleep.'

'Perhaps your Grandmama Kingsley would like to come with us,' he said. 'I expect she has been invited too.'

'I remember the Marquess of Dorchester from the spring months I used to spend in London,' she said, 'though he was plain Mr Lamarr then. He is fearfully handsome.'

'Fearfully?'

'Yes,' she said. 'Fearfully. I suppose you did not notice. I still find it hard to believe that Mama is going to marry him.'

'Or anyone?' he asked.

'I suppose so,' she said after thinking about it. 'It is hard to imagine one's mother wanting to marry anyone. We will go, then?'

'Of course,' he said.

And of course Mrs Kingsley was happy to go with them. 'I need to take a look at that young man,' she said. 'I do not like the few things I have heard of him.'

In Dorsetshire, the Reverend Michael Kingsley conferred with his wife. He had just taken a far longer leave of absence than he had originally intended. They had gone to Bath supposedly for a few days to attend the christening of his great-nephew and had stayed for a few weeks after the disappearance of his sister. He would need to take leave again over Christmas – the very worst time, with the exception of Easter, for a man of his calling – in order to attend Viola's wedding. He really could not make a good case for going all the way to Northamptonshire in October just to attend her betrothal party.

'*Could* I, Mary?' he asked.

'She is your only sister,' his wife reminded him. 'When she came to live with you here for a while a couple of years ago, she was dreadfully hurt. She was all locked up inside herself, as I remember you telling me. And I agreed, though we were not married at the time and I did not see a great deal of her. You want to go, do you not? You want to see him. You are worried.'

'Riverdale – her husband – was the lowest form of human life,' he said, 'and may I be forgiven for passing such judgment upon a fellow mortal. I could not abide being within ten miles of him. Consequently, and to my shame, I did not see much of Viola during those years, or of my nieces and nephew. I cannot bear the thought that she might be making the same mistake all over again, Mary. I spoke with the present Riverdale while we were still in Bath and with Lord Molenor – husband of one of the Westcott sisters, you will recall – and the Duke of Netherby. Dorchester is the sort no man of sense would wish upon his daughter or sister. But there is nothing I can do, is there, if she is determined to have him?'

'Except be there,' she said. 'You cannot be certain that your presence will be meaningless, Michael. If nothing else it will assure Viola that she is loved, that her family cares. And perhaps you will be surprised. Perhaps all your fears will be put to rest. The marquess is, after all, willing to do the decent thing.'

'But only because he was caught red-handed,' he said.

'You do not know that,' she said, taking his hand across the breakfast table. 'You will be miserable if you do not go, Michael. You will feel that somehow you have failed her.'

'Again.' He frowned.

'Besides,' she said, smiling at him, 'I cannot wait until Christmas to get my first glimpse of the notorious Marquess of Dorchester. Camille told me he is fearfully handsome.'

'Fearfully?'

'Her very word,' she said.

It was she who sat down a little later to write an acceptance while her husband stood behind her chair. His hands were clasped at his back, a frown on his face, as he resisted the inappropriate temptation to lean down to kiss the back of her neck.

At Morland Abbey, country seat of the Duke of Netherby, Louise Archer, née Westcott, the dowager duchess, waved her invitation in the air as the duke and duchess joined her and her daughter, Jessica, at the breakfast table.

'You have one too,' she said, indicating the small pile of mail that had been placed between Anna's plate and Avery's.

'I am overcome with joy,' Avery informed his stepmother, his voice sighing with ennui. 'And what exactly is it we have one of? You may save Anna from having to read it for herself.'

'An invitation to Redcliffe Court,' Jessica blurted, 'to a betrothal party for Aunt Viola and the Marquess of Dorchester. I thought only Aunt Viola and Abby were invited, but I think we all are. Lady Estelle Lamarr would hardly send invitations to us and to no one else in the family, would she? We must go, Mama. Please, please, Avery. I cannot wait to see the marquess. Camille says he is fearfully handsome despite the fact that he must be *old*.'

'My love,' her mother said reproachfully.

'*Fearfully?*' Avery's quizzing glass hovered near his eye.

'It is the very word she used,' Jessica said.

He looked pained. 'It would be a long journey for Josephine,' he said, looking at Anna.

'She has always traveled well,' she said. 'Besides, I really must meet this fearfully handsome man. It is too long to wait until Christmas.'

'I must say,' Louise added, 'that Camille chose the perfect word to describe the man. I cannot, however, like the idea of Viola marrying him. Perhaps my sisters and I can frighten him away, though I doubt he is a man easily intimidated.'

'Shall I answer the invitation for all of us?' Anna asked.

'Yes, do,' the dowager said while her daughter clasped her hands tightly on the edge of the table. 'I shall have no peace from Jessica if I deny her the treat. Besides, I cannot deny myself.'

At Brambledean Court Wren found Alexander in the steward's office and showed him the invitation. He said a few words to the steward and followed her out into the main hall before reading it.

'You must not do any unnecessary traveling while you are in a delicate condition,' he said.

'*Must* not?' She was smiling.

He looked up sharply. 'Am I being the stuffy autocrat again?' he asked.

'*Delicate?*' She raised her eyebrows.

'You are with child, Wren.' He looked at her ruefully. 'To me you are delicate. So is my child – *our* child. You both bring out my worst instincts to coddle and protect.'

'Or your best.' She set a hand on his arm. 'I have never felt better in my life, Alexander. And you *are* head of the family.'

'If that were a physical thing,' he said with a sigh, 'I would hurl it from the highest cliff into the deepest depths of the ocean.'

'But it is not.' Her eyes twinkled at him.

'But it is not.' He sighed again. 'Let me go alone. You remain here.'

'I would pine away without you.' Her eyes were laughing now. 'And you would pine away without me. Admit it.'

'Hyperbole,' he protested. 'But I would be horribly inconvenienced and out of sorts.' He grinned suddenly. 'I suppose you want to meet the infamous marquess before Christmas.'

'Camille described him as fearfully handsome,' she said.

'Did she really?' he said. '*Fearfully?* I suppose he does have a way of instilling fear in anyone who tends to be intimidated by pretension.'

'But you are not. My hero.' She laughed, and he laughed with her.

'We will go, then?' he said. 'You are quite sure, Wren?'

'I am very fond of Viola,' she said. 'She was not in London long when we got married, but there was an instant bond between us. Apart from your mother and sister, who were incredibly kind to me from the start, Viola felt like the first real friend I have had in my life. I am a little upset about her, for I fear that circumstances are forcing her into doing something she does not really want to do. I cannot do anything about that, of course, but I can . . . *be* there. It is not much to offer, is it?'

'It may be everything,' he said. 'Why have we

258

been standing here for so long? You will be getting dizzy. You will answer the invitation? And say yes?'

'I will.' She kissed him on the cheek. 'You may return to what you were doing.'

'I have your permission, do I?' he asked.

'You do, sir,' she said. 'You may have noticed that I can be a stuffy autocrat too.'

At Riddings Park in Kent, Alexander's home until he inherited the Riverdale title and Brambledean with it, Mrs Althea Westcott, his mother, read the invitation aloud to Elizabeth.

'I must have seen the Marquess of Dorchester a hundred times over the years,' she said, 'but I cannot for the life of me put a face to the name.'

'Even though Camille describes him as fearfully handsome, Mama?' Elizabeth asked, her eyes twinkling. 'And she is right too. I have to agree with her. He is both handsome and fearful. I would not like to cross his will. And he was not the Marquess of Dorchester until a couple of years or so ago. He was plain Mr Lamarr before that.'

'Is Viola out of her mind agreeing to marry him?' her mother asked.

Elizabeth thought about it. 'No,' she said, though there was some hesitation in her voice. 'Although the marriage has undoubtedly been forced upon them – good gracious, his young son and daughter and her daughter were among the eight of us who came upon them there. It *has* been forced upon them, but I am not at all sure they would not have got there on their own, given time.

There is something . . . Call me a romantic if you will. There is just . . . something. Words have deserted me this morning.'

'They are in love?' her mother asked.

'Oh,' Elizabeth said, 'I am not at all sure about that, Mama. He is definitely not the sort of man one would expect to fall in love. It is widely believed, on good evidence, that he is a man without a heart. And I am not sure Viola is the sort of woman to fall in love. She is far too disciplined, something that has been so forced upon her all her adult life that it may well have become ingrained, I fear. But . . . Well . . .'

'There is *something*,' her mother said, smiling.

'Just the word I was searching for. Thank you, Mama.' Elizabeth smiled. 'There is something. We will go, then?'

'Certainly,' her mother said. 'Was there ever any doubt?'

In the north of England, Mildred Wayne, née Westcott, was still in her dressing room having the finishing touches put to her morning coiffure when Lord Molenor, her husband, came in with their invitation dangling from one hand. He waited until his wife had dismissed her maid.

'Dorchester's young daughter is inviting us to a betrothal party for Viola and her father at Redcliffe,' he said. 'We have just returned home from Bath. With the boys away at school, perhaps behaving themselves, perhaps not, we have more than two months of quiet conjugal bliss to look forward to before we all take ourselves off to Brambledean for Christmas and the wedding. But I suppose you will insist upon going to Redcliffe as well.'

'Well, goodness me, Thomas,' she said, taking one last look at her image before turning from the glass, apparently satisfied. 'Of course.'

'Of course,' he said with mock meekness, and offered his arm to escort her downstairs for breakfast. 'And you may answer the invitation, Mildred.'

'Of course,' she said again. 'Don't I always?'

He thought about it during the time it took them to descend five stairs. 'Always,' he agreed.

And at the home of the Dowager Countess of Riverdale, one of the smaller entailed properties of the earl, Lady Matilda Westcott, spinster eldest sister of Humphrey, the late Earl of Riverdale, offered her mother the vinaigrette that she took from the brocade reticule she carried everywhere with her to cover all emergencies.

'We will not go, of course,' she said. 'You must not upset yourself, Mama. I shall write and decline the invitation as soon as we have finished eating.'

'Put it away,' her mother said, batting impatiently at the vinaigrette. 'The smell of it makes my toast taste vile. Viola is an important member of this family, Matilda. She was married to Humphrey for twenty-three years before he died. It was not her fault the marriage turned out to be irregular. I have loved her as a daughter for twenty-five years and I will continue to do so until I go to my grave. What I need to know is whether she is making a

261

foolish mistake. Again. I understand this young man has a reputation every bit as disreputable as Humphrey's was.'

'I would not know, Mama,' Lady Matilda said, holding the vinaigrette over her bag, reluctant to let go of it. 'I have always been assiduous about avoiding him and gentlemen like him who really do not deserve the name. And he is not so young either. But Viola has no choice, you know.' She flushed deeply. 'They were caught living in sin together.'

'Ha!' the dowager said. 'Good for Viola. It is about time that girl kicked up her heels a bit. But I am concerned about her marrying the rogue. Why should she when all she did was kick up her heels? Half the *ton* – the female half – will feel nothing but secret envy if they ever find out, which I daresay they will. We will go, Matilda. You may write to Lady Estelle. No, I will do it myself. I want to take a good look at the young man. If I do not like what I see, I shall tell him so. And I shall tell Viola she is a fool.'

'Mama,' Lady Matilda protested. 'You are over-exciting yourself. You know what your physician—'

'Nothing but a quack,' the dowager said, thereby signaling an end to the entire discussion.

CHAPTER 15

After two weeks at home, Marcel was still feeling savage. He had never spent so much time at Redcliffe. He had spent enough time here now, however, to have learned something disturbing about himself. He was nothing but a weakling. It was a nasty realization for a man who had always prided himself upon being just the opposite.

He had come home to assert himself, to restore his household to order, to put an end to all the petty bickerings, to make himself master of his own domain. But he wondered at the end of the two weeks if he had accomplished anything at all – and this was even before his life was to be further disrupted by the arrival of Viola Kingsley.

His aunt Olwen, the marchioness, was a very elderly lady. She did not move about with any great ease, but her mind was sharp and there was something stately about her heavy figure. Her daughter, his cousin Isabelle, Lady Ortt, was an overblown blond fading to gray and liked to bully all around her, including her daughter, Margaret. And including her husband. Irwin, Lord Ortt, was a reedy individual, one-quarter head shorter than his wife, with receding fair hair, a chin that had never been anything else but receded, and an Adam's apple that bobbed with unfortunate frequency since he swallowed whenever he was nervous and he was habitually nervous.

It should have been the easiest thing in the world to gather them all together and announce a move to the dower house for the lot of them. It would not even have been a cruel pronouncement. The dower house was within the park one mile away from the main house on the far side of the lake. It was sizable and in good repair – he had taken a walk there and looked it over for himself. There was room to spare for all of them. They would be away from the constant aggravation of Jane and Charles Morrow's presence in the house with their adult children.

'Those people,' Isabelle told Marcel when none of those people were within earshot to defend themselves, 'do not possess a title among them, Cousin Marcel, and they are not even Lamarrs but only relatives of your long-deceased wife.'

'Who was a Lamarr,' he reminded her. 'And they are the appointed guardians of my daughter and my heir.'

Isabelle had looked somewhat disconcerted, perhaps at his tone and the fact that he was holding his quizzing glass only just below the level of his eye. She was not ready to concede defeat, however. 'But they do not take precedence over Mama,' she said, 'or over Irwin and me. Sometimes they behave as though they do.'

'I looked at the dower house this morning,' he said in an apparent non sequitur, though it became quickly clear that both ladies understood him perfectly well.

'It was built too close to the lake,' his aunt said. 'It would be very bad for my rheumatics over there.'

'We have dear Margaret's wedding to Sir Jonathan Billings in early December,' Isabelle said. 'The house is going to be full of guests. You were not here to consult when we began planning, Marcel, but you could not possibly begrudge her a wedding befitting her rank and fortune.'

No, Marcel could not, though he did wonder why, if Ortt was in possession of a fortune, he was living off Marcel's bounty at Redcliffe and not putting on a grand wedding for his daughter in his own home. Marcel would certainly broach both that subject and the removal to the dower house after Margaret's wedding, but it did seem a bad time to do it now with the wedding plans well advanced. He could not help the niggling feeling, however, that if he were the man he thought he was, he would not have waited even one hour.

Jane and Charles Morrow's children – his nephew and niece – were both grown-up. Oliver had been seven or eight when the twins were born, Ellen only a few years younger. Yet they were both permanently ensconced at Redcliffe. Marcel intended to have a word with them, or with the young man, anyway. Ellen was her mother's concern, though it was hard to know why she was not already married. She was neither ravishingly pretty nor notably vivacious, but she was not an antidote either. Charles Morrow, though not poverty-stricken, was not a notably wealthy man. His son could surely not afford a life of permanent idleness – unless he continued living at Redcliffe, that was. That was out of the question. Marcel was going to be living here himself – with his wife.

Upon which topic his mind preferred not to dwell.

Oliver liked to trail about the estate with Marcel's steward, giving unsolicited opinions and suggestions and advice, which on more than one occasion Charles had tried to convert into orders – which the steward resented, as was to be expected.

The matter ought to have been easy to resolve. Marcel ought to have backed his steward, counseled Charles not to interfere where he had no business interfering, and given his nephew his marching orders. However, nothing was easy these days. For the truth was that after some long talks with his steward and a bit of tramping about the farms, and after a close look at the books, all of which activities went severely against the grain, Marcel could not help coming to the conclusion that his nephew had a point. The steward was an elderly man, not doddering exactly, but certainly past his prime and set in his ways and unaware of the fact that his domain was no longer running as efficiently or even as sensibly as it ought.

What he really needed to do, Marcel realized, was sack the steward and hire a new one – and then give his nephew his marching orders. He would write to his man of business in London when he had a moment. He was half aware, of course, that he had any number of moments. Life in the country was not exactly characterized by its hectic schedules. He would do it after this infernal party, then. Meanwhile, he noticed that Bertrand was rather fond of his older male cousin and looked up to him with some admiration. And Charles, though more than a bit on the stuffy side, was a decent sort and doubtless meant well.

André had remained at Redcliffe despite the fact that there was nothing there to entertain a man of his tastes. Marcel had paid off all his debts and increased his allowance from the estate, but he had done nothing to force a permanent solution to the problem of his brother's extravagance and gaming. As André had pointed out, it was a family failing, though Marcel had got his own habit under control, damn it. He had been given no choice. He had had two children to support long before he inherited his title and fortune. His income, though more than adequate, had not been limitless.

The housekeeper, closely backed by the cook, complained that too much was expected of them – *by too many people*. Lady Ortt's wedding plans for her daughter were becoming more and more demanding *even though she was not and never had been the mistress of the house.* Mrs Morrow consistently refused to hear of extra help being taken on, as those who worked there already never seemed very busy. *And* Mrs Morrow demanded that they all attend morning prayers in the drawing room before breakfast every day. *And now* there was this party Lady Estelle was planning . . .

Their problems at least Marcel was able to solve. 'There is only one person in this house with the authority to give orders,' he said, regarding them in some amazement, his eyebrows raised. 'You are looking at him. If you need extra help in the house, Mrs Crutchley, then you must get it. If you need any extra help in the kitchen, Mrs Jones, then you will inform Mrs Crutchley and she will provide it. And from this moment on attendance at morning prayers is to be voluntary.' He had voluntarily absented himself from the daily ordeal since his return. 'I shall inform Mrs Morrow. Will that be all?'

It seemed it was. Both women bobbed curtsies, thanked his lordship, and went on their way, looking vindicated.

It was a small success among too many weaknesses.

And now this.

He came across Jane and Estelle in the morning room one day two weeks after his arrival. He had gone in there looking for a book he had put down somewhere but now could not remember where.

They were both standing, Jane close to the window, Estelle not far inside the door. He could see her in only partial profile, but she was the picture of docile dejection. Her aunt, in contrast, was looking majestic and annoyed. She was waving a letter in one hand while she held two or three more in her other hand. She stopped midharangue when the door opened. Estelle, significantly, did not turn.

'I really do not know what has got into Estelle lately,' Jane said as he stepped into the room and closed the door behind him. 'She has always been the most obedient and biddable girl. She has never given me a moment's trouble. But first she insisted upon pursuing you all the way to Devonshire, a decision she has no doubt regretted bitterly ever since. Then she insisted upon this *party*, which even you must admit is excessive, Marcel.'

'Must I?' he asked softly.

'And now,' she continued without perceiving the danger in his tone, 'she has gone beyond the pale. I am at a loss to know what to do. A simple punishment seems inadequate, though a few hours or even a full day of quiet reflection in her room would certainly do no harm. But all this—' She waved the letter that was still suspended in one hand, and then waved the others too. 'All this is irreparable, Marcel. She did it entirely on her own, without seeking anyone's advice, and she did it on the sly too without anyone noticing. I am extremely vexed. Charles will be infuriated when I inform him. You doubtless will be too.'

'Will I?' He strolled farther into the room and stood facing his daughter, positioning himself between her and her aunt. 'And what have you done, Estelle, that is so heinous?'

'She has—' Jane began. But he held up one hand without turning.

'Estelle?'

She did not raise her eyes to his. 'I am sorry, Father,' she said. 'I wrote invitations I did not have permission to write.'

She was back to calling him Father. She had been doing it ever since they arrived home.

'To your party?' he asked. 'Why would you need permission when it is your event?'

'Marcel,' Jane said. 'Estelle is still a *child*. You seem to forget that.'

'I forget nothing,' he said. 'Her mother was the same age when she married me.'

A loud silence from behind assured him that his sister-in-law did not think that much of an argument. Estelle raised her eyes to his face for a moment before she lowered them again.

'I wanted them all to come,' she said. 'I wanted it to be a proper betrothal party, a real celebration. Abigail gave me all their names that evening at the cottage. I did not expect that they would all accept the invitation, though. I only hoped that a few of them would – Abigail's sister, perhaps, with Mr Cunningham. I would not have been at all surprised if none of them had come or even answered.'

Good Lord!

'And some of them are coming?' he asked.

'I sent nine invitations,' she said. 'I had five replies yesterday and the day before. Four more came today. Aunt Jane saw them before I came down this morning. I was delayed when one of the tapes at the back of my dress snapped.'

'I see,' he said. 'And how many have accepted?'

He scarcely heard her answer, but she repeated it a little more loudly. 'All of them,' she said.

All . . .?

He held up a hand again when he heard Jane draw breath.

'And when,' he asked, 'did you intend to reveal this information?'

It was some time before she answered. He waited. 'I do not know,' she said. 'I was a little frightened.' But she looked up suddenly, and she looked more like the angry little daughter who had all but launched herself upon him outside the cottage in Devonshire. 'I am not sorry I did it, Papa. If I had asked, Aunt Jane would have said no. You would have said no. But they ought to be here, or at least given the opportunity to be here. They are going to be your family. They are going to be my family and Bert's. I want them here for Miss Kingsley's sake and Abigail's. It ought to be a celebration for both families, not just ours. Oh, I know the wedding is going to be that, but I want everyone *here*. If you are angry with me, I—'

He held up his hand and she fell silent. *Was* he

271

angry? Was there a part of him that had been hoping that somehow he could wriggle out of this marriage? It had been all very well at the time to do the honorable thing, even to insist upon it when Viola had resisted. But now? Truth to tell, he had been avoiding thinking about her and about it – *it* being his betrothal and his looming marriage. And when he could not block all thought, perhaps he had considered that if she came alone or with just her younger daughter for company, and if she still felt as strongly opposed to the marriage as she had the last time they spoke, then perhaps . . .

If there had been any faint, lingering hope, it had now been snatched from him. The whole damned lot of them were about to descend upon Redcliffe to celebrate his betrothal. Unless they were all coming here to boil him in oil or otherwise express their displeasure. It was a distinct possibility, but he would not rely upon it. Either way he had lost control over his life and the conduct of his business. Again.

'Why would I be angry with you?' he asked. 'But your aunt believes you ought to be punished, Estelle, and I cannot help but agree.'

She lowered her eyes again and stood meekly before him. And good Lord, he thought, was *this* how she had been raised? Was this the way all young ladies were raised? She ought to be coming at him with both fists flying and both eyes flashing. It was how her mother would have behaved.

'You,' he said, 'are going to find Mrs Crutchley

as soon as I have finished speaking, and confess all to her. And then you are going to find Mrs Jones and confess all to *her*. And then you are going to wear your slippers into holes and your fingers to the bone helping them prepare for this houseful of illustrious guests we are expecting. Even if it means getting down upon your knees and scrubbing a few floors.'

'Marcel—' Jane protested from behind him. He ignored her.

Estelle's eyes had flown to his again, and she smiled radiantly, transforming herself into a considerable beauty, the little minx. 'Yes, Papa,' she said, and whisked herself out of the room before he could draw breath to say more.

He strode out after her before Jane could launch into speech.

His mind was reciting every blasphemy and swear word he had ever heard. Again. He even made up a few extras.

And yes, he was an abject weakling.

When Viola had returned home to Hinsford, in her own carriage and with her own servants this time, she had urged Abigail to remain with Camille and Joel and the children. She was happy there, Viola knew, with her sister and nieces and nephew and the constant comings and goings of artists and musicians and writers and children from the orphanage, among others. Abigail had insisted upon returning home with her mother, however.

What Viola had really hoped for was to go alone to Redcliffe. As the days passed the events of those few weeks became more and more unreal in her mind and the predicament in which she found herself more intolerable. Why *on earth* had she not spoken up for herself in Devonshire and told her own family and his that they might make what they would of their discovery but there would be no marriage? Did she really care that her behavior might be the subject of drawing room gossip for weeks or months to come? She no longer mingled with polite society except in the very small circle of her friends and neighbors at home. What was said about her elsewhere would not hurt her.

Why had she not stood up to Marcel more forcefully and flatly refused to be bullied? It was not as though he wanted to marry her, after all. It was just his sense of honor that had driven him to it, and she doubted even that would have mattered to him if his children had not been among those who had arrived on the scene. Except that he had announced their betrothal before his children came. Had he done it because of Abby, then? It certainly would not have been because he feared a challenge from Alexander or Joel.

But of course the reason she had not spoken up was precisely the reason he had. *Their children had discovered them,* and their children must be protected from the sordid nature of what they had seen. They must be persuaded that it was all in fact very nearly respectable, as their parents were betrothed and had been even before they came there.

That they must now end the charade of the betrothal was, of course, imperative. But they must find a way of doing it that would cause the least pain to their children. Whatever pain she caused herself would be fully deserved. It was one thing to snap after years of discipline and general unhappiness and two years of intense misery and to make the impulsive decision to run away for a short spell with a man notorious for his womanizing. It was another to be caught and thereby to pass on her misery to her children, who had suffered enough, and to his children, who seemed to her to be very innocent and therefore vulnerable. She was not, alas, alone in this world. Who was it who had said . . .? She had read it somewhere. William Shakespeare? John Milton? No, John Donne. He had written something to the effect that no man is an island, that everyone is a part of the mainland, that everyone's suffering affects everyone else. She wished she could remember the whole passage. There was something about a bell tolling and someone sending to ask for whose death it tolled. *It tolls for thee.* She could recall those exact words, at least.

He had been quite right, Mr Donne. Her great adventure had also been her great selfishness.

But she would extricate herself. She must. She must not compound one wrong with another much worse wrong. She wished, then, that Abigail had chosen to remain in Bath with Camille, so that she could do it alone. It was not to be, however, and so she must make the best of the situation.

There had been two weeks of almost relentless rain after they returned to Hinsford. But at last the sky had cleared and ever since they had been enjoying glorious crisp weather with the trees in the full glory of their autumn colors. It was the perfect time to be traveling, Viola thought. It was just a pity she dreaded the end of the journey.

She was troubled by her brief acquaintance with his children. Lady Estelle Lamarr, with the wildly varying emotions of a very young lady and the obvious hurt she felt at her father's unpredictability, was particularly vulnerable to anything that might bring her pain. Her twin seemed on the surface to be quite the opposite – a quiet, dignified, controlled young man. Viola suspected, however, that he was far more like his sister than had been apparent. It was Estelle who was organizing the betrothal party. Viola hoped the plans were not too elaborate or the guest list too large, though neither was likely for a country entertainment. Fortunately – very fortunately – it was also to be a slightly belated birthday party for her father. It could still proceed as that, then, even after the ending of the betrothal.

The girl would be disappointed, though. She was the only one among the eight of them who had seemed unreservedly delighted to learn that her father was about to marry. She had assumed, of course, that if he was married he would settle down at Redcliffe and give her the sort of home life she had probably always craved. Viola could cheerfully shake Marcel for that alone. It was hard to forgive fathers who took no responsibility for their children except – in some cases – a monetary one. As if that were in any way adequate.

But she could not marry him just to please his daughter.

Harry did not know yet, though she had written to him. She had considered withholding the news of her supposed betrothal in the hope that he might never have to know. But she was not the only one who wrote to him. Camille and Abigail wrote frequently. So did young Jessica and probably a few of the aunts and one or both grandmothers. It would be impossible to keep him in the dark. There had been one letter awaiting her when she returned home, and another had arrived two days later. She called them letters, but they were his usual brief, cheerful notes, in which he claimed to be enjoying himself immensely and meeting a lot of capital fellows and seeing a lot of impressive places. One would hardly guess that he was in the very midst of a vicious war. But there was no point in worrying.

Or, rather, there was no point in trying *not* to worry.

'I think this must be it, Mama,' Abigail said, and sure enough, the carriage was making a sharp turn just short of a village onto a wide, treelined driveway partially carpeted with fallen leaves, though there were plenty more still on the trees.

They wound through woodland for a couple of minutes before emerging between rolling, tree-dotted lawns stretching in both directions. The grass had been cleared of all but freshly fallen leaves. Viola could see the marks of rakes on its surface.

And the house. She glimpsed it for a moment before the driveway bent away from it. It was a massive classical structure of gray stone with a pillared portico and a flight of wide stone steps leading up to massive front doors. It had been built to impress, even perhaps to inspire awe in visitors and petitioners. Viola could feel her heart beating faster. She was very glad of the long years of experience she had had of dealing with situations she would rather avoid. She remained outwardly calm and aloof, while Abigail sat with her nose almost touching the window as she gazed ahead.

'We must have been seen approaching,' she said. 'There is the Marquess of Dorchester. And Lady Estelle. And Viscount Watley.'

For a moment Viola could not recall who Viscount Watley was. But of course it was Bertrand's courtesy title as his father's heir.

And then the carriage turned before slowing and coming to a halt below the portico. She could see for herself that there was indeed a reception party awaiting them.

She saw only one of them.

Her stomach clenched tightly and tried to turn a somersault all at the same time, leaving her breathless and nauseated. He was dressed as immaculately as he might be for a reception at Carlton House with the Prince of Wales. He looked austere and was unsmiling. It would be ridiculous to say she had forgotten just how handsome he was. Of course she had not forgotten. It was just that . . .

. . . ah, she had forgotten.

It was he who stepped forward to open the carriage door and let down the steps. He reached up a hand to help her alight and . . . oh, she had forgotten the dark intensity of his eyes. And the breath-robbing feel of his hand closing about hers.

'Viola,' he said in that light, quiet voice she could always feel like a caress down her spine. 'Welcome to Redcliffe.' He was still not smiling. Neither was she. When she was standing on the cobbled terrace before him, he raised her hand to his lips, and oh . . .

She knew him intimately. She knew his body, his voice, his mannerisms, his likes and dislikes. Even his mind. Yet it was like a dream, the knowing of him. The austere aristocrat standing before her was a stranger. She did not know him at all.

'Thank you,' she said.

His son, she was aware, was handing Abigail down from the carriage. His daughter was flushed and bright eyed and bursting with suppressed energy.

'Miss Kingsley,' she said, hurrying to her father's side and smiling warmly at Viola. 'At last. I thought the three weeks would never go by. They have seemed more like three months. You are the first to arrive, of course. I was sure you would like a day or so with just Papa and us before all the excitement.'

'That was thoughtful of you.' Viola smiled at the girl. 'I hope you have not gone to too much trouble.'

'Aunt Annemarie and Uncle William will be arriving tomorrow,' Estelle said. 'And so will everyone else if there is no bad weather to delay them.'

Everyone else?

'I cannot wait to meet them all,' Estelle continued. 'Your other daughter and her children, your mother, the Countess of Riverdale, the Duke and Duchess of Netherby, the . . . oh, everyone.'

Viola's eyes met Marcel's, which were hooded and blank – with perhaps a hint of mockery in their depths.

'From the look on Miss Kingsley's face,' he said, 'I would guess this is all news to her, Estelle.'

'Oh, Abigail.' Estelle turned to hug Viola's daughter. 'How lovely it is to see you again. I cannot wait . . .'

Viola had stopped listening. She stared into Marcel's eyes.

'This was your doing?' she asked.

'Oh, not at all,' he said, raising his eyebrows. 'It

seems I have a daughter who has stepped out of the schoolroom and out of her cocoon and has not waited to grow accustomed to her wings before spreading them and taking flight.'

She was speechless.

He offered his arm and indicated the steps up to the front doors.

Even her mind was speechless.

CHAPTER 16

It struck Marcel only after Estelle had taken the new arrivals up to their rooms and they had come back down to the drawing room half an hour later that he had been remembering Viola as she had been fourteen years ago – young, slender despite the fact that she had three young children, poised and coolly dignified. It was almost as if his heart had shut off all memory of her enjoying herself at that village fair, decked out in the gaudy jewelry he had bought her, waltzing on the village green, demanding that they stop for every castle, church, and market they passed on their leisurely journey to Devonshire, buying him a black umbrella only because the hideous gold tassels amused her, giggling in their inn room when his wooden staff cracked in two, running downhill through the ferns with her arms spread wide, pirouetting on the bridge, glowing with animation, making love with uninhibited delight.

It all came flooding back now along with her somewhat more mature figure and her less youthfully lovely face. And he remembered, and felt again, that he found her more attractive now than he had then, perhaps because he had aged with her. She was now, quite simply, beautiful. Even, perhaps, perfect.

And with his memories of those weeks came the full force of the realization that he was still not over her. He ought to have been happy to realize it. She was, after all, going to be his wife. But he did not want a marriage in which there was sentiment involved – on either side. A leg shackle was one thing. A loss of oneself was another, and it seemed to him that he would lose something of himself if he could not get over her. Lust would be acceptable. And lust was all he had felt for any woman since Adeline. For almost twenty years he had been free, safe, his own master and master of his world. He liked it that way.

He deeply resented the fact that Viola Kingsley threatened his world.

Everyone was gathered in the drawing room for a formal presentation to his intended bride. He met her at the door, made her a slight formal bow, and offered the back of his hand. She set hers lightly upon it and he conducted her first to his aunt Olwen, the marchioness, who was seated in state in her large chair by the fire.

'I understand, Miss Kingsley,' his aunt said, 'that you had the misfortune to discover after the death of the Earl of Riverdale that your marriage to him had been bigamous.'

'It was a distressing thing to discover, ma'am,' Viola said. 'For my children more than for me.'

That was all she – or anyone else – said on the subject. She did not wade into explanations and assurances that she had been an innocent victim. She was, in fact and to her very fingertips, still the Countess of Riverdale as he had known her. She appeared perfectly relaxed as he continued to take her about. She repeated the name of everyone to whom she was introduced – a device for remembering, of course – and said everything that was proper. Her manners were impeccable, her demeanor poised.

After all the introductions had been made, she seated herself between Charles Morrow on one side and Cousin Isabelle on the other, accepted a cup of tea from Ellen Morrow with a nod of thanks, and proceeded to engage both her neighbors in polite conversation.

Her daughter meanwhile had been led about by Estelle while his relatives had eyed her with a certain wariness, as though they feared her illegitimacy might somehow contaminate Estelle.

He was not over Viola. By God he was not. He wanted to run away with her again, but so far away this time that they would never find their way home or want to. He longed for those days and nights back when there had been nothing to think about, nothing to brood upon except each other. There was no point in wanting, though. He had felt her gradual withdrawal during their last day or two at the cottage even before that final confrontation on the beach. Pleasure had become less enjoyable to her. *He* had become less enjoyable. She had told him it was over, that she was going home.

He was not over her, but she was over him.

The atmosphere in the drawing room was stifling, the chatter intolerable. Margaret had joined her mother and was telling Viola about the plans for her wedding to Sir Jonathan Billings in early December. The other young people – the twins, Abigail Westcott, Oliver and Ellen Morrow – were in a group together and talking rather loudly and not always one at a time. André was holding a conversation with Irwin, Lord Ortt. And Jane's tight-lipped silence as she sat behind the tea tray even after everyone had been served and most had even had a second cup was somehow as loud as any of the actual sounds in the room.

Marcel got to his feet rather abruptly. 'Viola,' he said, 'come for a stroll outside with me.'

She looked up at him in some surprise before her eyes strayed to the window.

'It is almost dark out there, Marcel,' Jane pointed out.

'It is only early dusk,' his aunt said, for the mere sake of contradicting Jane, Marcel suspected. He ignored them both.

'Thank you.' Viola got to her feet. 'I shall go and fetch a cloak and bonnet.'

'Do dress warmly,' Isabelle advised. 'Once the daylight goes at this time of year, it can feel like the middle of winter out there.'

'I shall,' Viola promised, and she left the room without another glance at Marcel. He followed her out without paying any attention to André's grin.

She was wearing half boots when she came back downstairs five minutes later, and a long gray cloak of winter weight and a bonnet and kid gloves. Her eyes met his, but she did not smile. Neither of them spoke until the footman on duty in the hall had opened the door for them and shut it behind them.

It was actually lighter outside than it had appeared to be from the drawing room. He gestured to the path on their left as they came down the steps. It meandered across lawns and among scattered oak and beech trees on its way to more dense woodland and the lake and the dower house beyond that. They would not go as far as the woods today, though. Darkness came rather early this late in the year, and darkness in the country could be quite total.

He searched his mind for something to say after she had taken his arm and they had set out along the path, but he could not think of a blessed thing. It was quite unlike him, and he resented it. He resented *her*, which was quite illogical and even more unfair. He almost hated her - at the same time as he was not over her. If he was not careful, he thought, he would be having a childish tantrum, throwing himself to the ground and drumming his heels and his fists on the path. And that would be more than a little alarming.

She took the responsibility for choosing a topic of conversation from him. 'It is *insufferable*,' she said, and he could hear that her voice was vibrating with anger.

'*It?*' There were a number of *its* to which she might be referring.

'All my family and the Westcotts coming here tomorrow,' she said. '*All?* My mother? My *brother?* The dowager countess, my former mother-in-law, who is in her seventies? All of them are coming?'

'If their replies to their invitations are to be believed,' he said.

'It is intolerable,' she said again. 'You ought to have forbidden it.'

'The invitations were sent and the acceptances received before I got wind of it,' he said. 'Or anyone else for that matter. Jane was puce in the face when I came upon her – she had just intercepted a few of the replies. I am not sure Estelle told even Bertrand, which would be most surprising.'

'Then you ought to have put a stop to it as soon as you did know,' she said. 'Have you *no* control over your children?'

He was getting a mite annoyed now too. 'I imagine it would be beyond the pale even for the notorious Marquess of Dorchester to uninvite houseguests when they had already written acceptances,' he said. 'And Estelle did it with the best intentions, you know. She wished to please you. Strange as it may seem, she actually likes you.'

She appeared not to have been listening to those

last words. 'Why did you not tell me you are the Marquess of Dorchester?' she asked.

Had they not dealt with this matter before? Perhaps not. 'For some reason I have not quite fathomed,' he said, 'people treat the Marquess of Dorchester rather differently from the way they treat Mr Lamarr. I thought you might treat me differently.'

'You thought I might be frightened away?' she asked.

'Would you have been?' He could not see her face fully about the brim of her bonnet.

'Yes,' she said.

He was a little taken aback, though he had withheld the truth from her for precisely that reason. 'Why?' he asked.

'I was not exactly a fallen woman when you met me again, Marcel,' she said, 'but I was and am a *tainted* woman. I lived, albeit unknowingly, in a bigamous marriage for twenty-three years. I gave birth to three illegitimate children. I took back my maiden name when I learned the truth and retired to a quiet life, as far from the *ton* as I could get. The closest I have come to returning since then was this past spring when I went to London for Alexander and Wren's wedding. I went to the theater with them one evening. It was not an enjoyable experience, though there was no gasp of outrage when I stepped into the Duke of Netherby's box. I was glad to retire to my quiet life again. And then a few weeks ago I discovered that you are a marquess.'

'You ran away with *me*, not the marquess,' he said. 'Just as I ran away with *you*, not with the tainted former Countess of Riverdale. But what a ridiculous word, Viola – *tainted*.'

'You made an informed decision,' she said. 'I did not. You withheld pertinent information from me.' Her voice was shaking a bit again, a sure sign that she was still furious.

'You would not have enjoyed me so much if you had known you were making love with the Marquess of Dorchester?' he asked. They had stopped under the branches of a large beech. 'He makes love in the same way as Marcel Lamarr does. If our love nest had not been discovered with the two of us more or less in it, would my title have made a difference, Viola? If you had discovered that fact after you had returned home? Would it have made a difference?'

'But that is not what happened,' she said. 'We were discovered, and you made that stupid announcement that we were betrothed, and now look at the mess we are in.'

'*Stupid?*' he said. 'And *are* we in a mess?'

'Yes, stupid,' she said, her eyes flashing too now. 'We should have told the simple truth – that we had gone there for a week or two of relaxation and that we were about to return home. Let them make of it what they would. Good heavens, we are not children or even young adults. It was none of their business why we were there. And any unpleasantness and awkwardness would have blown over by now. We would both have been free.'

'And living happily ever after,' he said.

'And living *separately* ever after,' she said, 'as we had planned and as we wished. We had reached the end, Marcel, but your stupid announcement complicated and prolonged it. And now *this*.' She gestured with one arm toward the house. 'My own family and all the Westcotts arriving tomorrow to celebrate our betrothal in grand style. Do you understand how impossible you have made life for me?'

He gazed at her with narrowed eyes and a cold heart. 'You would take pleasure from sleeping with me,' he said, 'but not from marrying me?'

'Oh, stupid,' she said. *'Stupid.'* It seemed to be today's favorite word.

'You will probably survive the ordeal of marrying a marquess,' he said. 'It is actually quite a coup for you – or so the *ton* will be sure to say.'

Dusk really was gathering about them now. Compounded by the shade of the old tree, it made any clear sight of her face difficult. But every line of her body suggested outrage.

'You arrogant—' She could not seem to find a cutting enough noun to slap up against the adjective.

'Bastard?' he suggested.

'Yes,' she said, her voice colder than the air was getting to be. 'You arrogant bastard.'

He wondered if that word had ever passed her lips before.

'For wanting to marry you?' he asked. 'Am I so inferior to you, then, Viola, that I cannot aspire to your hand?'

She stared long and hard at him and then turned back to the house in obvious exasperation. But before she could take more than one step, he reached across her to grasp her arm.

'*Am* I?' he asked her again, and he could feel her fury recede.

'Marcel,' she said, 'it is impossible. You saw the reaction of your own family toward me – not to mention Abigail – in the drawing room. Can you imagine taking me to London? During the Season? It cannot be allowed to happen. And for more personal reasons it cannot be allowed to proceed. We are going to have to think of some way out, and it is not going to be easy, especially now. We *both* need to think. I am perfectly well aware that you do not want this marriage any more than I do.'

'I can think of one reason why I might find it very tolerable,' he said.

'Oh, life is not all about . . . *that*,' she snapped.

'Sex?'

'Yes,' she said. 'Life is not all about sex.'

'But an important part of it is,' he said.

'*Monogamous* sex?' she asked him, and even in the half light he could see that her eyes were looking very directly into his.

It was something he had committed himself to

once upon a time. Once upon a long time ago. It was something he had assiduously avoided since Adeline's death. It was something—

'I thought not,' she said curtly, and this time when she moved off in the direction of the house, he did not try to stop her. He fell into step beside her after he had caught up, but they did not speak another word.

The next morning after breakfast, Bertrand Lamarr, Viscount Watley, offered to show Viola and Abigail the lake, which he explained was among the trees to the east of the house. His manner was stiff and formal, and Viola suspected he made the offer out of duty rather than inclination. But appearances must be preserved, at least for now. She said she would be delighted. His father, he told her, would be busy for an hour or so with his steward. Lady Estelle decided to come too, as none of the guests could be expected to arrive until the middle of the afternoon at the earliest.

The two young ladies walked ahead, arm in arm. It looked as if Estelle was doing most of the talking, though Abigail was smiling. Viola did not really know how her daughter felt about this whole situation. Strange as it might seem, they had somehow avoided the topic of Viola's betrothal and what had led up to it during the three weeks prior to their coming here. Outwardly their relationship had not changed, but there had been a certain constraint between them.

Bertrand and Viola followed behind. He did not offer his arm but held his hands behind him. He walked close beside her, however, matching his stride to hers and bending his head politely toward her when she was speaking. And he had conversation at the ready – some details about the park, questions about Hinsford, a hope that she found her accommodations here satisfactory. He was perfectly willing to answer her questions. They had lived at Elm Court in East Sussex until two years ago, when they had moved here. He had had a tutor there, a retired scholar who had lived close by and given him excellent instruction in all subjects, particularly in the classics and classical history. Having to leave his tutor behind was what he had most regretted about coming here. Since then he had shared his sister's governess, a worthy lady who had forced him to spend more time and effort on his least favorite subject, mathematics.

'I will be forever grateful to her for that,' he added in all seriousness. 'Children, and adults too, I believe, should always be willing and eager to stretch the limits of their minds in uncomfortable directions as well as in comfortable ones.'

'Most people,' Viola said with a twinkle in her eye, 'are not comfortable with *any* stretching of the mind, Lord Watley.'

'Oh please,' he said, 'call me Bertrand.'

They walked past the beech tree where she had quarreled with Marcel last evening, and on toward the woods and then among them. The path was wide, though at present it was almost obliterated by fallen leaves, which crunched underfoot. There was a lovely feeling of seclusion.

Bertrand was going up to Oxford next year and was looking forward to it immensely even though he had never been away to school and would doubtless be quite nervous at first. And it would mean leaving Estelle behind.

'You are very close to your sister?' Viola asked.

'We have been constant companions all our lives,' he explained. 'There have always been our cousins, of course, but they are older than we are. Not by many years, it is true, but I have been told an age gap seems far wider to children than it does to adults. Estelle and I are the same age. We are twins.'

'Which of you is the elder?' she asked.

'Estelle, by thirty-five minutes,' he said. 'I have never been allowed to forget that fact and never will be, I daresay.' He flashed her a grin, and for a moment he looked the handsome boy he was. And very, very much like his father. Was she seeing Marcel as he had been at the age of seventeen? But no father was quite replicated in his son, and she doubted Marcel had ever had the gravity of mind and manner that his son had. He had gone to Oxford University, but he seemed to have used his time there just to get into trouble, or rather to avoid the trouble his wild exploits ought to have brought him. She doubted he had ever taken his studies seriously. Though he was a reader, she remembered.

They came upon the lake suddenly and unexpectedly. It was surrounded by woodland, a large kidney-shaped body of water, very calm today, its still surface reflecting the myriad colors of the leaves on the trees. There was a sloping stretch of sandy soil ahead of them, which was probably used as a beach during the summer, and a boathouse off to their right. The woodland did not completely surround the lake, however. On the far side some of it had been cleared for a house with large windows and a garden that sloped down to the water. It was not at all like the cottage in Devonshire, but something about it was similar. Its size, perhaps. Its secluded location, perhaps. There was no other building in sight apart from the boathouse.

'The dower house,' Bertrand said. 'I love it. It always makes me feel a bit homesick.'

'For Elm Court?' she asked.

'Yes,' he said. 'Aunt Jane believes Great-Aunt Olwen ought to move here and drops frequent hints to that effect. That is what it was built for, you see – as a *dower* house for older members of the family after a new marquess moves into Redcliffe.'

'But she does not want to live here?' Viola asked.

'No,' he said. 'But I think perhaps it is more that Cousin Isabelle does not want to move here. Perhaps she will feel differently after Margaret marries and moves away with her husband. I am not sure her feelings are going to matter, however. They really must move here after Father's wedding.'

They stood looking at the lake and the house beyond it while Estelle and Abigail made their way toward it. And Viola broached the topic she had been avoiding with her own daughter.

'How do you feel about that, Bertrand?' she asked. 'About your father's marriage to me, I mean. And please be honest.'

'Oh,' he said, 'how can I be?'

Viola winced inwardly, but it was honesty she needed. She wanted to be armed with ammunition the next time she tackled Marcel. 'By simply doing it,' she said.

'I am furious with him,' he said after a short silence, his voice quietly intense. 'Everything has always been just about him. He was supposedly too grief-stricken over our mother's death to spend any time with us when we were children. He was still too grief-stricken when we were older. But we heard things. Children do, you know, no matter how well shielded they are – and we were very well shielded. We heard things that did not make him sound very grief-stricken. Estelle had her heart set on giving him a fortieth birthday party this year. I tried to warn her. So did Aunt Jane. But she would not listen. And then she chose to be *delighted* when we found him and he announced his betrothal. She is *still* delighted. I have never seen her this . . . ebullient. She has always been quiet and docile except sometimes when we are alone together. She thinks all will be well now even though our childhood is over. She will probably be married herself within the next year or so and I will be gone. But she still believes in happily-ever-after. She still believes in *him*. He had no intention of marrying you, did he?'

Well. When one asked for honesty, one had better be prepared for just that. Viola tried to frame a suitable answer but could not think of anything to say.

'Please be honest,' he said, echoing what she had said to him.

'No,' she said. 'What we did was very selfish, Bertrand. I will not try to explain to you why I felt the overwhelming need to escape for a short while and why I took the opportunity when it presented itself. There is no reason why you would care. I did not know that you were waiting so eagerly for your father's return home – I believe you were waiting just as eagerly as your sister was. It seemed harmless, that escape, of no concern to anyone but the two of us. I ought to have known better. I have thought recently about something John Donne wrote in one of his essays.'

'*No man is an island?*' he asked, surprising her.

'Yes,' she said. 'I ended up hurting my family, and your father ended up hurting his. He is not entirely selfish, Bertrand. As soon as he saw Abigail outside that cottage, he believed he must make reparation. And as soon as he saw you and your sister, his resolve was hardened. It was not for himself he made that announcement and not for me. I thought at first it *was* for me, to protect my reputation. But I do not believe he would have said it if Abigail had not come with my son-in-law and the others. He did it for your sake and your sister's and Abigail's. I am sorry. No, that is too easy to say. Apologies usually are.'

'He said that you fell in love with each other years ago,' he said. 'Was that true?'

She hesitated. 'Yes,' she said. 'But I was married then – or thought I was – and we both respected that marriage bond. *Both* of us. There was nothing between us then, except those feelings, which we resisted by avoiding each other.'

'Thank you,' he said after a short silence. 'Would you like to walk around to the dower house?'

Abigail and Estelle were wandering about the outside of it.

Should she tell him, Viola wondered, that she was not going to marry his father? Or would that be unfair to Marcel before they had worked out how it was to be done?

'Yes,' she said, but before they could resume their walk they both turned at the sound of foot-steps crunching on the leaves behind them. It was Marcel.

She had avoided him last evening after they had returned to the house. She had not seen him this morning. He had already been shut up with his steward when she came downstairs to breakfast with Abigail, dreading seeing him again.

He looked as he had in Devonshire, dressed warmly in his many-caped greatcoat and top boots, his tall hat pulled firmly onto his head. And her insides turned over even as she despised herself for the pleasurable awareness the mere sight of him aroused in her. No, it was *not* pleasurable. Not when it was something that involved only her body while her mind and her very being told her otherwise. If she was in love with him, then being in love was mindless and not at all something to be desired and reveled in.

His eyes held hers before moving to his son. And in that look, unguarded for the first moment, she read something that pulled at her heart and shook her resolve yet again, though she could not put a name to it. Pride? Love? Longing? Did he see something of himself in the boy? Something better than himself?

'Thank you, Bertrand,' he said, 'for entertaining our guest.'

His son was stiff and formal again as he inclined his head. 'It has been my pleasure, sir,' he said.

Marcel looked across the lake to where his daughter was pointing upward toward the chimney or roof of the dower house, or perhaps an upper window while Abigail looked upward too.

'Would you like to see the dower house?' he asked Viola.

'Bertrand was about to escort me there,' she said.

'Good.' He offered her his arm. 'And I have brought the key. It is a pleasant house. Sometimes I think perhaps I should move there if my aunt does not wish to. With my children. And you.'

His eyes came to rest on her as she slid her hand through his arm. 'What do you think, Bertrand?'

'I think being the Marquess of Dorchester imposes obligations that necessitate your living at the main house, sir,' his son said as they set off along the path about the lake.

'Rather than the dower house or anywhere else,' his father said. 'One cannot escape duty, then? Or ought not?'

'I can only speak for myself, sir,' his son said. 'Living at the dower house – or anywhere – with you and your wife would be a dream come true for Estelle.'

Viola felt a slight twitch in Marcel's arm.

'You do not believe in dreams?' he asked his son.

Bertrand did not answer for a few moments. 'I believe in dreams, sir,' he said. 'I also believe in the reality of the fact that very few come true.'

Marcel's eyes moved to Viola. 'And what do you think, my love?' he asked.

'Dreams cannot come true if the dreamer does not have the resolve to make them reality,' she said.

'*The resolve*,' Marcel said. 'Is it enough?'

No one ventured a reply, and the question hovered like a tangible thing over their heads.

CHAPTER 17

Viola had gone upstairs with the young people to see the bedchambers. Marcel could hear them talking up there – all four of them. He had missed that time when his son's voice had changed from a boy's to a young man's. And he had missed the change in his daughter from demure, rather colorless girl to eager, forceful young lady, though he suspected that change had been far more recent. Indeed, perhaps he had not missed it at all. Perhaps it had begun with her disappointment that he had not come home when he had said he would come, and the resulting anger had propelled her into adulthood.

He had remained downstairs in the drawing room – if the room in which he stood could be dignified with so grand a name. It was a large sitting room but cozy too – or would be if a fire were burning in the hearth. As it was, he was glad he had kept his greatcoat on when he removed his hat and gloves after stepping inside. He stood gazing through the large window upon woodland and the lake and the boathouse and more woodland beyond.

Something about it all reminded him of the cottage, where he had been so happy.

Happy?

That was a strange word to use. He had enjoyed himself there. Enormously. He could have stayed for another week at least without being bored or restless – if she had not grown both, and if their families had not descended upon them when they had.

He had also been *happy* there, damn it all. He pushed his hands into his pockets for warmth and listened to the voices, though he could not hear the actual words, coming from above, and he felt like . . . crying?

What the devil?

What the devil had he done with his life?

He had enjoyed it – that was what.

Living at the dower house – or anywhere – with you and your wife would be a dream come true for Estelle.

I believe in dreams . . . I also believe in the reality of the fact that very few come true.

Dreams cannot come true if the dreamer does not have the resolve to make them reality.

It was strange how one seemingly insignificant decision could cause turmoil and upset the whole course of one's life. Less than two months ago he had decided quite upon the spur of the moment to send André home with the carriage while he stayed to speak with the former Countess of Riverdale, to persuade her to spend the afternoon with him at the village fair, to coax her into spending the night with him. One small decision, quite in keeping with what his life had been like for the past seventeen years.

It had led to this.

If he had decided differently and been content merely to nod civilly to her across the width of the taproom and dining room before leaving with his brother, he would have come home, suffered through the unspeakable horror of the birthday party Estelle had planned, and been gone from here already in search of new amusement. He would have been safe.

'I cannot understand why Great-Aunt Olwen does not want to come here to live,' Estelle said from behind him. 'I would in her place. I could be very happy here, Papa. It is not really small, is it? There are eight bedchambers. But it is cozy.'

He turned from the window. 'And what would you do for amusement?' he asked.

She looked blankly at him before shrugging her shoulders. 'What do I do now?' she asked. 'I could read and paint and embroider and write in my diary and pay visits and receive visitors just as easily here as I can there. But it would be peaceful here. It would feel more like a home.'

'The dower house is not quite as cut off from civilization as it may appear to be,' Bertrand explained to Viola and her daughter. 'Just through the trees behind here there are stables and a carriage house, empty now, of course, but still quite serviceable, and a wide pathway that connects with the main drive.'

'Come and see the stables,' Estelle suggested, and she led the way from the room. Abigail and Bertrand followed her. Marcel did not move, and neither did Viola. The front door opened and closed.

They gazed at each other for several silent moments.

'Does it remind you?' he asked, nodding toward the window and the view beyond. 'Even just faintly?'

'Of Devonshire?' she asked. 'Yes. But we were alone there.'

'It was good,' he said. 'Was it not?'

She turned her head to gaze out the window. 'It was,' she said. 'It was exactly what it was intended to be, Marcel – a brief escape from our lives. It was never intended to be converted into anything permanent. Neither you nor I wanted that. And it had run its course. You told me on the beach that my telling you I wanted to go home saved you from having to hurt me. You told me that you hated hurting your women.'

Good God! Had he really said that? But he knew he had. 'Could I possibly have been so unmannerly?' he asked anyway.

'You were merely being honest,' she said. 'I know you have other women, Marcel, and always have – and always will, I daresay. I had no illusions when I decided to run away with you. It was a temporary arrangement, and I was contented with that. I am not contented with . . . with this.'

'The *always will* part is unjust,' he said. 'When I marry, Viola, it is for all time. Until death do us part.'

She turned her head away from the window to frown at him. 'What happened?' she asked him.

He raised his eyebrows and felt a chill about his heart. He knew what she was asking.

'What happened with your marriage?' she explained. 'With your wife. How did she die?'

He did not want to talk about this. He did not want to think about it. The air in the room suddenly felt too thin to breathe.

'She fell out of an upstairs window to the terrace below,' he said curtly. 'She died instantly.' He swung about to face the window, though he was unaware now of the view beyond it. He willed her to go away, to follow the young people. But he could not hear her go. So he added the final detail. 'I killed her.'

Silence. Except for the dull thudding in his ears of his own heartbeat. He wished he were sitting down. He wished he were alone. He wished he were dead too. He wished . . .

'You cannot possibly leave it at that,' she said from behind him, and he swung about again to glare at her, fury almost blinding him.

'Why not?' he asked her. 'What happened is none of your damned business, Viola. Unless, that is, you think I may do the same thing to you when I grow tired of you or when you annoy me. Go away, or I may do it now.'

Her frown was back. 'I am sorry,' she said. 'I am so sorry to have ripped open such a deep wound. But you must tell me.'

'Why?' he asked. 'You are determined not to marry me, it seems. And even if you change your mind, you have no business prying into my first marriage. I do not pry into yours.'

'How can I believe you killed her,' she asked, 'when you did not hang or even spend time in prison?'

'It was ruled an accident,' he said. 'A tragic accident. Leave it alone, Viola. I will not speak of it. Ever. As for now, you tired of me in Devonshire before I had quite tired of you. You did not want to be saved from scandal when we got back to the cottage. You would have preferred to brazen the situation out rather than betroth yourself to me. You have not changed your mind since then. You made that perfectly clear last night. So. Make the announcement today, tomorrow, whenever you choose. I will not try to stop you.'

It was one hell of a time to realize that his heart would be broken, that it probably already was. When had he suddenly acquired a heart? Perhaps she had not really meant her dismissal of him; perhaps she did not resent their betrothal as much as she said she did; perhaps . . .

Perhaps nothing. She had made herself perfectly clear.

He could only make an ass of himself by telling her now that he had not got over her at all, that he did not believe he ever would. He could only make a nuisance of himself by begging her to marry him anyway. Though he knew that for the sake of his children and her own he would keep pressing her to do just that.

Good God! He had just told her he killed Adeline. Which he had done.

'You will be glad,' she said. 'You do not want to marry me, Marcel. It was never part of our plan. Very far from it.'

'A thousand miles from it,' he agreed. 'But we are in the devil of a coil, Viola. My sister is arriving this afternoon, along with all your family. A big party is imminent. Our children appear to like one another.'

They both turned their heads to watch the three young people make their way back about the lake in the direction of the main house. Bertrand was in the middle, Estelle on one arm, Abigail on the other.

'So,' she said, 'we take the easy way out and celebrate our betrothal here. And at Christmas we take the easy way out and celebrate our wedding. And then we face the rest of our lives.'

'You make it sound like a bleak prospect,' he said.

They looked at each other, and their eyes held.

'I cannot face another marriage that might be anything like my first nonmarriage, Marcel,' she said.

He winced inwardly but said nothing.

'And you—' she said, and circled the air with one hand, in search of words that would not come.

'And I am an incurable libertine,' he said.

'Well.' She frowned once more. 'Aren't you?'

'Except when I am married,' he said, 'as I pointed out earlier. But I have not been married for a long, long time, and during that time I have indeed been a libertine. I daresay you are right, Viola. I daresay I am incurable.'

But he felt hurt. He wanted to beg and protest and justify. He wanted to . . .

She did not want him. She had enjoyed their idyll and had tired of it and wanted to go home. Just as he ought to have done.

Damn him for a fool for having sent his brother home in his carriage instead of going with him and forgetting the former Countess of Riverdale.

'I am going back to the house,' she told him.

'And like the gentleman I am I will escort you,' he said.

But they did not touch as they walked, or exchange another word. He was reminded of their walk back from the beach to the cottage in Devonshire. He ought to have grabbed her then before the cottage came in sight and had it out properly with her – the truth, the whole truth, and nothing but the truth, just as he wanted to do now.

But it would be unfair to her and humiliating to himself to pour out his love now and his commitment to fidelity and forever-after and love eternal and all that drivel. She had tired of him. She had never given the smallest hint that she loved him or wanted a future with him.

Humility attacked him like a hammer blow to the stomach.

She did not love him. She had told him that in so many words. He was going to have to allow her to go free, to extricate herself from this mess somehow. He could not do it himself. A gentleman did not repudiate a betrothal once he had committed to it. Or once he had invited her to his own home, and all her family and his were gathering to celebrate with his neighbors.

Good God! It was enough to make the hair stand up on the back of his neck.

The walk back to the house seemed interminable.

After she returned from the dower house with Marcel, Viola retreated to her room and wrestled with the temptation to leave, to send word that her carriage was to be before the doors within a half hour, to send word to Abigail that she must pack up her things without delay. She wanted to be gone. She wanted to forget.

Two months or so ago she had run from Bath – to escape from the suffocating love of her family. Two days after that she had run again – to escape from herself to the mindless pleasure of a love affair with a libertine. Much good it had all done her. It had brought her to this, to an entanglement far more complicated than anything she had known before.

For this time, of course, she could not run. Estelle had gone to a great deal of trouble to plan this house party and the betrothal party tomorrow evening. And she was bubbling over with excitement, a girl of seventeen who had lived a sheltered existence with her uncle and aunt but who had longed for her father's presence in her life and now thought she was about to get it.

She could not run. Her mother was on the way here. Camille and Joel and the children were on the way. So were Michael and Mary. So were all the Westcotts, even her former mother-in-law. Even Anna, Humphrey's legitimate daughter. And Wren, with whom she had struck up such a lovely and unexpected friendship back in the spring. Wren was pregnant, but she was coming anyway. Viola could not possibly not be here herself when they arrived.

And there was Marcel. He had accepted reality this morning, telling her that he would not stand in the way of her announcing that there was to be no betrothal. And only she could do that, of course. Honor dictated that the man could not.

And this morning he had told her how his wife died and had claimed that he killed her. She did not for a moment believe him, though she believed he did. What had happened? She ached to know, but she had no right to insist. They were not going to be married. She had felt in him this morning, however, an unbearable pain at the memories he had held close all these years and refused to share now.

What had happened?

She had ached to tell him she loved him, that when she had said down on the beach that she needed to go home, she had not meant that she was tired of their affair, that she had no feelings left for him. But she had not said it. He had not announced their betrothal because he loved her and wanted to marry her. She could be absolutely sure of that, having known him and his reputation for many years. He was not a settling man. He had told her he was glad he had not been forced to speak up first. He had told her he did not like to hurt his women.

His women.

Plural.

As she had always known. As she knew when she agreed to run away with him.

She could not run, then, but she could not stay either. She could not marry him, but she could not break the betrothal either. She could not love him, but she could not stop loving him either.

She stayed. Of course she did. And she prepared for the arrival of his sister and her own family. She drew about her the long-familiar mantle of the Countess of Riverdale and waited.

But what was she to do? She could not marry Marcel.

What was she to do?

Annemarie and William Cornish were first to arrive, early in the afternoon, bringing their two young children with them. Marcel and the twins met them on the terrace. Estelle hugged the children, aged seven and five, while Bertrand shook William's hand and Marcel found himself being hugged tightly by his sister.

'I am so very happy that you are to remarry at last, Marc,' she said. 'And not before time either. I have hardly stopped talking about it, have I, Will?'

Cornish exchanged a sober glance with his brother-in-law but said nothing.

As usual Annemarie filled the drawing room with her presence as soon as they stepped inside it. She hugged everyone gathered there, including Abigail and Viola, talking the whole while.

'I was just telling Marc how delighted I am,' she told Viola. 'Marriage will be good for him. It is high time he settled down. Gracious, he is *forty*. Just imagine! And you will be able to bring Estelle out during the Season in London next spring, and your daughter will be good company for her. They will be stepsisters. It will be a dream come true, I am sure, for Estelle to have her own stepmother sponsoring her.'

William cleared his throat, and she looked at him inquiringly before wheeling about to smile at Jane. 'I am perfectly sure you were willingly and self-lessly prepared to take Estelle to London yourself, Jane. But I am sure that now you must be eager to resume your own interrupted life at last.'

'Well, it *was* interrupted, Annemarie,' Jane

admitted, 'quite suddenly and unexpectedly when our own children were no older than yours are now. But Charles and I would do it again and for twice as long if we had to. I was dearly fond of Adeline, and I *am* dearly fond of her children.'

Marcel had never really thought of the past seventeen years in terms of any sacrifice Jane and Charles Morrow had had to make. He had always recognized his need of them, but he had always seen it from his point of view. Never from theirs. He had resented their influence over his children even though he had chosen not to raise them himself. They had left behind a home of their own in order to move to Elm Court – theirs had been leased out until very recently by a retired admiral and his wife.

The thing was, though, he did not want to start looking at things from other people's point of view. His own was quite bothersome enough.

And this was just the beginning. Viola's own family, Kingsleys and Westcotts, would be here before the day was out. Not counting children, Estelle had informed him, there were to be seventeen of them. *Seventeen.* And that was in addition to Abigail and Viola herself.

He felt an almost overwhelming urge to leave. Just to walk out, get his carriage, or even just saddle a horse, and leave. His baggage and his valet could follow him. No explanations to anyone. No warnings. No goodbyes. He had done it before – more than once. Just a couple of months or so ago he would not have hesitated, or looked back, or suffered a qualm of conscience.

This time it just could not be done. For his daughter – and his son too – stood squarely in his way. He looked from one to the other of them as chatter continued around him – and felt an equal measure of resentment and aching love. Estelle was flushed and bubbling over with excitement now with the arrival of her uncle and aunt and the imminent appearance of the seventeen. He was not certain how many neighbors were expected to come to the party tomorrow evening. He had not asked. He did not want to know.

Why had she done it? Why the birthday party? Because she *loved* him? How was it possible? He was the most wretchedly bad father on the face of the earth. And why the betrothal party?

And Bertrand. Not quite eighteen. An awkward, often rebellious age, not quite a youth, not quite a man. Quietly backing his sister every step of the way. Courteously entertaining the woman he had caught with his father at that wretched cottage. Conversing now with his uncle and Ortt. Treating even his despicable father with unfailing courtesy.

No, he would not run. He was increasingly certain that he would never be able to run again. It was one of the most terrifying thoughts he had had in the past seventeen years. His eyes rested upon Viola as she spoke with Annemarie and Ellen Morrow. He wished this morning had not happened. Last night was bad enough, but now there seemed

314

little doubt that this betrothal everyone was gathering to celebrate was about to be ended. He must continue to behave as if it were real, however, until it was not. And then? He would think about that when it happened.

Annemarie was explaining to Viola that their mother had been French and had insisted that all her children have French names. And Adeline had admired her mother-in-law so much that she had insisted upon giving *her* children French names too.

'My sister is Camille,' Abigail said. 'I do not know why she has a French name.'

'I liked it,' Viola said, 'just as I liked *Abigail* when you were born.'

'Here comes another carriage,' Bertrand said, turning from the window and looking across the room at his father.

And so it was continuing. And again there was the urge to leave the drawing room and turn left toward the back stairs, used mostly by the servants, instead of right toward the main staircase and the hall below. To run away. As he had done seventeen years ago and had continued to do ever since.

Until now.

'It will be someone from your family,' he said to Viola. 'Will you come down with Estelle and Bertrand and me? And Abigail too?'

These arrivals were Lord and Lady Molenor – she was a Westcott, former sister-in-law to Viola. But everyone else came hard upon their heels – the Earl and Countess of Riverdale; the Duke and Duchess of Netherby and their baby with Netherby's half sister, Lady Jessica Archer, and the dowager duchess, the girl's mother, also a former sister-in-law of Viola's. Why did family relationships have to be so complicated? Then came Mrs Kingsley, Viola's mother, with Cunningham and his wife, Camille, Viola's elder daughter, and their three children; Viola's clergyman brother with his wife; Elizabeth, Lady Overfield, and her mother, Mrs Westcott, Riverdale's mother; and, as a grand finale, the Dowager Countess of Riverdale, Viola's former mother-in-law, and her daughter, Lady Matilda Westcott. Seventeen of them, not counting the children. Not that Marcel counted off the seventeen. The number seemed more like seventy to him.

Seventeen further complications to what was going to have to happen before they all took their leave again. To what Viola was surely going to make happen – with his blessing. Why *the devil* had he behaved with such totally uncharacteristic chivalry outside that damned cottage in Devonshire and announced their betrothal?

The last two carriages had arrived almost simultaneously. Marcel offered his arm to the elderly dowager countess and led her slowly up the steps to the house while Bertrand and Abigail came behind with Mrs Westcott, Riverdale's mother. Estelle chatted merrily with Lady Overfield as though they were old friends, and Viola made soothing noises as Lady Matilda Westcott shared her fear that her mother had overtired herself.

How was Viola going to tell these family members that they had come all this way for nothing? And why *had* they done such an asinine thing when the wedding was supposed to be celebrated within two months?

Because they loved her?

'Young man,' the dowager countess said in a voice that was pitched low, for his ears only. 'I will be wanting a private word with you before the party your daughter has planned for tomorrow and what I suppose will be the official announce-ment of your betrothal. I have not seen it in the papers yet. Viola will try to insist that she is not my daughter-in-law and never has been, but that is arrant nonsense. She is as precious to me as any of my three daughters, and they are precious, as daughters always are. You will know the truth of that for yourself, I daresay. I want to hear from your own lips how precious my daughter-in-law is to you.'

Good God! So he was to be interrogated by a frail old dragon, was he? She was the first one to speak up – if one discounted Riverdale and Cunningham, who had spoken up back in Devonshire. But Viola's mother had given him a long, measured look upon her arrival, and her clergyman son had regarded him gravely, as though he were merely biding his time until he could find a suitable moment during which to unleash a sermon. Lady Matilda had looked sour out there on the terrace when Viola introduced them, and Lady Overfield had twinkled at him as though in sympathy for what was in store for him.

For what we are about to receive . . .

'I shall look forward to a private conversation with you, ma'am,' he assured the dowager countess, lying through his teeth.

Yes, by God, they loved her.

And no, by God, he could not run. Estelle was looking near to bursting with pride and happiness. He was going to have to stay to cope with the opposite when it happened, as it surely would sometime within the next twenty-four hours or so. Not run from it, but stay to deal with it.

Good Lord.

CHAPTER 18

'I hear there is a pretty conservatory here, Lord Dorchester,' the Dowager Countess of Riverdale said the following morning after breakfast. He had been hoping to escape into his steward's office for a while, but it had always been a forlorn hope when today was going to be frantic with activity before it culminated in an early family dinner and the grand party in the ballroom to follow.

'There is, ma'am,' he said. 'Would you care to see it?' He had seen the conservatory a time or two, but he knew nothing about the plants that grew there. He did not suppose she wished to see it in order to have each plant identified, however.

'I shall go and fetch your warm shawl, Mama, and bring it to you there,' Lady Matilda Westcott said.

'You will do no such thing,' her mother said. 'When I need a warmer shawl, Matilda, I shall send a maid to fetch it. And I do not need any company but Lord Dorchester's.'

Lady Matilda, Marcel had observed, was the

spinster daughter who had remained at home as a prop and stay to her mother, who needed neither.

The conservatory was full of greenery rather than flowers. It was rather cleverly done, large plants mingled with small, broad-leafed plants mingled with narrow, plants with light green leaves alongside those with dark leaves. And lots of glass – three walls of it as well as a roof. It was a sunny morning, and the conservatory was bright and really quite warm. It would make a wonderfully romantic setting for a tryst. There were window seats with soft cushions, but he seated the dowager on a firm-backed sofa before perching on the window seat across from her.

'You wish to interrogate me, ma'am.' There was no point in launching into a conversation about plants he could not even name. He looked very directly at the dowager without a glimmer of a smile, an expression he knew many people found intimidating on his face, though he was not expecting it to have that effect upon her. It was perhaps a defensive expression, as was his nonchalant posture.

'My son,' she said, 'was the greatest disappointment of my life, Lord Dorchester. And that was while he lived. Afterward he was the greatest shame of my life. Because of his misdeeds one of my granddaughters grew up in an orphanage, without the comfort of any family at all. Two other granddaughters and a grandson grew up with a false idea of who they were and suffered the overturning of the world they had known when the truth came out. Because of his misdeeds my daughter-in-law endured unspeakable humiliation and was cut asunder from a whole family of people she had considered her own for almost a quarter of a century. *In her own mind* she was cut asunder. Not in ours. She is a Westcott as surely as any of the rest of us are, even though she took back her maiden name and has clung to it ever since.'

She stopped and glared at him as though to say – unnecessarily – that she did not find him in any way intimidating.

'Miss Kingsley is fortunate to have such a loving and loyal family, ma'am,' he said. His words sounded lame and fell quite flat.

'I want you to give me one good reason, Lord Dorchester,' she said, 'why we should entrust one of our own into your keeping. One good reason why we should welcome you into the family, as we welcomed Joel Cunningham last year and Wren Heyden earlier this year.'

He looked steadily back at her. 'I cannot, ma'am,' he said.

That certainly had its effect. She leaned farther back into the cushions, rather as though he had reached out a hand and shoved her.

'I do not doubt you are aware of my reputation,' he said. 'I do not doubt all of you are. It has been hard-won, and I apologize for none of it. If I regret anything in my life, the regrets are mine. They are not the property of a disapproving *ton* or even of the disapproving family of the woman to whom I am betrothed. That I have the birth and rank and fortune to support your daughter-in-law for the rest of her life is beyond question. But that is *not* the question, I know. You want her to be happy at last because you love her.'

'And do *you* love her, Lord Dorchester?' she asked.

It was the inevitable question. He had been hoping even so to avoid it. He could not even answer it for himself. He knew he had been in love with her fourteen years ago, but fourteen years was a long time. He was not the same person now he had been then. Anyway, what did being in love mean? Anything at all? He knew that he had wanted her when he took the madcap risk of sending André away with his carriage, that he had enjoyed her more than he could remember enjoying any woman before her, that he had not been nearly done with her when she was done with him, that he was still not over her. But love? Love was a forever-after thing, was it not? An in-sickness-and-in-death thing – or was that in sickness and in health? It was a steadfast all-or-nothing thing, or rather an all-in-all thing. It was an amputation of everything he had been for almost twenty years and . . . But his mind would not take him further. It did not matter anyway. He was not going to marry her.

'Yes,' he said softly.

There was a lengthy silence.

'I have no control over what any member of my

family does,' she said at last. 'Least of all with Viola. And you know that, Lord Dorchester. You might have invited me to go to the devil rather than agree to bring me here. Instead, you have listened to me and answered my questions with what seems to me to be blunt honesty. I thank you for that. Whether you can bring Viola happiness remains to be seen, but no couple can ever know that for certain when they marry. I am going to trust you not to break an old lady's heart as well as hers.'

'Thank you, ma'am,' he said, getting to his feet.

But he was not free even after returning her to the morning room, where a number of other people were gathered to stay out of the way of the servants who were dashing about to prepare the house for the celebrations later. Before he could excuse himself, Mrs Kingsley discovered an urgent desire to view his library, and her son, the Reverend Michael Kingsley, thought he would rather like to see it too since he had not brought more than one book with him from home.

It was much the same sort of interview as the last one. Mrs Kingsley told him how delighted her late husband had been when the Earl of Riverdale, a slight acquaintance of his, had broached the possibility of a marriage between his son and Viola. The earl had made no secret of the fact that his son was sowing some wild oats and was impecunious to a fault, but both fathers had agreed that marriage – with a great infusion of money from the deep Kingsley coffers, of course – would be a steadying influence upon the young man. And the *young man*, she added rather bitterly, had doubtless been pressured into agreeing with the threat that there was no other way to settle his astronomical debts. He had agreed despite the fact that, unknown to his father or anyone else, he was already married to a woman who was dying of consumption and they had a daughter.

'I acquiesced, Lord Dorchester,' Mrs Kingsley said, 'even though Viola fancied herself in love with the son of a friend of mine and he with her. It is easy for parents to brush aside very young love when they can convince themselves that they have the greater good of their child at heart. I have never forgiven myself. My weakness has haunted me even more during the past couple of years.'

'Unfortunately, Mama,' the Reverend Michael Kingsley said, 'we can never look ahead to see the consequences of the decisions we make.' And never were truer words spoken, Marcel thought. 'We can only make them with the best intentions in mind and with love in our hearts.'

He was a bit of a pompous man, Viola's brother. But he had come all the way from Dorsetshire, abandoning his flock there, because his sister was of great immediate concern to him. There was a story somewhere in the Bible, Marcel seemed to remember, about a shepherd who left his whole flock to fend for themselves while he went in search of the one lost sheep. A rash thing to do, that, though the story illustrated a point. Good God, was he about to start quoting Scripture? The mind boggled.

'I understand,' Marcel said, 'that you are afraid Viola is about to step into another marriage that will bring her as little happiness as the first one did. That perhaps it will bring her actual misery.'

One thing to be said in Kingsley's favor was that he did not beat about any bushes. 'We are mortally afraid, Dorchester,' he said. 'I was a moral coward during my sister's first marriage. I did not like or approve of Riverdale, and so I avoided him. In doing so, of course, I avoided her too. I am ashamed of that neglect. It will not happen again. If you do any harm to my sister, I will find you and call you to account.'

He ought to have sounded ridiculous. Marcel had a mental image of pacing out the steps of a duel and turning, pistol cocked, to face this man, who had possibly never held a gun in his life. But try as he would, he could not make the clergyman in that mental image into a figure of fun.

'I will not hurt her,' he said.

'Tell me, Lord Dorchester,' Mrs Kinglsey said before asking the inevitable question, 'do you love her?'

He did not even have to think about it this time, though he knew the answer no better than he had an hour ago.

'Yes,' he said curtly.

★　　★　　★

Viola kept out of the way of the busy preparations for the party as much as she could all day. It was not difficult. She spent an hour after breakfast in the nursery with the children. Winifred was in her element playing mother to Annemarie's two children, who were both younger than she and were quite happy to be organized by someone they looked upon with evident admiration. Sarah was happy to play a clapping game with her grandmother, while Camille and Anna rocked the babies and talked with each other. It was good to see those two grow ever more accepting of the fact that they were half sisters. It had been difficult at first, especially for Camille. And Viola herself was beginning to love Anna, partly because she was determined to do so and partly because she could not help herself.

She drank coffee in the morning room with her former mother-in-law, who informed her that if she must marry a rogue, she could do worse than the Marquess of Dorchester, who was clearly prepared to turn over a new page in his life and who was just as clearly in love. Afterward, Viola went for a walk with Elizabeth and Wren and Annemarie. Viola and Elizabeth walked ahead while Marcel's sister questioned Wren about the glassworks she had inherited from her uncle and ran herself.

'I was worried about you after Jacob's christening,' Elizabeth said. 'It seemed to me that everything from the past couple of years had come over you all of a sudden and overwhelmed you. We all felt helpless to console you, for of course we were part of the problem. Sometimes people just need to be alone, and the best those who love them can do to help is simply to leave them alone. But it is very hard to do.'

'It is,' Viola agreed. 'Watching those we love suffer can be worse in some ways than suffering ourselves.'

'But you found the perfect solution.' Elizabeth laughed. 'Oh, I was very prepared to be horrified when I saw who it was you had run away with to that cottage in Devon. I had a slight acquaintance with the Marquess of Dorchester and was fully aware of his reputation. He is, of course, extraordinarily handsome, and that can be a dangerous attribute in a man who is also devastatingly attractive. But it was clear there and has become clearer here that he feels a sincere attachment to you. You should see how he looks at you when he believes you are not looking at him. It makes me quite envious. It is equally clear that you return his feelings. I do love a happy ending.' She sighed theatrically and laughed again. 'Your mother and brother are having a word with him.'

'My mother-in-law already has,' Viola said.

'Poor man,' Elizabeth said, and they both laughed.

Annemarie and Wren caught up to them at that point and conversation became general.

Viola spent the early part of the afternoon in the portrait gallery on an upper floor with Camille and Joel and Ellen Morrow and her brother. While Joel studied the family portraits and Ellen identified them, Camille smiled at Viola and strolled with her to the end of the gallery, where there was a window overlooking the park behind the house.

'It is beautiful here, Mama,' Camille said, 'and you are going to be happy. I came determined to dislike the Marquess of Dorchester, you know, for he was always so fearfully handsome and . . . well . . .' She smiled again. 'I have changed my mind. Not that that matters anyway. You have chosen your happiness just as I did last year with Joel. And I *am* happy, Mama. Happier than I ever dreamed of being. I can only wish the same for you. And for Abby. And Harry.'

They caught at each other's hands at the mention of his name and squeezed tightly. They both blinked back tears.

Viola went for another walk later with Michael and Mary, and her brother told her gravely that she had his blessing, but only if she promised him that she would be happy this time. He said it with an uncharacteristic twinkle in his eye.

'Michael still feels guilty about not voicing his concern over your first marriage, Viola,' Mary explained. 'He wanted to come here so that he could speak up this time if he felt he ought.'

Viola looked inquiringly at her brother.

'I feel that I *ought* to object,' he said, frowning, 'both as a man of the cloth and as your brother.

The Marquess of Dorchester did not endear himself to me by reputation. But I have the curious feeling that I might be making an unpardonable mistake if I did so. Mama agrees with me.'

And her mother did indeed pat her daughter's hand when Viola joined her and the marchioness and Isabelle for a cup of tea in the morning room and heard yet again all about the plans for Margaret's wedding.

'I admire your energy, Lady Ortt,' her mother said. 'I feel I should be similarly busy over Viola's wedding to Lord Dorchester. However, I am content to leave it all in younger hands, and the Countess of Riverdale is eager to organize the wedding at Brambledean over Christmas.' She smiled at her daughter.

Viola's three former sisters-in-law bore her off to look at the conservatory during the afternoon.

'I will envy you this, Viola,' Mildred, Lady Molenor said. 'I wonder if I can persuade Thomas to build on to our house.' She laughed. 'Perhaps it would be easier to come and visit you often.'

'I cannot tell you in all honesty, Viola,' Matilda said, 'that I approve of what you did after leaving Bath so abruptly. However, we all understood that the family celebration of young Jacob's christening somehow opened up old wounds for you. So I am willing to grant that your meeting the Marquess of Dorchester when you did was fortuitous, and I wish you happy. You are still and always will be our sister, you know, so you must expect plain speaking from us. Your marrying again will not change that.' She looked severely at Viola.

'And since it was Humphrey, *our brother*, who caused you all your distress,' Louise, Dowager Duchess of Netherby, added, 'then we can only be happy that you are having your revenge, Viola. We still wish fervently that he were still alive so that we could throttle him ourselves.'

'Indeed,' Mildred agreed. 'Oh, just *look* at these cushioned window seats. I could spend hours here just gazing out.'

Nobody urged Viola to end her betrothal before it was too late. *Nobody.* It was quite incredible.

But what of herself? She could not marry Marcel, of course. No one but the two of them knew the whole story of why they had run away together and what their intentions had been. No one knew that it had been a regular sort of sexual fling for him and an impulsive self-indulgence for her. No one knew that there was not and never had been any declaration of love between them or any intention of prolonging their liaison beyond its natural end. It had reached that end. She had yearned to return to her life, and he would surely have tired of her very soon if she had not spoken up when she had. Indeed, his words on the beach had been a clear indication that he was close to that point. He had already begun speaking of her as just one of his women.

That still stung.

Everyone was mistaken. Her relatives, who loved

her and wanted her to be happy, were seeing in Marcel what they wanted to see, and he, as a gallant gentleman, was playing up to their expectations. After all, if she did not put an end to their betrothal, he would be compelled to marry her. But he could not possibly be happy about being so trapped – trapped by his own outrageous announcement, it might be added. He did not love her. He could not possibly settle down with her in a marriage that would bring her or himself any lasting contentment. She was not even young or youthfully pretty. She was older than he. And even if he did settle down to a certain degree, how could she settle for less than love? And she did not need to marry. She had been essentially alone all her adult life. She could continue alone. The only thing – the *only* one – that might induce her to marry was love. She could not even define it. But she did not need to. She *knew* love even if she could not describe it.

She loved Marcel.

But he did not love her. He had never said anything to lead her to believe that he did. Everyone was mistaken. Oh, they were all wrong.

At least she did not see much of him during the day. He was being interviewed by her well-meaning family members during the morning, and she believed he was with his children during the afternoon. She felt sick as the day wore on. Time was running out. The official announcement of their betrothal was to be made tonight, yet she had still said nothing of the truth to anyone but Marcel himself.

What would she say? And when?

Time was running out. She could not allow that announcement to be made. She was going to have to speak up at dinner. Just before the party.

She felt sick.

And when she thought of Estelle, who had been flushed and bright-eyed at breakfast, she felt even sicker.

Why, oh why, had she not simply spoken up when Marcel made that outrageous announcement to her family outside the cottage? It had seemed impossible at the time. But compared with now . . .

Well . . .

After luncheon, Marcel decided that it was time he initiated an interview of his own. He found Bertrand in the billiard room with Oliver Morrow, the Duke of Netherby, André, and William Cornish. They found Estelle in the housekeeper's room, going over one of her endless lists for tonight's party and doubtless delaying that lady from getting on with business. She threw the two men an almost openly grateful look when they took Estelle away.

They went to the ballroom, the three of them, to see how preparations were proceeding there. It was clean from top to bottom. The wooden floor gleamed from a new coating of polish, though parts of it were overlaid with sheets upon which the two grand crystal chandeliers rested. The crystal shone, and the silver was its rightful color again rather than the black it had been the last time Marcel had looked. Each candle holder had been fitted with a new candle.

'They will be raised later,' Estelle explained, 'and flowers will be brought in and arranged. They are to be left as long as possible so that they will look fresh tonight.'

Tables in the adjoining anteroom had been spread with crisply starched white cloths, upon which refreshments and punch bowls and other beverages would be placed later.

'I expected that we would make do with the pianoforte,' Estelle said, looking toward the orchestra dais at the other end of the room, 'but Bert told me about a trio that plays for the assemblies in the village and we have hired them.'

'There will be a violin and a cello and flute to add to the pianoforte,' Bertrand said. 'At first I suggested this room rather than the drawing room merely because there will be so many of us. But then it occurred to us that there could be dancing.'

'And Aunt Jane thought it would be acceptable even though Bert and I are not yet quite eighteen,' Estelle said. 'I have never danced at an assembly.'

'Then you will dance with me tonight,' Marcel said. 'You have done well, both of you.' He clasped his hands at his back and abruptly changed the subject. 'Tell me. Does your apparent approval of my marriage plans stem mainly from your desire to have me live permanently here at Redcliffe with you?' He wheeled about to look at them. They were standing side by side, very much alike apart from height and gender, and very, very youthful. 'Or perhaps I ought to ask first if you *do* approve. And if you *do* want me living here?'

They reacted differently, though neither spoke immediately. Bertrand's posture stiffened and something behind his face closed. Estelle flushed and her lips parted and her eyes grew luminous. Bertrand spoke first.

'Miss Kingsley is a gracious lady, sir,' he said. 'I like her, and if you believe you will be happy with her, then I am happy for you. As for your living here, I will be going up to Oxford within the year, and the question of where you make your home is immaterial to me.'

'Bert,' Estelle said reproachfully, but Marcel held up a hand.

'It is all right,' he said. 'I did ask. And you, Estelle?'

He saw her swallow and then frown. 'Why did you leave?' she asked. 'Why did you never come back except on brief visits?'

Ah. He had hoped to avoid this, at least for now. It was not to be, it seemed. 'I left you in the care of your uncle and aunt,' he said. 'They were prepared to remain with you and raise you, and I thought they would do a good job of it. I still think it. They have done a very good job. You are fine young people. Have you not been happy with them?'

'Why did you leave?' she asked again. 'Aunt Jane has always said it was because you were grieving. She said it when we were five and when we were ten and when we were fifteen and every time in between that we asked. Does everyone grieve for so long when they lose someone? Did you not think that we would grieve too? For our mother? For you? We cannot remember missing you, of course, because we were not even a year old when it all happened. We do not even remember our mother. But I think we must have missed you both. We used to play a game when we were children. We set up the empty attic room at Elm Court as a lookout point with blankets and biscuits and an old telescope that did not really work. We took turns keeping watch. We watched for your return and told stories of all the adventures you were having and all the dangers you had to overcome before you could come back to us. Remember, Bert? You had been told the story of the *Odyssey* and how it took Odysseus many years to return to Ithaca and his wife and son. We used to hope and hope and hope it would not take you so long.'

'It did not take us that long to understand that you were not coming back at all,' Bertrand said, 'except for brief visits, which always turned out to be even shorter than you promised. You always had an excuse for leaving – except when you did not. Sometimes you just left.'

'Why, Father?' Estelle asked.

Marcel was asking himself a different question.

How had he managed to dodge his own life for seventeen years? He had always thought he was living every man's dream – free to go where he wanted and do what he wanted, unencumbered by strong attachments or a troublesome conscience, uncaring of what anyone thought or said of him. Rich and powerful, the one inconvenient little package of love and conscience neatly balled up and taken care of by the Morrows.

Then he had met Viola.

And again fourteen years later.

If he could go back . . . right back. But that was the one impossibility in any life. One could not go back to relive it.

'I thought I was not worthy of you,' he said. 'I was afraid of . . . hurting you.'

They were both looking pale. Bertrand stood very straight, a hard look about his posture and face, the sort of look Marcel had seen sometimes in his own looking glass. Estelle lifted her chin, her face troubled.

'Not worthy?' she said.

He turned and strode across the ballroom floor to sit on the edge of the orchestra dais. He set his elbows on his knees and ran his fingers through his hair. 'What do you know of your mother's death?' he asked.

'She fell,' Estelle said, coming to sit beside him. 'Out of a window. It was an accident.'

Bertrand had remained where he was.

'I had been in the nursery with you through much

of the night,' Marcel said. 'You were both cutting teeth and were cross and feverish and unable to settle to sleep. I held you in turn and sometimes both of you together, one on each arm, one head on each shoulder. I adored you. You were the light of my life during that year.'

Good God, had he just spoken those words out loud? He could not look at them to see the effect his speech was having, not if he hoped to continue.

'Your mother adored you too,' he said. 'She played with you endlessly whenever we were at home during the daytime. We both did. We loved your smiles and your giggles when we tickled you or pulled faces at you, and we loved your excitement when you saw us, your little hands and feet waving in the air. But she was cross with me that night for staying up with you. That was why we paid a nurse, she told me. But I had sent your nurse to bed because she was on the verge of exhaustion and complained of a blinding headache. I had just got you both to sleep when your mother came into the room at dawn. She snatched you away from me, Estelle, to lay you down in your crib, but you woke up and started to wail again. She came for you, Bertrand, but you had woken up too. She was annoyed. She wanted me to summon the nurse and come to bed and reminded me that we had a picnic to attend later in the day and I would be too tired to attend.'

He drew a deep breath and let it out on a sigh. 'I was frustrated,' he said. 'It had taken me several hours to get you both to sleep. I shoved her away with my free hand. Her foot . . . I think her foot must have caught in the hem of her dressing gown. I think that is what must have happened. She staggered backward and reached out a hand to steady herself on the wall behind her. Except that it was the window, and I had opened it wide earlier because you were both feverish. I tried— I— But she was gone. She fell. She died instantly. I was unable to grab her. I was unable to save her. She was my own wife, but I was unable to keep her safe. I caused her harm instead.'

'And so you went away,' Bertrand said after a short silence. He had come a little closer, Marcel could see. His voice was cold and hard. 'And you stayed away. You left us.'

'Bert,' Estelle said, distress and reproach in her voice.

'No,' Marcel said. 'It is a fair comment, Estelle. Yes. I went away immediately after the funeral. Your aunt Jane and uncle Charles and the cousins were there. So, I believe, were your grandmother and uncle André and aunt Annemarie. I left.' There were no excuses. 'I left you. I was unable to keep my own wife safe, even though I loved her dearly, because I lost my temper with her and pushed her. How could I be sure I would keep you safe?'

'I hope you have been happy,' Bertrand said with stiff sarcasm.

Marcel raised his head to look at his son – tall

338

and hard and unyielding and hurt to the core of his being. By an absentee father.

'I am sorry,' he said. 'I know those words are easily said and entirely inadequate. But I *am* sorry. No, I have not been happy, Bertrand. I have not deserved to be. In punishing myself, in fleeing from myself, in convincing myself that I was doing what was best for you, I committed perhaps the greatest wrong of my life.'

He lowered his head into his hands.

'I loved your mother,' he said. 'She was vibrant and pretty and full of fun and laughter. We quarreled frequently, but we always worked out our differences without really hurting each other. *Almost* always. We were over the moon with happiness when she discovered she was expecting the two of you. Two! Oh, the joy of your arrival, Bertrand, after we thought the labor safely over with the birth of Estelle. I already thought I could well burst with pride, and then . . . out you came, cross and squalling.' He swallowed once, and then again. 'And then she died in an accident I caused, and I fled and left you to the care of people who would raise you to be better than I was.'

There was a lengthy silence. Estelle slid her hand through his arm and hid her face against his shoulder. He could hear her breathing raggedly. Bertrand had not moved.

'Papa,' Estelle said, her voice trembling with emotion. 'It *was* an accident. I shove Bert all the time and he shoves me. We do not mean anything by it, even when it is done in real annoyance. We never mean to hurt each other, and we never do. It was an *accident*, Papa. You were not a violent man based on that one incident. You are not violent. I am sure you are not.'

He closed his eyes. Was she offering him forgiveness? For depriving her of her mother? Could anyone do that? She had called him *Papa*.

'And now you have fallen in love again,' Estelle said after another silence. 'Your life will change again and you will come home to stay. And next year or the year after – I am in no real hurry – my stepmother will sponsor my come-out in London. In the meanwhile, Bert will come home from Oxford between terms, and we will be a family.'

And live happily ever after.

'I will indeed be coming home to live,' he said. He had decided that during a largely sleepless night. He did not know if it was going to be possible to turn his life around at the age of forty, but he did know something with absolute certainty. He could not go on as he was – or as he had been two months or so ago. It was strange that he could know that with such certainty, but he did. That life had come to an abrupt end. 'And when I do go somewhere else – to London or Brighton or wherever – I will take you with me, Estelle. Until you marry and set up your own home, that is. You too, Bertrand.'

His son had still not moved. By neither word nor gesture nor facial expression had he indicated how he felt about all this. Not since his sarcasm of a few minutes ago, anyway. He was not so ready to forgive, it seemed. Justifiably so.

Estelle squeezed his arm. 'Or to Bath,' she said. 'Mrs Kingsley lives there as well as Camille and Joel and the children. They will be my nieces and nephew. The baby, Jacob, is such a—'

'Estelle,' Marcel said, cutting her off. 'I will not be marrying Miss Kingsley.' The final hammer blow.

Estelle leaned away from him to look into his face, though she did not relinquish her hold on his arm. Bertrand did not move a muscle.

'I forced the betrothal on her,' Marcel explained. 'She had just informed me that she was going home, that she wished to return to her family, when Riverdale arrived at the cottage with his sister and Viola's daughter and son-in-law. And you two were not far behind. I acted upon impulse and announced our betrothal – without any consultation with her. She protested as soon as we were alone together and again before we all left Devonshire, but I remained adamant. She has not changed her mind since then.'

'But—' Estelle began. He held up a staying hand.

'And to be quite frank,' he said, 'I do not really wish to marry her either.' He was not at all sure he was being frank, but he was not sure he was not either. His mind and his emotions were a jumble of confusion.

'I thought you *loved* her,' Estelle cried. 'I thought *she* loved *you*.'

He drew his arm free of hers in order to set it about her shoulders. 'Love is not a simple thing, Estelle,' he said.

'Just as it was not in our case,' Bertrand said, his voice quiet and flat. 'You adored us but you left us. You love Miss Kingsley but you will repudiate her. Or she will repudiate you. Which is it to be?'

That was the thorny question and the main cause of his sleeplessness last night. If a betrothal was to be broken, it must be done by the woman. Honor dictated that on the assumption that no true gentleman would break his word and in the process humiliate a lady and quite possibly make her appear as damaged goods in the eyes of the *ton* and other prospective suitors. But was it always fair? His family and hers were assembled here at his home to celebrate an event that was not after all going to happen, and he must force *her* to explain? Merely because it would be ungentlemanly for him to do it himself?

Estelle had just realized the implications of what he had told them. 'Oh,' she cried, jumping to her feet. 'I brought her whole family here as well as Aunt Annemarie and Uncle William, and I have invited everyone from miles around, but there is to be no betrothal after all. Oh. Whatever am I going to *do*?'

Bertrand stepped forward at last to wrap an arm

about her shoulders and draw her against his side. 'You did not know, Stell,' he said. 'No one told you. You did not know.'

'But what am I going to *do*?' she wailed.

'Did you announce the celebration to our neighbors as a betrothal party?' Marcel asked.

'N-no,' she said. 'Bert is to make the announcement at the sit-down supper later tonight. Everyone believes it is a birthday party. But—'

'Then a birthday party it will be,' he said. 'My fortieth. As you planned it originally. With a grand guest list of neighbors and valued house guests from farther away. A lavish and precious and quite undeserved gift from my children.'

Or so they must make it appear to their guests.

It was Bertrand who answered him, his voice firm and dignified but with more than a tinge of bitterness. 'Perhaps love does not have to be deserved, sir,' he said. 'My sister has always loved you regardless.' He swallowed awkwardly, and his next words seemed grudging. 'So have I.'

Marcel closed his eyes briefly and grasped his temples with a thumb and middle finger.

'I am sorry, Bertrand,' he said once again. 'I am sorry, Estelle. So very sorry. I do not know what else to say. But let us put a good face on the rest of today. And let me try to do better with the future. Not to make amends. That is impossible. But to . . . Well, to do better.'

'There will still be a party, then?' Estelle asked. 'But a birthday party instead of a betrothal party?'

'It had better be the best party ever,' Marcel told her. 'A man turns forty only once, after all. But I am sure it will be. You have worked hard over it, Estelle. So have you, Bertrand.'

He gazed at his children, and they gazed back, one of them wistfully, the other troubled and still faintly hostile. None of the three of them were happy, but . . .

'But our family?' Bertrand asked. 'And hers? And Miss Kingsley herself?'

'You are going to have to leave all that with me,' Marcel said.

He knew something at that most inappropriate of moments.

He loved Viola, by God.

And he would set her free, even at the cost of his claim to be a gentleman.

CHAPTER 19

There had been exactly this many people at the table last evening, Marcel thought, gazing along its length to where the marchioness, his aunt, sat at the foot with Viola on her right and the Reverend Michael Kingsley on her left. He had not particularly noticed then what a vast number it was. He noticed now. And somehow or other they were all relatives – his and hers – gathered to celebrate a merging of their families. He wished there were not a meal to contend with and polite conversation to be made with Mrs Kingsley on his right and the Dowager Countess of Riverdale on his left.

Estelle, roughly halfway down the long table, was flushed and looking a bit anxious. Bertrand, on the other side of the table, was grave in manner. But he always was. He was also bending his head attentively toward Lady Molenor, who was talking. He turned his face toward her even as Marcel watched, and he laughed.

'It must be one of the loveliest views in all Europe,' Mrs Kingsley was saying, speaking of what she could see from the front windows of her house on the Royal Crescent in Bath. 'I am very fortunate.'

'I know the view you speak of,' Marcel said. 'I spent a few days in Bath a couple of years ago.' He had not stayed long. He had found very little there with which to amuse himself. Bath had become largely a retreat for the elderly and infirm.

The meal seemed interminable and came to an end all too quickly. He almost missed the moment he had decided upon. His aunt was getting slowly to her feet at the foot of the table as a signal to the ladies that it was time to leave the men to their port. The first outside guests would begin arriving in an hour's time. Viola stood too and turned to look along the table. She was drawing breath to say something.

Marcel got to his feet and held up a hand. 'Do sit back down for a while longer,' he said.

His aunt looked at him in some surprise and subsided back onto her chair. A few other ladies who had begun to rise did likewise. Viola locked eyes with him, hesitated, and then sat. He gave the signal for the servants to leave the room.

'I have something to say,' he continued when the door closed, 'that will surprise most of you and perhaps distress a few.'

If he had not had everyone's full attention before, he had it now. He tried to gird himself with his famous disdain for anyone's opinion of what he said and did. But it would not work this time.

'I hold Miss Kingsley in the deepest regard,' he

said, 'and I flatter myself with the belief that she returns it. However, a little less than a month ago I forced a betrothal on her when I made the unilateral decision to announce it to four members of her family and then four of my own. It was wrong of me, for an hour or so before I made that announcement Miss Kingsley had expressed her wish to return home to her own family and her own life. With my impulsive announcement I placed her in an impossibly awkward situation, and she has become more enmeshed in its consequences ever since. She has told me a number of times that she does not wish to marry me. So I am making another announcement now to correct the first. There is no betrothal. There never has been. There will be no wedding. And I must stress that Miss Kingsley is entirely blameless.'

Everyone had listened in absolute silence. There were a few murmurings when he stopped, and it became something of a babble when it was clear he had finished. Marcel took no notice. His eyes were locked upon Viola's. She was looking like the marble goddess, the ice queen of memory, her chin raised, her face pale and utterly devoid of any expression except that which lent her unassailable dignity.

No one asked questions. No one voiced any protest. No one challenged him to a duel. He held up his hand after a few moments and looked along both sides of the table as silence fell again.

'My daughter has planned tonight's party with

meticulous care,' he said. 'It is the first such event she has organized, and she has done it on a grand scale. She decided upon it because I have reached the milestone of my fortieth birthday and she wished to do something special for me. It *is* special, and I trust you will all help us celebrate.'

'I certainly will,' Viola said, the first to speak up. 'I wish you a happy birthday, Marcel, and Estelle a successful party.'

'I will echo what Aunt Viola has said,' Anna, Duchess of Netherby, said. 'Happy birthday, Lord Dorchester. And, Estelle, thank you for inviting us all to be participants in your party. It is a delight to be here, and I must confess to having peeped in at the ballroom earlier. I thought perhaps I had discovered a glorious flower garden instead.'

The duke, across the table and a little way down from his wife, was cocking an eyebrow at her and looking faintly amused.

Bertrand was on his feet, a glass of . . . water in his hand. 'I hope everyone has some wine left,' he said. 'Will you join me in wishing my father a happy fortieth birthday? I know you do not particularly like to be reminded of the number, sir, but enjoy it now. Next year will be worse.'

Bertrand making a joke?

There was general, perhaps embarrassed, perhaps a bit overhearty laughter and the scraping of chairs as everyone stood and raised a glass in a toast. And dash it all, they were going to bring this thing off in a civilized manner, it seemed, when everyone must surely be wanting a piece of his hide.

'Thank you,' Marcel said. 'I believe the gentlemen will be willing to forgo the port tonight in favor of getting ready for the party. I will see you all in the ballroom in one hour's time.'

And just like that, he thought as he turned to offer his arm to the Dowager Countess of Riverdale, the worst of it was over. He had in the nick of time saved Viola from having to make the announcement herself.

André caught his eye from across the room and winked and grinned.

'Well, young man,' the dowager said amid the babble of voices around them. 'I have never heard anything more ridiculous in my life. You will regret this. So will Viola. But that is your business, I suppose.'

She took his offered arm.

Viola had always known that something immeasurably good – or, rather, three things – had made every difficult year of her marriage worth suffering through. She was not a demonstrative woman – another result of her marriage – and perhaps her children did not know fully how adored they were, but *she* knew. She had often thought they were the only good thing to have come of her marriage. But she had been wrong.

During those twenty-three years she had learned to endure in full sight of family, friends, and society at large. She had learned to drag a gracious sort of dignity about herself like an all-enveloping mantle whenever she was not alone, and that meant most of her waking hours. That ability was her saving grace this evening.

With palpitating heart and shaking knees she had been about to make the announcement herself. She had drawn breath and opened her mouth to speak. A few heads had begun to turn her way. Yet even at that moment she had not known quite what she was going to say. She had not prepared any speech, or if she had, she could not remember a single word of it. She had only known that it must be done – *now*. Suddenly time really had run out. It was now or never, and *never* was a temptation that must be resisted.

Marcel had saved her by speaking up himself and risking all sorts of repercussions for violating his gentleman's honor. It had not happened, however. To her knowledge, Joel had not challenged him to any sort of duel. Neither had Alexander nor Avery. And Michael had not denounced him. Everyone, in fact, had absorbed the shock of the announcement with remarkable civility despite the fact that a large number of her relatives had been dragged half across the country under false pretenses. Her daughters had hurried to her side before they left the dining room, and she had smiled at them both.

'Everything he said was true,' she said. 'It was noble of him to make the announcement himself and take all the blame. I do not hate him or even dislike him. Neither does he hate nor dislike me. We just do not wish to be married to each other.'

'Mama,' Abigail said, and could not seem to find anything else to say. She looked her concern and distress instead.

'We so wanted you to be happy,' Camille said, looking equally forlorn.

'We have a party to attend and enjoy,' Viola reminded them. 'For Estelle's sake. And Bertrand's.'

'They must have known,' Abigail said. 'He must have told them before tonight.'

'Yes,' Viola agreed. 'I think he must. Now, I promised to kiss Winifred good night before the party. I am going to go there without further delay before you and Joel go up, Camille.'

And the party proceeded an hour later as a grand and noisy reception in the ballroom, followed after a while by some country dancing for the young people and eventually a lavish sit-down supper during which there were toasts and speeches and birthday greetings from Bertrand and various neighbors – and Marcel, who praised his daughter and son and thanked his guests and made a few dry remarks about being forty. He made the first cut into a very large iced fruitcake, which fortunately looked suitable for any occasion.

If any of the neighbors had heard rumors of a betrothal announcement to be made tonight, none of them alluded to it or afforded Viola any more marked attention than they showed any other of the house guests. All was well, and Estelle's party had been rescued from the disaster it might have been.

'How very fortunate it is,' Louise, Dowager Duchess of Netherby, remarked to Viola soon after the party began, 'that there was a birthday also to celebrate tonight.'

'I daresay Dorchester will remember it for the rest of his life,' Mildred, her sister, agreed. 'So will you, Viola. I must confess to some disappointment, though I came here quite prepared to line up with my sisters and subject the marquess to an interrogation that would reduce him to a quivering jelly. However, I daresay you know your own mind as he knows his.'

'I am so *sorry*,' Viola said, 'that you were all dragged here for nothing.'

'Kicking and screaming,' Louise said after clucking her tongue. 'It is a pity Bertrand is so very young. Jessica seems rather smitten with him, does she not? And who can blame her? That young man is destined to break a few female hearts before he finds the one for him.'

Lady Jessica Archer had made her come-out during the spring. She could probably have made a brilliant match before the end of the Season if she had wished. She was both pretty and vivacious – *and* the wealthy daughter and sister of a Duke of Netherby. Instead, she had insisted upon returning to the country even before the end of the Season, upset that Abigail, her very best friend, could not make a come-out with her. She had been unable to accept the fact that Abigail's illegitimacy disqualified her from entering society on a level with her own.

'He looks exactly like his father,' Mildred said.

Viola seemed to spend half the evening apologizing for what had not been her fault.

'I would rather have the two of you admit your incompatibility now, Viola,' her brother told her, 'than in the middle of next January.'

'But I am so glad we all came,' Elizabeth assured her a little later, and Cousin Althea, her mother, nodded agreement. 'I think this evening would have been dreadful for you if you had only had Abigail for moral support.'

'Aunt Viola,' Avery, Duke of Netherby, said with a languid sigh after she had expressed her regret at his having come all this way with Anna and the baby for a nonevent. He had wandered her way to rescue her from a gentleman farmer who had settled into a lengthy description of all his livestock and the bounty of his recent harvest, which somehow surpassed that of all his neighbors. 'People who are forever begging one's pardon are almost invariably crashing bores. I shudder at the unlikely possibility that you might become one of them. Do come and dance with me. I believe I may remember the steps of this one well enough not to disgrace you.'

'You must not apologize, Viola,' Alexander told her not long before supper. 'It is not your fault that we were invited as a surprise for you and ended up being a bit of an embarrassment instead. And we are glad to be here to lend you some support.'

'If you are truly sorry, Viola,' Wren said, a gleam of mischief in her eyes, 'then you will come to Brambledean for Christmas regardless of what has happened tonight. Everyone else will still come even though there is no longer to be a wedding. I know you well enough to predict that you will not want to be there. But you must. Family is so very important. I know. I grew up without any except my aunt and uncle. At least now I have my brother back in my life – and I have all of Alexander's family. As you do. Your mother is still going to come, and so are your brother and sister-in-law. I just asked them. You must come too.'

'Wren is an expert at twisting arms,' Alexander said. 'I have the sore muscles to prove it.'

Viola was horrified at the very thought of yet another family gathering in little more than two months' time. But she would not think about it yet. She *could* not. 'I will let you know,' she said.

'That will have to do for now,' Wren said. 'But do remember how we dared each other back in the spring to step out into the world, and how we did it and felt enormously proud of ourselves.'

But she was not being dared to step out into the world, Viola thought. She was being asked to step *into* her family and accept their collective embrace.

'Come and dance with me, Viola,' Alexander said.

And then, after supper, just when Viola was wondering if she could slip off to her room without appearing unduly bad mannered, Marcel appeared before her and Isabelle and the vicar and his wife. They had successfully avoided each other all evening. Yet she had been aware of him every interminable minute. He looked elegant and almost satanic all in black and white with a silver embroidered waistcoat and his solitaire diamond winking from the intricate folds of his neckcloth. He looked austere and a little intimidating, though he had made an effort to mingle with all the guests and make sure that refreshments were brought to the more elderly among them. He had begun the dancing with Estelle, and Viola had watched, feeling sick at heart as she remembered dancing the very same country dance with him on the village green a lifetime ago.

She was horribly, painfully in love with him, and resented the fact. She was no girl to be made heartsick by a handsome face and figure. Except that it was more than that, of course. Far more.

She wanted to be gone – from the ballroom and from Redcliffe. She wanted to be home. She wanted . . . oblivion. It was the worst wish of all and something that must and would be fought. But she would be gone from here tomorrow. She had decided that. All the houseguests had expected to stay for a few days after the party, of course – a few days in which to enjoy their surroundings and celebrate a new family betrothal in a more leisurely way. She had no idea how her leaving would affect everyone else. Staying after the betrothal was ended and she was gone would be more than a little awkward, and – good heavens – her family had arrived here only yesterday, after a few days of travel in most cases. But she would not think of that or of them. Sometimes – yet again! – she could think only of herself. She must leave, as soon in the morning as it could be arranged.

Yet now he was standing before her. Well, before all four of them actually, but it was at her he was looking, as though he were unaware of his cousin or of the vicar and his wife.

'Viola,' he said, 'will you do me the honor of dancing with me?'

Ah, it was unkind. It was cruel. He was doing it no doubt in order to demonstrate to their families that there were no hard feelings between them, that – as she had told her daughters after dinner – they did not hate each other but just did not wish to marry each other. But he ought not to have chosen this particular way to do it.

'Thank you.' She set her hand in his, and his long fingers closed warmly about hers as he led her onto the floor.

'We are perfectly coordinated, you see,' he said. 'Had we announced our betrothal tonight, Viola, the guests would have assumed it was planned.'

She was wearing her silver lace over a silver silk evening gown. She had always considered it elegant in an understated sort of way, and modest without being prim, and flattering to her figure. She had always thought it suited her age without making her look frumpish. It was, in fact, her favorite, and she had chosen it to boost her confidence.

'Thank you,' she said.

'For?' He raised his eyebrows.

'For speaking at dinner,' she said.

'And saving you from having to do it yourself?' he said. 'It was what you were about to do, wasn't it? I assume you would not be thanking me if that were not the case. You were not about to announce your undying love for me and your commitment to a happily-ever-after that would stretch into our old age and beyond into eternity?'

She could not help but smile, and his dark eyes fixed with some intensity on her face. 'You did not misunderstand,' she told him.

'Ah,' he said. 'I did not think I had.'

The musicians played a chord and Viola looked about her, startled. They were not in line. She had not heard the announcement of what dance they were to perform. There were a few other couples on the floor, none of them the very young people and none of them in line. There were Alexander and Wren, Mildred and Thomas, Camille and Joel, Anna and Avery, Annemarie and William, and two other couples. Almost before the chord had finished she understood.

'It is a waltz,' she said.

His right arm came about her waist and his left

hand, raised, awaited hers. His eyes never left her own. She set her hand in his and raised the other to his shoulder, and . . . Ah, and they waltzed again. As they had on the village green in that other lifetime when all had been carefree adventure. They had danced on uneven ground there and in semidarkness. Here they danced on a polished floor among banks of flowers with the light of dozens of candles flickering down upon them from the chandeliers, and with other couples twirling about the floor with them.

But she saw only Marcel, felt only his body heat and the touch of his hands, smelled only his cologne. His eyes never left her face – he had always had that way of making his dancing partner the full focus of his attention. It was part of his masculine appeal. She smiled, though there was a totally unreasonable sort of bitterness inside her. She had nothing of which to complain, except perhaps his announcement of their betrothal outside the cottage – surely one of his rare forays into gallantry.

Music engulfed them.

'I did love you, you know,' he said when the dance was almost at an end.

'Fourteen years ago?' she said.

He did not reply.

'You did not even know me,' she said. 'Love cannot exist without knowledge.' She did not know if that was true or not.

'Can it not?' he said. 'Then I did not love you,

Viola. I was mistaken. It is just as well, is it not?'
There was a curious twist to his mouth.

And a thought struck her – *was* he talking about
fourteen years ago? But it did not matter.

The music ended and he led her from the floor
in the direction of her mother, who was seated on
a love seat with the marchioness, his aunt. But
Viola did not stop beside them. She hurried away,
trying to slow her footsteps, trying to smile and
make some eye contact with people she passed on
her way to the door. Once she reached the door,
however, she broke into a near run and did not
stop until she was inside her room, her back to
the closed door, her eyes tightly shut.

Her heart breaking.

CHAPTER 20

Aparty involving dancing and unlimited refreshments and a lavish supper would have gone on until dawn in London. Fortunately, this was not London. Guests began to trickle away soon after midnight and then the trickle became a steady stream. Houseguests began to slip away quietly in the direction of their bedchambers after thanking Marcel for his hospitality and Estelle for the splendid party.

It really had been splendid, even though Marcel had hated every moment of it. Though that was not entirely true. Despite the fact that she was upset about the betrothal, Estelle had been flushed and bright-eyed and exuberant tonight at the success of her party. Bertrand had comported himself with dignity and charm. Marcel had been filled with pride over both of them, though he had done nothing to earn the feeling. And then there had been that waltz . . .

He went down onto the terrace to see the last of the guests on their way. Inevitably neighbors discovered things they absolutely must tell one another even though they had had all evening

360

during which to converse. And everyone wanted to thank him again and again and yet again.

It took a while longer to see the stragglers inside the house off to bed and then to hug Estelle and shake hands with Bertrand and thank them for that most precious of birthday gifts – the party. But finally he was able to retreat to the library alone after favoring André with his most forbidding look when it seemed his brother might follow him. He stood in the middle of the room for a couple of minutes dithering, trying to choose between sitting down to read for a while and going straight up to bed.

So he went to Viola's room and stood outside her door to dither. He could not be sure, but it seemed to him that there was a thread of candlelight beneath it. Or perhaps she had left the curtains open and it was merely moonlight. It must be half past one at least by now. He had not looked at the clock before leaving the library. But one o'clock, half past one, two o'clock – the actual time was not important. The fact was that it was far too late to be paying a social call, and even if it had been one o'clock in the afternoon it would still be improper to call upon a lady in her bedchamber. Which was a mildly ridiculous thought under the circumstances.

He tapped lightly on the door with one knuckle. He could hardly hear it himself. If she did not come before he counted at medium speed to ten, he would go away. One . . . two . . .

The door handle turned noiselessly and the door opened a crack – and then a wider crack.

It was candlelight. A single candle burned on the dressing table.

She was wearing a nightgown. Her hair waved down her back. She was also wearing her marble expression. The bed behind her had been turned down for the night but did not look as if it had been slept in yet. The candlelight winked off something at the foot of the bed. Some *things*, rather. A hideous pink drawstring bag was there too.

Someone had better say something soon, and he supposed it ought to be him. 'You had better invite me in,' he said softly.

'Why?' Her voice was just as soft.

He tipped his head slightly to one side but said nothing more. She had choices – open the door wider and step to one side, shut it in his face, or stand there for what remained of the night. He left it to her to decide.

She turned and walked away, leaving the door ajar. So she had chosen the fourth option. He stepped inside and closed the door quietly behind him.

'I interrupted you while you were estimating the value of your treasures?' he asked, nodding toward the bed.

She glanced at the cheap jewels spread there and looked mortified.

He strolled over and looked down at them. 'I noticed,' he said, 'that tonight you wore a string of pearls that were rather small and insignificant in comparison with these.'

'I have no taste at all, do I?' she said.

'And you had no diamonds or emeralds or rubies to add some color and sparkle either,' he said. 'You looked almost—'

'Genteel?' she suggested.

'That is it,' he said, turning to look at her in her nightgown and slippers. 'The very word for which my mind was searching. Ever and always genteel.'

'Not always,' she said softly, and stepped up beside him, gathered the jewelry as though it was precious indeed, put it away inside the bag, and tightened the drawstrings.

He had the Hideous Handkerchief – he always thought of it as though the two words began with capital letters – in an inside pocket of his evening coat. He had put it there to lend himself the courage to speak up at dinner.

'You will stay for a few days?' he asked her.

'No,' she said. 'My things are packed. So are Abigail's. We will leave tomorrow – or today, I suppose I mean. Our leaving will make life very awkward for my family, but I cannot cope with everything.'

'They will be made welcome here,' he said.

'Thank you.' She set down the pink bag. 'You will be able to leave here soon and resume your life where you left it off a couple of months ago. That will make you happy.'

He felt a spurt of anger and . . . hurt? 'That will

be pleasant for me,' he said. 'And you will return home and be respectable and genteel.'

'Yes.'

It was the very thing she had been fleeing when she left Bath in that sad apology for a hired carriage. She had come full circle after an aborted adventure courtesy of himself and a lot of embarrassment courtesy of himself and his daughter. Now she was content to crawl back to safety. But why be angry? He had just had a very fortunate escape from an entanglement that would have adversely affected the whole of the rest of his life. And that was courtesy of her. She had made her feelings quite clear on that windswept beach. She wanted to go home. The affair had served its function, but she had tired of it – and of him. She had never told him anything different in all the times they had talked since then.

He took a step closer to her. He could still smell the subtle perfume she had been wearing earlier – the perfume she always wore. He could feel her body heat, the pull of her femininity.

'The answer to the question you asked earlier is yes,' he said. 'I loved you fourteen years ago, Viola. If I had not, I would not have left when you told me to go.' A strange paradox, that. But true. He had not thought of it before.

She did not raise her eyes to his as she lifted a hand and set it against his chest. She looked at her hand instead. He could feel its warmth through his waistcoat and shirt. 'I loved you too,' she said. 'If I had not, perhaps I would not have told you to go away.' Ah, a matching paradox.

'And I loved you again this year,' he said while her eyes came to his for a moment. 'It was very good while it lasted, was it not? That absurd village fair and the night that followed it in the saddest apology for an inn it has ever been my misfortune to encounter. Though in this case it proved to be good fortune. And the unhurried, meandering journey, which would have driven me mad under any other circumstances. And the cottage and the valley and all that ghastly fresh air and exercise and nature appreciation. And what happened inside the cottage at night and occasionally by day. It was very good, Viola, was it not?'

'Yes,' she agreed. 'It was very pleasurable. While it lasted.'

He gazed down at her in silence for several long moments while the candle cast shifting shadows on the wall behind her. 'It could not have been expected to last, of course,' he said. 'It never does. You grew tired of me, and I was in the process of growing tired of you. It was time to go home. We would have done so and parted on the most amicable of terms if our families had not come in pursuit of us. I am still not sure how they found us or why they went to all that trouble. However it was, it was unfortunate, and I am sorry I made matters worse.'

It could not . . . last. It never does. I was in the process of growing tired of you. What he said was surely true. Why, then, did it feel like the most barefaced of lies?

'You have made amends by setting them to rights,' she said.

'Thank you,' he said, 'for attending the party. You must have wished yourself a thousand miles away.'

'I did it for Estelle's sake,' she said, looking up into his eyes. 'And for Bertrand's, since he is exceedingly fond of his twin. And because it was the *genteel* thing to do.'

'Thank you anyway,' he said. 'And I will endure being reminded by all my neighbors that I am forty years old.'

There was nothing more to say. There had been nothing even before he came here. They gazed at each other, her palm still against his chest. He raised a hand to hook a fallen lock of hair behind her ear and left his hand there, cupping one side of her face. She did not jerk away.

'Sometimes,' he said, 'it is a curse to know that one is beneath the same roof as one's children and grandchildren and parents and aunts and cousins and siblings.'

'And sometimes,' she said, 'it is a great blessing.'

She was quite right. Without that knowledge he would probably try to entice her into bed, and that would be enormously wrong. It would be quite in keeping, of course, with the way he had lived and conducted himself for many long years. But now? The earth had shifted on its axis when

Adeline died. Recently and for reasons he had still not fully fathomed, it had shifted again.

'You are not a romantic, Viola,' he said.

'It is not romance you have in mind,' she told him.

'No.' He rubbed the pad of his thumb along her lips. 'But, regardless, you are safe. My children are beneath this roof. So are yours. And your grandchildren, one of whom I met in an upstairs corridor this morning. An extraordinary child. She introduced herself as Winifred Cunningham, introduced me to herself as the Marquess of Dorchester, shook my hand with the dignity of a dowager, and informed me that she was praying for her grandmama's happiness and my own.'

'Winifred is given to the occasional flight of piety,' she said. 'She is a very dear child.'

'She asked if she might use my library,' he said. 'When I informed her that to my knowledge and regret there were no children's books there, she told me that was quite all right. She had recently read *A Pilgrim's Progress* and now felt ready to tackle anything in the literary realm. She might have been my grandchild too if I had married you.'

He wished he had not said that. Good God, why had he? And why did he feel a sudden yearning for . . . for what? It had been a mistake to come here. But of course it had. He had never thought otherwise. That was the whole trouble actually. He had not *thought*.

'I had better be going,' he said.

'Yes.'

So of course he did not move. He sighed instead. 'Viola,' he said. 'I wish to God this had not happened.' He did not specify what he meant by *this*. He did not know himself. His fingers slid through her hair to the back of her head and his other hand went about her waist while her own arms came about him. And he kissed her. Or she kissed him.

They kissed.

For long, timeless moments. Deeply, their mouths open, their arms like tight bands about each other. As though they were trying to *be* each other or some third entity that was neither and both and something uniquely one. When he drew back, she looked as he felt, as though she were rising to the surface of some element from fathoms deep.

'It is a sad contrariness of the human race,' he said, 'that desire often remains even after love is gone. And yes, it is an enormous blessing that innumerable relatives are beneath this roof with us.'

. . . *after love is gone.* Had he ever spoken more asinine words? And would he believe it if he said it often enough?

He took her hand and raised it to his lips, making her a deep bow as he did so. 'Good night, Viola,' he said. 'You have only a few hours to endure until it is goodbye.'

He turned and left the room, holding the door closed behind him as though some force were trying to open it and tempt him beyond his endurance.

You have only a few hours to endure until it is goodbye. Good God, those hours could not pass quickly enough for him.

It was, he supposed, poetic justice that he had fallen in love with a woman who would have none of him. He was sure he thoroughly deserved every moment of misery he was about to endure. However, he would push past it. He had a great deal to do, much with which to distract himself.

To start, he had two children . . .

He would go, then, and start getting on with it. So of course he turned about, opened her door again, stepped inside, and closed it behind him.

Viola was holding the pink bag of cheap jewelry against her mouth, her eyes tightly closed, fighting a bleakness so powerful it felt actually like a physical pain. And then she opened her eyes abruptly and turned her head. She felt a welling of fury. Oh no, he could not do this to her. Surely . . .

'We were hideously, horribly, dangerously young,' he said. 'We were in love and swinging from stars half the time and squabbling the other half like a couple of—' He sawed the air with one hand. 'Like a couple of . . . what? Help me out here.'

'Marcel,' she said, 'what are you talking about?' She knew, though. But why now?

He strode across the room, thrust back the curtains, and stood gazing out the window – into total darkness.

'You wanted to know,' he said. 'I came to tell

you. She was eighteen when we married. I was twenty. There ought to be a law. We were no more ready for marriage than . . . than . . . I am having trouble with analogies tonight. We were children, wild, undisciplined children. Would we have settled into a mature relationship given time? I will never know. She died when she was twenty. I killed her. Adeline.'

She set down the bag on the edge of the bed and sat beside it. She folded her hands in her lap. He was right. She had wanted to know. Now it seemed she was going to.

'I adored my children from the moment of their conception,' he said, 'or from the moment she told me she was expecting them, I suppose would be more accurate. Not that we knew at the time there would be two. We did not suspect that until almost half an hour after Estelle was born. I had a daughter and a son all within one hour and they were red and wrinkled and ugly and bawling and I thought I was in heaven. We both adored them. We cuddled them and played with them and taught them to squeal with laughter. We even changed a few soggy garments. But we were restless, irre-sponsible children. We were soon back to our busy social life, dancing, drinking, attending parties until late into the night. It did not matter, of course. We had hired a competent nurse and could safely leave the children to her care whenever we had better things to do than be their parents.'

He braced his hands on the windowsill and

rested his forehead against the glass. Viola's hands tightened in her lap.

'They had been teething for some time,' he said, 'but usually one or the other of them would be crying from it but not both together. But this particular time it was both of them and their nurse had been up most of several nights in a row with them. When we got back late from an assembly, Adeline went to bed while I looked in at the nursery. I was supposed to follow her immediately. We were feeling . . . amorous. But the poor little things were in distress, and the nurse was pale and heavy eyed and admitted when I pressed her that she had a splitting headache. I daresay it had been brought on by exhaustion. I sent her to bed. When Adeline came to find me, I sent her away too. She was furious with me – and with the nurse for going. She returned at dawn when I was still in the nursery. I had just got the two of them to sleep, one on each shoulder, and was wondering if I dared try putting them down.'

Viola spread her fingers in her lap and looked down at them when he stopped. He did not resume his story for some time.

'She was still furious,' he said. 'She told me she had not had a wink of sleep and was going to dismiss the nurse as soon as morning came. I told her in a whisper not to be ridiculous and to hush, and she came rushing at me, all outrage, snatched Estelle from my arms, and set her down in her crib. To be fair, I had not spoken nicely to her even though I had whispered. Estelle woke up, of course, and started crying again, and then Bertrand woke up and started crying too. And when Adeline tried to snatch him away from me, I—' He stopped a moment and drew an audible breath. 'I shoved her with my free hand and she stumbled back and . . . and I think she tripped on the hem of her dressing gown and reached behind her to steady herself against the wall. Except that the window was there and it was wide open. I had opened it earlier because the children were feverish – even though both the nurse and Adeline strongly disapproved of fresh air under such circumstances. She—' He stopped again to draw a ragged breath. 'I tried to reach her. I tried to grab her, but she was gone. I do not know what I did with Bertrand. I do not know how I got downstairs and out on the terrace. I did not know who was screaming. I suppose I thought it was her until I realized she could not scream because she was dead.'

'Marcel.' Viola was on her feet though she did not approach him. His head jerked away from the window as though he had only just realized he had an audience.

'I cannot remember much of the following hours or even days,' he said. 'I do not recall who pulled me away from her. I do remember her sister coming and her brother-in-law – Jane and Charles. I cannot remember what they said to me, though they said a great deal. I can remember the funeral. My mother was there – she was still alive then – and my brother and sister, though they were still very young. I cannot remember their leaving, or if, indeed, they left before I did. I can remember not daring to go near the babies lest I lose my temper with them and harm them too. I cannot remember leaving. I can remember only being gone. And remaining gone.'

Viola had closed the distance between them and laid a hand against his back. He did not turn.

'Marcel,' she said, 'it was an accident.'

'I caused her death,' he said. 'I opened the window. I shoved her away from me. If I had not taken either of those actions, she would not have died. She would still be alive. My children would have grown up with parents. All this would not have happened. I would not have caused you unutterable embarrassment.'

He turned and looked at her, his face hard and bleak in the candlelight. He had been blaming himself all these years for what had been essentially an accident. Yes, he had pushed his wife, and there was never any real excuse for that. But his punishment had been vast and all consuming. He had judged himself solely responsible for his wife's death and for depriving his children of their mother. And so he had deprived them of their father too, the foolish man. He had cut out his heart and become the man the *ton* knew and she had known.

'I want you to promise me something,' she said.

He raised one eyebrow.

'No.' She frowned. 'I do not want a promise.

Only an . . . assurance that you will give serious thought to something. Had nothing happened that morning, the quarrel between you would have been long forgotten by now, replaced by layer upon layer of other memories. You were not to blame, Marcel, except for pushing your wife out of the way. The catastrophic consequences were unforeseeable and quite accidental. You did not intend that she would die or even be hurt. I want you to forgive yourself.'

'And live happily ever after, I suppose.' One corner of his mouth lifted in a parody of a smile.

'Forgive yourself,' she said. 'For the sake of your children.'

They gazed at each other for a few moments and she wondered why on earth this was happening. Why had he set her free tonight if this was to follow? What did it mean? She supposed it meant nothing beyond a certain need in him to unburden himself. But why her?

'And I want you to promise me something,' he said, 'or *not* to promise. Merely to give it serious thought. You learned when you were very young and married a scoundrel to suppress love. Not to kill it, but to push it deep. You love your children far more than they probably realize. For two brief weeks in Devonshire you allowed yourself some temporary escape, but now you have command of yourself again. I want you to think about . . . loving, Viola. About allowing yourself to love a man who will love you in return. There is such a man for you. You will find him if you will allow yourself to.'

She gazed at him in amazement. 'This,' she said, 'from *you*?'

'It is as suspect as all the wisdom Polonius poured out to his children, I must admit,' he said. 'Wisdom from a foolish man. But it *was* wisdom, nevertheless. Shakespeare was perhaps a perceptive man – and I am hardly the first person ever to have noticed that.'

He was referring to *Hamlet*. And he was mocking himself. And surely her too – *there is such a man for you. You will find him if you will allow yourself to. I want you to think about loving . . . a man who will love you in return.*

He took her right hand in his, raised it briefly to his lips, released it, and walked past her and out of her room without another word. He closed the door quietly behind him.

Viola turned blindly back to the bed and snatched up the pink bag to hold against her mouth again. If it was possible to feel more wretched, she did not want to know it.

CHAPTER 21

For the first half hour Viola could do nothing but draw air into her lungs and expel it, over and over again. If she did not concentrate upon breathing, she felt she would simply forget to do it – or perhaps she would be too tempted to let herself forget. If she watched her breathing, counted her breaths, kept her eyes on the scenery passing by the carriage window, perhaps she would be able to put enough distance between herself and . . . and what? But she would not let her mind search for the appropriate word. There was only the feeling that if she could allow enough distance to pass by all would be well again.

Abigail, gazing from the window on her side, was mercifully silent.

It had been awkward. No one in her family had seemed to know if they would stay a day or two longer as originally planned or follow immediately after her. Her leaving before any of them must have appeared incredibly bad mannered since she was their reason for being there. But she could not worry about that. She seemed to have established the habit in the last while of leaving when she ought to stay, of making an utter pain of herself to those whose worst sin was that they loved her.

She had shaken hands with all of Marcel's family and thanked them for the welcome they had extended. Bertrand had surprised her by kissing her on the cheek. Estelle had hugged her tightly and clung wordlessly for several moments before doing the same with Abigail.

Viola had hugged her own family amid bustle and overly cheerful farewells. Sarah had kissed her on the lips, her own little ones puckered. Winifred had hugged hard and raised a plain, shining face.

'I wanted to tell you about the start of *Robinson Crusoe*, Grandmama,' she said. 'But maybe by Christmas I will be able to tell you about the whole book. We are all going to Cousin Wren's for Christmas.'

'Or you could write to me after each chapter,' Viola had suggested.

'Mama says I have better penmanship than she does,' Winifred had replied. 'But I do not think that is correct, for hers is perfect.'

Jacob had frowned and released some wind.

Marcel had not appeared at the breakfast table or during all the bustle of leave-taking that followed it. Viola had willed him to stay out of sight until after she left. And she had fought panic at the possibility that he would do just that. She and Abigail had been inside the carriage, the door closed, her coachman climbing up to the box, when he had finally appeared at the top of the steps under the portico – remote, austere, immaculately elegant. He had not hurried down the steps to bid her farewell. Instead, meeting her eyes through the window, he had inclined his head, raised his right hand not quite to the level of his shoulder, and shifted his gaze to give the coachman the nod to leave.

And that had been that. That *was* that. Inhale, exhale, watch the miles slip past. Home and safety awaited, and broken hearts mended. Indeed, it was a silly concept – a broken heart. It was all *feelings*, and feelings were all in the head. There was no reality to them. Reality was her daily life, her friends, her family, her many, many blessings.

Harry. She swallowed and wondered if there was a letter from him.

And finally, after half an hour or so, she let go of her concentration upon her breathing and trusted it to look after itself. She turned her head to look at Abigail.

'It is young people whose lives are expected to be tumultuous a time or two before they settle,' she said. 'It is they who are supposed to need the calm comfort of a mother's wisdom. Our roles appear to have been reversed lately. I am so sorry, Abigail. I will do better. It feels good to be going home, does it not?' She reached for her daughter's hand.

'I thought you loved him,' Abigail said. 'I thought he loved you. Perhaps I am too much of a romantic.'

'What I am is selfish,' Viola said. 'Your life

would have undergone great upheaval yet again if I really had been serious about marrying.'

'Yes.' Abigail frowned. 'But, Mama, a woman does not have children in order to give up her life and happiness for their sake, does she? Why is it selfish for her to want to do her own living too?'

Viola squeezed her hand. 'You see what I mean about our roles reversing?' she said.

'The point is,' Abigail said, 'that Camille found her own way forward. Grandmama and I were horrified when she decided to take employment as a teacher at the orphanage, and we were even more upset when she decided to go and live there. But – she found her way all on her own. She found Joel and Winifred and Sarah and she has had Jacob and, Mama, I believe she is as happy as it is possible to be in a life that is always changing.'

'You are saying that I am not as important as I sometimes think I am?' Viola asked ruefully. 'But you are quite right. Harry chose a military career, and Avery made it possible for him by purchasing his commission.'

'Oh, you are more important than *anything*,' Abigail cried. 'But as a *mother*. All we want is your love, Mama, and the chance to love you. We must do our living ourselves, just as you have always done, and as I hope you will always do.'

Viola sighed. 'But what of you, Abby?' she asked. 'You were deprived of the chance to make your come-out during a London Season and of the chance to make a suitable marriage. You were—'

'Mama,' Abigail said, 'I do not *know* what my life will be. But I am the one who must and will live it. I do not expect you to organize it for me or make decisions and plans for me or . . . or *anything*. It is *my* life and you must not worry.'

'You might more easily get me to stop breathing,' Viola said, and smiled.

Abigail smiled back, and for some strange reason they found her words uproariously funny and laughed until tears rolled down their cheeks.

'Mama,' Abigail asked, drying her eyes with her handkerchief, '*do* you love him?'

Viola curbed the easy answer she had been about to give. She sighed as she put her own handkerchief away in her reticule. 'Yes, I do,' she said. 'But it is not enough, Abby. He does not love me, or at least not in any way that would allow for a lifelong relationship. He is not the sort of man who can settle to anything or with anyone. He was once upon a time, perhaps, but he changed after his wife's untimely death, and too much time has passed to enable him to change back or to change at all in essential ways. We never expected permanence, you know, when we decided to go away together for a week or two. I needed to . . . escape for a while, and he is always ready for an adventure that will bring him some pleasure. As he said last evening, I had already decided to return home and would have done so without fuss or bother if you had not turned up at the cottage with Joel and Elizabeth and Alexander.'

'I am sad,' Abigail said. 'Life *is* sometimes sad, is it not?'

And for some absurd reason they found that observation funny too and began to laugh again, but somewhat ruefully this time.

The really odd thing, Marcel discovered over the following couple of months, was that he did not once feel tempted to dash off to London and his old life or to accept any of the invitations he received to join shooting parties or house parties or, in one instance, an unabashed orgy at the shooting lodge of an acquaintance of his – *in the company of only the loveliest, most alluring, most accomplished young ladies, Dorchester. You must come, old chap.*

The houseguests all left within two days of the party, including Annemarie and William.

'I must confess to you, Marc,' Annemarie told him privately, 'that I am not overfond of Isabelle, and I find Margaret insipid for all she is to be a bride in December. And if I have to make excuses much longer for avoiding morning prayers with Jane, I shall forget my manners and give her a truthful answer. Though she has done splendidly with the twins, I must confess. Bertrand is positively dream material for all the young ladies who will be coming on the market in five or six years' time. And Estelle is going to be a beauty after all. I did not think so for a long time – she was all eyes and hair and teeth too large for her face. She did a magnificent job with the party, thanks to Jane's training. She is going to have suitors queued up outside your door as soon as she is let loose upon society. Next spring, will that be?'

'She says she is in no hurry,' Marcel told her. 'I will allow her to decide. I am in no hurry to be rid of her.'

'*You* will allow?' she said with a lift of her eyebrows. 'Not Jane?'

'I am going to remain here,' he told her.

'Oh, for how many weeks?' She laughed. 'Or days? I am going to start counting.'

André left a few days after everyone else.

'I do not see why you will not come with me, Marc,' he said. 'If I had to stay here one more day, I would be climbing trees to alleviate my boredom.'

'But no one is forcing you to stay one more day,' Marcel replied. 'Or even half a day.'

'Oh, I say,' his brother said. 'You are serious about staying. I will give you another week, Marc, and then expect to see you in London. Have you heard about the new brothel on—'

'No,' Marcel said. 'I have not.'

'Well.' André grinned. 'You never did have any need for brothels.'

No, he never had. And never would. He doubted that he would ever need another woman, but that was a rather rash thought, brought on, no doubt, by the damnably flat, heavy feeling with which his latest affair had left him. Damn

Viola Kingsley – which was grossly unfair of him, but in the privacy of his own mind he damned her anyway.

He spent the two months sorting out the unsorted threads of his life. He gave his aunt and his cousin and her daughter free rein to plan the upcoming wedding – upon one condition. Under no circumstances whatsoever was he to be bothered by any of the details. In addition, he told them, after the wedding, by the beginning of January at the latest, they were to remove to the dower house. Again they might have a free hand about preparing it and the carriage house and stables for their comfort, but the move must be made.

None of them argued.

He had a word with Jane and Charles and suggested that they might wish to resume their own lives at last now that the twins were more or less grown-up and he was living at home with them. Jane looked skeptical.

'But how long will it be, Marcel,' she asked, 'before you take yourself off again?'

'I have no such plans,' he told her. 'But if and when I do, then Estelle and Bertrand will go with me.'

The tenants who had leased their own home for the past fifteen years had recently moved out. The truth was, Jane confessed, they had been longing to return home and had only remained because they had felt their first duty was to Adeline's children.

The whole situation resolved itself easily and

amicably within a couple of weeks. Ellen went with them. Marcel suspected that she would choose to remain at home as the prop and stay of her parents in their old age, though that was some way in the future yet. Oliver did not go. Marcel gave notice to his steward, who was to be allowed to remain in his cottage on the edge of the estate with a generous pension. And, before he sent to his man of business in London to find a replacement, Marcel offered the job to his nephew. Oliver, who was eminently suited to the job and who, Marcel had observed during the birthday party, appeared to be sweet on the daughter of a neighboring gentleman, accepted. Bertrand was happy about it. He obviously looked up to his older cousin as some sort of role model.

Marcel tried to take up the role of father. It was not easy. He had had very little to do with the upbringing of his children and did not want to be too intrusive now. On the other hand, he did not want to appear to be aloof or indifferent. He did not know if they loved him or even liked him, and was well aware that he had not earned either. But thanks to Jane and Charles, they were neither openly hostile nor rebellious. They had been brought up to be a lady and a gentleman, and that was exactly what they were. They were invariably courteous and deferential to the man who was their parent, even if he had no real claim to the name of father.

It would take time. And he would give it time.

Sometimes it puzzled him that he was willing to remain and try. How could his whole outlook upon life have changed so radically and so completely in such a short while? It had happened seventeen years ago, of course, but there had been a definite, catastrophic reason then. But this time? Just because he had fallen in love and had not been given the chance to fall out again before she tired of him? Such a notion was ridiculous.

But his heart ached a little bit. Well, a whole lot if he was going to be honest with himself.

On the whole it was easier not to be honest.

Despite all the turmoil of the past few months, Viola quickly settled down to her old life and became her old self again. The need to run, to escape at all costs had left her – and she was a bit depressed. For what had changed? Had all the upheaval accomplished anything at all? She had perhaps proved to herself that she could be bold and defiant and adventurous and passionate. And happy. But now she had been caught in the return swing of the pendulum, as had been inevitable. She remembered Marcel saying that what went up had to come down.

She tried not to think about Marcel.

She mingled with neighbors and friends. She worked with the vicar and a few other ladies to arrange a Christmas party for the children. She stitched and embroidered and tatted and wrote letters and read and walked, within the park about the house and along country lanes. She started playing the pianoforte again after neglecting it for a couple of years. She organized tea parties for Abigail and her young friends and several times played for them in the music room while they danced.

She slept poorly. She could discipline her mind during the daytime and scarcely think of him more than once or twice an hour – and then only fleetingly until she realized where her thoughts were wandering. At night, when her mind relaxed, it was harder to keep the memories from flooding in. And it was not just her mind the memories attacked then, but her body too and her emotions. She ached and yearned for what she had found during those weeks. But not just for *what* she had found. She yearned for *whom* she had found.

It had been hard to recover fourteen years ago, when she had been a young, unhappily married woman. But at least then she had only been *in* love with him. She had not *loved* him. She had not known him in any of the meanings of the word. It had taken her a long time to forget anyway. It would take longer now. She understood that and set out to be patient with herself.

Her clothes began to hang a bit more loosely about her, but that at least was a positive effect of heartache. She had been intending for some time to lose a bit of weight, to get back the figure she had always had until her courses stopped two years ago.

And she was going to Brambledean for Christmas. She felt obliged to go – for Abigail's sake and for her mother's and Michael's and Mary's. They would feel awkward being there if she was not. And of course everyone had written – as she had written to everyone – and all, without exception, had variously hoped, urged, or begged or wheedled her to come too. She wondered why they bothered. She really had not treated her family well since Humphrey's death. And while it was understandable that they would make allowances for a while, there surely ought to be limits. It was closer to three years than two. Yet it must seem to them that she was still sulking and behaving erratically and even discourteously. And good heavens, she had dishonored them. She had been discovered in the midst of an affair with a man who was not her husband.

Did love really know no bounds when it was true love? Was it really unconditional? She felt ashamed of something she remembered telling Marcel one day when he had asked her what she wanted most in life. She had told him she wanted someone to care for her – for *her*, not just for the mother or daughter or sister or whatever else label could be put upon her. She was ashamed, for they had proved over and over, her family, that they cared indeed – for her and for one another. What Humphrey had done to wreck the structure of the family had not wrecked what lay beneath it – love, pure and simple.

She would go to Brambledean out of gratitude

and a returning love. And because she missed the children – Winifred and Sarah and Jacob. And even Anna and Avery's Josephine. And Mildred and Thomas were to bring their boys, whom she had not seen for several years. They had been mischievous little boys then. Now they were apparently boisterous big boys, forever getting into scrapes at school and causing their parents mingled anguish and wrath. She was missing Elizabeth with her unfailing calm common sense and twinkling eyes, and Wren, who had grown up as a recluse, her face always veiled to hide the birthmark that covered one side of it, but who had found the courage to face the world and fall in love with Alexander. She was missing her mother and Camille. And her former sisters-in-law. Oh, *all* of them.

She had fled the stifling affection of her family a few months ago. Now she was ready to embrace it. Perhaps something good *had* come from all the turmoil and heartache.

She would go because she was lonely. Because her heart was broken and she could not seem to find the pieces to fit it back together.

She would go to show them all that she was neither lonely nor heartsick.

They worried about her. She would show them that they did not need to, that she was fine.

Marcel was in the boathouse down by the lake, looking at the two overturned rowboats inside. It was not a happy sight.

'They look as if they have not been used this side of the turn of the century,' he said.

'I do not know,' Bertrand told him.

Marcel turned to look at him. 'You have never wanted to use them yourself?' he asked.

'Aunt Jane thought it would be unwise, sir,' his son replied.

Jane had not allowed much that was joyful into his children's lives, it seemed. Every day he discovered more examples. Not that the twins ever complained. They were amazingly docile young persons – with the exception of Estelle's grand fury and rebellion and epic journey to Devonshire. He wondered at that now, at the feeling that had burst the bounds of a lifetime of training. She must have been very angry indeed with him. A promising sign? There were not many such signs from either of them, though they were the most dutiful children any father could ask for.

'Let me guess,' he said. 'It was because Estelle was a delicate girl and you were the heir.'

'Well, I am the heir,' Bertrand said apologetically. 'The only one, sir.'

'My fault, I suppose,' Marcel muttered. 'Yes, my fault. Perhaps you were so perfect, Bertrand, that I did not believe you could be replicated.'

'I am not perfect,' his son said with a frown.

'To me you are,' Marcel said. 'I will have these looked at in time for summer next year. I will test them myself before I allow you to row off to the far shores of the lake. If I sink and leave nothing but a bubble behind, at least I will have left an heir too.'

Bertrand looked slightly shocked. Estelle, who had come to stand in the doorway, giggled. Yes, really. She did not just laugh. She giggled. It was music to her father's ears. And Bertrand, after a glance at her, laughed too.

'I daresay you can swim, sir,' he said.

'Yes, I daresay I can,' Marcel agreed.

They continued on their walk about the lake. He tried to spend time with them each day and had felt some easing of their very formal relationship. Bertrand had become almost enthusiastic when he learned that his father had not idled all his time away at Oxford but had actually earned a first-class degree. Estelle had looked at first dubious when he had suggested that they invite some young people to the house occasionally. Apparently Jane had believed the son and daughter of the Marquess of Dorchester must hold themselves aloof from inferior company. Perhaps now they were close to eighteen, Marcel had suggested, and their characters were fully formed, they might relax that rule somewhat. Estelle was ecstatic. Even Bertrand had looked pleased.

'My sister will be happy, sir,' he had said. 'She enjoys company. So do I,' he had added after a short pause.

Marcel stopped on the bank below the dower house and stood looking at it – specifically at the large drawing room window, behind which he had stood with Viola. He determinedly avoided thinking of her – except when memories crept up on him unaware, which was far too often for his peace of mind. His son and daughter had stopped on either side of him.

'She is going to Brambledean Court for Christmas,' Estelle said, jolting his attention from the memories. He looked sharply at her. 'In Wiltshire,' she added. 'The Earl of Riverdale's home. She is going there for Christmas.'

'Indeed?' he said. It would be foolish to ask who *she* was. His tone was deliberately frosty. He did not want to hear more.

'Yes,' she said. 'Abigail told me so.'

He turned to walk onward, but she did not move. Neither did Bertrand.

'I write to her and she always replies,' Estelle said. 'So does Jessica.'

Jessica. He had to think for a moment. Ah, yes, she was Abigail's young cousin and friend – Lady Jessica Archer, Netherby's half sister.

'She is unhappy,' Estelle said.

'Jessica?' he said. 'Abigail?' He did not want this conversation.

'Miss Kingsley,' Estelle said. 'She will not admit it, Abigail says. She is always determinedly cheerful. But she has lost weight, and she has dark circles under her eyes.'

He turned on her. 'And of what possible interest can this be to me, young lady?' he asked. 'What is her unhappiness to me? She did not want to marry me. She would have been happy enough to leave me back there in Devonshire before you discovered us. She was happy enough to leave here. She left before any of the rest of her family, if you will remember. She could not leave here soon enough. Her mood and her plans for Christmas are of no concern to me whatsoever. Is that clearly understood?'

Her face paled and her lower lip quivered, and he half expected her to collapse in an abject heap at his feet. She did not do so.

'And you are unhappy too,' his daughter said.

'What the devil?' He glared at her.

'It is true, sir,' Bertrand said from behind him. 'You know it is. And we know it. And a proper gentleman does not blaspheme in a lady's hearing.'

What the *devil*? Marcel wheeled on his son. 'You are quite right,' he said curtly. 'My apologies, Estelle. It will not happen again.'

'You are looking almost gaunt,' Bertrand said. 'And you wander alone and go riding alone and stay up half the night and get up before anyone else.'

'What the devil?' Marcel frowned ferociously at his son. 'Is a man not allowed to do as he wants in his own home without being spied upon by his children? I beg your pardon, Estelle. It will not happen again. Perhaps I have always walked and ridden and stayed up late and risen early. Have you thought of that? Perhaps it is the way I like to live.'

'Perhaps you want to go back to your own life,' Bertrand said, 'and that is why you are so unhappy. But Stell and I do not think it is that, sir. We think it is because of Miss Kingsley. And we think she is unhappy because of you.'

'And . . .' He looked incredulously from one to the other of them. 'And you think you ought to appoint yourselves matchmaker to your own *father*.'

They both stared back, identical stern looks on their faces. Bertrand spoke first.

'Someone has to, sir,' he said.

'Someone *has* to?' He felt as though he were in the middle of a bizarre dream.

'You are going to ruin your life, Papa,' Estelle said, 'and she is going to ruin hers. All because you are both too stubborn for your own good. Have you told her that you love her, that you *want* to marry her?'

'I would wager you have not,' Bertrand said. 'And you cannot expect her to say it first, sir. No well-bred lady would.'

It was either explode with wrath or . . .

Marcel threw back his head and laughed. Estelle's lips twitched. Bertrand frowned.

'And why would my, ah, love life be of such concern to my children?' Marcel asked when he had sobered.

Bertrand was still frowning. 'We are still *children* to you, are we not?' he said. 'I am not *concerned* about you or even much interested. You may return to London for all I care, or wherever else it is you go when you are not here. You may waste the rest of your life as far as I am concerned. You seem to be very good at that. I wish you *would* go away. We have grown up very well without you, Estelle and I. We can do the rest of our living very well without you too. Why did we ever think you cared for Miss Kingsley or anyone else? You do not care about anyone except yourself. *Sir.*'

'Bert,' Estelle wailed, and tried to catch his arm. But he jerked it free of her grasp and turned to stride off back the way they had come. For a moment Marcel thought she would go running after him, but he set a hand on her arm.

'Let him go,' he said. 'I will have a talk with him later.'

She gazed at him, her eyes troubled. 'We have no memory at all of our first year,' she said, 'though we have strained to put a face on Mama from Aunt Jane's descriptions. We have tried remembering you too as you were then. It is hopeless, of course. We were just babies. But always, as far back as we can remember, we have waited for you to come back. To stay. We have waited to love you. And for you to love us. We have been puzzled too and angry, and we have told ourselves with each passing year that we no longer need you or want you to return to upset our lives. But it is what we have always wanted, Papa. Perhaps Bertrand more than me. He wanted – no, he *needed* a father to look up to, to admire, to emulate, a father to praise him and encourage him and do things with him and look at him with pride. He has always known he looks like you. He used to stand in front of a looking glass whenever you were here, trying to imitate your posture, your facial expressions, and your mannerisms. I just wanted a papa, a sort of rock of strength and dependability. Uncle Charles is a good man, but he was never you.'

Marcel was wishing she had gone after her brother. Truth was beginning to be spoken among them, but it was halting, difficult, necessary, hurtful, endearing . . . He could go on and on. Sometimes it came blurting out all in a flood, as now with Estelle. Sometimes it was denied with some bitterness, as a moment ago with Bertrand. But he would endure it all if there was a chance of getting his children back, totally unworthy though he was.

'We have loved you anyway,' Estelle said. 'It was something we could never choose to do or not to do. It just . . . *is*. And call us foolish if you wish, but we want to see you happy.'

'I can never make amends for the lost years,' he said, 'but I will try to give you . . . now. It is all I can offer – now on into as much of the future as we are granted. I *am* happy, Estelle, or was until fifteen or twenty minutes ago.'

'No, you were not,' she said. 'Not really. We will never be quite enough for you, Papa, just as in time you will not be quite enough for either of us. I do not feel any burning wish for a Season yet, but I surely will in time. I will want a husband

and a family and a home of my own. And Bertrand will want a wife. He and I will not even be enough for each other, though we always have been and still are. We wanted you to be fully happy, and it seems to us that you gave up the chance because for once in your life you wanted to do something noble.'

'For once in my life?' He raised his eyebrows and she flushed.

'I am sorry,' she said. 'I am sure you must have done other noble things. Even when you announced your betrothal in Devonshire, you were being noble.'

He gazed at her, this daughter of his who had so recently found her voice and revealed herself as a young woman of firm character and principle and considerable courage. She had blossomed before his eyes.

'I will tell you this, Estelle,' he said. 'I am as proud of both you and Bertrand as any father could possibly be of his children. I will tell Bertrand that too. But . . . what exactly is it the two of you want me to do?'

She smiled at him, linked her arm through his, and turned them back in the direction of home.

'I assume,' she said, 'that was a rhetorical question, Papa.'

CHAPTER 22

Viola and Abigail arrived at Brambledean Court four days before Christmas. They had come sooner than planned because heavy clouds had loomed overhead for a few days and the blacksmith, who had a reputation in the village for forecasting weather with some accuracy, had predicted snow for Christmas and lots of it.

Brambledean was the principal seat of the Earls of Riverdale, but Viola had never lived there as countess and so felt no awkwardness about going there now. Alexander and Wren had been busy since early summer repairing the damage that neglect of years had caused to both the park and the house, though they had concentrated most of their efforts upon restoring the farms to prosperity and making repairs to the laborers' cottages. There was still much to be done. The park looked very barren even for December, though the lawns were neat and much deadwood appeared to have been cut away from trees and hedges. The driveway had been resurfaced and the wheel ruts of years smoothed out. The house was still shabby, but curtains and cushions had been renewed in the main rooms and walls had been painted or papered. Everything gleamed with cleanliness and liberal doses of polish.

'It is not yet a showpiece,' Wren said as she took them up to their rooms despite the increasing bulk of her pregnancy. 'But it is cozy, or so we tell ourselves. It is home. And now it will have a sort of housewarming. Oh, I am *so* glad the two of you have come. My first Christmas with Alexander would not have been complete without the whole family here.'

But Harry would be absent, Viola thought without saying the words aloud. There had been one letter from him since she returned from Northamptonshire. In it he had wished her happy in her upcoming marriage, though he had expressed a wish that he had been able to interrogate the Marquess of Dorchester before the betrothal became official. He remembered him as Mr Lamarr, but while he and his young friends had looked up to him with some awe as one devil – his exact word – of a fine fellow, he had not been the sort of man a son would want to see his mother marrying. There had been no letter from him since. Viola assumed her son would express some relief in his next one.

'Except for Harry,' Wren added. 'Let us hope that the wars will be over by this time next year and we can all be together. Including this babe,' she added, patting her abdomen.

They were not the first to arrive, early though they were. Althea and Elizabeth, Alexander's mother and sister, had come the week before, and Thomas and Mildred, Lord and Lady Molenor, had arrived the day before with their three boys, who had been let loose from school for the holidays – that was how one of them described their presence to Viola anyway. She loved them instantly – Boris, aged sixteen, Peter, fifteen, and Ivan, fourteen. They were polite, charming boys, who looked to her like three kegs of powder just awaiting a spark so that they could explode into activity and mischief.

Camille and Joel arrived the next day with Viola's mother and the three children. Sarah fell instantly in love with Boris, who lifted her to one shoulder almost as soon as her feet were inside the nursery and galloped about the room with her while she clutched his hair and shrieked with fear and joy. Winifred eyed Ivan and informed him that he was her first cousin once removed since he was her mama's first cousin and that he was four years older than she. If he would tell her when his birthday was, she would be able to tell him exactly how many more months than four years. Ivan looked at her rather as if she had two heads.

'March the twenty-fourth,' Peter told her. 'Mine is May the fifth.'

'And mine is February the twelfth,' Winifred said. 'I think.'

'You *think*?' Ivan said.

'I am not quite sure. I was an orphan before Mama and Papa adopted me,' she explained. 'I was in an orphanage. Papa grew up there before me. And Cousin Anna.'

'Really?' Ivan's interest had been caught, and Viola went back to the drawing room to speak with her mother.

Most of the other guests arrived before dark – and an unexpected one in the middle of the evening, long after dark.

'Whoever can that be?' Matilda asked when they heard the unmistakable rumble of wheels on the terrace below the drawing room.

'I hope it is not Anna and Avery and Louise,' her mother said. 'The baby should be in her bed already.'

'And it is never safe to travel any distance after dark,' Matilda added. 'Surely it is not them. Louise is far too sensible. Or perhaps they were afraid it would snow and so pressed onward.'

Alexander laughed. 'There is one way of finding out,' he said, getting to his feet. 'I shall go down.'

He came back less than five minutes later with a single traveler, a young man who strode into the room one step behind him, looked about him with eager good cheer, and went striding off toward his mother, arms outstretched.

'Hired carriages are an abomination,' he said. 'I am convinced every bone in my body is in a different place from where it was when I started.'

Viola was on her feet without any awareness of how she had got there.

'Harry!' she cried before she was enfolded in his

arms and hugged tightly enough to squeeze all the breath out of her.

'So,' he said, looking down at her while noise and exclamations of pleasure erupted about them, 'where is the happy bridegroom?'

Viola felt as if at last she had come to the end of a tumultuous journey of close on three years. She was in the drawing room of Brambledean in the early evening, two days before Christmas, surrounded by her family – *all* her family except for the very young children, who were upstairs in the nursery, and she was thoroughly contented. She tested the word *happy* in her mind, but decided that *contented* was the better choice. Contentment was a good thing. Very good.

Finally she was able to accept with her whole being that Humphrey's family was indeed hers too, even though their marriage had never been a valid one. They were her family because they had chosen her, not only during the twenty-three years when really they had had no choice, but in the close to three years since when they could have disowned her. And at last she had chosen them to be her family.

She gazed about the room from her position on a small sofa beside Althea, Alexander's mother. They were all here – the Kingsleys, the Westcotts, and their spouses and older children. Ivan and Peter were playing a duet of dubious musical distinction on the pianoforte, and Winifred was leaning across the instrument on her forearms, watching their hands and making what were probably unhelpful suggestions when they hit one of their frequent wrong notes or contested the middle keys with some sharp elbow work. Viola's mother and Mary were in conversation with Humphrey's mother. Jessica and Abigail were squeezed onto another sofa on either side of Harry, while Boris was perched on a pouf in front of them. They were all absorbed in some tale Harry was telling. Camille and Anna had their heads together, talking about something. Wren and Joel and Avery were in conversation together.

It was, in fact, a warm family gathering. And there was even an extended family member present – Colin, Lord Hodges, Wren's younger brother, who was currently living eight or nine miles away at Withington House, Wren's former home, where Alexander had met her less than a year ago. He was a good-looking, good-humored young man who had caught the attention of both Abigail and Jessica earlier in the day. He was currently standing by the window, talking with Elizabeth, who was perched on the window seat.

The room was lavishly decorated for Christmas and smelled wonderfully of pine. Alexander and Thomas, Lord Molenor, had gone out to the stables and carriage house after luncheon to look at the sleds that had been stored away for years to see if they could possibly be used if it should indeed happen to snow. Most of the rest of them went out to gather greenery from the park – pine boughs and holly, ivy and mistletoe. Then they had all set to with a will to decorate the drawing room and the banisters of the main staircase. Matilda had marshaled a group to make a kissing bough, which now hung from the center of the ceiling and had been visited accidentally on purpose – as Avery phrased it – by several couples and a few noncouples. Harry had kissed Winifred and his aunt Matilda, who had told him to *mind his manners, young man*, and then had tittered and blushed. Boris had kissed Jessica and turned a bright red, even though she pointed out that they were *cousins, you silly boy*. Colin had gallantly kissed both Jessica and Abigail, and *they* had turned bright red.

The Yule log would be brought in tomorrow, Alexander promised, and then it would be Christmas indeed. The carolers would surely come from the village – they had promised anyway to revive that old tradition – and there would be a wassail bowl awaiting them and mince pies and a roaring fire in the hall.

Christmas was a happy time, Viola thought, content to be quiet while Althea knitted beside her and smiled about at the scene before her eyes. It was a family time, a time to count one's blessings and fortify oneself for the year ahead. For the new year would bring changes, as all years did, some of them welcome, some a challenge. One needed to grasp the happy moments when one could and hug them to oneself with both arms.

Her blessings were many indeed. Someone from

Harry's battalion had needed to come back to England for a month or so to select recruits from the second battalion and train them rigorously for battle before taking them out to the Peninsula to bring the first battalion up to full strength again. He had volunteered for the unpopular task so he could attend his mother's wedding. The letter in which she had informed him that there was to be no wedding after all had not reached him before he sailed for England. The armies moved about a great deal within Portugal and Spain. Often the mailbags were redirected several times over before they were delivered into the correct hands.

Viola was very glad that letter had not arrived. Harry looked healthier and more robust than he had looked several months ago when he had insisted upon going back earlier than he ought after recovering from his injuries. He was also leaner than he had been and . . . harder. There was something about his eyes, the set of his jaw, his very upright military bearing . . . It was impossible to put it quite into words. He had matured, her son, from the carefree, rather wild young man he had been at the age of twenty before his world collapsed along with hers and Camille's and Abigail's. He was a man now, still energetic and cheerful and full of laughter – with that suggestion of hardness lurking beneath it all.

But he was here, and she felt it would be impossible to be happier than she was right now. After Christmas, when she went back home, she would carry this feeling with her. She would make her happiness out of her family, though they would be dispersed over much of England. Not too far for letters, however, and she liked writing letters.

'*Now* who can be coming?' Matilda asked, and they all stopped what they were doing to listen. There were the unmistakable sounds of horses and a carriage drawing up outside the front doors. 'Are you expecting anyone else, Wren?'

'No,' Wren said. 'Perhaps one of the neighbors?'

But it would be a strange time for a neighbor to come calling uninvited.

'I shall go down and see,' Alexander said.

He was gone for several minutes. When he returned, they all looked at him inquiringly. There was no one with him.

'Harry,' he said. 'Can I trouble you for a moment?'

'Me?' Harry jumped to his feet and strode toward the door. Alexander ushered him through it and closed it from the other side. The rest of them were left none the wiser about the identity or errand of the caller.

'If there is something I cannot abide,' Louise, Dowager Duchess of Netherby, said when neither man had reappeared after a few minutes, 'it is a mystery. Can it be army business? Whatever can Harry do to help?'

At least ten more minutes passed before the door opened again. It was Harry this time, looking every inch the hardened military officer.

'Mama?' he said, and beckoned her.

'Well,' Mildred was saying as Viola left the room. 'Is this some new sort of party game? Are we all to be summoned, one at a time?'

Viola stepped outside and Harry closed the door.

'The Marquess of Dorchester wishes to speak with you in the library,' he said. 'If you wish to speak to him, that is. If you do not, I shall go and tell him so. I have made it quite clear to him that I will not allow you to be harassed.'

She stared at him in the flickering candlelight of one of the wall sconces.

'Marcel?' she said. 'He is *here*?'

'But not for much longer if you do not want to see him,' he said. 'I shall show him the door, and if he is reluctant to move through it, I will help him on his way.'

'He is *here*?' she said again.

He frowned. 'You are not about to faint, are you, Mama?' he asked. 'Do you *want* to see him?'

The reality of it was just striking her. He was *here*, at Brambledean. In the library.

'Yes,' she said. 'Perhaps I ought.'

He was still frowning. 'Are you sure?' he asked. 'I will not have you upset, Mama. Not at Christmas. Not at any time, actually.'

'He is here,' she said. She did not phrase it as a question this time.

'Good God,' he said, 'do you *care* for him, Mama? He looks like the very devil.'

'I want to see him, Harry,' she said.

He was here. He had come.

But why?

She went downstairs on her son's arm and waited while a footman opened the library door. She slipped her arm from Harry's and stepped inside.

And, oh, she could see what Harry had meant when he told her he looked like the very devil. His face was surely thinner than it had been, and harsher. He was wearing his many-caped greatcoat – she never had counted the capes – and looked large and menacing with the light of the fire behind him, his hands at his back. His eyes, dark and hooded, met hers.

'Marcel,' she said.

'Viola.' He made her a stiff half bow.

Marcel had been feeling savage – a not unfamiliar feeling whenever Viola was concerned. This was *not* something he ought to be doing. It was not something he *wanted* to be doing. He had never enjoyed making an ass of himself, and to do it deliberately, as he was doing now, was insanity.

Good God, that puppy had treated him as though he were a worm he would squash beneath his foot at the slightest encouragement. And Riverdale had stood just inside the door, as he was still doing now, hard faced and silent, like a damned jailer.

What he ought to do, he thought after the son had gone back upstairs, was leave right now without another word. And without waiting to be dismissed. He should stride from the room and from the house while some shred of dignity remained to him.

But no, it was too late for that. There was no shred left.

He had made a prize ass of himself.

All because he had wanted to prove something to his twins. That he loved them. And even that was a head scratcher. How could he prove he loved them by proposing marriage to a woman who had been about to leave him while they were having an affair, who had told him with perfect clarity after he had announced their betrothal that she was having none of it, who had repeated that rejection when she had come to Redcliffe, who had not uttered one word of protest when he had announced that they were *not* betrothed, and who had left his house the following morning as though she were being pursued by the hounds of hell?

Sometimes he wondered after all about the upbringing Jane had given those two. How could they have grown up so muddleheaded that they could believe that she *loved* him? How could they think he could possibly love *her*? And want to *marry* her? And why did they care after the way he had neglected them?

But here he was, and there they were, established in two far-from-luxurious rooms at the village inn nearby. They had seen him on his way as though they were sending him to his execution, Estelle teary eyed as she gave him a hug, Bertrand with tight lips and an unreadable expression and a handshake that might have ground to a powder all the bones in a lesser man's hand.

'Good luck, Papa,' he had said.

It had almost been Marcel's undoing. It was the first and only time his son had called him Papa. He had never managed even a *Father* before, but only a deferential *sir*.

Riverdale had had a servant come in to light the fire and had lit two branches of candles himself before he went upstairs to fetch Captain Harry Westcott and then took up his silent vigil inside and to one side of the door. The fire was warm at Marcel's back now, but he did not remove his greatcoat. He felt damned silly. Here they were, two grown men standing silently in the same room, as though they had never heard of making polite conversation. The weather at least ought to have been a decent topic. It was surely going to snow, though it had not happened yet.

The door opened.

Estelle was quite right. Viola had lost weight, though not enough to detract from her beauty. And she did have dark shadows below her eyes, though they were not as pronounced as he had imagined. There was not a vestige of color in her face. Even her lips were pale. Her posture rivaled that of her military officer son.

'Marcel,' she said, her lips hardly moving.

'Viola.' He made her a half bow and looked from Westcott to Riverdale, his eyebrows raised. 'Do we need nursemaids?'

It was probably not the best start he might have made, but he was damned if he was going to deliver a marriage proposal in the hearing of two men who would as soon run him through with a sword as give him the time of day.

'You can go back to the drawing room, Harry,' she said. 'And you too, Alexander. They are all very curious up there to know who the visitor is.'

'There is a footman in the hall outside should you need him,' Westcott said, and they left, shutting the door behind them.

Marcel stared at Viola and she stared back before he pulled impatiently at the buttons of his great-coat and tossed it onto a nearby chair.

'I am not going to ask questions,' he said. 'Not yet, at least. That would put the burden upon you, and I have been told that doing so would be unfair. I am going to make statements. To begin, I will say again that I thought it was going to be a brief, thoroughly enjoyable affair. I was right about everything except the *brief* part. I was not finished with you. I was annoyed when you were finished with me. That had not happened to me before. If only you had given me another week or so, I would have been done with you and ready to move on.'

'Marcel,' she said.

'No,' he said, holding up one hand, 'I will not be distracted. That was what I thought. Then I made that rash and foolish betrothal announcement and felt angry and injured and blamed you. I had not been given the time to work you out of

410

my system. You were still there when you came to Redcliffe. You were still there when I told everyone I was not going to marry you after all – and after you left. I could not rid myself of you.'

'Marcel—' she said again.

'I am not doing very well, am I?' he said. 'I had a speech. At least I think I did. I do not think I planned to tell you that I could not rid myself of you. What I meant to say was that I could not forget you because you were there to stay. Because you are *here* to stay. In me. I hesitate to say in my heart. I would feel too much of an ass. And I suppose I should apologize for using that word. I am never going to be over you, Viola. I suppose I am in love with you. No, I do not suppose any such thing. I *am* in love with you. I *love* you. And if there is any chance, any remote possibility that you have changed your mind since that day on the beach, then please tell me and I will ask you to marry me. If there is no change, then I will go away and you need never see me again or listen to any more of this drivel.'

He stopped, appalled.

'Marcel.' She had come a few steps closer, and her eyes were bright. She blinked them. 'I had not *tired* of you.'

He frowned at her in incomprehension. 'Then why did you say you had?' he asked.

'I did not.' She came one step closer. 'I told you I needed to go home. I felt disconnected from my family and my life. I was afraid because my life

411

had become so vivid and so happy and I was so in love with you and I knew it was not in the rules of the game to become too emotionally involved. I sensed the end coming, and out of a sense of sheer self-preservation I wanted some control over *how* it ended. I thought perhaps I could keep my heart from breaking if I ended it.'

'You did not say you had tired of me?' he asked, frowning more deeply and trying to remember her exact words.

'No,' she said.

He closed his eyes and tried hard to remember, but all he could recall was the terrible hurt and the inevitable anger.

'I lashed back at you, did I not?' he said.

'You told me you were glad I had said it first,' she said, 'because you never liked to hurt your women.'

'Oh yes. I did.' He closed his eyes as if to shut out the horrible, embarrassing memory of his pettiness. 'Why did you not shoot me between the eyes at that very moment?'

'I had no pistol with me,' she told him.

'You must hate me by now,' he said.

'Why must I?' she asked. 'What have you been doing for the past two months, Marcel? Punishing yourself with riotous living in London?'

'Not at all,' he said. 'I have been lashing out at Redcliffe, setting everyone and everything to rights, sending Jane and Charles and Ellen home, attending Margaret's wedding and seeing her on her way. Sending my aunt and Isabelle and Ortt to live at the dower house. Sending my steward into retirement and putting Oliver in his place. Getting to know my children, being tyrannized by them.'

'You stayed home?' She frowned. 'But now you have left your children alone for Christmas?'

'They are here, at the village inn,' he said. 'We went to London first. It occurred to me that I would need to bring a special license with me if we are to be married over Christmas as originally planned. And then we came here, hoping we would beat the snow, which we did. I spoke with the vicar here, and tomorrow will be fine with him. I had a talk with your son, who gave his blessing to the extent that he threatened to throw me out if I tried to bully you and to do dire and painful things to my person if I should ever cause you pain.'

'Marcel,' she said, 'I am a tainted woman.'

'Good God,' he said. 'I suppose you are referring to what that scoundrel did to you and your children. The taint is not yours, and I will be interested in having a word with anyone who says it is. Don't be ridiculous, Viola. The only thing that matters to me is *you*. Do you recall telling me that what you wanted most in life was to have someone who cared for you? *You*. Not a tainted woman or a former countess or a mother or grandmother or a woman two years older than myself. Well, you have what you wanted if you choose it. You have me. I do not only love you. I *care* for you.'

He watched her swallow and sighed. 'I almost

forgot to explain that,' he said. 'I believe it was to have had a prominent role in my speech. In my imagination this was going to be a fearful but wondrous scene, Viola. It was to be romantic. It was to be touching. It was to proceed in an orderly fashion. It was to culminate in a proposal upon bended knee and then the affecting revelation that I had brought my children and a special license with me. And it was to end up with us locked in an embrace.'

'And?' she said.

'And?' He raised his eyebrows and looked blankly at her.

'I have not seen the bended knee yet,' she said.

'Viola.' He frowned. '*Do* you love me?'

Her eyes, gazing at him, grew luminous. 'Yes,' she said.

He drew a deep breath, held it, and let it out on a silent sigh. 'And *will* you marry me?'

'I will have to think about it,' she said.

'Have mercy,' he said. 'Knees become rheumatic, you know, when one passes the age of forty.'

'Do they?' She smiled. And, God help him, he was a slave to that smile. It got him every time.

And so he did it. And did not even feel too much of an idiot. He went down upon one knee and took her hand in his.

'Viola,' he said, looking up into her face, 'will you marry me and make me the happiest of men? And that is not even a cliché in this case. Or, if it is, then it is a true one.'

Somehow this time her eyes and her face smiled before her lips caught up to them. She had never looked more dazzlingly beautiful.

'Oh, I will, Marcel,' she said.

And he remembered to fumble in his pocket for the box with the diamond ring he had bought in London, using Estelle's finger and both her and Bertrand's opinions to estimate the size. He slid it onto her finger, and it neither got stuck on her knuckle nor fell off again.

'The diamond is not as big as the other one I bought you,' he said, 'but this was all I could afford after that extravagance. Now, would you like to tell me how I am to get up again?'

'Oh, silly,' she said. 'You just turned forty, not eighty.'

And she came down on both knees before him and wrapped both arms about him and smiled into his eyes. And he wrapped his arms about her and kissed her.

And everything was perfect after all. Just as it was. He was home. At last. And safe at last. And at peace at last.

Except that—

'I suppose,' he said, drawing back his head with the greatest reluctance, 'we had better go up and make the announcement and face the music.'

'You should not find it difficult,' she said as he got to his feet and helped her to hers. 'After all, Marcel, you had some practice in Devonshire.'

CHAPTER 23

'You are quite, quite sure, Mama?' Harry asked. He was standing in the doorway of her bedchamber, looking achingly handsome and smart in his green regimentals, which someone had brushed and cleaned so that they looked almost new. 'I know almost everyone was delighted to see Dorchester last night and greeted him and his announcement as though Chr— Well, as though Christmas had come. It was extraordinary. Even Cam and Abby were delighted. Even *Uncle Michael* shook his hand with great heartiness. But—'

'Harry,' she said, 'I am quite sure.'

He relaxed visibly. 'Well, then, I am happy too,' he said. 'We had better be on our way. You do not want to be late for your own wedding, I am sure.'

'I think,' she said, smiling at him, 'it may be the fashionable thing for a bride to do. But you are right. I do not want to be late.'

They were the last two members of the family to be still at the house. Her mother had left with Michael and Mary a few minutes ago, and Alexander and Wren had gone with them. Harry was to give her away.

'I must say,' he said, looking her over from head to foot, 'you look as fine as fivepence, Mama.'

She was wearing a cream-colored dress of fine wool, plain, high waisted, high necked, and long sleeved. She had thought it was perhaps not quite festive enough for the occasion. But she was no blushing young bride to be decked out in frills and flounces, and the dress was new, purchased in Bath when she was there a few months ago. She had fallen in love with it on sight and had intended to wear it for the first time on Christmas Day. She was wearing it one day early instead, for her wedding.

'Thank you,' she said, and he strode forward to help her on with the heavy wool cloak that matched the dress in color.

'Those are not the pearls you usually wear, are they?' he asked.

'No.' She smiled quietly to herself. 'They were a recent gift. And the earrings.'

'Well.' He eyed them a bit dubiously. 'They are very fine.'

And they were on their way to the church in the village under skies heavy with snow clouds that had stubbornly held on to their load for several days now. But even as she thought it, one flake and then another floated down beyond the carriage window.

'Oh look,' Harry said. 'Snow. Many more flakes and we may be able to use those old sleds after all.'

But Viola would think of the possibility of a white Christmas later.

Harry handed her down at the church gates and she walked along the churchyard path and into the church porch on his arm. There she removed her cloak and hung it up on a hook while she ran her hands over her dress to smooth out any wrinkles. Someone must have been on watch. The old organ began to play within moments of their arrival, and they proceeded into the church itself and along the nave toward the altar, where the vicar waited.

'Gamamama,' Sarah said, and was immediately hushed.

They walked among family and soon-to-be family. Estelle was sitting in the front pew on the left-hand side beside Abigail and Camille and Joel. Bertrand was on the right-hand side, handsome and dignified in his role as his father's best man. And . . . Marcel, halfway into the aisle himself so that he could watch her come with intense dark eyes and austere expression. He was wearing a brown coat with a dull gold waistcoat and fawn pantaloons and white linen.

All was right with the world, Viola thought. Sometimes one did feel that way, as though one's heart expanded to fill with all the love and well-being in the universe. As though nothing could ever happen to shake that inner tranquility no matter what troubles lay ahead. And how fitting it was that she should have that feeling now on her wedding day.

Her only real wedding day.

With Marcel.

Who had come for her and told her he loved her and asked her on bended knee to marry him.

He had even remembered to bring a special license with him.

She smiled inwardly and his eyes grew more intense and his face more austere. She was not deceived for a moment.

And then she was beside him, and his eyes were still focused upon her and her own remained on him even while she allowed her awareness to expand to feel the presence of all who were nearest and dearest to her and of his children, for whose sake he had eventually returned home.

Oh yes, all was right with the world.

The organ had stopped playing.

'Gamamama,' Sarah said again into the silence. Someone shushed her again.

'Dearly beloved,' the vicar said.

Marcel had not stayed long in the drawing room at Brambledean the evening before, just long enough to make his announcement and endure numerous congratulatory handshakes and more than enough hugs and several backslaps and to wish there were a big black hole into which he could step. What had startled him most, however, was the ecstatic pronouncement by young Winifred, who had apparently been allowed to spend the evening in the drawing room with the adults, that he was going to be her new grandpapa. As soon as he decently could, he had slunk off back to the village inn after a quickly exchanged kiss with Viola in the hall, in full view of an impassive footman. At the inn he had been met by a visibly anxious Estelle and a determinedly *un*anxious Bertrand and hugs and kisses from the former after he had announced the success of his mission. And another bone-crunching handshake from his son.

'You see, Papa?' Bertrand had said. 'We were right.'

And indeed they had been.

And then it was morning, his wedding day, and he would have bolted for the farthest horizon if he could have taken Viola with him again, as he had done on another memorable occasion a few months ago. Oh, and the twins too. And, to be fair, her daughters and son-in-law and the three children, including the one who clearly had every intention of calling him Grandpapa. Good God, he was only forty. He did not even have rheumatic knees yet. Oh, and her son could come too if he wanted to desert from his regiment.

On the whole it had seemed wiser to stay and endure all the tedious pomp of a wedding and a wedding breakfast and more hugs and kisses and whatnot despite the fact that he had brought a special license and so avoided the horror of a meticulously planned wedding of the ilk of Margaret's at Redcliffe recently. Isabelle had even wanted him to repaint the dining room to match the color of the flowers she and her daughter had planned. He had suggested they change the color of the flowers instead, an idea that had been greeted with faint shrieks and upflung hands and an exclamation of *'Men!'*

And now here he was at the church, intensely aware of Bertrand at his right and Estelle across the aisle to his left. And of the strange transformation his life had undergone in the few months since he had looked beyond a taproom door to the newly arrived guest who was bent over the register the innkeeper had turned for her signature.

And then he was intensely aware of the vicar coming from the vestry and of the organ beginning to wheeze and produce music, and of the arrival as he got to his feet and turned to look back of the fierce young puppy, who looked really quite formidable today in his full regimentals. And . . . Ah . . .

Viola.

Understated in an unadorned cream dress, allowing all her elegance and beauty to speak for themselves. And they spoke loudly and clearly to the deepest chambers of his heart. Or rather they shone and warmed his whole being. He gazed at her as she approached on her son's arm, no longer aware of anyone or anything else. He gazed as though only by doing so could he keep her here and prevent her from disappearing while he awoke from a dream.

She was not smiling. At least her lips were not. But she had that ability he had noticed before of smiling with her eyes and her whole face and rendering the curving of lips redundant.

Viola, the love of his heart – which sugary language he did not stop to analyze.

It was only as she took her place beside him that he noticed the only adornments she wore – the large, cheap pearls about her neck and at her ears.

And she smiled, a full-on smile that everyone would see. And he became aware of everyone again – of his son on his other side, of Viola's son on her other side, of Estelle beyond him, of all Viola's family members, soon to be his, half filling the church behind them. He was aware of the silence as the organ stopped playing. He heard the infant granddaughter – *soon to be his* – identify her grandmother aloud before being shushed.

'Dearly beloved,' the vicar said.

And then it began – the rest of his life.

It was snowing when they stepped out of the church. Thick white flakes were descending and melting as they landed, but the heat of the ground was fighting a losing battle against the onslaught the clouds were unleashing upon it. Already the grass was turning white, as were the roofs of the carriages. But despite the weather, a number of curious villagers had gathered beyond the church gates and cheered, some of them self-consciously, when it became obvious to them that a wedding had taken place – that of the former countess, in fact. Who was now, the innkeeper's wife was not shy about explaining, the Marchioness of Dorchester, since that was the marquess with her. He was the grand gentleman who had stayed at the inn last night.

Mildred's boys and Winifred were out on the church path armed with colorful flower petals they had wheedled out of a reluctant gardener proud of his hothouses. They threw them over the bridal couple as they hurried along the path toward Marcel's carriage, cackling and whooping as they did so.

'Young jackanapes,' Marcel said, brushing at his greatcoat and shaking off his hat before joining Viola inside the carriage. He was too late, as it happened. Young Ivan had kept back one fistful of petals for just this moment.

And then they were in the carriage alone, and it was moving off from the gates so that the next carriage could draw in behind it, and a grating, banging, clanging, dragging sound assailed their ears.

'We began with carriage trouble,' Marcel said, raising his voice above the din. 'We might as well continue with it. I suppose there are boots attached back there and other paraphernalia. There is at least one pot. Anyone would think we had just got married.'

He turned toward her and smiled, and she smiled back.

'I think that is exactly what has just happened,' he said.

'Yes.'

He gazed at her. 'And there is a wedding celebration to come,' he said.

'Yes,' she agreed. 'And carolers this evening and the Yule log and the wassail bowl. And Christmas tomorrow. And probably sledding and snowball fights and snow angels and goose and plum pudding.'

'And there is the time between this evening and tomorrow,' he said. 'Just for you and me.'

'Yes,' she said.

'Could we practice just a little bit now?' he suggested.

She laughed and so did he.

'Just a little bit,' she said.

But he gazed at her for a few moments longer.

'I will spend the rest of my life proving to you that you have not made a mistake, Viola,' he said.

'I know,' she said. 'And I will spend the rest of my life proving to you that you do not have to prove anything at all.'

He blinked. 'I will have to think about that one,' he said. 'But in the meanwhile . . .'

'Yes,' she agreed. 'In the meanwhile . . .'

He slid an arm about her shoulders and she turned into his arms.

'Lovely pearls, by the way,' he murmured against her lips.

'Yes,' she said. 'My favorites.'